Also by
Steven Shrewsbury

Novels
Hell Billy
Thrall
Stronger Than Death
Tormentor
Hawg
Godforsaken

With Nate Southard
Bad Magick

With Peter Welmerink
Bedlam Unleashed

Collections
Thoroughbred
Bulletproof Soul
Depths of Savagery
Nocturnal Vacations

Novellas
Whore of Jericho
Widowmaker's Apprentice

overkill

overkill

Steven Shrewsbury

SEVENTH STAR PRESS

Editor: Joshua H. Leet

Published by Seventh Star Press, LLC.

ISBN Number 9781937929800

Library of Congress Control Number: 2012935047

Seventh Star Press
seventhstarpress.com
info@seventhstarpress.com

Publisher's Note:
Overkill is a work of fiction. All names, characters, and places are the
product of the author's imagination, used in fictitious manner. Any
resemblances to actual persons, places, locales, events, etc. is purely
coincidental.

Printed in the United States of America

First Edition

ACKNOWLEDGEMENTS

Thanks to Mark Boatman, Mark Hickerson, Peter Welmerink, Angie & Christopher Fulbright, Stephen Zimmer, Matt Perry, Josh Leet, Louise Bohmer, Brady Allen, Mark Shrewsbury Sr, Mark Shrewsbury Jr (the Godson), Amy Shrewsbury, Jim McCleod, Joe Howe, Rhonda Harris, Michael Knost, R. Thomas Riley, Kimmi Jo Greenwell, Bob Freeman, Cheryl Lynne Staley, Randy Chandler, Gina Ranalli, Roy Booth, Jodi Lee, David Wilbanks, Martel Sardina, Ginger May, Donnis Lovell, Ty Schwamberger, Rhonda Wilson, Evyl Ed, Andrew Wolter, Michael West, B.J. McPherson, DezM, Elizabeth Hetherington, Jeremy Bulloch, Shawn Reeder, Debi Hulbert, Mark Johnson, Kelli Miller, Elizabeth Donald, Scott Nicholson, Laura Long, Dean Harrison, Stuart Bergman, Cat McMinn, Gail, Minh, Noigeoverlord, Mike Ko, Stephannie Scott, Wulf, D.J. Weaver, Brandon, Rita Scarlet, Justin Chiang, Angela Bodine, Andrew Leonard, Keevah, Amy Simpson Seel, and Brian Knight.

Special thanks to Norm Partridge, Ron Kelly and Bryan Smith for words of encouragement.

Lastly, but most of all, thank you to my family, Stacey, John and Aaron.

Shrews
Rural Central Illinois

DEDICATION

For those that pass me in the Ether-realm

You know who you are

And

Mark Worthen

A Friend Who Passed

CONTENTS

"Some costs are too lofty, no matter how greatly you may crave the accolade. The article one can't swap for one's heart's desire is your heart."

-From tablet Fragment found at Larak

PREFACE

THEN

Nykia opened her door and watched her bodyguard's head roll past. She took one step out into the hall and looked to her right following a trail of blood to where it originated. Vanda's body laid on the rug woven by her aunt, Mavik. Jets of blood shot from the ragged stump on Vanda's shoulders, each beat firing less of a volley as his heart realized it no longer was needed. Clothed in lighter leathers, and no armor, Vanda's right hand wilted, dropping a short sword as his killer stood over him. This intruder, naked, save for leathery moccasins on his feet, bellowed and swung a crude bronze-tipped axe down onto Vanda's headless body. Nykia recognized a ruddy Pryten savage when she saw one, mostly from paintings and one at an execution back home in the capitol of Qesot. Nykia couldn't understand why the Pryten buried his axe in Vanda's chest. At eight years old, even Nykia could tell her guard wasn't getting up soon.

The Pryten warrior locked eyes with hers. His eyes, black, burning and shallow, made her freeze in place. "She's here," he grunted, barely understandable in her own tongue.

Nykia broke from the shock and stepped back into her room. She shut the door fast. A tiny trigger allowed a thick crossbeam to drop across the doorway. Nykia used little effort to trip the switch Vanda installed when the family first took up vacation residence there in Perpignan. Such delicate fingers created a great obstacle for the Pryten warrior to get through as the curses at his first failed attempt testified.

A great many things raced through her mind, like if she really would die at the hands of Pryten barbarians at a coastal retreat in Perpignan, Transalpina or if they'd take her back to their sacred woods to sacrifice her. She wondered after her parents and the others in the royal party and how the invaders could've made it through

1

the grounds, into the house and up the stairs. Nykia retreated to her bed, hands pressed to the sides of her painting smock as she pondered why the savages bothered to speak her tongue at all. But the hammerings on her door blotted these thoughts out.

Nykia backpedaled to the corner of the room. Beyond her bed mat Nykia knelt by the shrine she'd erected. As the axe struck the planks that made up her sturdy door, Nykia didn't pray to any god or goddess. Her thoughts of her savior filled her mind, the object of her shrine: Gorias La Gaul, fabled warrior from afar off lands. All the splintering of wood and curses at her door couldn't get her eyes from the drawings and paintings of Gorias on her shrine, nor the tiny clay rendering of the great hero that slew the last of the dragons.

"I love you, Gorias," she said, folding her hands, eyes on the bearded images for a moment, then closed, recalling the time she saw her grandmother speak to the legend himself…how amazingly tall he stood, the ruggedly handsome figure he cut even if his long hair and beard had turned gray. 700 years would do that, she reckoned with a grin as the door started to leave its hinges. She'd heard whispers the legendary warrior would hunt with her father in the coming weeks and the possibility of meeting Gorias dominated her dreams. However, Nykia reasoned with sadness, she needed him now, not in a few weeks.

Her dreamy state shattered just like the crossbeam. The Pryten, who smelled like horses and urine to Nykia, stood in her room at last, but his axe hung at his side. Behind him, someone in a cloak drifted past the ruined doorway. Nykia only got a glimpse of this person, but enough to realize the figure wasn't a Pryten. Hands from the cloak with milky white skin gestured to the savage, but the figure didn't speak before disappearing into the shadows.

Nykia didn't recall much about being armed up under the Pryten's left armpit, but she closed her eyes at the gore in the house. The cook, nursemaid, the man who kept the horses and the other guard all missed limbs & their lives. The cook really put up a fight by the state of the dead Pryten at his feet, but they'd chopped off his right hand, which lay on the rug by the pantry door, still clutching a cleaver.

Once outside, she saw more Prytens, but only a dozen, not the army she expected. At their feet lay a few of their brothers' bodies, so Nykia smiled that some died in the exchange. The Prytens quickly put the luxury home on the coast to the torch, unconcerned if nearby trees or fields of autumn would catch in the blaze.

When they threw her to the ground, the air left her body. This moment became her first taste of terror. She couldn't breathe and flipped over, arms flailing in the air.

The person in the hood stepped forward and admonished the Pryten who dropped her. "Fool. Be careful. She's of no use to Tancorix damaged."

The Pryten spoke in his own tongue as he grabbed Nykia up by the hair. He swatted her back and she gagged, air rushing back to her lungs.

Tancorix, the Pryten queen and high priestess of the Wood... Nykia didn't like the sound of that. She'd heard tell of evil Tancorix around the hearth in tales to scare children, but what would that crazy woman across the channel want with her?

The hooded person, a woman, she thought by the voice, said acidly, "Getting the wind knocked out of you is the least of your worries." The woman whose voice rang familiar turned to the Prytens. "Prepare her for the journey to Pergamus."

Her heart spiked with terror at that name: Pergamus, the land from where the dragons came. She imaged a proper sacrifice back in the Pryten wilderness on a stone slab to their Queen Tancorix, but Pergamus? It sounded impossible and unfathomable. Would she be fed to dragons?

Nykia always loved to braid her long hair and the way the ebony locks shone in the sun. It took but a few moments for the Pryten to shear off her tresses down to the scalp with a curved blade. She'd not cried until then, and words from the throaty woman about lice didn't fill the void when Nykia mourned her long locks.

Once the warrior removed her hair, he ripped her painting smock off in a single swipe. He then pulled a textured sack over her head. Nykia nearly giggled as her head and arms found holes in the rough sack to pop out from.

The smelly warrior mumbled something about "the sea." Nykia only understood him when she saw their series of small crafts wedged in the sand down the coast. It stood to reason they'd cross the channel and her heart screamed at that idea. Though not afraid of the water, she wouldn't trust venturing out on such a tiny ship.

Again, the warrior carried her under his arm and she looked away from the sea. Flames crept around their large home and the thatch in the roof started to smolder. She couldn't understand how such a thing happened, her in a place where they were so safe. No one could approach the lands from roads nor through the dense forest nearby. Dogs patrolled the grounds and many guards held a leisurely post all about. Transalpina was at peace; even a little princess such as Nykia understood that.

The closer they drew to the boats, the more she put it together that these savages crossed the channel from Albion, probably the Pryten wilderness to the west, to reach this spot. Though she'd sailed on larger vessels, she couldn't comprehend how they'd performed such a feat on bitsy boats.

It took the snorting of a horse to make the hurried Prytens stop and turn their backs to the sea. The man carrying Nykia also twisted, causing her to face the water. Only after he dropped her did Nykia turn to claim the same sight as the abductors.

An enormous black stallion, as big as a draft horse, stomped down the coastline. The animal carried a huge figure encased in a faded navy blue cloak. At first, she thought this man another one of their party, but soon abandoned this line of thinking due to the unrest caused amongst the Prytens. A few jumped in the boat on the left, another fumbled with his shield, trying to get the crude buckler made of twine in the correct spot on his arm.

The warrior guarding Nykia turned to square his shoulders to the oncoming rider. This move sent Nykia rolling. In the sand, she looked up and thought a dream materialized. It couldn't be possible, outside a fable or a bedtime tale by her grandmother the Queen Garnet, that Gorias La Gaul would ride in to save her.

And yet, there he was...the legend his own self, revealed as his hood and cloak started to part. He wore his bluish armor rumored created from the skin of a wyrmling dragon, and his helmet didn't hide the flowing gray hair out the back.

Even if she dreamed, Nykia reasoned, it was a good dream, for the arrival fought and killed like the legend. The horseman put the reins in his teeth and threw a small object at the first man to step up. The article appeared at first like a tiny ball, but opening to spin long cords that encircled the arms of the Pryten. While this bolo wouldn't subdue the savage forever, it only had to until the rider disengaged two swords from a pack on his back and sliced one through his target's forehead. The horse thundered on and the slit-open man stood, shaking, brains running down his face, before falling to his knees in the sand.

Nykia's heart came near to bursting when she saw the swords come free. The rider, close enough now to see the reins disappearing in a slit on the helm, had to be La Gaul. All the tales of his twin swords that came from angel's wings and were lodged in scabbards on his huge back. They cleanly passed through the crude swords the Prytens offered up and swiped on down through flesh like they were spreading butter. La Gaul slew two that approached him on each side, standing in his stirrups and slashing down, not only cutting through bone and metal, but also twisting as he withdrew, ensuring neither blow dealt a simple injury. Nykia swore she saw part of a rib cage pull out when La Gaul yanked back from a Pryten on her left side.

The huge man slung his legs from the horse and tossed free his cloak, sending it over the head of the robed woman who directed the Prytens. While she struggled with this obstruction, Gorias turned to the other warriors. One already advanced and stabbed at his right side with a spear. The blade glanced off the dragon scales. Gorias' back swipe with the sword in his right hand sent the Pryten's jaw flying. A bubbly scream echoing in the throat of the maimed warrior, his terror didn't last long as Gorias brought his blade around and inserted it in the man's heart. Gorias turned the blade and pulled, near to a good handshake

A Pryten managed to parry the left sword arm of La Gaul with his shield, but drew close, getting out a small stone axe and

5

slamming it into Gorias' midsection. The axe head broke off and the Pryten stopped. Up close with the big man, Gorias drew his right forearm across the neck of the Pryten and shoved him away. Blood spouted from the Pryten and his face wore a confused look, not comprehending what Nykia saw: the armored forearm of La Gaul held a dew nail of the wyrmling dragon, now decorated with the Adam's apple of the Pryten.

Gorias shook off the gore as a smaller Pryten jumped on his back. This man held a dagger in each hand. Legs wrapped about Gorias' waist, he stabbed down wild, like he beat on a drum, both blades crashing into Gorias' shoulders. The daggers both broke off on the armor and Gorias twisted once. Not dislodged off him, the man remained intent on pounding at him with the handles of the broken knives. Gorias raised the visor on his helmet.

Free of the cloak, the woman screamed at the warriors, "Get him! He's one man!"

One closed on Gorias on each side and another to his front as the small man on his back worked on to no avail. Each of the men charged in like the savages they were and Gorias spread his arms, stabbing each flanking Pryten in the stomach. However, when he struck the two, the woman screamed a guttural chant and flung a glowing ball of glass at Gorias. The ball imploded in the air as he stabbed through his two attackers, and he froze in place. For a moment, Gorias couldn't move, but then he released his swords and stepped forward. The two dying men remained standing, blades in their guts, and the man on Gorias' back remained paralyzed. This time when he pivoted his shoulders, the man on his back fell off.

Nykia thought she heard Gorias curse wizards as he planted his right sword in the smaller warrior on the ground, relating a Mage's parentage to donkeys and swine.

The woman gaped, unable to move herself at first, stunned that her magicks didn't stop Gorias.

Gorias moved on the man in front of him, who staggered to move as well under the effects of the magick ball of the witchy woman. Gorias grabbed each wrist of the stunned man, raised a boot to the Pryten's chest and fell backwards on the sand, arms extended. Two loud pops echoed as Gorias dislocated both of the Pryten's shoulders and kicked him back. His fall also smashed the frozen man on his back into letting him go. Gorias got to one knee and drew two daggers from his belt. He glanced Nykia's way and then reared back, burying the blade in his left hand in the small attacker's chest. The small Pryten's frozen legs twitched but he never moved as Gorias pushed off his body to get up.

Up on his feet, Gorias used his right forearm to wave off a couple flying tomahawks thrown by Prytens as they cautiously fell back. He put his knives back in their holsters and turned around to take his swords by the pommels. After he pulled them from the frozen dead men, Gorias squared up to the Pryten with two dislocated arms and criss-crossed the blades, removing the throat of the injured man so fast Nykia gasped. The Pryten moved his mouth many times, trying to gag, but couldn't make a sound, save for the one his body let out when he hit the sand.

As Gorias made this move, two more savages attacked, one hitting him in the back full on with a tackle. He stumbled forward, helmet coming loose and falling forward, but Gorias stayed on his feet. One Pryten grappled Gorias' left arm, hugging it to make sure he couldn't use it for a sword strike. The Pryten drew back with his stone-headed tomahawk, but hesitated when he locked eyes with Gorias. The old fable pivoted, facing Nykia at last. Her chest filled with cool air. Gorias' strong face would make anyone stop and question a move, Nykia reasoned. She also saw that in the tackle from behind Gorias had dropped his right sword, but held his helmet by the edge in his right hand. He used the helmet on the stunned warrior, smashing it into the Pryten's face, causing him to spin away, drop his weapon and put both hands to a bleeding countenance. Gorias staggered a little when his tackler planted a stone tomahawk on his right hip, but Nykia saw the head of the weapon shatter. Gorias used his left saber to strike out and impale this attacker who backpedaled away from his destiny.

"C'mon," Gorias grunted. "Ya wanted me." The Pryten fell, dead, like the rest, only with Gorias accidentally stepping on his head as he caught up to his prey.

Gorias' grim face turned to the last warrior, the one near Nykia, his lips parted as he said, "Your benefactor is dead." Gorias gestured back at his horse, and swiped away another of the glass balls the wizard woman threw. "Yer startin' to piss me off, honey. Just stop it."

The Pryten, the witch and Nykia cocked their heads and saw that the great mount dragged something behind it. What lay in the sand wouldn't pass much for a human anymore, but it wore a purple sash, something Nykia recognized as a member of the royal house.

Gorias crossed his swords in front of himself. "Yer luck is bad. If I hadn't been bringing back a gift to the Queen, ya may have got away with yer treasure."

The Pryten gripped a bronze sword, stabbed out at Gorias. It took a swish of the legend's swords to cut the savage's weapon off at the hilt.

Gorias voice dropped, full of resignation. "Some men in the Queen's party objected to torturing that piss-ant traitor I saw tattooed with Pryten god markings. I wasn't one of those men."

The Pryten scrambled back as Gorias swung. The blades missed as the savage ran past Nykia and the boat and into the surf.

He turned to the hooded woman. Her arms free of her robe, she raised her hands and started to conjure. Gorias turned, eyed Nykia, winked and then stepped between her and the woman. She couldn't exactly see how Gorias slew the conjuring woman, but suffice it to say, her spell remained mostly in her throat as she fell.

Swords wiped clean on the robe of the dead woman then returned to their housings, Gorias turned to Nykia and knelt beside her. He watched the Pryten out in the surf, intent on escaping into the sea.

"I'm Gorias…" he started to say, but she quickly reached out and touched his beard.

"I know. You've come to save me."

A wry smile crept onto his face, as her tiny fingers gripped his beard. "I'd have been here sooner, but that Pryten spy proved stubborn."

"Will you take me to my mommy?"

8

Gorias lifted her up and cradled the child to his armored chest. "No."

As they turned to the horse, Nykia wondered, "Why not?"

He sighed a little before saying, "Because she's dead, that's why. You're old enough to understand the world is a bad place, even though you grew up in such luxury. Forces have come to slay enemies of your grandmother, the Queen. Your mom is dead. Sorry I had to tell you that."

The reality of *never* seeing her mother again sank into Nykia and she started to cry.

"Your father…" Gorias began, but she again cut him off.

"He's not my father, only the man who took his place when Papa died on a hunt years before."

La Gaul didn't finish his words and many years passed before Nykia understood all that happened this day. She oft wondered if Gorias really would've confessed that he slew her stepfather when he was revealed as one conspiring with those in Albion to kill the royal family of Transalpina. Gorias killed a dozen conspirators that day, her stepfather just happened to be one of them, but the cruel reality was that this man caused the death of her real father in order to invade their home, their mother's bed, to spy on the family.

"I'll take you to your grandmother, Lady Garnet Peverall, the Queen." Gorias promised as he climbed back into the saddle.

The girl wept for a long while as they rode back past the blazing home and into the wilderness around the estate. They stopped to navigate better through some ditches leading to a main road and she touched his face again.

"I'm going to marry you someday."

Gorias couldn't suppress a chuckle.

"I'm flattered, young lady, but in time the princes of the continent will line up at the palace door. The Queen will see to it. She'll watch out for ya now."

"I already love you, Gorias La Gaul. Why would I want another?"

As they rode, Nykia got comfortable in the lap of the legend, her hair lost in his beard. Only after a few miles did he look down to see her drawing on her palm with a red object.

"It's like paint and ink but in a tube," she explained to him and showed her palm to him. "See? That's my profile."

The old warrior squinted and nodded. "Not bad. You're an excellent artist."

"I can draw you," she said with confidence. "I often do. Let me see your hand."

They stopped and Gorias opened his right hand. The rough, scarred palm of Gorias became her canvass and she drew a fine profile of the legend on his flesh. She then slapped her hand over it, tight.

"Are we married now?" Gorias smiled.

"Forever." Her eyes gleamed.

"That's a long time, sweetheart." He kicked his mount, heading them toward the distant banners of the Queen's retreat.

Later, she understood his words were that of an aged fighter, probably one always doled out to females…but the articulation of Gorias calling her sweetheart rang in her ears forever.

❖❖❖❖❖

Reality destroyed her vivid memory with only a few words.

"Do you like that, sweetheart?"

These words came from the husky voice of the she-pirate Noguria, the whip mistress, after the dropping of a leather lash over Nykia's bare backside. She couldn't move to escape the shot. More leather bound up her ankles and wrists.

The voice persisted. "Thinking of him again, are you? Gorias La Gaul? I can live with that competition. It's only fencing with a dream." Again, her leathery tie fell across Nykia's hips. "Although I envy the fighter." Her gloved hand gripped Nykia's. Noguria raised her head to face her. Tears rolled down her cheeks and onto Noguria's leather-clad fingers. Noguria let her face go and licked her fingertips. "I make you cry, but he makes you cry out, doesn't he?"

Nykia sighed. "Isn't this game over? You are taking a long

time tonight, even for you."

Again, the whip fell, but Nykia hardly moved away from her place strung up on the wall.

"Gorias and I have a few things in common. We both saved you from the Pryten savages, he when you were a little girl, me, a year ago when we raided the shrine for Tancorix. How many years had you been their prisoner?"

"A few. Tancorix is dead and her daughter Adraste too young to make coherent choices. I blended in the crowd."

"Until I came," She said, her right index finger running down the tattoos on Nykia's left arm. "These marks are blended from what the savages gave you to make you mine."

"Yes, you rescued me, mistress Noguria."

"He's in Albion, that La Gaul. Go ahead, think of him all you want. I don't care."

Eyes closed, Nykia's tattooed flesh quivered at the touch of Noguria and the thought of Gorias La Gaul.

CHAPTER 1

REMEMBRANCE OF THINGS PAST

"Gorias La Gaul will solve this riddle of the dragonfire and make my household complete," Lady Garnet pronounced, reading the scroll held in her withered hands. She placed the parchment on a mahogany end table and stepped away from the burning lamps. Only the rustle of her gown on the tiled floor and the breathing of her young servant were audible in the vast throne room.

"Yes, my Queen," the young man answered as he imparted a small bow. The guards behind him didn't move an inch. Tall women, clad in leathers and emotionless, stood rigid, ready to pounce in defense of their Queen. The other man, an aging Castellan clothed in the rich robes of a councilman, folded his hands and said nothing.

Garnet stepped away from the raised dais of the vaulted room, her gaze focused out the yawning window. Lady Garnet soon stood by the huge shutters, took in the sky and then the grounds around the castle. Eyes focusing on the guards meandering on the second curtain wall, she said to the young man, "Orsen, Yannick has seen that La Gaul is across the channel in Albion. Only Gorias can handle this case to my complete satisfaction."

Orsen nodded, eyed the guard for a moment and said, "So you say, Mum. I know he supported your wishes in the past and saved princess Nykia twenty-five years ago from the Prytens before the Albion war." He paused and clasped his hands in front of his tunic, shooting the towering women guards a steady look. "While he supposedly slew all the dragons in the world, Mum, surely La Gaul is well over seven centuries old by now."

Still at the long window, she answered, "There is no supposedly about it, Orsen. It wasn't that long ago and they did exist. Surely, you've seen the bones in the museums and the platelets in beer halls."

Orsen nodded. "Many say those are fanciful stories, Mum,

and that one man couldn't possibly kill such a great beast."

Garnet paused, eyes to the skies before saying, "And yet Gorias was strong enough to see all of the dragons extinct as well as my enemies."

His words chosen carefully, Orsen said, "That was before my birth, Mum."

The Queen's right hand reached over to her left wrist. Lady Garnet's thumb rubbed on her golden bracelet. "They were real. I was a princess, a hundred years ago, when I saw La Gaul help in the battle of the Somme." She twirled and addressed the auburn-haired guard on Orsen's left. "Alena's father was there as well."

The tall woman bowed her head once, but said nothing.

Orsen swallowed before saying, "I've heard many stories about that day, Mum. I wish I'd lived to see it."

Eyes closed, the Queen said in a low voice, "No, you don't."

On the walls of her mind, the day so long ago played itself out again. Of course, the Princess Garnet stood nowhere near the massive battlefield dissected by the Somme River. However, from the broiling caldron of the seer Yannick, she perceived everything that happened miles distant. Through the churning waters and multicolored bubbles of his pot, Garnet saw the image of the man her father paid to fight with the army of Transalpina.

Gorias La Gaul sat atop his great black stallion in the thick of the cavalry. Though a long cloak billowed out behind him, Garnet could see his body clearly through Yannick's foam. Unlike the rest of the cavalry who donned chain mail shirts and metal leg guards, Gorias wore a strange covering of plated armor, dark blue in hue. Garnet understood little of protective coverings, but thought he stood out more than just due to his age and the fact he didn't wear the insignia of Transalpina.

The other fighters, probably aged twenty to forty years if a day, dark-haired or shaven of head, stood firm. Gorias looked carved from stone, his pronounced features unreal like something an artist dreamt up. His flowing gray hair billowed from his shoulders and framed in his somewhat craggy face. Yes, the caldron of Yannick let her get a good look at the hero from afar before the view widened out to include the entire field of battle. Garnet's heart raced at the stern forehead scarred several times, and the arched nose protruding above high cheekbones. His beard and mustache ran white and very thick, but not brutally unkempt as some of the forward infantry of their enemies from Albion.

Gorias' blue eyes glimmered and he smiled at the enemy formations. From a horse that stood a few hands higher than the rest of the cavalry, Gorias nodded as the young men around him shouted and taunted the Albion forces falling into their formations.

"They are a bunch of mutts," a soldier on foot said to the rest of the assembled cavalry. "That pervert King of Albion has bitten off more than he can chew, crossing the channel to fight us here in our own yard."

Gorias' voice thudded deep and wise to his fellow horsemen, "The distant King has gathered a Confederation of Transalpina's enemies. By the edges of the forward infantry I see the standard of the archers of Andorra. They've come a long way to piss in King Peverall's breakfast plate."

Laughter rippled through the lines and Garnet smiled her own self at the mention of such an act to her revered father.

Gorias continued, "Most of his men are foreigners here to a grab a piece of the grand kingdom. Those tan-skinned footmen with short swords? They are from Atropatene, so far away."

A man nearly as big as Gorias stopped his horse next to him and said, "This will get ugly." This graying man held a scope aloft and then handed it to Gorias.

Eyes scanning the front lines of the massive Albion army, Gorias said, "General Appra, I see it. Behind their spearmen units, foot soldiers and the wave of pikemen lies something else…" Gorias squinted through a looking glass. He grinned as he lowered the viewer. "Hot damn, gentlemen, they brought wizards and wyrmling dragons instead of cavalry."

As trumpets sounded across the Somme, General Appra donned a chain mail headdress and said to Gorias, "Then paying you to be here is a good idea, no?"

Gorias stowed the General's looking glass in a saddlebag

and adjusted the sheathed broadsword to the left of his saddle horn. "You have employed the Belenos Kelt tribe to be berserkers in the front lines. Those hairy bastards'll do a great bit of damage." Gorias then donned a helmet, made of the same blue material as his armor. Visor up, he glared at the others and reached back with both hands at his waist. He disengaged two swords from their housings on his back. Since Gorias was quite tall, the long pack held two long blades nearly a yard in length each. "So will I."

At the sight of these two gleaming blades, many in the cavalry shied back. As Gorias put his reins in his teeth, the whispers flooded the crowd. Though many watched the enemy advance, several still murmured about Gorias and his swords. Aside from many rumors about the weapons, the main issue was that the soldiers could see the blades weren't made of any sort of metal.

Gorias' horse stayed with serried lines of cavalry, ranks of berserkers and regular infantry as bowmen in leather jerkins stepped forward, bows in their left hands, ready to strike. Pikemen secured their basinets and gripped long lances, screwing in their courage like the rest.

Across the Somme, Albion's squadrons of death dealers swung into formation, armed and dressed likewise.

Though his reins were in his mouth, Gorias muttered the words, "Deliverance will come."

Through the morning mists across the Somme, the forces started toward each other, each army with their strength in its middle. The knights and cavalry full of grizzled veterans in the center flanked by wings of berserkers, pikemen and archers that curled around mimicking the enemy. Only the center of the Albion army possessed several dozen creatures under the control of bald men in robes. From a distance, they looked like horses, but as they approached the shallow muddy water of the Somme, their reptilian bloodline shone through. No hooves touched the ground, but clawed fingers stabbed at the earth. Though bitless bridles held these beasts in check, sparks and smoke emerged from their nostrils. Their wings, folded down, bobbed with movement as they advanced.

One of the solders muttered, "If those are wrymlings like La

Gaul's armor, then why aren't they blue?"

Another grunt replied, "Maybe those are just stories about his armor. Those things out there are red and green."

"Blue dragons aren't from around these parts." Gorias said to his fellows nearby, "I doubt they can fly just yet. They're young, easier to control and subdue."

"They can die if they breathe," a loud horseman proclaimed from behind La Gaul.

The divisions came together as the archers unleashed their volleys. Though several troopers on either side held up shields to ward off the missiles, several shafts found their targets. Bodies fell all around and a few horses howled on either side of the Somme's banks as the center of each army met. Many a young man from Albion gaped at their wounds, stunned that such a thing could actually happen. A graying veteran, however, took a bolt to his side, looked down like he contracted an insect bite and broke it off, never ceasing in his charge.

He may just bleed to death and fall, Gorias mused, *but at least he'd fall forward*. Garnet shook for she could hear Gorias' thoughts and that unnerved her deep.

A few arrows struck Gorias as he charged, but blunted on his armor. His swords struck fast, removing the wing of a wyrmling to his left while slicing off the arm of the bald rider to his right. Squeezing his knees, his horse ducked low. Gorias criss-crossed his blades in the open space at the oncoming creature. The young dragon's head stayed in place for a moment, then teetered, falling from its neck.

"They hardly bleed," General Appra hollered from Gorias' right, but never slackened his advance and strikes against the wizards.

All along the lines, the horsemen didn't have great success against the dragons, but the Keltos berserkers did. With their great lances, they used the creature's momentum against them. Planting the brass ball at the end of the lance on the ground, the onrush of the wyrmlings aided the strike, inadvertently pushing the weapons through their chests. In many cases, the Keltos spears went through the dragons and into the wizards that rode them. One held up his like a prize, and then trashed them to the ground. Removing the lance became a bother, so the berserker took up the curved blade of the wizard and charged again, making certain they were dead.

Besides Gorias in the caldron, the Princess saw one such impaled foreign wizard, off his saddle by a foot, stunned that he hung up on the spear tip in his groin. La Gaul didn't take the time to kill this confused man as he passed by. He had others to slay.

A dragon roared at La Gaul, long neck slithering out of his sword's slash, almost to Gorias' face before it stopped abruptly. Though Gorias missed with his left-handed, roundhouse swipe, something on his left forearm stopped the dragon's bite. The beast blinked and felt the dew nail on his forearm rip its throat out. Garnet absently wondered if the recognition in the dragon's eyes saw that Gorias' armor was made from a wyrmling's flesh…and the dew nail on his arm spelled this monster's death.

Though the Somme ran shallow here, many were dragged under the muddy water after being knocked from their mounts. Frantic horses inadvertently drowned a few of the knights of Transalpina. The stunned men struggled to rise in the water and had their brains dashed out by war hammers from Albion.

Not checking back to see if the attacking factions behind him held or not, Gorias continued on in his war against the young dragons. Over a dozen of them fell, but a few more dozen remained, easily taking out the legs of many horsemen and biting the faces from several crazed berserkers. A small company of pikemen lowered their thick weapons and skewered one dragon, but the beast refused to die. Gorias rode by, clipped off its head and moved on. The pikemen exchanged looks and continued as well.

Garnet even understood the dragons, while rare, could be used as fodder in this conflict. They weren't the important thing as the center of the opposing army held in reserve huge lines of archers and men with slings. Mostly, these were annoyances, set to scatter the Transalpinian middle. From her studies Garnet thought such men should have been deployed to soften up the lines of their forces and couldn't comprehend why they hung back.

17

Gorias shouted and rallied the scattering men to charge the center anew. At his words and example, many broke from the weakening wings and stabbed forth into the center. Led by La Gaul, the lone man on horseback in this charge, the shouting soldiers raged on into the bloody fray.

He struck, flanked by running, berserk Kelts and green pikemen with something to prove. The field opened up, letting them near opposing lines of archers who only wore leather jerkin, not thick armor. Their ranks, arrows notched, were easily penetrated as many ran at the sudden shift in the battle. The spearhead move bit deep, dividing the middle of the Albion forces, driving Gorias to within sight of several older men on horseback, generals, he surmised.

* * * * *

"Mum?" Orsen said.

The Queen blinked and found herself back in her main throne room with the youth she'd called.

Orsen tilted his head, concerned, "Mum? Are you well?"

Broke from her memory, but unable to stop smiling, "Yes. Fine." Her manner turned stern and she faced Orsen, then glanced at the two women guards. Neither set their eyes on the Queen, but stared down. "Convey my thoughts to Gorias."

"You're certain he'll do it?" Orsen's voice sounded wary. "The stories of his lack of interest in any conflict for the past ten years are many."

"Aside from the dragonfire, which will get his interest, convey the other matters in due course. He'll do it."

"How can you be so sure?"

She turned away, eyes closed, saying, "Gorias La Gaul is a great many things. I saw him return the heads of two Generals and three wizards due to their slighting of a princess, over a century ago. He has a soft spot for girls who love him, be he bitter and old now."

"He will see the program through to the end?"

Again, she looked at him with stern eyes. "Only Gorias can

18

be trusted in full. Only he will execute it all with impunity." Her bony hands fists, she looked to a rendering on the wall and said, "I won't leave the throne to that bitch and her offspring."

"Yes, Mum."

"Is there something else?"

Orsen's shoes shifted. "What was the slight to you, then the princess? What would make Gorias lead an army over?"

Eyes dancing, Garnet replied, "Ask Gorias sometime. He may even tell you."

After a bow, Orsen departed.

The Queen waved at the Castellan and said, "You are dismissed Turenball. I'm glad you have not fallen to the fire in the night."

He too left after a bow, leaving the Queen with her guards.

Garnet never turned but said, "Speak, Alena. I feel your mouth wanting to burst."

"Mum," Alena said, her throaty voice steady, eyes still pointed to the floor. "Your affection for Lord La Gaul is clear."

Again, Garnet's eyes closed, remembering the night of the battle of the Somme, how Gorias came unto the chambers of the Princess, a lower quadrant to towers near the inner walls to this day, and went to his knees before her. He'd helped regain her honor that day and it felt beautiful.

"Yes? What is it you wish to know?"

"Why didn't your father choose him for your husband? Isn't Gorias of royal blood?"

Eyes open, manner curt, the Queen replied, "I'd been promised to another since my fourth birthday. The marriage of my consort was wonderful and I produced many lovely children. Unfortunately, they cannot aide me now. Gorias, well, every young maiden has her first love, no?"

Hand resting on her sword pommel, Alena said nothing.

"I saved my virginity for my husband, but mind you, young lady, Gorias La Gaul was the first man to touch me." She turned to Alena, an impish smile on her lips. "Would that every girl had a tender lover as I had for her introduction to the arts of love." Her smile disappeared and Garnet's rigid way returned. "Still, that was a long time ago. We shall soon see if La Gaul is truly a Lord or the dirty dog many say."

✶✶✶✶✶

Orsen Riva met Gorias La Gaul in an Albion whorehouse. The young man Orsen came to Rhiannontown in hopes of contacting the legendary mercenary for a service for his Queen, the much-feared Lady Garnet Peverall of Transalpina. La Gaul attended the whorehouse to purchase a harlot. The two men, nearly seven hundred years apart in age, met when La Gaul's twin swords sent a head flying into Orsen's delicate hands. At the bottom of the stairs, the youth caught the hairless orb like a ball in a child's game. An erudite palace servant, Orsen's shock froze him. He let the head, slick with blood and sweat, turn in his hands. The eyes of the decapitated man blinked. Orsen screamed and dropped the head on the red carpet. Unlike a ball, it only bounced a few inches off the floor and didn't roll over but once.

"Try and cheat me out of the last whores," the deep baritone voice of Gorias La Gaul echoed in the foyer of the candle-lit brothel. The looming legend swore and spit on the corpse of the man he had just killed. Streams of blood painted the velvety tapestry to the left of the grand staircase of the house of ill repute, but not a drop struck the imposing, armored figure of La Gaul.

The dead man's corpse flailed, slapping at a tattooed chest in terror, unable to deal with the reality of his own death. Ominous in his stance over the body as it grew still, Gorias' grim face frowned at the display. His white beard drooped as his teeth ground together.

"Now I gotta pay to clean the damn place up." His heavy leather boot kicked the dead body and he spat on it again. "Ask to flip a coin for the services of the Mallory twins, ya prick," La Gaul snorted, blue eyes afire. "Lucky I didn't cut ya deep and let ya bleed to death."

Orson wiped his mouth and accidentally rubbed blood into his teeth. He dropped to his knees, seized the bronze spittoon in the entranceway of the whorehouse and vomited. After his spasm ceased, he looked up the stairs at the towering fable, La Gaul. The old man's massive body obscured Orsen's view of the two harlots on the stairs. He saw their flowing hair and heard them giggle. Orsen felt embarrassed at his weak moment. Even the aged Madam, graying, swathed in burgundy samite robes gave him a sympathetic look from across the room.

"You killed a man for that?" Orsen rasped, checking his tan cotton breeks to see if he tore the knees on the trip to the floor.

Gorias replied, "Turak there was a wanted man." He pointed at the deceased man and made an obscene gesture. "Besides, he could've waited until I was done." Sweeping back his mane of white hair with a jerk of his head, the old fighter turned to the red-haired women. No words were spoken as they started to ascend the stairs. Suddenly, he stopped and turned back to the youth. "Who are you, kid, and what the hell are ya doing in this place? Somethin' tells me it ain't for a game of hide the manhood."

Orsen stood, straightened his jacket and said clearly, "I am Orsen Riva from the service of Her Majesty, the Queen of Transalpina across the channel, in the name of the goddess Ernytel. She requests your skill in hunting down a suspect that has confounded the local guard and Constables back in our land."

La Gaul blinked and seemed lost in thought as the Mallory sisters walked their long fingernails up his substantial cloak-covered arms on opposite sides. "The goddess or the Queen?" He laughed at his own joke and then said, "Huh. Lady Garnet Peverall of Transalpina? She's still alive, by God? Damn. The gal paid me a fortune 'bout a hundred years ago. Well, I can use the cash if ya really are from the old lady."

"I can prove I'm from Her Majesty."

He turned and started to walk up the stairs. "You can wait a while, all right?"

"But…" Orsen sighed, realizing he wasn't going to change what La Gaul had on his mind.

At the top of the curved stairs, La Gaul let his cloak open, revealing the blue armor. The candlelight glinted off the shiny plates from his neck to his boots. The Madam gazed up after him and sent the renowned combatant a wink.

Gorias said, "You coulda hired Turak there, I guess, he's as much a rogue as me in this enlightened age of the judgmental goddess ya mentioned."

"The Queen desires your service, La Gaul," Orsen explained calmly, glancing at the lifeless man. "Turak was near to five hundred years old and hadn't as many kills as you."

Gorias grunted, "Time he was dying anyway then, wasn't it?" A few men entered to carry out the body of Turak. Dressed in russet gypons, these men made no eye contact, and pulled their gorgets closer, having shielded themselves from the night's chill with the musterdevilliers fabric. A few servant girls in drab, flaxen tunics started to take down the bloody tapestries.

Just before he disappeared upstairs, Gorias called down, "The Madam there owes me a favor. If she does it wrong, tell me and I'll take her head as well."

The swaggering marvel left Orsen confused by his words. The older woman, not unattractive, ample of bosom and supple of hips, now winked at Orsen. She waited until the others left and sighed. "He wouldn't do that to me, the hoary sinner." She then walked over, pulled up a chair and started to undo Orsen's pants. She held his trousers firm and there was no escape, though he struggled. "He knows I do quality work."

Orsen tried to get out of his mind what he saw disappearing upstairs with Gorias…how the twin Mallory sisters sported three legs and were joined at the hip.

Orsen Riva faced the chandelier and blessed the perks of being the servant of the Queen.

❖❖❖❖❖

In an hour's time, Gorias staggered down the stairs and fell onto a reclining couch in the receiving room of the brothel. A portly girl with a disfigured right cheek handed La Gaul a flagon as he groaned, stretching out his long frame. He gazed up into the placid face of the auburn-haired youth Orsen and paused a moment before drinking.

Orsen said, "I'm flabbergasted the couch can hold all of your weight with the armor and all."

Gorias drank, then coughed, but didn't answer.

"Surprised I'm still here?"

His mane of white hair shaking from side to side, Gorias cleared his throat. "No. After what the Madam gave you, I figured you'd wait and see if she owed me any more favors."

"Your friendship with the Madam was much appreciated, sir, but the matter of the Queen remains."

Another drink fell; Gorias put his head back, adjusted the armor by his hips and sighed. "I gotta great joke here kid, but I'll leave it go."

Orsen raised his right hand and then extended it, showing Gorias what he held.

The old man squinted and then leaned forward long enough to snatch the object from the youth. "Huh. Been a long time since I saw this. Garnet was wise to send this along, as there's no way to doubt where it came from."

"She said you would listen after seeing this. What is it, exactly? She wouldn't tell me."

Gorias ran a thumb over the object, and then held it up. "The main hunk of the bracelet is gold, of course, but the piece that surrounds it is off a dragon's eyelid. Kind of pretty really, ya see, some of them had double lids like crocs. I handed it to her about a hundred years ago."

"Very kind of you."

Though his eyes got lost on the bracelet for a moment, Gorias soon snapped out of his trance. "I was a bit of a romantic back then, not just whores and no feelings like now."

"I see."

"What's so damned wrong that she needs me? Doesn't she have guards, a police troop near the coast and some necromancer assface telling her which way is north? All of the royals have that kinda stuff to lean on. I'm sure that's how ya knew I was in Albion, anyway, some idiot rolling bones. Why call on an old killer like me in a petty criminal case?"

Hands on his belt, Orsen admitted, "Yes, the Queen now refers to Yannick as her chief prognosticator. His abilities are more to portent horoscopes for the Queen and make her balms for various ailments."

"I never saw a wizard yet that wasn't rolling the wrong bones when he should be doing his regular job."

"The Queen wants to usher in an enlightened age, one under the edicts of the pure goddess, Ernytel, via the abbess Niva." Orsen stated as if reciting a pledge.

"I've heard of Ernytel," Gorias related with little breath left in himself. "Nosy bitch who tells ya how to live your life, what to think and where to piss. I'd bend a knee to someone else if I were young."

"She's the one true goddess from which all purity and light flows."

The old man looked at him curiously but let him talk.

"That's why the act of selling curses, and various acts of wizardry, are forbidden in Transalpina, land by the ocean. Transalpina's old feuds with Albion are no more and our place will be a realm of brightness and good breeding, not one of darkness. It will take time to shrug off the bonds of old magic and primal fears, but the Queen is determined to see it happen."

Gorias drank before saying, "Yeah, I heard you all will burn them if caught, the necromancers and such."

"Mostly a token gesture at first, just to drive the practice off the street corner."

"And back into the privy where it belongs?" Gorias stifled a laugh. "Better than selling babies on the street corner like they do in the far East for such ceremonies. I'd sooner all wizards went the way of the dragons, if I had my say."

Orsen's keen eyes studied La Gaul's dragon skin armor and fumbled for his words, then blurted, "Are the legends true that it was you that killed the last of the dragons?"

Gorias sipped the drink again. "Ya believe everything you

24

hear around the campfire or at a mead hall?" Again the old man laughed before saying lowly, "Funny, there aren't any dragons around any more, are there?"

Eyes on the nail of the dragon on Gorias' forearm, Orsen blinked. "Odd that you mention dragons, La Gaul, for part of this may involve them in a rather strange way."

"There aren't any more dragons," Gorias said with a firm voice, watching the disfigured server trim the lamp near the doorway. She curtsied before leaving, smiling at Gorias. The warrior waved under his chin at her and took another swallow. "All right, ya have my interest, kid. What makes ya think that a dragon could be involved in any of this trouble you talk of? What's happening, anyway?"

"Oh, it wouldn't be a dragon, per se, Lord La Gaul..."

"Call me Gorias." La Gaul stared at the back of his right hand and his eyes traced a crossing of scars there. "I haven't been a Lord in hundreds of years."

"Fine, then, Gorias, a dragon couldn't fit into the bed chambers of these politicians who are being burnt to death."

His head snapped back on the plush pillow, Gorias roared with laughter. "By the God of Heaven, kid, yer a riot!"

Still serious, Orsen stated, "It's not without good reason the dragon idea was postulated, sir. These men were of high office, usually castellans for the Queen herself or her family's households. They were found in small rooms burnt alive, yet the fire didn't consume the entire establishment. You see, dragonfire..."

"...isn't like regular flame," Gorias completed his sentence and sat up on the couch. He winced and rubbed his back-brace. "Dragon fire is gelatinous like a dessert dish and will eat away what it gets deposited on like an acid. Yet, it has a strange combustible quality that'll only go until the substance burns out."

"Your help is requested for a great sum," Orsen said and fell quiet when Gorias stood up. The big man lost none of his menace in his old age, the youth thought. "I can take you to the latest scene across the channel if you are up to it."

A sour look spread on the harsh features of La Gaul as

25

he snapped, "I'm ready for more than just sniffing after a Queen, the goddess Ernytel, and her trouble, ya damned runt. Must be a real problem if yer Queenie sent ya after me. These politicians her friends or family?"

"Friends, of course," said Orsen as La Gaul stretched.

"Is there something else she wants?"

Orsen hesitated and then said, "It looks rather bad if the Queen is trying to create a better world and her castellans are found dead in rooms above taverns."

"You're right there," Gorias agreed, watching Orsen amend the cuffs of his jacket. Great reflexes undiminished, La Gaul snatched the young man's right hand and turned it over. "That's some tattoo for a house servant," Gorias jabbed at the mark on Orsen's wrist. "Why would a pretty boy like you have such a thing?"

His hand pulled back, Orsen wore an angry look. "It's a tattoo of good fortune, endowed on me by Yannick, the Queen's Prognosticator."

Gorias raised an eyebrow as he wrapped his cloaked about himself. "Yeah, if ya paid enough, I wager that wizard endowed you with special rites in that mark, to ensure good fortune."

A mild shrug later, Orsen said, "That's no one's business but mine."

"Take me to one of these scenes, kid...I..." the old eyes of La Gaul looked up and he said quietly, "wonder why I gave ya that favor from the Madam? Maybe the necromancy of that there Yannick is strong enough to give ya good luck."

Orsen frowned. "Such major arcane powers are illegal in Transalpina. What of it then?"

Gorias smiled and slapped him on the shoulder hard enough to make the boy take a step. "No real reason, just curious that's all. Hell, ya better walk slow with me, kid, if yer lucky. I need all the good fortune I can get these days." He tossed the bracelet to the Madam of the house and performed a perfect bow. Orsen stared for a long time at the bracelet as it slid on the whore's wrist, but said nothing.

They departed the large house and the few newcomers to the

establishment provided Gorias a wide berth. As Gorias was about to ascend his horse tethered outside near the stables, his head snapped toward the alleyway behind the brothel.

This action caused Orsen to look away from his own colt. "What did you see?"

"Cart of the dead going by, wait a second here." Gorias jogged gingerly toward a large cart of corpses pulled by a pair of horses. Orsen followed him, anyway. The alleyway route netted the gatherer of the dead three bodies that night, one of which was Turak whom Gorias slew earlier.

"Gorias, sir, why…?" Orsen stammered as the old legend shouted at the driver to halt and then proceeded to dig into the pile of dead bodies on the back.

"They're mine now," the chubby driver squalled at Gorias in the moonlight, his head wrap starting to unravel as he lost his temper. "If you want a bounty on them for being dead, it's too late. I have them fair to rights!"

"Ya can have the corpses," Gorias shot back, loud, clearly impressed at the pluck of the fat man with little ability toward the greatest warrior alive. "I just want to see something. There, look kid." He pointed at the shoulder of Turak. "See that tattoo?"

"Vaguely in this light. What of it?"

"Do ya see what it is? A bag, a potion bottle and the rainbow?"

"Difficult to see in the darkness and that image…"

"…has faded," Gorias affirmed. "That's a tattoo oriented with some magical properties. When he had his head cut off, Turak kept slapping that spot up by his chest, that tattoo. Well, it's a balm for healing, which is why a stubbornness to die set in and more blood shot out."

Orsen nodded, rubbing his chin. "Very likely, sir. His wound was too grievous for a mystical tattoo to heal."

Frown deepening, Gorias turned toward the stables. "What'll they think of next? Maybe the edict to burn the wizards isn't so harsh after all. That's just unnatural. Your Queen should watch who she employs and lets do tats."

Once they walked to the horses, Orsen glanced at the

backpack that was close at Gorias' spine. "Is it true your double swords are really made from an angel's wings?"

With a swift move, Gorias reached in his cloak, disengaged the twin blades and held them up in the moonlight. "Aw, more tales, eh? What do they look like to you?"

Eying the gleaming blades in the light, Orsen said, "They are alight, yet do not reflect the moon. Their texture doesn't look like steel."

Gorias returned his swords to their housings. "Get drunk once and tell the truth and it follows ya forever. C'mon, let's go." After a single step, Gorias halted. "What else is it?"

"Excuse me?"

"Just dragonfire on bad politicians, nothing else?"

Orsen hesitated and Gorias grabbed him by the shoulders. "Ya little prick, I'll kill yer ass and send that good fortune tattoo back to Lady Garnet under glass. Don't screw with me!"

"There is a matter of secession in the land."

Gorias' eyes narrowed. "The Queen's heirs? They're threatened?"

"One might say that. Her sons and daughters are dead."

"I kinda wondered about that, but she had grandchildren." Gorias grimaced. "Are they all dead, too?"

"Save for one, but she's no longer in the realm. The Queen's nephew stands to inherit the realm, but..."

Gorias cut in, "Garnet hates her younger sister's guts. I know." He took a few steps back toward his mount and then stopped once more. "Her sister, Mavik?"

"Yes."

"Huh. Back in the day, Mavik was a real piece of work and couldn't have kids due to her lifestyle."

Orsen wore a confused look.

Gorias smirked. "She couldn't keep her knees together as a younger gal and the King ordered so many bastards aborted, Mavik couldn't have a kid later when she wanted one. She musta got lucky, huh?"

"I hadn't heard that. Dowager Mavik is a lady of high class."

"Old age and no witnesses can do that to ya. It'll make ya forget ya bedded the servants, the chef, the stable guys and their buddies. The sitting monarch gets pissy when royal blood ain't on the menu opposite another royal."

Orsen's face darkened. "I'll explain more as we go."

✵✵✵✵✵

Sometimes, Nykia dreamt she woke up in her bed, back in the vacation home the Prytens burnt. That dream made her angry enough to wake up for real, usually not talking like a princess but the pirate fighter she'd become.

In the dead of night she woke up, swaying in a hammock, covered in sweat, tears running down her face. Nykia swung her legs down and hopped from the swinging bed. Bare footed, Nykia walked up the wooded steps and stood on the deck of the larger schooner.

"Out of the way, Allard," she told an aged man scanning the waters with a spyglass. Clad in filthy breeks and a vest, the coarse-skinned man performed a mock bow and stepped aside.

The sea air in her lungs, Nykia's hand ran down between her breasts and stopped at her abdomen. Her fingers drummed as the wind off the sea struck her face, the flap of the sails keeping time with the rush of the sea.

A few men tending the rigging and watching out on the deck noted her, but paid her little mind. Allard took a hit off a small flask and moved on down the way.

Her fingernails clenched tighter on her belly and she mumbled, "You're very close, Gorias." Eyes closed, she licked her teeth. "Why are you here?"

"Ho, there, Nykia," came a gruff voice from over her head. She never turned to see who spoke. "Early for even you to rise."

"He's near, Noguria. Gorias La Gaul, he really is I know."

A tall woman with waist-length blonde hair and amazingly long legs slowly descended from the deck behind her. On each hip, leathery coils of whips slapped the bare portions of Noguria's hips

29

just above her high boots "I haven't heard you speak of him for quite a while and you didn't react when I told you he may be close by." Noguria cracked her knuckles and then stretched, watching Nykia scanning the endless waves. "I figured him long dead by now, but we heard tell of him near the temple of Rhiannon in Albion the other day. Hell, didn't we hear a story by those drunken sailors that La Gaul died in the great Dagon sacrifice at Nineveh a few years ago?"

Her face sour, Nykia shook her head once. "I didn't believe that then, nor do I now."

Noguria looked her up and down and then shared Nykia's stare across the water. "You feel it in your bones, do you?"

Nykia folded her arms and hugged herself for a moment. Noguria slipped a slender arm about Nykia and pulled her tight. Nykia's dark eyes closed and she said, "I feel it, under my skin."

CHAPTER II

CHANNEL CROSSING

At the outer reaches of the hamlet of Rhiannontown, Orsen said, "It's only thirty minutes' ride to Portcity."

In the saddle, Gorias glanced back at Rhiannontown and remarked at Orsen's words, "Can't fault the Albion's for their originality in naming."

Facing the dirt road, Orsen related, "Rhiannontown is known for the temple to Rhiannon, the great goddess of Albion and the stone circles outside it. Portcity is where one disembarks, hence the name. No need to draw fault with everything."

Gorias muttered, "So much for casual conversation." They rode for a few minutes before Gorias said, "Rhiannon isn't a deity to break one's balls, though. Her and her initiates, they keep to themselves, get some oil from the masses, pour it down the well for the goddess and pray for good things. No mess, no big rules or anything. Rhiannon kinda helps when she can." Gorias voice had a lighter air, almost comical. "Kinda cute, no?"

In the moonlight, Gorias could see Orsen's jaw tighten before he declared, "Rhiannon is a gutless choice for a goddess. There's no sacrifice, personal or literal, just everything is all right." Orsen spat on the ground as if he could hit Rhiannon herself. "Gutless."

Amused, Gorias related, "I didn't say she was a god for real, kid. The priests of Rhiannon are a quiet bunch. For the regular fella in the street, yeah, simple goddess to call on either in swearing or hopes for good performance on the bed mat. Her priests are fanatics, like any other followers of a god, though."

"She's a false god, an idol."

Gorias adjusted his thick belt and made sure his pouches stayed snapped down. "Never know, son. Rhiannon might be closer than ya think."

They rode on in silence for several minutes, navigating the

well-trod road made wider by wagons and many hooves. Once they'd passed along the outer ridges of the sleeping Portcity, signs of life showed. The closer they drew to the dock, the chill of the sea made Orsen tremble and Gorias take a deep breath.

"Over this away," Gorias pointed at the series of docks stretching out from behind a tiny tree-line. "The sea air can't block the scent of Kazmur's stables and transports."

His nose wrinkling as he caught a whiff of what Gorias referred to, Orsen stated, "I have passage ready for us on the large barge there."

Gorias glanced over at the huge ship a few hundred yards past the galleons moored by the stables. "Nice, but I want Traveler to have a good ride."

They stopped in front of the stables and dismounted. A gagging cough echoed from within the domicile constructed with bricks on two sides and logs on the other. Gorias almost hammered on the wood plaque bearing the owner's name, but the door swung outward. Lamps lit inside, they saw a few men sitting, bored, drunk or both. A squat man with a round head made of pimples and greasy hair filled the door.

"By Rhiannon, you came back," the ugly man said and coughed violently. "You're good on for the gold, I have to admit."

"Kazmur, my word is usually good, unless someone kills me in the night and I can't follow through," Gorias told him with a smile and dismounted Traveler. "I won't be going across in the night, but please take my horse with other revenue, savvy?"

Kazmur nodded and gestured at Orsen's mount. "Same for yours?"

Orsen replied, "I'm not fond of a horse. Any one will do. I'll find another in my homeland."

Bloodshot eyes lit a bit as Kazmur grinned. "Suit yourself. Good luck with him, Gorias."

"He's a lucky little one, Kazmur. With any luck, he'll keep me alive another day."

The man stepped out of the stable and a wave of body odor hit Gorias and Orsen. Gorias didn't react, but Orsen covered his mouth. Kazmur stroked Traveler's mane. "Damned fine animal. I'll see to him."

Once they walked away from the stables, Orsen stopped, put his hands to his knees and wretched. The dry heaves stayed with him for a moment. Gorias waited patiently for him to recover or vomit.

"Through?"

"Yes, for now. I need to lay off the pipe and drink."

"That's all right. Ya got the rest of yer life to ruin yerself."

"Why did you tell him you weren't crossing tonight?"

"I don't have to tell everyone my business, do I?"

Orsen wiped his eyes and stayed with Gorias as they walked onto a closed shop's porch partially lit by lanterns. Nearby, a few locals warmed their hands over small bonfires and talked. "By the goddess, that was terrible."

"One gets used to filth in this world same as beauty. More rotten than good, I fear, but hey, yer young yet. True enough, that fella needs to take a step closer to the paper when he wipes his ass."

Just when Gorias was going to ask about passage and the barge looming before them, a commotion ensued amongst the people. Many of the robed men of the docks started shoving each other. Gorias stepped in front of Orsen, hands to his sword pommels, but he peered over the gaggle of little men.

"Another religious fanatic," Gorias told Orsen as the smaller man moved around his frame.

The crowd parted enough for them to see a figure in an orange-tinted robe pull back his hood. The old fellow, near to naturally bald and wearing a close-cropped beard, sat on the ground, legs folded under him. He held up a large gourd and undid the top.

Many muttered as to what would happen next but when Orsen gaped at Gorias. "This won't be as exciting as you think."

The priest opened his mouth wide and splashed the contents of the gourd over his face. The substance ran thicker than water, but not quite the composition of honey. The priest wavered little as the amber-colored fluid filled his mouth. In a moment, he started to gag and then convulsed.

"You thought he'd set himself afire, huh?"

Orsen confessed, "Yes. I've heard stories of men sacrificing themselves that way."

The priest flopped over, broke wind loudly and became still.

Gorias waved at the body. "That's the high priest of Rhiannon. He just drowned himself in on a dock."

"Why there?"

"So as not to befoul his land, I guess."

Orsen thought a bit before saying, "Gutless to the last."

"You'd have preferred a violent death and a self-consuming one?" Gorias chuckled and slapped the small man on the back. "Barbarian."

"You knew that man? You said he was the high priest?"

Gorias turned toward the barge. "I know of many people. Is this our ride?" He frowned at the method of transport Orsen acquired for transversing the channel. "I guess I've sailed in worse. What is this, a damned frigate?"

"A barge, technically."

The vessel stretched on, mostly with a flat bottom, but curled at the edges like a massive canoe. Huge sails loomed overhead, with smaller ones in the rear and a rudder on the side. "I guess it's just made for traveling the channel, huh? The side rudder negotiates the current either way. That thing'd be death in the open sea."

"Wonderful thing we aren't going that way then."

A whimpering squeal made them turn, seeing a man afar off the docks, his head and wrists bound across in a wooden set of stocks. Both of his eyes bruised, dried blood caked his cheeks and he hung from the stocks limp, his clothing in tatters.

Gorias asked a passing sailor, "What did he do?"

"Stowaway," came the answer from the scratchy voice.

Orsen wondered, "Hasn't he suffered enough? Look at the poor man."

Gorias turned back to the ship. "Ain't for me to say. Swift justice beats coddling 'em too long."

Orsen handed coins to the bosons. He turned from these men and said quietly, "I travel for Her Majesty, but a royal war ship might arouse, well, certain trouble in the ports of Albion."

"Yeah, I can see that." Gorias pulled his cloak tighter about himself, nodding to a few men dressed in baggy clothes and head wraps typical of merchants across the channel. He eyed two of them close, seeing them a trifle tall for sellers of wares and men obviously concealing weapons in their loose-fitting clothes. No law restricted them carrying weaponry, so he wondered after the stealth of their follow passengers

"Relations are good with the King of Albion, but not substantial," Orsen related as they looked the long ship over. "The sitting pretender on the throne is a better monarch to deal with than his pervert predecessor."

Gorias followed him to the dock and nodded. "Yeah, the Keltos usurper did the world a favor by butchering King Silex and all of his family."

At Silex's name, Orsen stopped, flared his nostrils and spat. His eyes wide at Gorias, he retorted, "Silex or Satan, no difference from the lessons in school. They should pin a medal on that barbarian drunk for his actions."

"I doubt he'd have one. But before ya ask, yes, Silex really was a freak. Not just bug-screwing crazy, but so beholden to the priests and wizards that they controlled his every desire, thus furthering their need for Mage materials." Once they stood aboard the ship, Gorias went to the handrail and looked back at the city as if he could behold all of Albion. "It'll take a few generations to replace all of the babies and children Silex used."

Orsen stiffened and motioned Gorias to follow him. They stopped at a series of cabins near the aft portion of the barge. "Can we discuss something else?"

"Yeah, whatever. I've left countries with better thoughts. I'm tempted to travel on the ship with the horses, I dunno why. I'll miss Traveler." He glanced at some of the crew. "Good sailors here, not a wormy bunch, well fed. I feel ready to slumber in the womb of safety."

"How much have you drunk today?"

"Not enough if I'm really crossing the channel on this fool's errand. Still, I feel better with a good crew of men than a bunch of navy washouts or pirate wannabes. They look apt to save their own asses, thus, mine will be comfy, too."

"You fought in the wars against Silex when Garnet was young?"

"Ya ask and yet, ya already know."

"What was the nature of the slight which started the conflict? What happened to make a war be fought for the honor of the Queen?"

Gorias shrugged. "Tits. Silex said Princess Garnet had nice tits. He'd never even seen her, but had a servant steal some of her girly clothes. One thing led to another…"

"A war over that? That cannot be."

"Kinda the start of it."

Orsen stopped, stared at the slabs of stone on the deck that the sailors threw tarps over and tied down.

One of the sailors said, "Big rocks for crown prince Vincent, Mavik's son."

"He likes rocks?" quipped Gorias, and the two men he'd noted earlier laughed with him from behind them.

Lips pursed, Orsen replied, "He's a sculptor."

The shorter of the two men in baggy clothes nodded furiously. "I've seen his work. Not bad if you're into nude fellas, uh, and I'm not."

A quick turn from Gorias made the two men tense up, but they relaxed when all he said was, "Congratulations."

The taller man did a brief bow. "I'm Coryll Masse, relation of the Lascaux Masse clan. This is Vallen."

Gorias nodded at the shorter man. "Vallen…what?"

"I don't have a dad so I don't have a last name."

Mirth spread over Gorias' face. "We all got a daddy."

Vallen answered, "Can't say who mine is, really. Don't know."

Gorias took a breath and looked over the other covered objects on the deck, one's with sharper edges and obviously not stone. "Guess that's what the world is coming to."

Coryll grinned. "The end, I hear." The two bowed again and walked away.

A sailor much older than the youths approached Gorias, stopped and took off his head scarf. "You are Gorias La Gaul?"

Eyes reading him over, Gorias admitted, "Yeah."

"My Pa told me many a story of you, of your defeating the dragons in the battle of the Somme. Just pleased to meet you, sir."

"Get me to Transalpina on this bucket and I'll buy ya a drink, son."

The heavily sunburnt man smiled a mouthful of rotten teeth and gingerly took Gorias' hand.

Once he left, Orsen said, "I bet he can drink as much as you."

"Hope so. Here's hopin' I wasn't his daddy."

Orsen did laugh. "How many women have you been with?"

"How many have you, palace boy?"

Stiffening, Orsen replied, "That's none of your business."

Gorias slapped him on the shoulder again, hard enough to make him take a step this time. "Ain't so fun being interviewed all the time, is it?"

Before entering the cabin, Gorias stopped and raised his chin toward the rear of the vessel. "Is that our Captain?"

Orsen strained to look from Gorias' angle. "Yes. His name is Cody, I believe."

"Now that skinny bastard is an ol' sea dog for sure."

"Yes, he used to be a Captain of one of Her Majesty's Naval vessels. Old age and drink sent him to retirement, but I think he's able enough to command a barge."

"Guess we're gonna find out, huh?"

Gorias ducked low as they stepped through the doorway into the cabin area. Several wooden benches, replete with worn cushions, lined the walls and many hammocks hung from the support beams, one of which Gorias pushed to make it sway as he passed.

Orsen put his hand in one of the hammocks. "This is fine luxury for a common ship."

Gorias gave a mild shrug, but due to his armor and cloak, it hardly showed. "Indulge if ya so choose." Gorias imparted a mock salute, then sat in the corner with a groan.

Orsen smiled as he climbed in the hammock. "This helps me as I'm not the best sailor. It'd probably be better on your back."

Gorias sat forward a little, hands on his knees. "I'm not dead yet, junior." He soon settled back and yawned. "Besides, I'd rather sit with my back to the wall, rough sea or no."

For a moment, Orsen's face twisted, perplexed. He soon lightened his countenance, understanding the caution of the old fighter. "I see."

Gorias shifted the pillows behind him, saying, "I never turn my back to a door. This way, if they come for me, they'll stab you first. That'll probably wake my ass up."

Orsen swung in the hammock, mouth open, but he soon shut it and said nothing.

"That tall kid on the deck was lying, by the way."

"Excuse me?"

"Coryll Masse he said his name was? The house and bloodline he claimed was exterminated to the last man in a war when I was two hundred years old, five centuries ago. I wasn't here but read of it on tablets in Jericho."

"I presume he wasn't obligated to tell us his genuine identity."

Gorias yawned. "I was gonna say I was Orsen Riva, Lord Governor of the privy, but the chance slipped by."

"Charming."

Eyes closed, fingers interlocked across his chest, Gorias asked, "How's the ol' girl?"

"Pardon?"

"Lady Garnet," Gorias said loud, not hiding his words whatsoever.

Others in the room looked up from their positions in the opposite walls, but soon lowered their heads again. Through the doorway walked Coryll and Vallen. They paused to stare at Gorias and then took up seats near the portal.

Frustrated that Gorias showed no tact, Orsen mumbled, "Fine, as good as can be expected, situation being what it is for her."

"Yeah?" Gorias said somewhat quieter. "What is that really?"

"The land has religion, a great revival under the goddess has taken place, and the Lady relishes the role she takes as the symbol of the land."

"Good for her. She always wore that position well."

"Quite so. However, as I intimated earlier, no heir to the Lady Garnet walks from her household, thus, her siblings and their offspring must be considered."

Bells and whistles sounded, warning all the ship would soon cast off so Gorias waited to say, "Gimme this straight, son. I knew her sons died long ago, and her daughter within the last ten years and such. But all her grandkids as well? Little Nykia is dead, too?"

Orsen waited a while before he said, "She isn't so little, but for all regular purposes, yes."

"But you say there are no heirs, but that sailor just said the Crown Prince was Mavik's son? I presume he means ol' Mavik, Garnet's sister."

"Yes."

Gorias opened his eyes and sat forward, noting the two skinny men with their faces pressed to the portal. "You're jerkin' me off with words, kid. First you lure me in with the dragonfire story…"

"It's no story. The politicians are dying from it! They feel the heart of Pergamus is lashing out from the great beyond."

"Yer breakin' my freakin' heart." The dark humor faded from Gorias' face, replaced by anger. "Pergamus! What do any of ya know about that? I'm more interested in how Nykia died."

Orsen sighed and interlaced his fingers behind his head. "Father wanted me to be a sailor. He thought I'd have made a good officer in time, as I took to ships and sea travel at an early age. That changed in time."

Gorias closed his eyes, letting his irritation at Orsen's diversions lighten. "Your father a sailor?"

"No, a castellan for the Queen. He thought I'd be toughened up by the experience."

Gorias cleared his head and tried to fine-tune to the rhythm of the ship as it moved into the waters. "I suppose military service does that."

Orsen volunteered, "I did join the regular army."

"Yeah? How'd that work out for ya?"

"I excelled at archery and the physical regimen, but qualified for the slingers brigades, better for a man of my height."

Gorias never spoke.

Orsen didn't remain quiet. "I only saw scant action until my term was up. We took on some Avars at the fringes of the mountains. I doubt my slings ever killed anyone."

"Firing from cover is different, I guess. One doesn't have to feel the blade in up close."

"It must be spectacular to fight something as grand as a dragon."

"Spectacular, all right. If ya can keep from crappin' yer trousers, it's alotta laughs. Every dragonslayer I ever met who had a hard-on for the hunt, for killing them for sport or for revenge, ended up in dragon-stool."

"How was it that you ended up being the last slayer?"

"Someone had to be. Some folks confuse being a survivor with being a hero."

"Why is it you do the things you do?"

"I'm still alive. Once I'm dead, I'll stop." Gorias took a deep breath before he said, "I'm still good at it, too. Find what you're good at, son, and stick to it. What are ya good at? Carrying messages? Ya must be a sneaky bastard."

Offended, Orsen shot back, "Why would you say that?"

Still placid, Gorias replied, "You got all the way to me in Rhiannontown without a knife in yer back or bein' skinned by the bandits. Ya must be sneaky, stealthy and tougher than ya appear." Gorias turned his head and grinned. "Or that fuckin' tattoo is workin' overtime. There must be somethin' to ya, kid. Nothin' in a wizard's blessing bag or scrotal sack is that goddamn powerful to see ya through all that."

Orsen swung quiet for a few minutes before saying, "The Queen speaks of you as if you're a god."

Gorias scratched himself. "You're unimpressed?"

"I hardly said that."

"But yer manners betray ya, young man, Yer eyes, nose and mannerisms all scream doubt at my godhood, hell, as well ya should. No one could live up to the Lady's tales, I reckon. But I've lived a long time, over 700 years, and after all that, one picks up a few pointers. I read folks really well."

Orsen swung in his hammock, eyes watching the ceiling. "I must be transparent to you then."

"Pretty much, but not everyone can be like me."

A half hour passed and Gorias guessed them far from shore when he noticed Vallen watching him, using his body to obscure Coryll's actions at the portal. Gorias ruminated what a terrible guard Vallen proved to be as he clearly noted Coryll holding a metallic object not unlike a sextant to the portal. At first, Gorias wondered if Coryll plotted their trip by the stars until he saw the crystal within the tiny bars of the sextant. The moonlight struck the jewel and a beam of light glittered back out across the waves. In moments, the two sat beside each other, stowing their objects, hands to their laps. They exchanged a nervous glance.

Orsen turned his head. "Do you hear that?"

Gorias' voice didn't betray that his defenses rose. "Sure. The sound rolls across the waves."

"Strange sounding thunder."

Gorias cracked his knuckles as the two youths sat forward. "That's because it isn't thunder. I'd hold onto something, Orsen."

Overhead the scramble of boots on boards coincided with the roll of thunder coming nearer to their ears. Coryll and Vallen rose up and made for the door of the cabin. The air split and the night exploded with sound, at the same moment the vessel shifted in the sea, causing Orsen to swing high in the hammock, slamming into the ceiling. The two youths flew back from the door, crashing into the beams that bisected the room. Orsen swung down, but never fell from the bed of netting. Gorias moved away from the wall and put his left hand up, stilling Orsen in his motions.

"What was that?" Orsen shouted as those others across the room scrambled, a few drawing their daggers, one stumbling into Vallen, impeding him from leaving the room.

41

Gorias muttered, "Not something ya can stab with a dagger. We were almost hit."

As he unfolded from the hammock, Orsen cried out, "Almost?"

"This thing is made of planking and logs across the belly," Gorias explained as the cabin emptied and they moved closer to the steps leading to the decks. "If they hit us, we'd have heard a whine in the air you'd not soon forget."

Orsen, frustrated, frowned as he reached the steps. "This barge is huge. Who'd want to sink it? Wait a moment! They? Who are they?"

"Pirates!" came the scream of the man in the upper deck, pointing to the east as the men flooded the deck.

Orsen stood above the hold, gaping at the three ships in the distance.

Gorias slapped him on the back so hard the palace servant stumbled. "Hear that? Pirates? Crummy aiming pirates, but pirates all the same."

As many scrambled all over the decks, Orsen stammered, "Why try to kill us?"

Gorias shrugged, still unruffled. "Maybe their aim sucks, maybe that was a warning shot. I can't say. Just in case they do sink us, can you swim?"

Orsen glared at Gorias. "Not the entire channel!"

"We're halfway across, ten miles, tops," Gorias said, looking south in the darkness as if he could see the shores of Transalpina. He noted the crew grabbing Coryll and Vallen, both them trying to get a leg overboard.

"You must be joking."

He pointed at the two being wrestled to the deck. "Those two punks thought it was a great idea. Let's hope it doesn't come to that. Glad my horse is on a different ship. I'd hate to lose Traveler." He then grinned at Orsen. "You? I can find another one of you anywhere."

"This is no time for jokes." He then took note of the violence the sailors used to subdue the two youths but still kept at Gorias.

42

"Can't you help the crew?" Orsen waved his arms as if Gorias couldn't see the desperate populace of the vessel scrambling.

Gorias grabbed Orsen and directed him back to one of the mast poles. "Hold on, kid, or yer gonna be wearin' yer ass for a hat."

The night didn't betray the projectile coming toward them, but their ears presently caught the thunderous echo just as the bundles of fiery explosive landed, ten yards below the bow, exploding on the surface but rocking them slightly.

Orsen exclaimed, "Goddess!" He then glared at Gorias and shouted, "Help them!"

Gorias scanned the deck. "I think that old sea bastard up there will do just fine." He thumbed up to the rear deck at the skinny man wearing the sash of a Captain, but no pants. "Well, it's freakin' late. Glad Cody got off a whore for this fight. Son, ever see what this barge is hauling on deck here?"

Orsen blinked. "Farm implements from Albion aside from the rocks for the Prince's sculpting."

His hand gripping Orsen's shoulder tight, Gorias said, "Since when did they plow fields in Transalpina with those?"

The large tarps securing many shapes on the deck slid back, revealing a series of catapults and siege devices. From the rear deck, the Captain shouted orders and pointed a three-fingered hand at the catapults. The sailors turned the devices, in places unbolting them and reattaching them to the deck in a hurried fashion.

"Goddess," Orsen mumbled. "What sort of madhouse is this?"

"Looks like the Captain knows what he's doing."

"That Cody, a wily fighter for certain. He lost one of his fingers as a prisoner in a camp."

Gorias wondered, "Torture?"

"No, they wanted his academy ring, so they cut it off to get it."

"Reckon he wouldn't give it up any other way. Hell, I can see doin' that."

"But this barge is unarmed, of no military significance."

"All the better reason to have pirates want to take her and the cargo."

Another shot from the lead pirate vessel missed them, this time going over their heads. Everyone dropped to their knees.

One of the sailors said, "The gods are with us. Praise Rhiannon!"

"Screw the gods," another shouted.

"We ain't got time," a third yelled and laughter rippled across the deck.

Gaping, Orsen struggled to find the words. "To laugh in the face of death."

"That takes balls," Gorias agreed. "Yer old man musta wanted this for you. Still think ya got what it takes to be a sailor? It ain't all about drinking and screwing crab-infested whores."

The sailors undid the tarps over the huge rocks and set about striking them with steel-headed mallets. In a few moments, the rocks fragmented. Several sailors took hold and loaded these pieces into the catapults.

Hand to his mouth, Orsen gasped. "Mavik will be livid."

Gorias sighed. "I think yer missin' the big picture here, kiddo."

Captain Cody moved down from the deck and raised his long scope. "Guide the settings by my words." He then shouted off ways to set the catapults.

Orsen shook his head. "How in the world can they do that? He uses no instruments!"

"He's using the tip of his nose, depth of his vision. He knows the sea, the curve of the earth and the breadth of waters he sails all the time." Gorias smirked. "Those fuckers out there don't have a prayer."

"Secure the rocks," Captain Cody called out, but the men had already started maneuvering the huge stones into their final places. Light rollers, no more than sanded logs, and manpower pushed the larger stones into the palm of the catapults. The sailors hurriedly stood back as the tension in the trigger mechanism got wound tight by a burly man on either side of the device. Already positioned back like giant mousetraps, the catapults extended over the length of the ship. The long arm of the weapons swung back, around like a weather vane, snapping into position far over the edge of the boat.

Orsen's mouth dropped open but no words came right away. "That's impossible. The arm will break."

Gorias looked from the weapons then toward the distant ships. "Get your faith tight, son. These artisans know what they're doing."

"Fire!" Captain Cody shouted and dropped his ruined fist to the handrail.

The sailors chopped at the lines securing the loads and the four catapults swung into action. Orson fell to his knees and even Gorias stepped back, so impressive was the recoil action and the spectacle.

The rocks flew across the waters and a hush gripped the barge. Over the water, they heard a huge splash, but this sound soon became overpowered by the crash of wood splintering and the cries of men in peril.

Orsen rose up, stunned. "The old bastard, he did it."

The sailors jumped up and down, hollering and screaming. Many praised their Albion god, Rhiannon, others made obscene gestures at the pirates, and still others dropped their trousers to show them their manhood or moons.

The Captain's hands beat a tiny rhythm on the rail as he stared. He didn't look through his scope, preferring to listen to those sailors who shouted, "Two of them are hit! They are tilting already! By the gods, I bet they are taking on water."

A smile on his weathered face, Cody remarked, "Damn straight they are. Screw with us, will they? Damn their eyes!"

The men cheered again and Gorias patted Orsen on the back. "Ya learn something every day, kid. It makes life worth living."

Cody addressed the men on the deck. "Now, which one of you bastards is the spy?"

Gorias set his boots, sizing up how many stood on the deck, but no sailor made a move. Suddenly, Coryll and Vallen slipped from their captors, making a run for the edge of the vessel. They nearly made a leap for the water before the sailors grabbed them again.

Held fast, the two men were displayed for Cody when he came down to look at them closer. "Planning to swim back?"

The two never answered as the sailors laughed.

Cody's face turned grim, the rough lines growing deeper to his chin. "You were, weren't you?" His nostrils flared. "Pretty boys, clean and shaven recent, trying to pass for regulars, but their bodies, no fat on them." Cody leaned in close to Coryll. "You've swam the channel before, haven't you?"

No answers came.

"Why spot us? Why finger us to the pirates? What could we have that was so much?"

Silence reigned.

His eyes flared in the dim light and he nodded at Vallen. "Cast that one by a line behind us. If he lives to shore, he can go free. He looks dimmer than this one." The men all grunted as they brought forth the steel-headed mallets again, this time shattering the knees of Vallen. Orsen moved behind Gorias, gasping, but the big warrior just watched as Vallen collapsed to the deck. The spy screamed, begging for mercy. None came. "Let 'em swim like that." Cody looked at the other man. "You're hard cases huh? Why bother with us?" Coryll remained silent despite the screams of his cohort. Cody said, "Work him over until he talks. If he doesn't, impale his ass on a pike and let him suffer until we arrive."

Vallen rolled, screaming, "Pergamus, we..."

Coryll slipped free of his captors, raging at his friend, "Shut up, damn you!" Gorias and other sailors moved toward the tall youth as he flailed at his fallen friend. Coryll made it to Vallen as the sailors tackled him, clasping his friend's right ankle.

Vallen still reeled from the blows to his knees, tears drenching his face as he wailed, "He's gotta die! He's gotta die!"

Someone shouted, "Who?" But Vallen screamed louder as Coryll pulled free of him. At Vallen's ankle, a ball of fire blossomed like a flower rapidly yearning for the sun. The fire spread, but only on his body, racing up his calf and over his ruined knee.

All eyes focused on Vallen save for Gorias. He stared at Coryll, who smiled at his handiwork, but his grin faded when he saw Gorias faced him.

The others stepped back as the fire raced over Vallen's

body, his voice screaming, "La Gaul!" But Gorias only imparted a momentary glance.

Gorias grabbed Coryll by the baggy shirt and shook him until his teeth snapped against each other several times. "That's right, skinny, I'm not impressed. They all got a hard-on watching him burn to death because they've never seen it before."

Coryll worked his mouth and Gorias anticipated him spitting in his face so he slammed his forehead down into the youth's mouth, smashing his lips and caving in two front teeth.

Face to face with him, Gorias growled, "Pergamus, aye? La Gaul has gotta die?" Again, Gorias shook the youth hard, the others still gasping at Vallen as the fire coursed over his flesh and ate away at his skin until soon, only bones remained, and they started to become dust. The fire surged, a vibrant yellow, surges of orange but occasionally a golden hue, but then back to its original color. As Vallen ceased to be, the fire started to ebb away, hardly scorching the boards of the barge's deck.

A few coins and a small straight razor fell from Coryll's trousers as Gorias thrashed him, turning out his pockets. Gorias' head snapped down as something else on the deck caught his eye. He threw Coryll into the sailors, who, though still stupefied by what they witnessed, caught him and held on. Gorias dropped to his knees, sweeping up the articles on the deck, and making his hands into fists. Back to his feet, Gorias' stare drilled into Coryll.

"You might as well talk," Gorias told him. "You're as good as dead already."

Still cocky, Coryll looked down and remarked through bloody teeth, "There are things worse than dying. Pergamus…"

A single step forward, Gorias kept his fists tight. "You know what Pergamus really is, don't you, kid?"

Head up, grin returned though ruined, Coryll stated, "Why the place where dragons come from, right?"

Gorias said, "Let him loose."

Cody barked, "What?!"

"This will only take a second. Let him loose."

The sailors unhanded Coryll, but he had little time to get his arms free before Gorias swung and connected with the youth's left eye. Coryll snapped around backward, his legs wavering and he fell back into the arms of the sailors.

Gorias turned to Cody. "I hate to hit a guy held by another. Do what you want with him now."

Cody stepped toward Coryll. "We will."

Gorias walked away from the rest and they started to arm up the youth. Orsen followed Gorias to where he stood near the edge of the barge, seeking out at the pirates in the distance. He opened his hands, shaking loose coins, lint, a hairpin memento of a lass, but keeping his fingers on a tiny object glowing yellow.

Orsen looked around him, but was careful to guard Gorias' discovery from the sailors. "What is that? A pill of some sort?"

Gorias held the tablet-shaped object up. He saw the tiny flicker of fire within. "This isn't good, kid. Coryll killed his buddy rather than let him talk, broke something like this against him, just enough dragonfire to burn a man to death. The tiny casing like glass but not as tough, see, it gives a bit if I squeeze."

"By the goddess," Orsen gasped.

"Yeah, goddess all right." He opened the pouch on his belt and pulled out a small glass vial. This vial didn't glow, but held a wriggling thing too dim to name in the moonlight. Gorias then pulled a silk scarf from the pouch, and wrapped both objects in the fabric. Once he closed the pouch, he turned to Orsen. "We all have our mementos."

"Would it matter if I asked what that is all about?"

"Nope."

The sailors set about tying down the spy and pulling out ropes for scourges as Orsen walked back to the cabin. The Captain and Gorias exchanged a knowing glance, but that was all.

Orsen said to Gorias as he walked into the cabin area, "That's one reason why I can't be a sailor."

"There's more to life than sailing. Hell, that can happen to ya in a desert."

"Cheerful sort, aren't you?"

"A long life does that to ya."

48

✿✿✿✿✿

Luckily, Nykia could swim. She'd been trained years ago by palace staff and the craft became keener to her nature when she came to live amongst the Prytens. Many of her fellows on the sinking vessel may have drowned, but she never looked back. She heard that was a sign of weakness. Nykia and dozens of others swam for the remaining vessel not struck by the Transalpinan Captain. Soon, she saw her mistress, Noguria, beside her in the drink, her blonde hair all washed out by the sea, turned back to its darker hue. The stout crewman, Allard, tried to help Noguria and received a backhanded slap for his trouble.

While they treaded water, Nykia stared up into the faces of those on the last ship. They let down ropes and ladders, but her eyes focused on the tall man who faced her. Dressed only in loose-fitting breeks and sandals, the man shouted, "I'm glad you survived." Behind him stood a broad-shouldered, thuggish man, who frowned at his leader.

"I should've stayed in the Pryten wilderness," Nykia remarked as she started to climb a ladder of rope.

"And why didn't you?"

Once on the deck, she gulped in air and said, "You pigs took me and I was drawn here."

"Tired of tribal life?" he jeered.

"You couldn't understand, dumbass, Dumas."

He roared with laughter. "I bet I understand just fine." Dumas struck a dramatic pose, one worthy of a thespian and said, "Your own true love, Gorias La Gaul, is nearby and heading to Transalpina."

Her boots flat on the wet deck, Nykia shook off her arms and promptly jabbed Dumas in the throat, causing the big man to grab his neck and falter a few steps. Fire burned in his eyes as Noguria hopped onto the deck and shook her locks off like a dog.

"Shut your mouth," Nykia sneered at Dumas. "I'd cut your balls off if you had any."

Allard and Noguria blocked Dumas from striking her.

Nykia faced across the waves, ignoring the distant men in the water and their screams. Her dark eyes rested on the barge. She could hear the cheering sailors over the waves, and even see a few of the figures in the half moonlight. Nykia swallowed hard, eyes focusing on a form taller than the rest, standing near a smaller man. She thought she could see gray hair blow in the night and her heart rose to her throat. "You're here," she gasped silently, hands gripping the edges of her tunic, thinking it not possible that she beheld him from such a distance. "You really are."

"Rotten bitch," said Dumas, rubbing his throat. "You have no humor anymore."

Noguria removed one of her coiled whips and slapped Dumas across the face, but more playfully than to harm him. "Ease up, Dumas. She's young yet."

"You just forget what connects us, pig dog," Nykia snapped at him.

The big man chuckled, "I'm not too bright but I get the notion of obsession."

"It's more than that," Nykia said, her right hand flat on her abdomen, slowly sliding to her pelvis. "It's magic."

Two men moved up to flank Dumas: one a head taller than the rest, skin & bones, but with eyes dancing like a fire; the other a stout man sporting a braided beard that draped his belly.

Comfortable with his two men near, Dumas said, "Why do you think we wanted that barge destroyed? The last deal with Pergamus, well, it was magic."

Hands becoming fists, Nykia raged, "You did it on purpose? You meant to kill Gorias!"

Dumas voice grew grave as he said, "You aren't a princess here, Nykia, barely the bedding for your bitch mistress. Mind your tongue or she'll have to find another."

CHAPTER III

PIE WITH THE QUEEN

The barge cruised on into the night, the men too hearty to sleep, and certainly, the ruckus of those torturing Coryll kept any who did try awake. Once they impaled the spy on a pole via his backside, his cries didn't help those attempting a nap. After an hour, the whistles blew when the watchmen spotted Transalpina's docks.

Stepping down the planks from the barge, Gorias glanced at the prisoner bisected by the pole, now silent, and then back to the dock.

Orsen said with frankness, "Coryll never made it."

"The waves made sure he'd slide down. Hell, on dry land he may have stayed up there for days." Gorias thumbed over his shoulder, but wouldn't look back. "That Captain knew what he was doing."

"Now they won't learn anything."

"I don't think Cody wanted to know any of it too badly. Sure, we wouldn't mind understanding the motives of all that, but this story about what Cody did will get around and that will be a warning enough. Fewer men will volunteer to be spotters or spies amongst the pirate ranks."

"You took note of Pergamus when they spoke of it."

Gorias kept walking and stretching, showing no great emotion to Orsen's words. "You play cards?"

"On occasion."

Eyes scanning the docks, Gorias didn't regard Orsen as he wondered, "You deal out all the cards face up, do ya?"

"Of course not. Oh, I see."

"Just because I ain't blurtin' it out, doesn't mean I ain't gettin' onto everything."

Once on the docks, Gorias hopped a little on the boards and Orsen gave him a sideways glance.

51

"Damned ocean," Gorias grunted, face flushing white for a moment. "It'll be the death of me."

"Missing your horse?"

"I'm missing anyone's horse right now. I'll be glad to get on Traveler again."

Orsen waved at a ship not far off down the line. "He's over there. We'll go collect him. Hopefully these men here have better hygiene than the handler in Albion."

"Dunno, kid. Not everyone can wash their ass so well as those in the palace, out here in the real world, don't ya know?"

Orsen eyed him as they walked. "You aren't a foul-smelling man."

"By the gods, ya know how to put ink in my marker, son. I was waitin' fer that compliment."

Teeth clenched, Orsen cursed under his breath, but Gorias only chuckled.

Halfway to the ship carrying animals the pre-dawn light showed them a few naval schooners and larger battle vessels in tow. Orsen gestured at a soldier guarding the nearest tie-up port and they exchanged niceties. Gorias noted the schooner and then turned to the sea.

"Gorias La Gaul," came a tight, strong voice down the docks.

Gorias turned to face a man on from the schooner, nearly as tall as he, clad in Transalpina naval garb of dark slacks, a white shirt and a navy blue jacket. This man sported officer's epaulets and unblinking violet eyes. His black hair, combed straight back, glistened in dim light. Behind this officer stood another dressed exactly alike, but he allowed a yard of space between himself and his superior officer.

"Of course you wouldn't answer," the officer stated with arrogance in his voice to spare. "You'd never show your hand."

"Did I kill somebody important to you or are ya just an asshole?"

Jaw open, words stuck, the officer froze for a moment. His look of contempt flared as he noted Orsen and the port workers nearby trying to restrain smiles.

"I am Admiral Rosman," he declared, hands pulling the edges of his short jacket down tighter.

"Good for you." Gorias stepped toward him but the admiral didn't back down. "So why do ya act like I pissed in your breakfast?"

"I've heard you were in Albion."

"Ya got great ears. So far, I'm all a twitter."

"Why do you sully our shores?"

"Just passing through."

Rosman's thin brows lowered. "See that you do."

"Admiral, huh? We coulda used ya out there on the seas. Lots of pirates, ya know?"

Rosman flared his nostrils. "I heard that Captain Cody saved your life."

"He saved all of our lives. Mine was accidental."

"A pity. See that you go about your business."

Gorias turned to Orsen. "See, kid? This is an example of one's mouth overloading one's ass for self-aggrandizement. He feels like more of a man because he can wave his prick in my face and live." Gorias laughed once and Rosman's sneer disappeared. The other officer fidgeted with his hands near his pockets, unsure what to do with them. "I killed my first before your birth, piglet, and I'll kill you if you cross my shadow again."

Undeterred, Rosman growled, "You'll eat those words, hero."

"What do ya know, Orsen? He recalls the nickname his mama gave me."

Ready to jump from his boots and strike Gorias, Rosman shook, but held his actions in check. He couldn't stop the blood from flushing his face and his hands balling into fists. The Admiral tore himself from his position and walked away, like a man yanking a boot from the mud. Stomping on the dock like he had a grudge against it, the Rosman departed, fellow officer still behind him at the same distance.

Gorias headed toward the ship that carried Traveler. Once Orsen caught up with him, La Gaul said, "Always throw a dig at their mother, Orsen. The strongest men hate that."

"Very good, sir."

"Unless of course, their mother really was a whore, and then the vain stab kinda loses its thrust, ya know?"

"Indeed, sir."

"Yer not gonna ask me about my mother?"

"I know who your mother was, Lord La Gaul."

Gorias peered down at him for a moment before saying, "I thought ya looked like ya read a lot."

"Nothing to be feared of, Gorias. She was a fine lady of great breeding."

"That she was," Gorias granted and scrutinized the waves again. "How long until we reach the capitol city?"

"Oh, you know it'll take all day." Orsen frowned as the man led Traveler to Gorias and then went to his own stables, producing a burrow for him. "You have no horses?"

The man threw up his hands and showed that his stable sat empty, save for three burrows.

Gorias paid the man a few coins and then got into the saddle. "Well, there ya go, son. Glad yer not emotionally attached to any animal like a foolish ol' fighter, huh?"

❖❖❖❖❖

They ate a quick breakfast of berries, cornmeal biscuits and jerky as the sun rose across the coast of Transalpina. Gorias pondered the long trip ahead, knowing the Queen resided further inland than coastal cities. True, this staved off easy invasion forces from the coast and even the lands beyond Transalpina.

"Gorias, why did you ask me how long the trip is? Surely, you've ridden it many times."

"But not recently. The mind forgets over a decade much less a hundred years. Besides, I didn't come by this way to Albion."

"I see," Orsen replied, pulling at the reins of the donkey.

"Borders beyond this land in good shape?"

Orsen nodded. "I know you fought in the battle of the Somme and then helped burn the great forest outside. The forces of

Transalpina have been at peace with their neighbors since that day, for the most part."

"Well, we did exterminate most of those in the neighboring lands aside from Silex country. We didn't invade Albion."

His nose up a little, Orsen said, "Other savages came in and have filled the lands left vacant to the east. They give us no grief when our forces travel beyond to trade or go aide in a war with an ally."

An hour passed before Orsen suddenly volunteered, "There are vast differences in Albion and Transalpina. Granted, Albion sits beyond the channel on a land mass in the north sea, on the very edge of the known world." He glanced at Gorias. "Surely different than the cradle of civilization where you visited and spent much time."

"Your seasons are rougher here, I'll grant ya that, but Transalpina has better summers than Albion. Pretty dreary there year 'round, but those folks don't seem to mind. Maybe it keeps the foreigners out."

Orsen glanced behind himself as if he could see Albion. "They are bordered by the Pryten wasteland on the west and glaciers to the north."

Gorias glanced across the lands away from Orsen. "I see yer pride swellin' over yer homeland. Take it easy, youngster. I get it." He didn't feel the need to argue over which land saw itself as better. In his eyes neither land ran much more cosmopolitan than the other. Granted, the regular buildings sported a different thatch and more mortar in Transalpina. In Albion, more working-class domiciles were made of logs and had a centralized chimney system, unlike the ones to the rear of the homes Gorias watched as they passed.

Gorias looked down the road, recalling how much rockier the avenues in Albion ran centuries ago. The farmers hemmed in their property lines with small walls composed of these bricks, showing that determined folks could make use of any obstacle.

"Most well-traveled dirt roads go to crap with great rains, but I gotta hand it to the Queen or whoever, the brick and stone streets in some cities are bound to catch on."

"The stones are not that difficult to quarry. They make them small and use filler. It's better on carts and they don't have anything like it in Albion."

"Must be harder on the horseshoes, though, but I reckon the blacksmiths do a good business because of it." Gorias' bored face broke and he mumbled, "And folks wonder why I travel and kill people. I wasn't made for the hearth and all this."

"I hadn't figured you for a farmer."

"I tried my hand at that for a few years when I settled in different places. The tree lines out here are scarcer than in Albion."

"There are different schools of thought on that. Many think the lines are better for the soil."

"Most hands that have ever turned a plow will agree."

"Quite, but several of the groves and whatnot have been gutted for timber. Plus, the sacred groves of the less-schooled have been done away with due to the goddess."

"Bet that went over well."

Orsen raised his nose as if he smelt something foul. "It's better this way. Such places are reminders of appalling ways and rites. It's better the innovative way and not dancing naked in a grove full of ticks."

They rode in silence for a few hours until Gorias asked, "Something on your mind, son? We can talk more about how red bricks are the fad in Albion rather than this whitewashing of rocks in Transalpina if ya want. I'm all about boring travel talk."

"While your mother came from a royal line, I know your father was a tribal chief from a backwater land."

Eyes forward, Gorias replied, "Your point?"

"Certainly, in my mind, your heart would have strove with the ruder folk vanquished by the erudite forces of Transalpina that day, on the Somme."

"Get to it, kid. What do ya wanna know?"

"What did you fight for us?"

"Your Queen, Lady Garnet, then a princess. I had to repay the slight. Time was, I'd have died for her."

"Not now?"

Gorias smiled. "Hell no. I'll only die for myself now. The way

I feel, the hole in the ground or the slot on the pyre will be comin' around soon. The value of my ass has increased in the last hundred years, both for those who want satisfaction in a hire or some punk who wants my pelt on his wall."

Evening fell by the time they reached the capital city of Qesot. Many times both men slept in the saddle. The outer rim of farms tightened up into gardens and thatched-roofed homes, usually built of logs like Gorias saw before. These simple, but cozy dwellings held many families who'd known much peace in their lives.

Gorias commented, "They really don't know they are there to be a buffer zone for invasions, do they?"

Orsen didn't answer.

"Kid, you've ridden in here how many times and never pondered that?"

"Not everyone thinks of dying, death and who they can kill for power every day."

Gorias spat to his right and then waved at a pair of stout girls weeding a garden. "That's why you won't live to be 700 years old."

"If the rumors on the wind are true, the world will end within a hundred years, so, what's to worry on?"

"I've heard that," Gorias remarked as a boy ran up and tossed Gorias an apple. The old man caught it and saluted the youth. A few children ran to them, but just petted Traveler as they went. One touched Gorias' leggings, drawing back fast at the feel of the dragon skin armor. "Transalpinan kids, gotta love 'em, huh?" He smiled at the rosy-cheeked children, their skin tan from much time in the sun after the spring plantings. At that moment, he thought of another difference from those in Albion. Those across the channel seemed pale of skin and fair no matter how much time spent in the sun. Was that a large enough difference to make them natural enemies?

"You are a coy man," Orsen said, watching the worshipful children,

"Excuse me?" Gorias said between bites of the apple.

"You act as if your fame has become a chore and you tire of being Gorias La Gaul, but I see a different yarn in your face when those little ones approach."

"Aw, they're kids. It's the best time of life." Gorias paused, looked to the distant earthen works about the main walls of the city. "No worries when you're a kid. Don't get me wrong, Orsen, being me has its merits. But there's only one of me and that's plenty. No one else should have to be me."

They passed through the guards, who let them all the way through the logs barring the gap in the works. The inner portion sat mostly empty, but Gorias saw where an army would gather their weapons for a siege at the earthen works, before falling back to the first curtain wall that surrounded the city. Gorias sighed, wishing he could sleep through the trip through that, the streets, and then the next series of walls that protected Queen Garnet in her castle beyond.

"It'll be dark by the time we see the Queen."

Orsen eyed the waning sunset. "This is true. Perhaps the morning would be a better idea."

Once inside the city, they traveled across the cobbled streets toward the castle. Orsen stopped them halfway to the castle and dismounted.

Confused, Gorias put both his hands out.

Orsen pointed to a shop made of bricks that belched great puffs of smoke. "You don't expect to see the Queen without a bath?"

"Yer killin' me, son."

"Seriously."

Gorias dismounted. "I guess I need one." He turned his head and grabbed his helm from the rear saddlebag. "I see a pie shop over there. Go get me some pie. I gotta eat something of substance. Don't get pissy, kid, I'll eat as I clean up."

Eyes rolling, Orsen sighed. "Yes, sir."

"And if ya bring me back a meat pie I'll break your damned legs."

❈ ❈ ❈ ❈ ❈

Once cleaned and fed, Gorias and Orsen headed to the series of walls that protected the estates of the Queen of Transalpina.

Orsen sighed, "I thought the bath house owner would bring himself to orgasm if he polished your armor any longer."

Gorias held out his left arm and feigned amazement at the shine. "He did a helluva job, no? That sucker'll tell that tale for the rest of his life."

The guards hovering around the entrance to the Queen's eastern tower wore rough looks. Gorias sized them up as young, brash, and easy enough to kill if the need arose, but dismissed such thoughts. He peered over Orsen's head across the vast gardens and grounds surrounding the tower, thinking how improbable performing a fighting exit might become.

"Well, we didn't beat the sunset, but I like the dark better sometimes. Our luck is holding out."

Orsen still struggled with the donkey. "I shall be glad to dispense with this thing."

"Yeah, I reckon." Gorias pulled his cloak over himself more the closer they came to the tower. The walls, though distant, felt nearer and the number of guards increased. In time, they stopped by the tower. Gorias looked up at the many tiers and admired the workmanship. He recalled climbing down one of these towers, the one over by the herbalist's wall, when he was a younger man with a greater passion for sex than living another day.

"Something funny?" one of the young guards gripping the pommel of a sheathed short sword grunted.

Gorias turned his head to face the guard and peered down. "I didn't realize I was smiling. I musta been thinking on something else." Gorias climbed from Traveler and the guard backed up a step. Eyes on the tower again, Gorias directed his words to Orsen. "Garnet still a handsome woman?"

Orsen's mouth popped open, but he couldn't find the words.

Gorias continued. "She used to have rich, auburn hair but more red in back like God grabbed it with bloody hands and wiped 'em off."

The guards exchanged glances and everyone remained silent.

"Hey, I'm a fighter not a poet."

Orsen said, "You could've fooled me. She's not had that color hair for my lifetime."

Another guard, practically a copy of the first, appeared from around the tower and ordered Gorias, "Leave your swords here."

Hands to his hips, long cloak billowing back to reveal more of his dragon-skinned armor, Gorias said, "That is something I cannot do."

Well aware these guards heard of Gorias' famed swords since their cradle, he placed the onus on them to go further.

Orsen spoke up, saying, "I believe Her Majesty will not object."

The gruffer of the two guards spat back, "To letting a professional killer into her chambers armed? Unlikely, even with all of the Appra sisterhood on duty."

Orsen pressed, "Then let the responsibility rest on me."

Gorias wore a modest look. "I'm gettin' tired of standing here. If you two wanna bugger yourselves over who gets to let me in…"

Metal scraped on stone as the locking bolts slid from the main tower door. The opening just up the steps swung out and a large form filled the frame. Near as tall as Gorias, the muscled woman leered at the guards, then cast her expression on Gorias. Her bronze eyes softened. Though clad in loose-fitting silk trousers and a vest neatly covering her small breasts, the tall woman stood ready to strike. On her left side dangled a thin sword and on her belt Gorias counted two daggers plus some sort of sharp instrument, probably a throwing star.

Gorias glanced at her leather boots and guessed the fixtures on the sides of them held thin blades, or pig stickers as he liked to call them. "Evening, or is it afternoon?" He checked overhead, trying to find the faded sun.

"Gorias La Gaul, you can be no other." Her voice, deep, but not off -putting, boomed in the cool air. "Come along inside. The Queen awaits you."

Gorias walked between the guards and ascended the steps. He soon stood next to the tall woman, who had to look up at him. "Pleased to make your acquaintance, Miss…?"

Full lips parting, the bodyguard stated, "Alena Appra."

After a single step further up the steps, Gorias paused, allowing her past him. As Alena passed, Gorias asked, "Are you related to General Appra from Lascaux?"

Her mane of golden-brown hair flipped back as she stood taller on the steps than him for a moment. "Yes. He spoke highly of you, even when the madness of age started to make him bleed from his ears."

"Sorry to hear that, well, that he has passed and all." He recalled the General well, his boxy facial features stuck out of the tall woman, but she was indeed fetching if somewhat plain.

Her voice echoing up the stone stairwell, Alena said, "It's a shame for a warrior to die in his bed with only the memories of past glories to keep him company."

"I hear you there." Gorias pondered the General, not what anyone would call a handsome man, but he had charm, macho bravado and guts. Gorias understood that such things could fill in the gaps for a man not so tender to gaze upon.

Alena didn't turn back as she asked, "Not your idea of a sweet death, Lord La Gaul?"

Watching her powerful hips shift as she climbed, he answered, "Not really, but call me Gorias."

"Are you contemplating your death now?"

He came near to responding, *I'm pondering you breaking my neck with those proud hips*, but held his tongue on that matter. "Just wondering how you've made this place smell like lilacs instead of stone."

They arrived on the landing of a floor a few stories up and Alena said, "It's better than musty stone, no?"

Hands to his belt, Gorias nodded. "Certainly." He glanced behind himself, seeing Orsen on the final step, waiting. "You're brave, sport. If my ass fell backwards, I'd have squashed you."

Deadpan voice low, Orsen replied, "I live to serve, Gorias."

Eyes drinking in the furnishing and everything on the level, Gorias saw a few more women dressed in a similar fashion to Alena in each doorway. "They your sisters?"

"The twenty daughters of Appra serve Queen Garnet. Loyal subjects are tough to find for an inner guard."

"I suppose." Gorias recalled Appra had no sons back when they fought side by side but that was a lifetime ago. "Your father was a great man."

Alena's head snapped around, her look one of testiness. "General Appra served his Queen as do I. While disappointed he had no legitimate sons, he didn't cry over it."

'"I never said…"

Her nipples stuck through her tunic as she declared, "Our bloodline is one of honor and we serve Garnet unto death. Beyond her death bad things may happen to the kingdom, thus, the reason for your calling."

"I've heard the world may end sooner than later."

Alena smirked. "I don't believe everything I hear. I heard once you were of royal blood."

"Don't believe everything you hear."

The other guards came in closer as Gorias stepped further into the chamber. "What is it she wants exactly?"

Arms folded under her scant bosom, Alena replied, "The Queen has lips and you shall hear from them." She then dismissed the other guards and Orsen, ever watching as they exited down the steps. Alena then marched across the room and opened the next door.

Gorias paused, hands to his sides, taking a few breaths.

"What is it?" Alena quipped in a bashful voice. "Preparing to see the Queen?"

"Nope," Gorias answered, taking a few steps toward her before stopping again. "I'm not accustomed to carrying the piss bucket." He then gave her a severe look. "Anywhere."

"Bad things will…"

Gorias cut her off saying, "I'm not from Transalpina so what do I care if this land goes into the shitter?"

Her mouth opened, but Gorias wasn't through.

"I don't need to be threatened or impressed to do my work. I came here outta past respect for your Queen. Now, if you'll kindly move the hell outta my way, I'll get this over with."

Jaw still open, quivering for a moment, Alena's face reddened as Gorias moved past her.

Cool air rushed to meet him as Gorias walked through the expansive terrace of the tower. While two walls hemmed in the floor behind his back, the rest spread out open to the air, only obscured by support pillars. He paused, ears picking up the silky sound of fabrics on the polished floor. Gorias turned slowly and saw the queen, Lady Garnet Peverall.

Probably a hair over five feet in height, the Queen stood, back erect, chin up, gazing across the vast courtyard and lands that butted up against the palace walls. Pretty as a painting, Gorias thought, her elegant yet simple gown one with the floor and tapering up her frame as if painted there by a master. She took a step to one side, head moving as if trying to see a sight in the distance, but her manner betrayed nothing feeble nor a lack of grace.

Gorias took a few steps forward, certain then that she heard his boots. He stopped, pondered that her hair was not as white as his, and waited.

"Come see her, Gorias," said the Queen, her right hand extended out from her powder blue, silken gown.

Trying not to smile that he obeyed an old rule of not speaking until spoken to by royalty, Gorias walked up beside the small woman. Right hand to his hip, Gorias leaned forward and squinted.

Outside the walls, a carriage drawn by white horses trudged along in the evening. Though guards flanked the ride, many shop owners and common folks were allowed to get near the wheels. They waved, laughed and bowed.

"What exactly are we looking at, Garnet? That's pretty far away."

Her steely eyes glancing up at him for a moment, she countered, "I wanted to show you what a bitch on wheels looks like."

"Oh, I know I've seen that before, but who is that down there?"

Hands folded in front of her, The Queen's scowl deepened. "My youngest sister, the Lady Mavik of Gordes."

"I hardly knew her." Right hand up to his beard for a moment, Gorias gestured out as he said, "I guess we all got old, huh? Holding a parade for herself this late, is she?"

Lips curling back, he thought the Queen two seconds from splitting apart. "Looks to be so, no? That carriage can hardly contain her ego and that fake son of hers, the supposed heir to my throne."

Hands to his sides, Gorias wore a rueful expression. "Mavik and Vincent? Big time phonies, huh?"

Her face focused up at the warrior, Garnet replied, "Of the worst kind. Her son isn't real whatsoever."

Gorias noted the young man beside his mother in the carriage, waving and his head turning. "Pardon?"

"He's a homunculus, not a real son, just a puppet with blood and some flesh, supposedly raised from the dead by the goddess herself."

Face hardening, Gorias nodded. "Well, that's sure something, then. I figured ya meant Mavik was fake because of her dyed hair and corset-aided big chest."

Garnet let her hands drop and her voice turned wistful. "I doubt he even knows, the crown prince Vincent. Everyone thinks him ill, weak of blood, not a one to be seen in the full sunlight."

"But you think Vincent is made from scraps and animated? Huh. Ain't that the crap sundae?"

Away from the guardrail, the Queen took a few steps and stated, "I don't think it. I know it."

"Not a believer in any sort of resurrection by the goddess?" He turned toward Vincent, replaying her words in his head. "You fear that fake thing in the carriage usurping your succession? How so? That'd be easy enough to prove if he's a reanimated piece of muck-up whatever it is."

Over near her writing table, her small hands rested on a porcelain cup and then moving to a taller piece of dinnerware, Garnet said, "One would think." She poured from a silver decanter into her cup, saying, "He's kept at a distance under great guard. Mavik's security man, Harlan, keeps a strict guard on every avenue to the Prince."

"I see that jar-headed prick in the carriage. Are you asking me to expose Vincent or pull him to pieces, thus foiling your sisters' claim to the throne?"

Garnet sipped her drink, swallowed and then gazed across the expansive floor as if Gorias wasn't there. "That would be wonderful, but no. I'm glad to see you still have the salt for such tasks. I have an undertaking for you to perform that will be more difficult."

"I figured as much. Orsen acts like money is no object."

She titled her head back and laughed once. "There was a time you'd perform my will for a chance at my bed."

Gorias shrugged, looking around the floor of the tower. "We could do that again, ma'am, but it'll be a bit slower."

Garnet's stiff face used muscles seldom put to action as she grinned and laughed to great excess. In a few moments, the Queen regained her composure. "Gorias La Gaul, you tempt me."

Cracking his knuckles, Gorias shrugged. "You're still a striking woman, but I doubt I ya can bear a new heir at this late stage in the game."

"That's precisely why you are here, mister hero for hire. There is an heir of mine, alive, but many think her dead."

"That's what little Orsen says, something about princess Nykia being alive somewhere. So knocking off this fake heir isn't on your mind?"

Garnet made eye contact with Gorias for but a moment before turning away to the outside world. "All in due time. I have many things in mind that will pay you well. The men that run Transalpina are having trouble with this dragonfire problem. They direct me like an old coot, yet I still have cards to play, hence, you."

"Thanks. Orsen told me about the castellans."

"He better have. I cannot have my trusted castellans all dying off. I need my friends even if they are politicians."

"This sounds like a mystical matter, ma'am, not one for a fighter or killer."

"There are no more wizards in Transalpina."

Gorias coughed and rolled his eyes heavenward. "So you

65

say, but I hear you retain Yannick, still alive after all these years. What do you call him?"

"My prognosticator and herbalist."

"You're funny and free with the truth."

"I am the Queen."

Gorias took a few steps as she started to walk across the room. "That you are. Well, what does Yannick say of this?"

"Not much as of late. He was just recovered from a long illness and a travel abroad. These deaths have been happening for a month. Your presence in Albion is a lucky occurrence."

"Lucky for you, sure. What does Yannick say?"

"I want you to ask him."

Gorias blinked. An understanding flowed over him as she figured his methods and presence would yield more than edicts by a monarch.

"Investigate this dragonfire matter with Orsen. That is your official reason to be in Transalpina."

"And my real reason is to find Nykia so the forces plotting for Mavik don't get wise? Got it. If Nykia were in this land, wouldn't she come forward?"

"She's nearby. An army couldn't have extracted her from the Pryten wilderness where she was lost to and grew up in, but she runs with the pirates now. I want you to bring her back to me."

"She runs with the pirates, and is now one of them?"

"Yes."

"Then perhaps she doesn't want the crown."

Garnet turned like a dancer, face like a stone and declared, "If she doesn't, I want her here, Gorias La Gaul, within my grasp. I won't be denied, one way or another."

He nodded, comprehending the fate of Nykia one way or another at his hands.

She said, "Take Alena for your guide in matters here as well as Orsen. He's a good youth but she will show you what you need and cover your back."

"I don't need back up."

"You are over 700 years old, Gorias. We all need help."

"I still can out-strut the roosters in the yard, ma'am."

She took steps toward him, her hand on Gorias' chest and then running to his waist belt. "I expect you still can."

"I can."

Eyes focused on his, Garnet said softly, "You wouldn't be much of a legend then, true?"

"A man has to eat."

She giggled, sounding much younger, and held her hand to her mouth. "You and your ways. If only you had stayed with me a century ago, we'd have bred a fine line for this land."

"Not my thing."

"I know. I had a wonderful life, but it's a terrible thing to be left alone in this awful world now."

Gorias shrugged. "It's not so bad if you're me, but I know what ya mean."

"So, do you still fancy redheaded ladies?"

"As often as my guile or pockets allow."

"To think you would have to pay for such things. Tarts, for the goddess' sake." Whereas her tone mocked him, a thread of humor strung in it deep.

"I don't have it in me to fall in love anymore, ma'am. It's easier and quicker this way."

"I'm sure you have a legion of adoring ladies or wannabe fighters prone to lie down for free."

"I get that, but, I'm gettin' too old for romance, ma'am."

An eyebrow raised, Garnet said, "Ma'am. There was a time when you'd never have called me that."

"Calling you Princess is kinda out now, right?"

Garnet walked to her changing alcove and sat on a cushioned chair beside the makeup table. After waving him to walk over, she asked, "Do you recall what you used to call me?"

His boots set on the rug by her chair, Gorias nodded once. "Firebrand, because of the spark in your eyes..." His voice trailed off.

"Oh, say it, man of renown." Her voice lost all of its stiff authority and purred. "You said my eyes flared when I arrived."

"They did, that and you were red down below, too."

"Yours always looked like you'd kill a man when you arrived."

Both shared a laugh as she sat back, opened her silk gown and parted her legs. "There are some things I can no longer do with a man, Lord La Gaul, but one thing I would not be remiss in asking is for you to kneel before the Queen. You always loved to do that."

Gorias stared down at her, seeing the age in her naked body, but that it hadn't lost complete attraction. Garnet still possessed a shaped form, sleek and comely even if decades past her prime.

"I'm not a man to kneel before any monarch, Firebrand, but…" Gorias went to one knee and then both, feigning a bad back, causing her to giggle again. He cupped her left hip and kissed her navel. "…but in your case, I will make an exception."

CHAPTER IV

CRYSTALS AND STREET FIGHT

"I know you," Noguria said to Nykia as the younger woman watched the sun-kissed waves.

Nykia couldn't face her mistress. "Are you here to chide me for my obsession, too? Even my so-called friends like Allard and Savage Chad give me grief."

Noguria shook her head and swept back a mane of blue-black locks as the wind caught hold of them. "Of course not. No, I can smell something else on you, what nips at your mind."

Eyes still on the waves and then the sky, Nykia replied, "Oh? Am I bored yet?"

Noguria stood beside Nykia and looked at the sea, then turned and faced the opposite way, toward the Captain's cabin. "I smell murder, very ripe indeed."

Nykia stayed quiet, so Noguria spoke instead.

"You're going to kill Dumas, aren't you?"

"What if I do? Dumas killed the last Captain, a proper Pryten, to be the leader now."

"You have the desire to lead?"

"No," Nykia admitted and turned to face her. "But Savage Chad does."

Noguria smiled for a moment but it dropped fast. She stepped away from the edge of the boat and started to walk, her nodding head leading Nykia with her. "Savage Chad wears ribbons in his beard for his bastard children."

"So?"

"He's awfully sentimental for a pirate."

"Aren't we all a little?"

Noguria took her hand, conceding the point.

"You oppose the idea?"

"No, I'll back you, of course. I just wanted to be sure of your actions."

"All right then."

"Better be quick about it as we'll be going to ground in the next phase as the moon is full."

Nykia's eyes became icy. "Oh, there will be no hesitation. Follow me."

Noguria whispered, "He'll have those two skinny bastards with him."

Never turning, Nykia shot back, "That's why you're with me."

They walked to the Captain's cabin. Nykia pounded on the cabin door with her fist, then stepped back.

The door swung open and a scrawny man wearing round spectacles and a loin cloth frowned at her.

"Yeah?"

"LaFeaur? Tell Dumas I need to speak with him, now."

The slight man turned to one side, showing that Captain Dumas and Savage Chad played cards with the other skinny second to the Captain, Ryder. "Oh Captain," LaFeaur mocked in a lilting voice. "The Princess would like to talk with you."

Well aware he could be heard, Dumas said, "Silly bitch." He pushed back his chair, upended the last of his drink and stood. "If her brains hadn't fallen out her twat she'd be resting for the coming actions."

Dumas made it to the doorway, his mouth open, and his eyes dancing with more mirth to be offered. That's how he looked when Nykia plunged her seven-inch dagger into his chest, striking through the bones and delving deep into his heart. Both hands on the handle, Nykia twisted, turning the blade counterclockwise, turning his heart into a ruined, spurting mass. Dumas didn't move at first, but a spew of ale erupted from his mouth as he fell forward, inadvertently tackling Nykia, falling and pinning her to the deck.

LaFeaur and Ryder drew their swords and charged out of the cabin. Savage Chad kept drinking and didn't rise up. The two men flanked their Captain, but looked at each other and then up at

Noguria just as she unleashed her whips. The long leather straps encircled both men's throats and they gaped, knowing what came next. Noguria yanked on her left whip, ripping the flesh and veins from LaFeaur's throat. He dropped his sword and grabbed at his neck. Soon, his knees hit the deck, as he couldn't get his life back into his body, and LaFeaur slammed into the boards, dead like his Captain.

Ryder dropped his sword as other pirates started to gather around.

Noguria offered him, "You have no problem with Savage Chad as Captain, do you?"

With minimal movement, Ryder shook his head form side to side.

Noguria moved closer and unraveled the whip from his neck. He breathed large gulps of air as Savage Chad's form filled the doorway. Whips both snapping down, she asked the crew, "Any objections?"

If any opposition existed, it wasn't voiced.

Nykia yelled, "Get this dead prick off me!"

❀ ❀ ❀ ❀ ❀

Orsen went to his knees and thought of his goddess. He gazed at the piece of crystal in the stone fixture before him. The holder for the elaborate object sat fixed in a pair of marble palms that topped a duo of arms traveling down to the floor of the temple. Hands on his knees, he glanced over at the tall lady in a hooded robe and the two rotund eunuchs that stood behind her.

"Show him to me, Orsen," her husky voice implored.

"Yes, Abbess Niva."

For a moment, he eyed the object before him, a large clear orb with a series of jagged edges on the sides to his right and left. He leaned in until his forehead touched the crystal's smooth surface. When Orsen's skin felt the crystal's cold touch, Abbess Niva moved around opposite him, but her guards stayed in place by the door.

"Show me your first sight of La Gaul."

71

All Orsen had to do was recall Gorias in Albion, but not in the whorehouse. That is where they first met, not where he first saw him in the flesh. Orsen never told the old fable how he'd observed Gorias and the reason the warrior came to Albion in the first place. He almost smiled at playing dumb with the great legend, trying to get him to admit it to him.

The crystal swarmed with images and they started taking on human forms. Within a few moments, a moving picture painted on the crystal, as real as if one looked into another room. A trail of dead bodies flanked the entrance to the large stone manse as Orsen's vision splayed across the crystal. His view jerked from left to right, showing one man, gaping, hands over his heart, shocked at his own death, eyes open. Another lay face down, quivering, blood pooled from his groin. Further up the steps Orsen saw a man with no right forearm, his last breath escaping as his blood stopped shooting from the stump.

Up the steps Orsen ran, but stopped at the higher level, seeing a group of men surround Gorias La Gaul. A man in felt trousers and a silk shirt cursed Gorias, pulled a bow from the wall rack and notched an arrow. Gorias swished his swords, not moving to stop the man as he drew back and fired. The arrow stopped in Gorias' helmet, but the old warrior didn't slow down.

Men clad in leather jerkins typical of guards surrounded Gorias. He paused, sliced the throat free of one with a left-handed swipe, and turned, stabbing his other sword into the foot of another enemy, pinning him through the wooden floor. This man screamed, but Gorias never regarded him again. Orsen couldn't believe this man forgot to even try and strike Gorias. A third guard leapt on his left arm, awkwardly removing Gorias' sword. As it clattered to the ground, Gorias drew back and chopped at the guard's head with a great roundhouse blow with his fist. The guard's helm flew, along with a couple teeth.

Orsen crouched at the last steps, just out of their sight, but he saw the man in the silk shirt fire another arrow just as Gorias moved forward. No swords, Gorias grasped the smaller man in a bear hug and belly-flopped toward the ground. They landed on a wooden chair and a small table, shattering both. A great groan escaped from the man under Gorias. Quickly, Gorias rose up, reached to his helmet for the arrow lodged there and broke it off. He sat up and held back the flailing man's arm so he could stab the arrow down into the left eye of his target. The man gagged, coughed, but no screams came out as the broken shaft passed through his eye and nestled in his brain.

Orsen shook, his body a bundle of nerves at the sight of such violence, and at the scent of brains.

The view twisted as a glass lantern flew into the scene, shattering at Gorias' side. A huge wave of flame spewed and rolled over Gorias' thigh and side. The big man rose up, flames all around him, and casually walked over to his dropped sword. These flames started to lick at the man pinned by Gorias' sword and the screams added more horror to the vision.

Orsen's view jerked away and he started to flee down the stairs again. Screams echoed in his mind as another man died. He pulled his head back and the vision ceased. While he sucked in breath, he opened his eyes to the face of Abbess Niva, standing only a few inches from the crystal.

"Incredible," Niva said with admiration, her long face almost glowing from her feline eyes that refused to blink. "The old man has lost none of his ability, though he relied on his armor protecting him from the attack from behind."

"The fire doesn't concern him whatsoever, Abbess."

The wonder receded and Niva's face showed no emotion. "It's made from dragon skin. He could walk through a furnace in that thing with his helmet on and feel no ill effects. He truly will be the answer to some prayers here in Transalpina." At last, she blinked, staring hard at him. "Is there something else?"

"Gorias holds something in his belt, a curious object in a glass vial. I saw it when he deposited the bit of dragonfire when we were on the ship."

Niva waved at the crystal and Orsen dutifully touched his head to the surface again. However, when the vision of the two on the barge's deck became clear, as soon as Gorias opened his pouch, the vision ended. Orsen moved back, confused.

Niva rubbed her chin with her right index finger. "Fascinating. Something magical blocks us from seeing it."

"The vial contains liquid and something floating, but I'm sorry I couldn't see it again."

"It's no fault of yours. A powerful enchantment blocks my eyes and the crystal, the Eye of the Dragon here. Keep me posted."

"Gorias holds his tongue often."

"He doesn't trust you?"

"He doesn't trust anyone." Orsen stood, adjusted his tunic and bowed. "I must go and tend to my duties, Abbess."

Niva put her hands together. They vanished in the baggy folds of her sleeves. Her chin rose as her aloft manner increased, the headpiece cuffing her scalp tightening at the edges. "Follow your orders, Orsen. I thank you for this vision. I always wanted to see him."

"I could bring him by the temple, Abbess."

"I said I wanted to see him, not necessarily meet him." She turned to address her guards. "Dola, Metrose, compline nears, my eunuchs."

He watched the slender lady begin to gravitate toward the exit. Dola and Metrose instantly parted to make way. She walked into the yawning sanctuary of Ernytel's temple, toward the towering image of the goddess, followed by the eunuchs. All about the goddess Orsen saw a yellow glow, but the corona effect wasn't even, as if whatever made the illumination wasn't uniform on the backside of Ernytel.

✤ ✤ ✤ ✤ ✤

Alena sat astride her dancing roan and looked up at the man hanging from the upper terrace of the boarding house. A stocky man, face bloated, a swollen tongue half bit off protruding from his lips, feces covering one leg of his trousers, never moved in the morning air. She dismounted, and hitched up her horse, half smiling at the grisly spectacle.

Once through the door of the boarding house, a portly lady approached her. "Young miss?" She asked, hands wiping on her apron. Both of them faced to the right, where Gorias La Gaul sat at a long table, eating, alone.

"I'm here for your lodger."

The old woman winked. "I hope you fair better than the man who came for him last night." Her eyes then pointed to the ceiling, toward the hanged man.

Swinging her long locks back, Alena offered, "I'd suppose Lord La Gaul enjoys the company of women in the night more than men."

A huge flagon at his lips, Gorias cleared his throat and waved her over. "Yer startin' to see the picture, little girl."

Alena walked to the table, noted his helmet in one seat and took the chair next to it. "I haven't been very little in years, Lord La Gaul."

"Yer small to me, sister, and call me Gorias."

"Call me Alena. I'm not one of Abbess Niva's vestal virgins."

Gorias picked up a round raisin cake and seemed to ponder that. "Ah, my words are what they are. I'm too old to be very sensitive anymore." Again, he cleared his throat. "Ya look better in the casual buckskin pants and leather vest. It suits a fighter."

"Thank you."

"Ya look like yer ready to kick someone's ass."

Hands resting on the pommels of her short sword and dagger, Alena replied, "It's early yet. I stopped to see where we'd be off to today."

"We?" he replied, chewing the cake. "Garnet wasn't kidding about you tagging along? Peachy."

"There are matters Orsen will direct you on, but I know things about this city and land. You'd be better for having me near in this search."

Eyes glancing over Alena for a second, he drank again. "Yer probably right there, so better to have ya at my back then."

"Of course."

He paused before saying, "You know where Nykia is, don't you?"

Hands folded on the table, she replied, "Pirates go to ground often. There are many ports where they take on supplies via tiny craft. They won't land as to arouse attention so they send in small boats. It's no secret where a few are, and the army regularly patrols them. However, when they go to ground, it's easy to predict which ones they use."

"How so and why doesn't the military nail 'em? Hey, who's in charge of the army these days?"

"General Thynnes is supreme commander."

"I'll be hanged, huh. That ol' cuss? Go on."

"I figure the pirates go by phases of the moon and how natural light can be best used. It only makes sense as seafaring folk use the sky well. Plus, they're a superstitious lot to the core."

"True. And yer convinced Nykia runs with a certain group that can be found?"

"We can try."

"It's a start."

Alena leaned back, intertwined her fingers behind her head. "Night visit from an admirer?"

"Not quite."

"Assassin?"

"Assfaced idiot."

She laughed, her smile expanding like her head would flip open. "He doesn't look bloody."

"Because I strangled him with a coat hanger."

"The same one he is hanging by?"

"Naw, I tried that and he fell a couple times. I had to use a baler wire from the stable out back. I wanted him up there for all to see. Keeps 'em away then."

"You slay me, Lord…um, Gorias." Her tough deportment gone, her face lit up and a toothy grin painted wide on her face, Alena suddenly tried to suppress her mirth.

"Naw, not you little girl. This happens at times, but it kinda pisses me off that they came for me so fast. I guess my presence in the city isn't a secret." He washed the last of the cake down. "So, why the hell are ya here again?"

Hands to her knees, she said, "I'll direct you to the pirate hideout, as the phase will be tomorrow tonight."

"Good. Orsen wanted to show me some scene of this dragonfire today and maybe see that Yannick guy later. Maybe he can gimme a clue on the mystery of the fire and Nykia."

She nodded. "Good. I'll get some supplies together."

"I hate to be an echo, little girl, but how can you be sure Nykia will be among the pirates?"

"She might not be, but we will compel them to tell us."

Gorias wiped his mouth on the napkin and then started to comb through his beard with his fingers. "This will be a great night."

✵ ✵ ✵ ✵ ✵

Just before noontime, Gorias and Orsen crossed the city. They delved into the outer boroughs, not drawing much notice. They hitched their mounts outside a tavern on a plain street choked with buildings hardly a yard apart.

"Quaint neighborhood," Gorias observed. "The stonework looks much older here than the inner portions of Qesot."

Orsen patted his horse, a fine mare with a non-descript saddle. "So?"

"It'd make more sense for the outer rings of buildings to be newer. It's ass-backwards."

"As if the castle is running away from the suburbs?"

"I suppose."

"The areas about the castle have been rebuilt a few times in the last decades. Various regimes get jaded and redo the city."

"Why?"

"When not at war monarchs must do something."

Gorias stretched and peered down the street at a few folks loitering near a rustic café. "Huh."

"Upstairs," the youth told Gorias as he walked to the door of the bar and stopped.

Gorias still eyed the neighborhood, full of hostels, stables and grim dwellings spewing rings of smoke. "Nice place for a high bred castellan to visit, much less die in."

Orsen shrugged. "All men have their desires, Gorias. No man is perfect, no matter how great the breeding, hence, the delicacy of this matter."

"Yeah." Gorias snorted as he stepped onto the porch of the saloon. "We wouldn't want the masses to think their Lords are just like them, now would we?"

"Quite," Orsen agreed and opened the door to the bar, yet offered to let Gorias go in first.

The warrior didn't hesitate, stepping into the smoky tavern and checking both ways as he did so. Sparsely populated, Gorias sensed no danger from the few older men and various shabby workers swilling down ale so early in the day. Gorias glanced down at Orsen. "Lead on, kid. So far, I'm underwhelmed."

Orsen gave the barkeep a knowing look and headed up a flight of stairs to the left of the bar. Gorias noted the chubby bartender in red woolen clothes. He mixed drinks like a butcher cutting up steaks. The bartender's bloodshot eyes seemed to know Orsen; probably from the incident they were going to see. Beholding La Gaul, his eyes widened and he pretended a sudden interest in drying mugs.

Gorias also saw that a group in the far corner didn't go back to their drinking. All four members of the ragtag party continued to stare at him. They stood out in his mind because they were all different in age, dress, and size, each gaping at him in a probing manner with eyes too stupid to hide their interest.

Ascending the stairs, Gorias held the handrail and lamented, "I liked it better when folks thought I was dead."

"Oh?"

"Yeah. Every swinging dick in the land wants to be a part of the legend of Gorias La Gaul, mainly the part where he dies. They hear a tale on the wind that I'm in town and then see a man like me, it's all over."

"You know, Gorias, it's not all about you."

"Funny, I thought it was. Ya know how many bands of unlikely dimwit heroes I've sent into the Great Hereafter?"

Oil lamps lit the hallway that greeted them. The ratty brown rug that ran the length of the hall muffled the sound of Gorias' boots. On either side of the hall, several doors led to various rooms over the tavern. Crossways wooden beams boarded up the doorway on the far right. Over the entrance, a series of paper banners, the intersection point bearing the seal of Her Majesty, warned people away. Under these bonds, there was no door. Orsen drew a slender, elegant misericorde from his frieze tunic and cut the waxen seal. He then motioned to Gorias and pointed at the boards.

"Glad I can be of service. I ain't doing jack-crap until I see some money."

Orsen's expression never changed as he fished into the inner lining of his jacket. He produced a half dozen gold pieces and handed them to Gorias.

"That's a good start," Gorias declared, put the gold coins in a pouch on his belt, and then slid that pocket around behind his back. He drew out the twin swords, squinted at the boards and put his left sword away. Gorias then inserted the other weapon behind the board obstruction. With a violent pull, the two planks popped from their moorings, but weren't sliced or broken. It was a matter of leverage, obviously, and Gorias understood his abilities.

Taking one of the hall lamps in with him, Orsen stepped through the door.

Gorias eyed the inner doorframe. "I wonder why this looks burned around here?"

Once through the doorway, Orsen waved at the scene. "What do you think, sir?"

Gorias stared at the bed; the humanoid shape imprinted there by a burn and then back to the doorway. "It looks like a localized blaze, all right. Whatever burnt the guy in this bed consumed only him and the area nearby." He knelt and touched the region by the foot of the bed. His index finger traced the depth of the singe on the wood and the mattress dilapidated by use. Eyes scanning the delineation on the bed, he looked up beyond the headboard. Two scorched areas singed the wall over the head of the bed. Gorias stood, stepped near to one side of the bed and touched the wall. He looked down and frowned.

Orsen had been smiling a bit.

"Ya happy I'm forced to accept the dragon anomaly? This is different than the spy on the barge, the pill-sized thing for sure."

"What?"

"Well, you're correct, kid, in that it sure looks like dragonfire and a combustion from such. I just cannot fathom how it was done on a localized level like this, aside from those pills, but this is different than Vallen's death." Fingers again on the wall, he said, "See how there are these two tiny marks, and almost like from two jets of it that hit the wall. Maybe that was a mistake or the first volley that missed, like a spurt, the fire was shot, not crushed open in pill form." Coughing, Gorias stared at the bed. "This fella in the bed when he died?"

"Yes, Gorias."

He glanced back at the doorframe and the slight singe around the frame. "Barkeep say who was with him?" Hands on his hips, Gorias' face turned severe. "Don't even sing a song that the bartender didn't see anything."

"Oh, he did. The man said the Castellan of Darian entered with a lady of the night and procured a room."

"Hmm. Color me shocked. What happened to this lady?"

"No one knows, save for the goddess Ernytel."

"Yeah, and she ain't talkin' now, huh?" Gorias pondered for a moment with his hand on his beard. "Then again, isn't the Darian sector of this city where the temple of Ernytel is?"

Since the answer was obvious, Orsen kept quiet.

Gorias put his hand on the wall by the two burn points. Spreading the hand, his thumb and ring finger met the impact points. He then made his hand travel away from the wall over the bed. With a grin, he then placed his hand in this way to Orsen's chest. Gorias chuckled and stepped away from the bed, dropping his hand.

"What do you find so humorous?" Orsen demanded.

"Ya folks may have a real problem on your hands, one I cannot completely fathom myself. I can see a lot of things in my mind, kid. I don't like a lot of 'em."

"Care to share any with me?"

Gorias shrugged. "Near as I can tell whatever burnt him alive was on top of him at some point. However the flame came out, it shot to the wall first, trailed down, and then enveloped the castellan."

"We surmised as much," Orsen related, arms folded.

"Then aren't ya'all throwing good gold after bad? Wonder what kinda gal of the streets can do that to a man, huh? Burn him with dragonfire. Damn. Maybe this is my lucky day I hadn't met up with her, aye?" He breathed again and said with a serious tone, "But she seemed to like the castellans."

Orsen rubbed his tattoo of good fortune and confessed, "We were hoping you could tell us. Is there such a thing as a dragon that masquerades as a woman?"

Eyes on Orsen's lucky tattoo, Gorias suggested, "My ex-wife? Huh. Perhaps we should go see Yannick."

Concern spread over the young man's face. "Why is that?"

"He's a prognosticator, yes? Maybe he can tell me a good fortune or a little something about this gal, much less where little Nykia is. Then again, if he were that bright, why call on me?"

As Gorias left the room, Orsen locked in place. Gorias looked back in at him and gave him a bitter look, wondering why he never followed.

"You think that wouldn't occur to me?" Orsen asked, somewhat indignant.

The left side of Gorias' mouth drew up some as he replied, "Maybe he'll be more forthcoming with me, huh?" Gorias' slight smile disappeared and his words turned dour. "Don't jerk me around, kid. The truth may hurt, but not as much as my uneven temperament if I find out I've been screwed, all right?"

"I wanted to see if you thought it was actually dragonfire. There has been great speculation and Yannick isn't a suspect in this matter, but..." Orsen's voice trailed off as Gorias motioned for him to head down the hall after him. He didn't bother to replace the boards.

Once downstairs in the tavern, Gorias checked the table

in the corner as they walked through. The odd party no longer occupied the spot. Gorias stopped and then went to the bar. He motioned for the bartender. "Brandywine. It's gettin' cold."

With no emotion, the man in flannels behind the bar poured a large cup of the purple liquid for Gorias.

After a sip, he watched Orsen stand stoically near the doorway. Gorias asked the barkeep, "You get a lot of varied parties in here?"

"What say you?" the bartender responded with a sly voice. "This is a tavern. We get nothing but odd parties."

"I spotted that bunch earlier," Gorias gestured at the vacant table. "The one with the big assed warrior in dented chain mail, the gal in the pointy brassiere with the rapier, the midget carrying a quiver and the old dude in the robe? That looked like some sorta joke. Who were they?"

Shrugging, the bar tender replied, "I never ask names."

"Did they ask my name?"

The bloodshot eyes flared at Gorias. "They seemed to know who you are, Lord La Gaul."

Hands on his hips, Orsen called out, "Well, now what is it?"

Gorias stretched, drank the brandy and then said, "Just the usual, kid. This is why I stay away from big cities. I think it's time to see Yannick."

Orsen almost stepped out of the tavern first, but Gorias grabbed him by the elbow, shook his head, and departed first.

As soon as the door opened, the air whistled. This hissing tone came fast and blunted quickly as an arrow struck Gorias' chest armor near to his heart. Gorias disengaged his twin swords, spotting the tiny man who fired the projectile. This individual, crouching behind the line of horses, notched and released another arrow. This shot flew toward his face, but Gorias tilted his head, deflecting the missile into the doorframe of the tavern.

"Deliverance shall come," Gorias muttered and stepped out onto the porch, setting his boots firm, swords up and ready.

Showing no fear of the legend, the woman warrior in pointed armor jumped out of the shadows with an elegant balestra hop, prepared to slay Gorias. Stabbing with her rapier, hiding behind a small triangular shield on her left forearm, the determined woman showed great courage by attacking. At first, she stabbed at him and moved past, executing a flèche move to perfection, but the blade brought no harm to Gorias.

Exhaling, sounding bored, Gorias let the woman's rapier glance off his stomach plates again. He swept the thin blade off once, using only his armlet armor, making her grit her teeth at his lack of respect for her. The girl hopped back, still poking her blade, trying to drawn him forward. Gorias recognized her motives, moves, and could smell her friends nearby. He saw the faces of those further down the streets, hiding in shop doors, gaping at figures out of his line of sight, ones over to his left and strangely, above his head.

He turned a moment to tell Orsen to stay in the tavern, but the young man needed no such instruction.

The woman backpedaled and hopped, a grin on her face as Gorias stepped forward. Over his head the wooden porch awning groaned and the scent of sweat and ale wafted on the wind.

"Amateurs," Gorias said loud enough for all to hear just before he stabbed both swords up into the roof of the awning. This action caused the barbarian warrior to swing down from the awning like a primate by his left arm, broadsword in the other, a pointed mace dangling from his waist belt. The huge man planted his boots on the porch, legs far apart and swung back with the weapon.

Gorias left his two blades stuck in the ceiling and simply kicked the man in the crotch.

Surprise and then pain traversed the barbaric fighter's face, his broadsword strike wavering and falling before ever reaching Gorias. As the barbarian's body started to seize up and he grabbed his fruits with his left hand, Gorias stepped forward. His own left hand gripped the wilted forearm that held the man's broadsword. Gorias struck the bearded man square in the mouth. The force of this clean shot and the weakness of the thug's legs caused the barbarian to fall backwards off the porch, shoulders flat on the street.

A step back, Gorias pulled his dangling blades loose and reached out, tapping the poles of the awning playfully as the girl in the street stepped over her fallen friend. No hesitation in her moves, she leapt forward as Gorias walked down to the steps. Again, she jabbed at his stomach and chest, trying to find a seam in the armor. Something flew past Gorias' face, a glowing orb and then what looked like ball of phlegm, but he didn't take his eyes from the woman.

Gorias lifted his left sword, not only parrying the rapier, but also cutting the stylish blade in half. Stunned, the woman gaped at her ruined blade but for a second. Gorias then raised his right sword and dropped it. Of course, she used her shield in defense. Gorias' sword passed clean through the metallic safeguard, sliced clean through her forearm and even cleaved into her jaw. He jerked back, ripping loose flesh, metal and teeth, Gorias stared at her bankrupt face as blood and gore belched from her torn mouth. He waved off another arrow attack by the midget fighter, avoided a third glowing ball and continued to look upon her pained expression. Green, her eyes were green like the southern sea, he noted in passing as founts of blood gray marrow gushed from her forearm stump. She stood on quivering legs, but he figured that wouldn't last long.

Once he kicked the suffering woman in the gut right under the cones of steel covering her breasts, Gorias hopped off the porch and checked to his left. A few yards away, the older man in billowing robes waved his arms. The palms of his hands generated an emerald hue and started to produce balls of glowing quality.

Behind his back Gorias heard the woman cry with her torn mouth and the barbarian growl, legs swishing on the street. With a grunt and a leap lacking in grace, Gorias attacked the mage, slashing through the spell caster's arms, removing both of the glowing hands. The wizard's mouth ceased its spell, frozen open at the suddenness of his destiny. He fell to his knees, rasping in agony, blood spurting from his wrists. Then, he started to scream.

Though people down the way at the shops and café applauded, they never came out into the open. Gorias winked at them, acknowledging them in passing and showing how little he feared his attackers. He told the mutilated man, "The policy of the Queen and her goddess is that nary a wizard should be spared the burning pile. However, she'll forgive me this sin of beheading." He criss-crossed his swords, cleanly removing the wizard's wailing head, sending his withered face to the street with a stunned expression etched on it forever. It stopped rolling, upright in the gutter.

Turning his back on the wizard's blood-gouting corpse, Gorias heard a rushing howl and got thrown back into the hitching post lines. The posts gave way under his back as the brutish warrior tackled Gorias. The fighter, much larger than even the thuggish La Gaul, knew how to fight, Gorias thought by how he hit him low. This man kept Gorias' sword arms from striking and pinned one of them down as he slammed his pointed mace into the dragon plates on the legend's chest. He blocked the attempt from Gorias' other sword by using the heavy broadsword.

Amid the displaced horses, the two struggled, neither gaining much advantage until Gorias kneed the burly fighter in the groin. This action sent the bulky man backwards and the mace to the ground. The barbarian staggered, struggling to get a grip on his aching manhood.

"Can't believe he fell for that twice." To his knees, Gorias sucked air in and held his chest. He looked up at Orsen, who had crept out on the porch.

The youth blinked, "What cheating deeds of the laudable La Gaul."

"Doesn't have to be pretty," Gorias murmured as he wobbled getting to his feet. "Only matters if ya win."

The barbarian stood, trying to shrug off the second shot to his manhood. He towered, his legs apart, shaking loose his manhood, but this proved his undoing. Gorias stepped forward, taking the swing of the broadsword to his left arm. His armor took the shot but it felt like a rhino charge to him. Placing his swords side by side, Gorias swung upwards, striking the savage between the legs before he could use the broadsword to block him off. The deep-voiced barbarian growled, but his tone was more in tune with a gelding than a manly shout of agony. The great sword dropped and blood ran from the barbarian's tongue. Drawing the twin blades out, Gorias stabbed one into his opponent's lower abdomen and sliced up, his motions raw because of Traveler bumping into him. When the barbarian's guts started to unravel, Gorias gave the horse an annoyed look, but a gleam lit in his eyes. Stabbing his swords into the dirt, he grabbed a handful of intestines and looped them over Traveler's saddle horn. The dying barbarian looked Gorias in the eye, knowing true terror as the old man slapped Traveler on the rump. The stallion galloped off, taking the guts of the Northern man with it. The barbarian gawked on in horror as his insides unraveled. Traveler ran on and there seemed no end to the barbarian's insides. Even after he fell to his knees, he kept losing his guts. Gorias took up his swords and made a slight motion, cutting the man's throat, ending his suffering.

The small archer, seeing himself alone, froze as he stared across the street at Gorias and Orsen.

Gorias joined his swords at the handles, forming a single, double-headed blade and proceeded to twirl it like a wheel.

The small man turned and ran.

"Ahh, ya wuss," Gorias shouted and faced Orsen, who was throwing up over the south side of the porch. Grimacing at the youth, he asked, "That tattoo of luck sure doesn't keep yer stomach in tow, does it?"

Orsen wiped his mouth, unable to face Gorias, his face pale and his hands shaking.

Coldly, Gorias said, "Now you see what it takes to be me." He gestured at the street, the sliced up mage, the dismembered woman, and at the trail of barbarian guts. "The burden of my life is with me at all times."

"This happens a lot?" Orsen stammered, his head turned to see Traveler stopping and beginning to trot back to them.

"Happens enough."

Looking at the body of the dead woman, Orsen asked, "Was she one of the famed guild of assassins from…"

Cutting him off, Gorias replied, "No, just a mean little bitch, trying to make a name for herself by killing an old man. She did make a name, though, and its *worm-food*. C'mon, kid, we're off to see a wizard."

Both men stopped cold as a tall figure emerged from around the corner of the saloon. Alena carried the small archer by the right ankle. The tiny one cursed her and flailed at his captor to no avail. She held the small bow in her other hand, patting her thigh.

"You missed all the fun, little girl," Gorias told her.

She offered the midget toward him. "Want to make a wish?"

CHAPTER V

TEMPLE VISIONS AND YANNICK

All on their horses, Gorias glanced at Alena and Orsen before looking ahead down the street. "I'm not buying this."

At first a dull silence reigned, but Orsen broke first, asking, "What do you mean?"

"The twerps on the ship, the band of goofs, the assassin last night with bad breath and shitty methods, all out to get me?"

Alena tilted her head to the left for a moment. "You said it does happen a lot."

"But seldom like a shark to blood in the water."

Alena and Orsen exchanged a glance.

Gorias sighed. "Ya dunno what a shark is?"

Orsen said, "We've read of them and seen sketches, but…"

"Suffice it to say when there is blood in the water out in the sea, a shark is drawn to it like a young man to a piece of tail."

Alena glanced at the people on the streets, many of whom ignored the riders as they moved on, but a few pointed at Gorias. "What are you saying?"

"I can't believe everyone has gotten stupid at once. I know the world is headin' down the privy hole and all that, but it seems a might convenient."

Orsen said, "If they are hired killers they are a poor lot."

"Yeah," Gorias said in a low voice, eyes still straight ahead. "Makes one wonder."

Frustrated, Alena spat, "What?"

"If someone doesn't really want me dead or is trying to distract me. That's a screwy game either way."

Alena sighed. "It isn't all about you, is it?"

Orsen put in, "I asked him that before."

"My life is, little girl. I take it pretty seriously even if killers come after me dressed like jesters."

"Oh, that'd be fun," Alena gushed, mocking him. "Can I kill a clown if they attack?"

Gorias eyed her briefly, struggling to rein in her humor. "Why are you along again?"

"To help you find the Princess. I think we should go to Yannick and wring it out of him."

"Not a bad idea," Gorias agreed to her violence.

She patted her right saddlebag. "I brought thumb-screws."

"Good night," Gorias said without turning. "You must be killer at parties."

They traveled several blocks, nearing the center of the city once more, but not by the route they traveled before.

Gorias said, "We must be gettin' near to something important. There are soldiers on every street corner."

Each of these men wore the insignia of the palace guards, not the regular army or the police. Gorias' curiosity was soon answered as many more guards and regular citizens flanked the street. Off to their left loomed the giant temple of the goddess. In front of this edifice passed the carriage Gorias saw the night before, the one carrying Mavik and her son, Vincent. A small crowd gathered near the outer wall of the temple, and applauded as the carriage stopped. A hulking man in black leathers emerged from the coach first. Though gruff in appearance, the man's tight black mane of hair stayed in place no matter how fast he snapped his head from side to side.

Orsen informed Gorias, "That's Harlan, the bodyguard."

Letting Traveler rest, Gorias said, "I doubted he was a baker with that build and look. He really loves himself--see how he sticks his chin out? What? Ya learn this stuff the older ya get."

Next came out Mavik, a much stouter version of Queen Garnet, her hair a fake blonde color. Her manner friendly, Gorias read weariness in her gait as she leaned heavily on Harlan's grip and her cane as she stepped to the paved area. Harlan then helped Prince Vincent emerge. Rail thin and delicate, clad in posh velvet trousers and tunic, he stepped down and waved to the crowd. Not a hair out of place, clean shaven and sporting flesh that came near to glowing, Gorias pondered the Queen's words about his artificiality.

He smiled, thinking Garnet paranoid as most royals had too soft of a life and had the tendency to come into view a tad dainty.

From the rear of the carriage, the driver produced a large wreath of flowers. He brought it to Vincent and the crowd whispered.

Gorias said, "Wonder if he outweighs the wreath."

Orsen's eyes riveted to Gorias, his desire for silence evident.

Vincent carried the wreath and placed it by the base of a pedestal showing a life-sized version of the goddess. Once the Prince drew back, the crowd applauded.

When the party turned back to the carriage, Mavik shouted, "Gorias La Gaul!" Thus causing the crowd to turn and face those on horseback. A few gasped, and Harlan moved in front of the Prince, hand resting on a sheathed sword pommel dangling from his belt.

Gorias gripped his reins. "Afternoon, ma'am. It's been a long time."

Her shock fading, Mavik waltzed over to Gorias, half dancing as her steps popped on the paved section of the street near the temple. "At breakfast dear Harlan said you were in Transalpina."

"It appears so."

Mavik smiled, her hands folded together in front of her stomach. "Will you join me for wine or perhaps dinner?"

"I have some things to attend to today." Gorias shrugged as Harlan relaxed, letting Vincent walk up beside his mother. "I might take ya up on that soon though, ma'am."

"You've seen my sister?"

"Hard to come here and not see the Queen."

A hint of distaste in her face, Mavik smiled and reached out to stroke Traveler's muzzle. "I'm sure the matters of state bore you as much as I."

"I hate politics."

Mavik turned to her son. "This is Crown Prince Vincent."

Gorias raised his head up to acknowledge the stoic Prince, and then climbed down from the horse. Many in the crowd retreated a step. Gorias stuck out his hand. "Young man, pleased to meet ya."

Vincent never hesitated to reach out and take the huge hand of the warrior.

Gorias shook his hand. After he released his grip, he reached up, touched the side of the Prince's face and then ran his hand to the side of Vincent's neck. "You'll have princesses from all over at your door, young fella. I'm sure your Ma will help ya choose wisely."

Prince Vincent smiled, but didn't blush.

Gorias patted him on the shoulder and let his hand drop for a moment. He soon took up Mavik's hand and kissed it gently. Though Harlan glowered at him Gorias never deemed him important enough to look at.

"Careful Mavik," a voice in the crowd shouted. "The dragonfire killing didn't start until that man came to our land."

Many started to murmur their agreement.

Gorias sighed and climbed back on his horse.

Mavik pressed the place Gorias kissed to her lips and fluttered her eyelashes. "I think that all preceded you, correct? Are you here to ferret out that problem?"

"Sure, why not?" Gorias winked at her and gently heeled Traveler to head down the street.

Orsen looked back, but Gorias didn't. "Not quite an angry mob."

Alena added, "Yet. They're stupid to think you had anything to do with this."

"Who the hell knows why all this is happening? If I threw my real reasons on the table to Mavik there, I bet Harlan's pecker woulda fell out his trousers."

Alena put her hand to her mouth, suppressing a laugh but Orsen didn't smile. He said, "We shall see Yannick and hear his words on our mission. Perhaps he has an idea on the dragonfire."

Alena patted her saddle horn and said flippantly, "Queen Garnet will be displeased."

Gorias frowned. "Why?"

"You had your hand on Prince Vincent's neck and never squeezed."

"He felt real enough to me."

Alena nodded. "Mavik had no issue with you touching him, did she?"

"If she's a card player, she's damned good," Gorias replied. "Damn, I need a drink."

"Another drink?" Orsen grimaced. "It's the middle of the afternoon."

"I'm late then, by God."

Alena stopped and held up her hand. "We need to go into the temple on the side route. They will let us in because of me." She faced Gorias and directed him to the doors by the outer wall. "I really want you to see something."

"All temples are about the same."

Alena shook her head. "I'll show you something on the memory crystal."

Gorias' eyebrows raised. "Recollection glass? A thing that'll let me see a memory of yours clear-like?"

"Yes."

His features darkened, brows drawing down. "What can ya show me that'll be that great?"

She rode ahead and dismounted. "Vincent's resurrection. I was there."

"Sweet," Gorias grunted as he climbed down.

Orsen stayed on horseback.

Gorias asked him, "Not coming along?"

"I'll wait out here."

The two walked to the temple and Gorias said, "I'd figured he'd break his mother in half to get in the temple, as religious as he sounds."

"Who knows about him? He's a court ass-kisser. If we are lucky," Alena said as she approached the twin double-doors, "we can see Niva."

"Niva? The Abbess of the temple? Sure are a progressive society here. Seldom do I see women running the temples, unless…"

Alena completed his thought: "Unless they are whores?"

"Temple prostitution is common enough out in the older regions of the world, where life sprang and all that."

Alena looked southeast as if she could see Shynar and the cradle of civilization. "I suppose it's alien that society progressed further away from where it sprang?"

"Oh, there are plenty of ideas on all that." He stood back as Alena pounded on the door using the iron ring hanging from it. "Some say tribes from after the creation went over the top of the world, as much as they could, hell, it wasn't so cold up there then, and had other revelations. I never have been that far north."

"But you are from the north, correct?"

"Sister, you know all about me, why ask?"

Alena smirked as they waited. "I hear tales of you in scrolls, in class, even in training, but the stories the drunks tell are more fanciful."

"Surprised I'm not ten feet tall?"

She let her smile break open. "I'd be disappointed if you were as little as Orsen, but you're a big man for this place. Or any other." The door opened and the young lady within blinked at Alena, who executed an elegant curtsey to the acolyte. The young girl let them inside.

"My dad was a big man, stronger than me, in many ways," Gorias went on to say as he noted the grassy lands inside the walls. "He was simple, not too complicated. Ya get out in the world, it bogs ya down with behavior, distractions and other crap like that. Dad lived in uncomplicated ways and doubtless never worried on too much." He eyed the inner courtyard, the cobblestone walks and brickwork.

"Niva is the one with all the visions, religious experiences and the mother of the new faith."

"A new faith? Stuff like that is hard to hoist on a people, much less an entire nation. How'd that happen? I'd not heard of that goddess until recently."

Alena frowned, her brown eyes sullen as she glanced at the pinnacle of the temple. Various ladies in white linen carried candles past windows making certain any who looked would see them. "Several miracles, healing of the sick and whatnot, added to a revelation that her faith is the true one, discovered in ruins in caves."

Gorias now grinned. "Ya don't believe it, do ya?"

Eyes shifting, Alena stated, "The people of Transalpina need this faith. It binds them together. Me? I follow what my papa taught, not the faith of a resurrectionist."

"Care to elaborate on that?"

"Prince Vincent."

"Yeah? Oh, c'mon. He rose from the dead?"

"He walked right out of his tomb. His body was destroyed, broken into pieces by a bear attack out in the Woodvine area. Good fishing out there."

"Apparently, good hunting too, if yer a bear."

"The Queen said herself she saw the pieces of Vincent plain as day. They wrapped him up in blankets and the next day, here he walks out of the tomb in front of the memorial party."

"Bet that put a damper on things."

Alena nodded. "Niva declared it a sign, as she'd prayed and asked for it. I'm always suspicious of those who gain such easy answers to prayers."

"Quick obvious answers to prayers aren't the way of the gods. Usually, they are content to let ya sweat it out for a while."

"Niva's faith isn't all bad, mind you, and the rules, disciplines have done great things for our land. I just..."

"...think it's rooted in manure?"

Her smile returned. "I like your words, Gorias."

"I got a few left in me. I'm awfully tired, little girl."

Alena exploded with laughter. "Your words, so endearing to many, and they bless me with a moniker like that?" Again, the tall woman couldn't contain her jollity.

Gorias stopped short of the place where Alena entered. Both hands on the styled outcropping of sculpted bricks, Gorias looked into the room dimly lit by surging light from the belly of the center of the room. Alena stood on the other side of a jewel held high on a set of alabaster stone hands. The jewel, bigger than a man's head, bore a jagged surface, as if pieced together from a hundred glass triangles.

"Amazing, no?" Alena said, her brown eyes alight in the glow from the jewel. "No one knows why they bear a slight bit of light."

Gorias nodded, stepping in, noting a robed figure that must

be Abbess Niva watched them from a distance. Gorias' mouth opened, but he stopped short of speaking.

Alena's bearing lost some glee. She whispered, "You know why there's the light in there, don't you?"

He shook his head, dismissing her words. "You don't even realize what this is, do you?"

"What?"

Gorias sighed. "Show me the vision so I can believe in the heir, too."

Right hand poised over the jewel, Alena replied smartly, "Your attitude is not very nice."

"I haven't been nice in centuries."

Alena's palm rested on the jewel and her fingers soon lay on the pointed edges. Eyes closed, she let her head go back. She reached out with her left hand, gestured for Gorias to come closer. "C'mon, let me touch you."

Gorias stood near her and held up his right hand. Their hands mirrored each other and adhered.

"It's intense at first," Alena warned him.

"I've done it before."

He blinked his eyes, but the room vanished once he focused. Gorias didn't expect to see it. The overcast sky outside the temple lent to the dreary mood. Gorias saw through Alena's eyes, the perception of a little girl as the black-clothed royal family of Transalpina walked to the tombs, but carried no body. Though he couldn't read her thought Gorias surmised this was a memorial for a soul already installed to the halls of the dead.

He noted Lady Garnet, her sister Mavik and a few of the usual military suspects, like Generals Appra and Thynnes. Appra, a slight limp in his gait, wheezed as he tried to stand as tall as the bushy bearded, fleshy brute Thynnes.

A huge crowd flanked the ladies as they walked several blocks to the edge of the city. The vision went fast and Gorias pondered that youthful times usually do. Soon, they all stood at the rocky hillside, probably a disused quarry now a holder for the bodies of rich families.

Artisans stood by, some holding waxen seals, others mortar and paste, ready to do a final seal on the tombstones.

Mavik walked forward alone, a wreath of lilies in her hands, trembling. Tears never came as the sturdy men moved the stone away and let Mavik come forward.

The crowd gasped as Mavik shook, dropping the wreath and going to one knee. Garnet ran up and took hold of her sister's shoulders. Tough as ever, Garnet glared into the open tomb, her face frozen with amazement but Gorias also saw she roiled with anger.

There he stood, the prince, his grave clothes off, bare-assed naked in front of God and all humanity. His body bore not a scratch. He took no shaky steps. The prince walked into the light and held up his hands.

From out of the crowd stepped Abbess Niva, declaring praises unto her goddess. With her stood two stout men with shaven heads, also declaring the wonders of Ernytel loud enough for all to hear.

The prince seconded her motion and thanked the goddess Ernytel for his resurrection.

A religion was born.

Gorias stepped back and the room returned.

Alena took her hand back and made a fist with it. "Amazing, huh?"

"Garnet sure looked pissed."

Alena smiled. "She usually does."

Head tilted, Gorias motioned her to leave the alcove. Immediately, they saw the pyramid shape of Niva bordered by her two eunuchs, the same thugs from his vision.

Niva, hands folded, looked at Gorias intensely. "You have a deeper understanding of our faith now?"

Gorias stopped and stared at her across the room for a long time but only said, "Yeah."

Niva blinked, openly shocked that no more words came.

Alena curtsied and explained, "We have to go, ma'am."

Niva nodded and dismissed Alena before saying, "Come, Dola, Metrose." She headed toward the main sanctuary. Gorias turned his back and walked away from them.

Once back atop Traveler, Gorias trotted away from the temple complex. In a few minutes, Alena joined him and Orsen.

"Mad that I'm rude?"

Alena's eyebrows rose. "You are who you are."

Gorias heeled Traveler a little and they started to trot down the street. "There are a number of things I couldn't much talk about back there."

"You've seen a jewel like that before?"

Gorias sent her a grave look. "They are the Eyes of the Dragon. Those aren't natural gems nor cut from raw materials. They are cut from magical sources from the ecstasy of Dragons themselves. The light inside them is a tiny flicker of dragonfire, sometimes no bigger than a bitten off fingernail."

"That is one theory."

"That's a fact," Gorias snapped. "A century ago these jewels were sold as tiny necklaces, sparkling bobbles for the unknowing. They're the portals of the dragons into our lives."

"But there are no more dragons."

Gorias nodded. "That's the theory."

Alena now shook her head. "Are there or aren't they?"

"Not as such, but there are different sorts of dragons than the winged beasts. The dragonfire in this city is an attainable item, but practically impossible to use or direct. It confuses me that someone can do it."

"Perhaps Yannick can make this clearer?"

Gorias looked away, quiet.

Alena wondered, "What is it? I get the feeling you know something."

"Your recollection of that day is from your mind, your actual memories, that is what the dragon's eye can pull out once it goes through your brain?"

"Yes, if that is how you say it."

"No magic of the goddess in those jewels, just a greedy spirit far away, locked up and wanting to see more of this world. Think about that. At some point, the spirit convinced the world that crystals are pretty. Since people are dim-witted enough to not believe that they are being used from afar, they swallow it. A dragon feeds off silly false beliefs and bleeds a spirit from that, living or dead. Unsettling? It ought to be. However, in that vision, I saw Prince Vincent keenly."

"Yes?"

"His grave clothes. The one's he dropped when he walked out, bare-assed?"

Frustrated, Alena slammed fists to her thighs. "What?!"

"They were dirty, green-stained, scruffy on the legs."

"They were clothes for a shroud, after all."

"But he'd been wrapped and laid in them, correct? Not walking around in the brush?"

Alena closed her eyes and thought for a moment. "I don't see as that is…" Her voice stopped. "By the goddess, you mean?"

"He walked before he got out of the tomb?" Gorias chuckled. "I don't think yer goddess has anything to do with it."

"Then what does?"

"I'm not so sure yet. I have a nasty idea, though. Let's see this wizard."

✦✦✦✦✦

It was late in the afternoon when Gorias, Alena, and Orsen reached the small cottage of the chief Prognosticator to the Queen, Yannick. His rather opulent home didn't sit in the main castle proper, nor in the great keep, but lay constructed away from the rest of the castle inner buildings, near the pilaster super structure that reinforced the eastern wall. On horseback, Gorias glanced up at the spires of the castle, wondering if any watched him from there. However, from the lower gatehouses, across the curtain wall to the various notches several eyes peered at him.

"Not many believe you're real," Orsen said about the great attention afforded La Gaul. He dismounted and marveled at the looks the ancient fighter received.

"Aw, bull crap, kid." Gorias snorted and even waved at one

young soldier nearby who seemed giddy at the sight of the legend. "They know I'm as real as the sun rising. Elsewise, they wouldn't be staring at me from every embrasure or loophole in the fortifications."

Once dismounted, Gorias saw the slender prognosticator open the door to his home and wave at them. Though an older man, Yannick wasn't the ancient crone Gorias had in mind by this day. He'd seen him years ago and Yannick had centuries on him then. Half expecting him to be dressed in a huge robe with a long hood covering his head, Gorias saw this was not so as Yannick was dressed smartly in form-fitting breeches probably made of rich brocade fabric by the raised patterns on them. The elegant doublet Yannick wore was also made from this material usually fit for the prosperous.

"Friendly as if it were high noon," Gorias commented in a low voice, taking in the wizard's deep wrinkles that started at Yannick's black eyes and flow downward over high cheekbones. "Then again, he'd be a piss-poor predictor if he didn't know we were coming."

Orsen tried to suppress a smile, put his hands behind his back and followed Gorias and Alena to Yannick's.

"Gorias La Gaul," Yannick said extending his hand to the old warrior. Clean-shaven face full of energy, dark eyes gleaming in joy, Yannick welcomed the fable to his entrance. "I'm honored that you have seen fit to visit me."

Shaking the smaller man's hand, Gorias smiled. "If ya have some wine handy, ya can be my friend, prognosticator."

Giving Gorias a sly wink, Yannick said, "I believe I can liberate some spirits I have bottled up, kept under wraps for medicinal purposes."

"God is merciful," Gorias remarked as they entered the front room of the small cottage. Gorias ducked his head low as the thatched ceiling was not made for towering folk such as Alena and him. "Yer awfully cleaned up since the olden days. Garnet make you cut yer hair and beard once wizardry was outlawed?"

"No, it just was too much trouble to take care of the older I became."

"Surprised ya aren't up in the main castle."

Yannick opened a lower oaken cupboard and reached into the shelves, saying, "One has to have their privacy. Besides, this separates me from the Queen. It makes me appear favored, yet effortlessly gotten rid of." Holding up a small flask, Yannick asked Gorias, "Wine from Massainla good enough?"

"Long as it's wet, yeah."

Sitting across the table from Gorias, Yannick eyed Orsen at the door, still standing with his hands behind his back, and chose to ignore him. Into two cups, he poured a generous portion of the ruby colored wine. He paused, looked at Alena, who also still stood, but who steadily shook her head.

Gorias sniffed it and then toasted Yannick. "To your health."

Yannick's dark eyes glowed as he replied, "To yours."

"Mine ain't so good," Gorias drank and his eyes flared. "But if I drank enough of this, I reckon I wouldn't care. Damn, it's strong."

"You come to me for answers involving these castellans and their unusual demises?" Yannick said in a short voice, abruptly serious.

Gorias nodded. "If ya were forthcoming, it would make my life easier."

Yannick stared at Orsen and Alena. "Could we have time alone? I'm sure La Gaul will make your dreams come true once I talk to him in private."

Orsen's mouth opened, ready to object, but held back his words and exited the home. Alena followed him, but sent a sullen look to them.

Yannick stated in a somber tone, "We all do what we have to in a bid to survive these days."

"Granted," Gorias said, sipping more wine.

Fingers drumming the polished wooden table, Yannick said, "I do as I must; you're a famed slayer for riches. You can be bought."

Gorias didn't looked at him, but took the flask and poured more wine into his cup. "Keep talking."

"I'm not sure how much Her Majesty is paying you for this venture, but I can add to that greatly if you see things my way."

Again, Gorias never looked at Yannick, just the wine.

Giving a sigh, Yannick said solemnly, "The victims of these events are just castellans and politicians, drawn into the web of peccadilloes by their own lusts. The world is better off without such men…" His face flushed and Gorias faced him at last. "…present company excepted, of course."

Gorias refused to betray confusion in his mind, for he really came to ask Yannick about the whereabouts of princess Nykia. "I don't allege to be better than anyone or have a right to rule anything, so yeah, hang them all if they're self-righteous bastards."

"You wouldn't be here if you haven't guessed at my involvement in this by now?"

Left hand drumming fingers on the table, Gorias tried to understand why the wizard appeared ready to blurt out information about the dragonfire. He decided that playing along would have to suffice.

"Not sure exactly, but when the kid said you imparted the tattoos on him, well, that set me to wondering, now that you mention it. Care to make it simple for me?"

"Tattoos?"

"Like the lucky one the kid has. Do anything similar recently?"

"The magic imparted in my tattoos as energy in art is simple really. Everything has a price, be it balms, oils, souls or the promise of more lives. The charms for good luck woven as tattoos have a mystical quality and can cloud some men's minds."

"Yeah, so I hear."

"Well, they are a simple force of nature to invoke." His eyes were scorching as he spoke these words. "Some young fool was a horrible lover, but had me tattoo a balm on him to make him more attractive…so the women hardly would note his inadequacy."

"I see."

"I did one of you, long ago," Yannick gazed at the ceiling, wistful of the memory.

"Do tell?"

"It was for royalty and in a rather rude place."

"Please don't tell me the Queen has my face on her ass."

"No, but a lost princess has one of you near to her heart, shall we say, or the seat of her passion."

Gorias swallowed hard, heat building up in his face. "You just may be able to help me with a few things."

"I can play timid, but I don't understand the motive for your stop in Transalpina. Surely, you don't dally unless you plan to kill someone."

"I've been hired before to find lost articles, but one never knows who I may be out to kill. You seem awfully convinced I came to ask you about the dragonfire."

"Didn't you?"

Suddenly, Gorias thought it unwise to show his hand in the pursuit of Nykia. Maybe the old wizard could help him find her, but something gnawed at him that this wasn't exactly what the Queen wanted.

"Just tell me how the dragonfire came into this world again, Yannick," Gorias said pointedly. "You're old enough to recall when dragons still were around, when they had just wrymlings for battle. They aren't something to unleash lightly."

Yannick admitted, "I was against the wall. My own existence was threatened, oh, not just my life in the short run. Even prognosticators, or wizards, can grow ill. I had a massive tumor growing in my belly. But my powers are limited and I couldn't secure myself without the proper palliative."

Gorias blinked as the wizard paused to take a drink himself.

"Everything costs money or blood," Yannick explained. "So when a refined lady approached me, wealthy and full of promise, I agreed as long as she fulfilled the program for me. I needed the money and the spell would require lives that I certainly had no means to go gather, due to age and my high station."

"I see."

"Secreted in the inks, in myriad spells, yes, I gave her the dragonfire from beyond, and true enough, she had to acquire the further sacrifices themselves for her bequest. Dragonfire is not an easy thing to acquire."

"I'd say it's bloody impossible."

"But you know of Pergamus?"

Gorias' eyes closed for a moment too long. "It's a legend, like many other tales, where the father of the dragons fell. I've heard of the tree, lights and tiny collection of dragonfire maintained and all that. I've been all over the world and haven't seen it nor tried to find it."

"The lady did know where it was, for a foundling in her employ found Pergamus by accident."

Eyes open, Gorias said, "She just happened to stumble across the land where Satan has his throne?"

"Don't be so dramatic. In a word, yes. The island isn't really far and is on all the charts off Albion. It's in a cave accessible by a lagoon certain pirates use."

At the mention of pirates, Gorias' skin crawled. "Go on. What about this lady? Why did she want such a boon?"

"She took to the venture like a famished dog, though." He drank more and related, "Gorias, you must understand, I've never used my wizardry for the darker, baser arts."

"Until now."

"You have to appreciate what we both can distinguish, that everyone can die, wizards and even legends. I had to stay the hand of death and defeat destiny itself."

Gorias stood and exhaled in disgust. "Forces beyond this realm always make men candy coat their words when defending why releasing evil is a good idea. You aren't snowing me, warlock. The sinister forces always want a baby or some such thing for this kind of art. Do you think I can just let that life slide for a few more gold pieces? No keeper at Pergamus just gave up the fire, for a soul has to feed the dragon-light to let it live on."

Yannick shrugged and stood up as well. "This particular lady was pregnant herself, so the infant was there for the sacrifice. The child was unwanted, so everyone won in the end."

Rubbing his right eye, Gorias muttered, "Except the baby, I guess. Who is she? Tell me, Yannick, and I'll see how good my disposition is by the end of this venture."

Yannick face turned insipid. "You'd never slay me, La Gaul…"

Gorias grinned. "Who would stop me, those rows of armed kiddies on the walls out there? Hardly a set a' balls in the bunch." He leaned over the table, "If my mind decides it, there will be no stopping me, old wizard. I'm not so infirm that I cannot take out a few dozen guards." His eyes were clear and focused when he promised the mage, "I'd kill myself to see you die."

Yannick didn't blink as he held his breath for several seconds before admitting, "I believe you."

"Then tell me where she's to be found and I may forget my way back here."

With a doubtful look in his eyes, Yannick confessed, "How can I know for certain that you won't double-cross me?"

Gorias adjusted his armlets and said, "You're a prognosticator, not a wizard, right? That should be an easy one to figure out."

"Noguria, the pirate mistress of Princess Nykia."

"She's the one killing the politicians? Noguria?"

"A crossbreed Pryten witch, a woman of some means." Yannick nodded, eyes closed. "Noguria poses as a lady of the night and entraps them. For what end I have no clue, but I cannot say anything as it will implicate me. She paints herself as a high-toned whore and they fall in line."

"Why not just a knife to the ribs? Why burn them? She must be makin' a helluva point."

Yannick took a few breaths, eyes open. "It's some horrific game, perhaps a contract with her soul to Pergamus, I cannot understand it all."

Gorias frowned. "I doubt that seriously, wizard."

"Noguria fences with Niva and the other religions. She is into some sort of religious domination game with the Pryten goddess, the dead Queen Tancorix. I cannot understand their fencing, but I was drawn into their conflict due to my illness. The deals I've cut to lengthen my life have spawned this petty conflict."

"Noguria is mistress over little Nykia?"

"She's not so little, I'd surmise, but if she still lives, yes. Nykia is hers now, body and soul." Yannick looked at the table and threw up his hands. "Finding Noguria may be difficult, but the pirates smuggle things into Transalpina at times. They land in a rocky outcropping to the northwest called the Keep."

Icy spiders walked over Gorias' shoulders as he recalled Alena's words. "Oh yeah? What sort of things?"

"Herbs, hallucinogens for the weak-minded, a base form of grain alcohol and whores. They move by phases of the moon." Yannick walked to his desk, fumbled for a sheet of parchment, tore it in half, then dipped his quill in ink.

His right hand running through the hair over his head, Gorias replied, "I think I've heard that."

Yannick handed him the paper. "In the region of Gabitril, west of Mysoline you will find the Keep. It's shaped like a crescent moon and hooks around the sea. There's no beach to make landfall. Much trading is done there under the noses of the authorities."

Gorias read the names on the paper. "I see."

"I think they will make a deal tomorrow night as the moon will be full. General Thynnes is even out to gain by this. Don't ask me to explain it all. That is my guess but I could be wrong."

Gorias turned, saying quietly, "Ya better not be."

CHAPTER VI

THYNNES AND THE PIRATES

Gorias, Alena and Orsen departed Qesot to ride all evening into the northern countryside away from the main highway. The Gabitril region they traveled to lay on a different plain away from the narrowest portion of the channel. Near Gabitril, the northern sea opened up in a jagged coastline before morphing into a tangled backwoods. Since this area descended into wilderness, it formed a natural border to the next land.

They stopped by a long mead hall and boarding house on the edge of the town. Orsen declared the village, "Tegitrol. A quiet place of no significance, save to water horses for the military and navy."

Gorias' eyes narrowed at him. "Excuse me?"

Orsen waved toward the northern hills. "Beyond Tegitrol lies Mysoline, great port and naval base by the sea. Far to the west lies the Keep where the pirates will arrive."

Gorias turned to Alena. "Are you sayin' the pirates will skirt territory of the navy and land just over the ridge in a rocky outcropping?"

She nodded. "Takes balls, no?"

"Or a navy on the take. I wonder if they aren't the only ones. Ah well. Time to rest. We'll have until tomorrow night."

Alena asked, "Do you think Yannick is lying?"

Gorias climbed down from Traveler and shook off the road dust from his cloak. "Sure, but he's afraid. He fingered quite a few people and may just be jerkin' me off. I do believe that he's been ill, though. Desperate men do stupid things."

Orsen dismounted. "From what you told me, he gave up everyone but his mother's banker, sir, even saying General Thynnes came this way to the naval base for an outing."

"Hard to trust a coward, but we are grasping at straws. I do wonder why he fingered General Thynnes and let out he was on a mission out here. Fighting the fuckin' army isn't on my plate."

Alena frowned. "Why come to this place he named particularly? I'd have chosen a different alcove than the region he specified. Why believe him about the spies and smugglers?"

"Because he may have known we were coming to see him, but readily gave up others. He's a survivor and wanted to save his own ass."

"Could he be sending us to our deaths?" Orsen wondered.

"We are from the Queen herself, but if we die, the inquiries from Her Majesty won't stop. But yeah, he could be, even if the General and some soldiers are nearby."

Alena offered, "Perhaps he knows better than to mess with a legend?"

"That may have crossed his mind, but he'd still kill me if it meant surviving another day."

Orsen took the reins of Traveler and nodded at the stables. "I'll get these mounts taken care of."

Gorias faced Alena, then reached in his belt and took out several coins. He handed them to her. "Now, let's get drunk. Go get us something to drink and ask about General Thynnes and if his troopers indeed came through here."

"They aren't likely to tell me the truth."

"They are less likely to tell me."

"Why? They fear a fable?"

"No, you have a nicer ass than me."

❖❖❖❖❖

Alena knocked on Gorias' room door and he twisted the latch to let her inside. Four long decanters pinned under her left arm, she held a platter of meat, bread and nuts aloft in the other. She paused at the sight of Gorias, his dragon skin armor on the floor opposite the bed. The old warrior, though scarred and sunburnt, didn't sport the body of an elderly man. Wearing only a wrap around his waist, he returned to the ceramic basin to continue washing himself down.

"Put that all down, I'm about finished, little girl."

Snapping out of her momentary shock, she put the flagons down and looked for a spot to lay the tray.

Gorias gestured to the foot of the bed. "Put it there." He wiped his chest and under his arms dry with a towel and pointed to the desk. "Plenty of water and rags if you wanna get clean, sister."

"Uh, all right."

He grabbed a flagon and sat on the bed, groaned and took a long draw on the tankard. "Ahhh, if God made anything better, he kept it to himself."

"You like honey beer?" She started to shed her mail vest and unbutton her leather blouse.

He eyed her oddly for a moment and then lay back on the bed. "The beer is ok. I smelt whiskey in one of the other ones."

She nodded, pulling off her top.

Gorias drank again, eyes mostly to the ceiling as she grabbed a rag and put it in the basin. "You're all right, little girl. Ya thought of everything."

She soaked the rag, started to wash her stomach and up between her small breasts. "Orsen heard tell in the stables that Thynnes' band is far up the road from us. He volunteered to go see them as a messenger."

"That little sucker never gets tired."

"Doesn't appear to, anyhow."

Gorias started to eat some of the sliced ham and Alena shed her pants.

Alena turned, smiling as she started to wipe off her long legs. "You aren't offended that I do this here?"

Gorias shrugged and took another drink. "I just figured you'd do it in your own room, but I ain't gonna tell ya what to do."

Alena wrung out the rag and dipped it in the fresher water. As she applied it between her legs, she shrugged. "I figured we'd eat and drink together, maybe you'd tell me a few stories."

He laughed once. "You ever hear the story about how I gutted the Orm of the Loch in the northern Albion wasteland?"

Dousing her hair in the basin, Alena said, "Yes."

He swallowed again. "Then there's no reason to bring it up

then."

Standing tall, long tresses thrown back, she laughed heartily. "You kill me."

"Oh, I'd never kill you. It's the red in yer hair. Ya get a pass on me killing you."

Wiping her neck, she asked, "You never would kill a redhead?"

"I'd feel shitty about it, but well…"

She stood before the foot of the bed, naked as the day she was born and put down the towel.

He stared at her and drank again.

Alena eyed the cloth over his midsection. "You stir because of me? I'm flattered."

"I'm old, but I ain't dead, and I'm still a man. But what would you want with an old fool like me?"

Her hands on the footboard, she climbed over the end and went to her knees between his legs. "What would any woman want with you?"

He placed the tankard on the nightstand. "Tell me."

Her long fingers ran up his legs and Alena moved closer to him. "I don't have a man. I don't have a vow of chastity, Gorias La Gaul. Do you have a problem with me and some informal enjoyment?"

"Of course not."

She smiled and ran her hands to his crotch. "You show no fear of a young lady? I'm no petite flower with a flat ass." She pushed his towel away to his belly and started to fondle him. "What if I don't say to my sisters that Gorias La Gaul wasn't the most rapturous match of my life?"

Gorias sat forward, nose to nose with her, and seized her waist. "You'd be lying, but really, I won't care. Within a few days, you won't see me again. But there are few things I want to do before I die."

"Such as?" she asked and kissed his lips softly, hands stroking his rigid manhood.

Fingers digging into her waist, he mumbled, "You."

Gorias lifted her off the bed and her eyes widened at his strength. He lay back, slid himself under her long splayed legs and dropped her sex over his face. She gripped his mane of hair, nails digging deep into Gorias' scalp, wet tresses flying back, slapping his waving erection.

A few times in the evening, the innkeepers thought the two slaying each other, but were relieved to see the tall young lady leave the room for more beer every other hour.

Just after midnight, a pounding at the door startled them both awake. Alena nestled in close, head under his chin, hand on his heart, she only moved a little.

"Lord La Gaul?" Orsen's voice cried out.

Gorias sighed. "Well, at least he was this late." He spoke up and shouted, "What is it?"

"I have spoken with representatives of General Thynnes. The pirates will make landfall this very night. I doubt he is on their side."

"Beautiful."

"I can't find Alena anywhere."

"Relax. I know where she is but gimme a chance to get dressed."

She feigned giggling and started to play with his member again.

Gorias muttered, "Don't you ever get tired?"

Alena kissed down his chest to his stomach. "Don't you ever stop getting hard when toyed with?"

Orsen called out, "How long will it be? These soldiers are testy to meet up with the General later on at a fixed point."

Gorias hand rested on her flowing hair as it bobbed over his midsection. "Gimme a few minutes, all right?" He let his head fall back on the pillow and ran his hand down her back. He didn't know if Orsen stood outside or not, nor did he care if he heard him say, "The hands on the hips pose you did while atop me? That was really special. I liked that. I saw you ride your horse like that, directing the roan with no reins." Eyes closed, Gorias relaxed back and said, "Special."

✾ ✾ ✾ ✾ ✾

Gorias and Alena joined Orsen near the stables. Traveler and Alena's roan were saddled and ready. Gorias gave little regard to the two soldiers mounted up beside Orsen.

"Why tonight? I thought Yannick figured the pirates moved by the phases of the moon or whatever the hell it is."

Orsen exchanged glances with the soldiers and stated, "The pirates aren't adherents to such things as many may think. They perform their mischief a day early to throw off those in pursuit or who may suspect them."

"Huh," Gorias grunted as he mounted up.

Alena related, "Kind of like celebrants of sects that do their holidays a day off to poke the establishment."

"So the pirates are zealots of a sort? Outstanding. Glad you made contact with Thynnes' men."

Orsen cleared his throat and explained, "They found me, sir."

His head snapping from soldier to soldier, Gorias' hands became fists on the reins. "Outstanding indeed." Traveler turned in a circle, but this move wasn't to launch him down the road. The horse reacted to his broiling anger. "That sonofabitch! He's playing me!"

All moved their mounts back from the raging man but none dared to speak.

"That damned wizard…"

Orsen amended, "Prognosticator."

Head snapping toward Orsen, Gorias shouted, "My achin' ass! I'll call that prick dead meat, I will. He has set us up!"

Alena held up her hand. "How could Yannick tell Thynnes? We've just arrived. He couldn't have spoke the words or sent a runner past, surely."

Orsen offered dryly, "Perhaps by carrier pigeon?"

Gorias still fumed. "I don't care if he tattooed it on a demon's backside and flew him over here. I'll shove my sword so far down

111

his throat that wizard will be able to use his cock to slice bread."

Alena dropped her hand. "What will we do?"

After a few deep breaths, Gorias eyed the troopers. "I'll kill that old bastard at my leisure. I wanna see Thynnes myself and see what awaits us. Kids, how many in your group traveling with the General?"

They looked at each other before the one on the left said, "I'm not at liberty to say."

Gorias wheeled Traveler about, facing the road out of town. "I just wanna know if you little pricks are laying in wait for me." He kicked Traveler and the horse leapt forward.

Alena faced the soldiers and said, "He wants to know how many of you he has to kill if this is real mischief."

*****

Two hours down the road, four horsemen approached them clad in the leathers and mail, but not like the soldiers with them. Gorias drew his swords. The riders drew short swords each and never backed down.

Orsen went forward on his mount, waving his hands, but not so far ahead to get between them. "Hold, Gorias! These are men from the General's elite strike force, the Black Ravens."

Gorias lowered his blades and smiled. The four Black Ravens didn't share his hilarity.

"How redundant," Gorias mumbled, putting his swords away in their housings, then pausing in his motions until the four horsemen stowed their blades as well. Gorias eyed Alena and said, "Black Ravens. How about Brown Pigeons or Green-Headed Ducks?"

Keeping her face stern, Alena replied, "They wouldn't be as intimidating to the ear, Lord La Gaul."

He gave her a wink as they took up riding along with the elite soldiers. One of them said to Orsen, "General Thynnes awaits, but has the area by the Keep surrounded. They're going to unload materials and exchange with traitorous dogs in Albion. We came by this information earlier today, so we are glad you arrived to help or at least watch."

"Dang, that is lucky, huh?" said Gorias, still annoyed. "I smell rats, lots of rats."

The speaker of the Black Ravens gestured toward a heavy copse of trees in the distance. "We must tie up our mounts there. The land rises to a ridge beyond the trees and then overlooks the Keep where the pirates are moored up. They have some ships farther out but are making a landing in small crafts."

As they rode on the man explained that traitors from Albion moved up a regular road in a caravan of wagons and waited on the opposite end of the Keep's crescent. These men were who the pirates were in with, not the General.

Nearing the trees, other soldiers emerged from the woods in the moonlight. Gorias wondered, "They traveled out here in a caravan of wagons? To where?"

The Black Raven climbed down and said, "They head toward Mysoline in theory and divert here."

The rest dismounted and tied their horse's reins to a fallen deadwood. As Gorias patted Traveler, Alena said, "The Keep is a half moon rock formation where the pirates can come ashore with ease." She motioned beyond the veil of trees at a distant object. "Their great vessel must anchor out there, but smaller boats can navigate into the keep without getting to a dock."

While they walked in the woods, Gorias said, "I remember hearing of the Keep a hundred years ago, not a natural beach, but a great abyss that dips down beside the crescent of rock. One can row up to it and step off into Transalpina, but many fear what lies below."

Orsen scoffed as the four soldiers took up behind them. "Childish nonsense. There's a gouge in the earth there and a shelf of rock sticking out, not a gateway to the abyss. Yes, I've heard that crock of dung story. Of course a pirate would use this as a dock as the farmers around here have no guile to interfere in such matters."

Gorias took a quick look back out of the woods at the sprawling farms that covered the land and then scanned the heavy shrubs hemming in the area where the long wall of the Keep began to rise. These bushes covered the bottom of the rising rock like a beard, sometimes pushing vines up to where the stony wall terminated. "Most old superstitions get there for a reason. I'm not saying there's anything evil about the Keep, but I've found its better not to put your peter out for sunshine in places with a bad reputation."

The elite soldiers exchanged glances, but Alena said, "Scholarly advice."

"There are more old drunken whoremongers than there are scholars, so ya better listen up."

They only walked a few hundred yards before several dozen troopers bedecked like the Ravens melted from the landscape. They ringed the outer edges of a mass of regular Transalpinan troopers.

Orsen whispered to Gorias, "At times like this, do you feel afraid? Knowing you cannot escape if they decide to kill you?"

Gorias shook his head. "Hell no. I'm ready to die, young man. Many of them aren't. I know I'd take eight or nine motherfuckers with me, so that cushion keeps many honest. Besides, ever see a seven-hundred-year-old man scamper up a rock face and leap into the ocean?"

The troopers parted and allowed them to walk through. The area of planning had only the dimmest of lanterns and a makeshift command area by a couch-sized boulder. On this potato-shaped rock lay a scroll with two graying men in officer's regalia pointing to it. The one on the left, a very tall man, partly due to an oblong head, was unknown to Gorias, but he recognized the other in a moment. Tall, but very thickset, with fingers so heavy Gorias wondered how he tied laces on anything, the man's shaggy white beard hooped around a worn face and balding head. The hair in the rear of his head flowed long over his chain mail in the back, a light armor that struggled to cover his barrel chest and thick belly.

"By the ass of Odin, Gorias La Gaul for real."

"General Thynnes," Gorias said and the two old warriors clasped right hands. They didn't let go. "It's been quite a spell."

Thynnes rolled his eyes and belched out a boisterous laugh. "Speak to me not of spells, La Gaul. There's wicked deviltry afoot here and I mean to stop it."

Gorias released his hand and turned to the map. "Yeah? How ya gonna do that?"

"Like always," Thynnes grunted. "I'm going to stomp its balls into oblivion like it was a common drunk in a bar fight. This won't be pinching off a stubborn turd, no, this will be a blow with finality. There's a ban on wizardry and spellcasters in our land."

"I've heard tell."

"Somebody is fucking around, though," Thynnes snorted, coughed and spat. "That's the only explanation for the goddamned dragonfire business." Thynnes looked to Gorias. "You know how this shit can be happening, don't you?"

"I have an inkling. There are no dragons and one can't carry a flint stone to create dragonfire in the twigs."

Thynnes nodded sharply. "Exactly. I'm so fucking glad to take council with someone with a few brains and who's been smellin' their piss for longer than twenty years." He then stared at the oblong-headed officer. "No offense, Colonel Schou."

The other officer smiled. "None taken, sir. I'm interested to hear and meet Lord La Gaul."

"Gorias is fine," he said and shook Schou's hand. "I'm only here as a favor to the Queen."

Thynnes cleared his throat and gripped the parchment again. "The old girl is coy, even at this late date. She keeps her damned friends close as the clap, don't you know?"

Gorias nodded. "So it's these pirates? What are they about?"

"They're smuggling something shitty into Transalpina. From what our sneaky pickets said, there was something sent out to them before we got in close, probably cargo from the goddamned traitors in Albion."

"You folks are sure there are traitors?"

"Ain't there always? Some sissy punk always wants to get the high ground in life by not doing a damned thing or by not fighting. Pirates, who'd deal with such scum? Goddamn navy, they polish their pricks and let these fuckers in close."

"I met an Admiral yesterday."

"Rosman?"

"Yeah?"

"Prick with ears. Anyway, I have a nasty idea what but not to who is supplying the pirates. I think we have them with their balls out this time. Maybe they'll roll under torture."

Thynnes motioned them all to follow as Gorias said, "What are the pirates smuggling in?"

They all climbed up a trail in the rising stone and soon peered over a crested rock cropping down into the Keep. Two small rafts stopped by the lip of the rock outcropping and several pirates climbed out, pulling their boats onto the land. In the distance sat a vessel anchored beyond the drop beside the Keep.

"See?" Thynnes asked Gorias. "You know what it is."

Gorias' eyes widened as he saw the pinpricks of lights, like glowing balls in the boats, each as big as a child's game ball. "Dragonfire."

Alena pushed up beside Gorias and whispered, "Where would they get such a thing? How?"

Orsen added, "And what is someone doing with it in Albion?"

Gorias stared a long time and Thynnes said at last, "You know the stories. You know where they are getting it."

"Pergamus."

Thynnes nodded. "There's no other place, even if it's a fuckin' legend. You know where it is, don't you?"

"Not exactly. It's been centuries, but granted, it's not far from here." Gorias rubbed his eyes and blinked. "That damned wizard, lied to my face."

Thynnes jeered him. "What? That never fuckin' happens to you?"

"Sure, but what makes me angry is, he wouldn't have done that if he thought there was a chance of me coming back alive."

Thynnes drew back on the dirt path and started to motion for his men to fan out away from them. "I guess we'll soon see if you get to die in the line of duty, huh?"

Alena stuck near Gorias as they moved back some, saying, "Pergamus, that's just a fairy tale like Lemuria on the other side of the world, not real like Atlantis, right?"

"Pergamus isn't a place, like they all think," Gorias said low so only she could hear. "They think it's an island, a special place, and well, kinda. Pergamus isn't an island."

Though she wore a questioning look, she stayed quiet as Gorias and the others started to jog to keep up with the troops encircling the edges of the Keep. He saw her watching Orsen as he hung back from the rest and disappeared into the troopers far behind them. Courage, Gorias mused, wasn't that kid's strong suit.

Gorias drew nearer to Thynnes. "Couple dozen pirates, probably all armed."

Thynnes nodded. "We'll take enough hostages." He then swept his right hand out, and near to fifty men spilled out of the brush into the moonlight.

Alena whispered, "Those aren't Black Birds."

"Ravens," Gorias corrected her with a droll voice. "Regular archers, correct?"

Thynnes said, "They're green troops but everyone needs practice. I figure firing down into the fuckin' darkness and any surprises that lurk will be a learning fuckin' experience."

The archers didn't let out a shout or a declaration to the pirates. The squad took a knee and leveled their longbows. The pirates saw them in the moonlight and stopped fast.

Gorias noted, "Longbows, damn, they'll slice them to the wishbones."

A hail of arrows released, probably leaving a few targets clean, but under such a barrage it appeared all of the pirates would die. Once the arrows released, the pirates also took a knee and pulled up tiny metallic shields on their left forearms. Near to all arrows were deflected by these small shields, save for one that found a home in the bent knee of the pirate nearest one of the boats. This man grabbed his knee and fell, screaming.

Thynnes looked at Gorias, "That was either a lucky shot or highly skilled."

Eyebrows raised, Gorias replied, "In the heat of battle, they are interchangeable."

Undeterred, the bowmen reached back and quickly notched another arrow.

One of the pirates stood up a tad, long hair blowing in the breeze. "Hail!"

Before another volley flew, a rain of projectiles struck the archer squad. Near to every shot went awry as many rocks, shiny balls and sharp objects rained on them, swooping up from the depths of the Keep's darkness.

Thynnes stepped back, frowning. "We are undone, fucking traitors out in the dark." He waved his left arm, indicating the Black Ravens should now descend unto the Keep. "Fucking pricks. I hate traitors, don't you?"

Half laughing at his obsession with traitors, Gorias followed Thynnes as he fell in behind more regular army troopers that in turn followed the Black Ravens disappearing into the night.

Alena hissed quietly, "Traitors?"

Gorias grabbed her by the wrist so they wouldn't get separated in the night. "Those pirates are coming to meet somebody with dragonfire. I guess they were still around and had slings to flummox the archers."

He released her and drew his swords. She did likewise, sliding out her blade and a dagger. The Black Ravens slithered into the brush where the party hid, and soon flushed out a group of men in regular clothes, armed with short swords and slings. The elite troopers cut them down for the most part, quickly chopping through their ranks like a gardener who discovered a snake. Gorias saw one of the men; turban tight to his head, mouth gaping, both arms hacked off, a scream caught in his throat, still running.

The archers stood and started to take better aim, but still only struck a couple of the pirates down, for the invaders still defended themselves well. Their attention now turned to the crop of men flooding in from the brush.

"Alive!" Thynnes shouted. "Leave some alive."

Gorias and Alena moved down the side of the Keep but she patted Gorias' arm, seeing Orsen staying up top. He shrugged. "We're probably stupid coming down here."

One of the pirates screamed out, "We're had!" The pirate turned and started to push the raft back into the sea, but a bowman struck him in the spine. The boat drifted off into the current as the pirate fell face-first into the sea. He never swam. The arrow in his back twitched twice.

"Surrender!" one of the Black Ravens shouted.

From the group of surviving pirates and their Transalpinan friends a thin pair of arms arose, holding a globe of flickering dragonfire. The sphere of fire illuminated a mound of blue-black hair.

Gorias grabbed Alena and pulled her behind him. "Aw, crap…"

The woman from the pirates shouted, "What shit!" and threw the globe at the largest mass of Thynnes' troopers.

Gorias had time to turn and push Alena far back toward the path on the steep drop they descended before he reached down to his belt and armed up his helmet.

The globe descended in the midst of the archers and Ravens, shattering like glass, but the contents spreading like the sun broke over the land. From out of the spot where the globe broke belched a huge flame that just kept growing. Like the billowing cloud of a furnace yet made of churning flame, the dragonfire arose, not caring who it touched, pouring over the archers and troopers like lava, giving them all several seconds to understand they were aflame and run a few steps before their joints turned to ash and they fell to flaming mush.

Thynnes and many more fled and took cover behind folds in the rocks, but a majority of the archers and several of the regular army died where they stood, melting away, their bones rattling on the floor of the Keep.

The pirates retreated to their rafts, many laughing, but the tall woman stepped from the group. Beside her was another slender woman with black hair, tattooed all over her flesh. The first woman stomped forward, hip boots flat on the rock surface, a dagger in her left hand and a coiled whip unraveled from her side. An archer who survived got to his knees and notched an arrow. She took note of him and he let the missile fly. Her whip lashed the object down as well as his second volley. The big gal stalked over and lashed the whip around the archer's neck, and yanked. The archer twisted as the whip ripped back, his neck and throat shredded of flesh.

She swung the whip back and snapped it down. The whip's tails glittered from the metal treatments affixed to it.

The dragonfire died down a little but amid the flames, only Gorias La Gaul, clad in his smoking armor, gauntlets and helm secure, stepped through the liquidy inferno. His cloak melted away in the fire as his heavy waist belt lost a few links and fell to the rock surface. He joined his twin swords at the handles and spun the weapon like a fan.

"You can die like any other," the woman screamed, whips snapping near Gorias. "Come dance with Noguria!"

"Deliverance will come," Gorias said, voice muffled in the helmet, still advancing, blade fan spinning slow.

Noguria took up an attack stance, left leg planted back and right bent forward, whip curled back ready to strike. She slapped the knife to a housing on her hip and it adhered. Noguria's hand slipped into one of her belt pockets and she threw out four metallic objects into Gorias' path.

His swords slowed in their spin, but skillfully swiped at two of the twisted objects, each whirling sword tip scooping one up and sending them back at their owner. Noguria dived out of the way and rolled back up into her defensive position. The two projectiles stuck into the side of the nearest boat just by the edge.

"Caltrops," Gorias named the wicked objects as he stepped over the others. "Meant to ruin a horse's hoof. Cute."

"Good enough for a horse's ass," Noguria shouted, pulling a second whip out in her other hand, lashing out, trying to encircle Gorias' knees.

So light on his feet, Noguria's mouth gaped, Gorias hopped back, legs apart more to avoid the caltrops, and he eluded the whips treated with jagged glass. "Yer outta yer league, sister," Gorias yelled and glanced over at the boat. He set eyes on the shorthaired pirate girl, but quickly refocused on his opponent.

Noguria's boots tapped like a dancer, trying to confuse him of her advance or intent to retreat. She kept lashing out with the whips, but her eyes betrayed her, darting past Gorias to the area where Thynnes hid, then to the tall guard of the Queen also coming into the open. Alena ran toward the crowd of traitors at the edge of the dragonfire burn.

Gorias seized her moment of panic and stepped forward, separating his swords back to his hands. His looming form made Noguria lash out to disarm him, wrapping both wrists in the whips. Gorias dropped his swords, not letting the whips slide down to his pommels, clutched the ends of the whips and pulled her to him.

Terror presented in her mind as she approached the warrior but her survival instinct rose up. She slammed into Gorias' frame, impacting on his chest, blood spilling from her jaw from the hit. His arms encircled her in a bear hug, but she quickly rotated, releasing one of her whips. Right hand into her other pouch, Noguria reached for his face as Gorias tightened his grip. Instincts running high, he flinched and pushed her away just as the hand slapped at his visor. Noguria meant to squash the diminutive tablets from her pouch into his open visor to his flesh, but his last-second jerk move made her gloved hand slap his helmet side instead.

Gorias' left hand let go and yanked down his visor just as the dragonfire from the tablets crushed on him started to flower. Noguria slithered from his grip and fell to the rocky surface, rolling over a dozen times to avoid the plume of dragonfire as it ran over Gorias.

Alena stopped in sword fighting one of those deemed traitors from Transalpina long enough to gawk at Gorias taking a few steps and shaking off some of the dragonfire. It snaked about him and nearly took on the shape of eels as it started to disperse, finding nothing to eat.

Gorias reached down, trying for his swords, not waiting for it to clear completely.

The girl in the boat screamed at Noguria, "Run!"

Her ego bruised, Noguria bit her bottom lip, started to get to her knees and faced the boat.

Gorias hopped, much of the fire off him, blocking her path to the tiny boat.

Noguria went at him again, lashing out with the last whip she held. The lash wrapped about one of Gorias' blade tips. He stopped moving toward her and let the blade she seized fall down to his right side. Gorias stepped on the blade, pinned her whip to it, and gripped his sword by the flat of the gleaming metal.

She held her whip too long, trying to pull it back, but did release at last. She drew back just as Gorias disengaged the handle, gripped the flat and swung his sword by the blade, cracking her across the cheek with the handle. The shot spun her around, but Gorias had her fast, holding her from behind by the shoulders like he meant to apply a gentle massage, but instead he drove his helmet into Noguria's skull. The dragon-skinned material broke through her hair, collapsed her cranium and hit the moisture of brain matter before Gorias drew back, and permitted Noguria to fall down. The whip mistress convulsed a few times before she lay still.

Seeing Gorias unarmed, one of the pirates leapt at him, dagger swinging. The knife broke in half as it impacted on armor near his neck. Gorias grabbed the pirate by the throat and threw him behind himself into the smoldering dragonfire mound. The pirate screamed in broken shouts, partially bathed in the runny bile, rolling until the blaze took his breath.

Alena took a knee, drew a pig sticker from her boot and drove it into the pirate trying to kill her with a curved sword. This man fell and she stepped away from the fray as the woman wielding the whips fell off Gorias. The confusion of bodies and swords flashing made Gorias turn, but he saw the same thing Alena did: The whip mistress' pouch fell from her belt, open, spilling out what looked like a handful of dead fireflies. Alena scrambled over by him, knelt, eyes darting around for an incoming target, but scooped the glowing objects back into the pouch. Her blade sliced through Noguria's belt and she took the pocket, just before she impaled a charging pirate. Gorias leaned down and grabbed his waist belt and swords. He then focused back on the fallen woman, using his swords to slice at the restraints of her leathery clothing.

"No tats," Gorias muttered. "Yannick, you die."

"Stop!" shouted the other woman with dark hair from the boat. She held a globe of dragonfire. She looked into Gorias' face. "I won't fight you. I can't fight you." She put the globe at her feet and held out her hand. "You're Gorias La Gaul." She turned her palm to him, showing a tattoo likeness of Gorias on her skin to him. "You're my husband, remember?"

Gorias pulled up the visor on his helm. "Nykia?"

The skinny pirate trembled all over. "It's really you."

"And it's you," Gorias said and stepped toward her.

"You know how to make an entrance," Nykia said, tears running down her face and then staring at the dead woman at her boots. Nykia gave her a kick. "She was my mistresses, Noguria. I belonged to her."

"Not any more."

Nykia wiped tears from her eyes, looked embarrassed that she cried in front of her men. "So I belong to you now?"

"I dunno, but you are free of them now."

Thynnes' troopers came forward, many leveling crossbows at the pirates. "Hold!"

Thynnes shouted from afar, "You have them, La Gaul?"

"Yeah," Gorias took off his gauntlet and touched Nykia's wet cheek. She started crying again. She moved closer and tested his chest to see if he was still warm from the fire, but threw herself on him anyway. "Yeah, I got 'em."

Nykia shook all over and said, "I love you, Gorias."

He patted her back, "I know, Princess. There's no future in it, though."

From her position, Alena pointed with her blade toward the ship and started to back up. She exclaimed, "Gorias! Look out!"

Gorias turned to see something in the air like a glittering ball coming away from the moored pirate ship. When he turned, Nykia slipped from his grasp and dived into the raft, along with many other pirates. The force of their bodies put the raft further back into the water. However, the group of traitors still alive ran for the edges of the Keep as the huge projectile fell from the sky. Gorias had no time to move much, but he took a couple steps to his right and flung his waist belt toward Alena. The belt flipped end over end and dropped short of her, for she had climbed down behind the rocks to hide.

When the flaming mass of scrap metal and flaming pitch struck the edge of the Keep, it killed a dozen Transalpinan troopers, a few more of the elite Ravens and the traitorous group. The ejecta spread out, cutting dozens of soldiers and traitors alike off at the knees. The blast struck far from Gorias, but this fallout swept Gorias over. The flaming pitch never scorched his legs due to the armor he wore. However, the force of the projectile knocked him down, slamming him into the stone beach. His helmet popped free and shot into the small craft.

Nykia caught the helm like a ball and then shouted orders to the other pirates in the boat.

"Get him! Help me with him, damn you all!"

Alena screamed, "Gorias!"

Nykia smiled, "We have him now!"

The pirates seized the form of Gorias and started to drag him to the small ship.

He turned his head to the flaming bodies and noted a large member of the traitorous band that fell, his bulbous body bubbling like fat in a skillet. Once the hood burned away, Gorias recognized the dying man.

The name "Dola" ran through his bleary mind, along with everything it implied. .

Gorias looked at Nykia with groggy eyes. He took a weighty breath and looked up at the full moon. He closed his eyes.

CHAPTER VII

ESCAPE, NYKIA AND PIRATES

Alena tried to run down into the flaming mass of the Keep, but General Thynnes grabbed her by the left elbow. "Hold your ass, child!"

"They're taking Gorias!" She yanked at her arm but the bear of a man held her fast.

Thynnes shouted out orders for his surviving troops to fire on the raft. "The old bastard's armor will protect him."

Alena used her leg to help pull free of the General, but she couldn't run through the seething pitch, even if the flames died out. She could see the crossbow missiles slay a few of the pirates in the boat with Gorias. Nykia, through, dragged the unconscious Gorias over herself, wiggling in behind him. The warrior's prostrate form proved an excellent shield against all attackers and missiles.

"Damn her," Alena cursed and swung about, glared at the General. "They're taking him away!"

Salty curses flowed free before Thynnes said, "We'll get them, I promise."

"But…" she protested.

His left hand up flat to her, Thynnes said, "The Admiral's ships were on the way up to Mysoline even before this operation happened. That pirate vessel won't reach open water."

"They let them past once. How can you be sure?" Her chest heaving, Alena stared helplessly at the raft as it traveled farther away. She turned angrily, stomping across the edge of the burning pitch.

Orsen stood at the crest of the descent for a moment and then he walked down near her.

Alena's face went sullen at the sight of him, "Fat lot of help you are, runt."

Orsen gazed across the sea, silent.

Thynnes' men gathered up what they could, and still had four living pirates as prisoners. The General said to Alena, "We'll go unto the coast and ride hard for Mysoline. The Admiral is taking on supplies, and after we talk, I'm sure he'll depart shortly to join his other men cutting them off at sea. I can put you aboard his ship if you so choose."

Alena's eyes locked on his. "I have a mission from the Queen..."

Thynnes got close to her, his nose near to touching the tall woman's nose. "I can only but guess at the true nature of your mission for my beloved Queen."

Alena blinked. The old man knew something of her assignment and vocation.

Thynnes said, "I shall do as I can to get you out to La Gaul again. Never fear, young lady, not all desire to have certain forces rule this land."

Alena then understood the old General not a disciple of the new way of Mavik or Prince Vincent. While many in the military paid unified lip service, Alena comprehended they wanted a different heir on the throne than Vincent and his controlling mother. Alena stood by the General, mildly amused that the deadly pouch on her belt, once belonging to the whip woman of the pirates, was out in the open. As they mounted up and rode toward the docks at the village a few miles distant, Alena thought the pouch weighed heavier all the time.

Thynnes shouted, "Take the fuckin' traitors that made it in for a damned public flogging and a proper execution. The pirates? We shall learn the fuckin' truth from them. Question them well."

Alena understood that meant torture and had no pity on them. Her anger boiled and her body seethed at the image of Nykia, her arms about Gorias, caressing him, saying she loved him. Alena tried to banish her thoughts but they refused to leave. She didn't love Gorias, nor did she have to. However, her innermost being still felt warm and wet with Gorias' seed. Alena wanted him, though she knew he lived unattainable, forever. Silly girl, she laughed at her own fascination with the legend. How many women did he have? He'd lost count. But his manner and method, she quivered at the memory of his touch, strong, gentle, forceful, almost sweet, yet could suddenly turn violent, like riding a wild horse.

Thynnes interrupted her thoughts, saying, "You're of the Queens guards. Wipe your damned tear, you're embarrassing yourself."

Alena shook her head and quickly pushed off a tear from her left eye that escaped. "I never…"

Thynnes nodded. "Just come along. We'll meet up with Rosman in a few hours. They won't escape. His ships can outrun those fools."

Alena rubbed her fingers hurriedly as if they'd exorcise her tear. Her sex quivered again. Had Gorias noticed she was a virgin at such an age? Had he cared?

❀ ❀ ❀ ❀ ❀

Somewhere in his concussed mind, Gorias heard Nykia's voice say, "Boy, we're in a world of shit now."

Gorias opened his eyes and felt hundreds of years younger. The reason for this proved obvious when he looked down at a body barely past puberty and running with a gaggle of other longhaired youths like himself. The moon, giant in the sky, stared down like the eye of God on that night when they all ran in the wild hunt.

He recalled the day well, very cold for the time just before spring, and the boys wore only their boots, trousers and a sleeveless tunic. Weaponless and freshly scourged by long reeds, the dozen youths sprinted across a broad field full of creeks, tangles, waterways, and crags in search of the other side. All around them echoed howls, whistles and animal sounds. Gorias wondered how many really were animals or just the other older warriors out to educate them. He reckoned the animals had lit it out by the time the warriors picked out a good spot to spring traps on the young boys on their mission in man-making.

Gorias loved that time, though some hated it. The training and regimen that came before this day, he loathed at first, but it hardened him, as it should. Many broke and couldn't make the grade, like Svien the redhead who had just caught his leg in a snare near Gorias and wailed for his mother. That was gonna hurt when the taskmaster beat him later. No mothers. Gorias didn't fear calling on his mother in distress. She died on the day he was born.

He leapt over a crag and rolled, but Haaken, the boy with white-blonde hair and low hanging balls, hesitated. Up from the muck in the crag loomed a hirsute warrior and grabbed him by the ankle. Down into the muck sank Haaken. He cried out, but tried to suppress it, then cried again as he realized the hunt ended for him badly.

A few others were picked off as well, but Gorias ran on. He smelt the warriors, their musky stank, men who needed to aim better when wiping their backsides. He knew them there as clear as if they were on fire. One stepped out from behind a tree, throwing a bolo at Gorias legs, so the youth leapt, dropped, rolled and struck the warrior in the groin before twisting away and going on with the hunt. A low groan echoed from the man he struck, along with laughter from his fellows that one of the young'uns had bested him.

On and on they ran until they were but four in number. Gorias didn't looked back as another fell, but that one cussed up a storm, angry at his falling. Gorias saw a series of trees and darted away from his fellows. He let the two left run into the open. One fell in a trap, not seeing the false ground before him as such…the other tripped, watching his friend fall. Soon, a warrior was on him, hog-tying the boy and hooting like an owl.

Gorias ran out from behind the tree and launched himself, drop kicking the warrior in the head. Not a small lad, near to six feet tall at thirteen years, Gorias' boots knocked the warrior askew, sending him tumbling into the trap the other youth fell in.

"Help me!" the hog-tied youth implored Gorias, but La Gaul didn't. He never looked back as he reached down and scooped up the three-headed morning star the warrior abandoned as he fell.

On he ran, seeing the hedge that denoted the end of the run. Gorias cursed, knowing that would be a trap as well, for the hunt was meant to exhaust the body and mind, to see that last easy obstacle and gleefully fall into the arms of stupidity. He ran on a diagonal line, away from the hedgerow, toward an ancient spruce tree. The moonlight shone bright and any watching could see his moves. He ran right for the tree then stopped.

The skirting of the wilted spruce trembled.

"C'mon out and fight, ya fuck!" Gorias howled.

Though the combatant hiding under the spruce skirting probably knew better than to let the challenge of a lad bother him, this night the stout killer Garretson rolled out of the tree. A shorter man than most warriors, Garretson was built like a tree trunk and could throw an axe damn near through an oak. Garretson smelled of whiskey, Gorias noted instantly, cocking his body back to hide the weapon he'd grabbed. The stout man took two shaky steps and Gorias understood his advantage.

Garretson growled, "You come here, little prick." In one hand he held a wooden board, just right for slapping down teen youths on a man-making trip, and in the other an almost-empty skin of liquor. Gorias didn't expect him to overhand the skin at him, but he dodged the blow, seeing the board swipe across the night coming on, fast.

Gorias cocked back and threw down the morning star, wrapping around the board and pulling it back, disarming the drunken fighter.

Astonished, Garretson grinned. "Sonofabitch."

Gorias snapped down the morningstar, freeing the board, and ran forward.

Garretson, a wily warrior even when drunk, set his feet and lowered his shoulders.

Gorias swung the morningstar, the long flails flying out. Garretson extended his left arm, partially covered in chain mail. The chains of the weapon wrapped around and the pointed ends stuck the chain mail. Garretson made a face. It hurt, but he was tough. Gorias figured he could take it. In fact, he counted on Garretson's pluck, for the warrior took the shot and cocked his arm, disarming the boy. Gorias, though, planned on that, too, for Garretson flung him out of his grip, past his self and toward the tree.

After a twist in mid air, Gorias flattened on the ground and crawled like a spider under the wilted skirting of the spruce. He quickly stood, and started to scale up into the pointed branches into areas Garretson couldn't follow. Not that he would, for the warrior stood, watching Gorias climb, curious. Garretson smiled as the youth got upright and leapt over the nearby hedge, thus navigating the field of the wild hunt.

Gorias lay on the other side, exhausted, seeing the campfires of the warriors and the shocked looks of the military men. They paused in their tales and drinking, stared at him and then stood. They all applauded. A few came over and picked him up.

"This day, you have proved your worth as a man," a hairy mammoth of a man called Tylr said, brushing Gorias off. "Thirteen winters you've survived, and now, it's time to show us if you are man enough to keep training."

Another of the soldiers, this one with an officer's rank, stared back at the hedge. "You worry not on the others with you?"

Gorias sucked in air and then stood upright by himself. "They will survive it someday. I can't help everyone."

The officer laughed. "Perhaps not good stock for a soldier, but a good warrior and tactician, this one."

Tylr guffawed. "Says you. He's a fighter, like his father, the chief. He would be proud to know he made it across on his first try."

The officer took a drink off a cup of wine. "His father would be proud if he takes longer than a minute to screw the whore we have for the victory later on."

Gorias breathed regularly, and his body tingled, but no fear birthed in him about the prospect of testing his manhood for the pleasure of these savages. Besides, he'd been performing that duty with the daughter of the neighbor lady for a year. Surely, whatever whore they had in mind would be different than Jenna, the red-haired lass near to his own age, but all the rest of it was gravy. He'd survived.

Garretson shambled into view, rubbing his shoulder, laughing. "Gotta hand it to ya, ya young buck, good move. You'll be all right someday."

Gorias nodded, no words spoken, as his father oft told him too many words amongst men showed a weakness. A great warrior like Garretson saluted him and didn't take the loss personally. Gorias chalked it up like a man and the others drank to it.

When he awoke, face cradled in the breasts of the pirate girl princess, he tried to remember the whore the warriors got for him. Reality jerked and his memory registered alarm as the boat was hoisted up the side of the pirate vessel on great chains. In moments, he was rolled from Nykia's bosom and to the deck of the ship.

"Belial wept," one of the pirates said, mouth gaping as he glared at Gorias. "You have La Gaul with you?"

Gorias rolled over and groaned, hearing Nykia say, "It was an accident, Savage Chad, but perhaps karma dictated it all."

Savage Chad grunted and then said with gusto, "Damn, we could use a man like him."

"Debna," Gorias mumbled.

Nykia and Savage Chad exchanged a look and then faced Gorias. She asked, "What is it? Who is Debna?"

"The whore the warrior guild got me as a kid." He coughed and tried to stretch. "Damn, I was big for a kid, but she had a cavernous vagina." Gorias stood and all of the pirates drew steel, shocked at his size. His eyes set on the pirate captain. "Not a tiny box like Jenna the neighbor girl."

Nykia said, "This is Savage Chad, the leader of the pirate ships."

Gorias didn't take Chad's extended hand. "Well, there, Savage Chad, I gotta take a wicked shit. Ya gonna gimme a pot? I ain't got sea legs for crap to hang my ass over the side." He then stared at the others and then the deck around himself. "Where the fuck is my helmet?"

❖ ❖ ❖ ❖ ❖

"Damn, be careful next time, asshead," Thynnes said in disgust to the sergeant. "Are their any more pirates you haven't killed under torture?"

"One," the sergeant admitted with a shrug.

Thynnes clocked the sergeant upside his head. "Shrug your shoulders at me, ya pissant. Stand at attention and mind your officers." He pointed at two corporals standing on the dock near Alena. "Crucify him for a day. Let him think about his fuckin' posture."

The sergeant's mouth gaped, but he never begged for mercy. The corporals dragged him away by the elbows and Alena pondered the coming crucifixion of the soldier. He would be stripped, flogged and tied up by his arms on a phallic symbol, barely able to push up to breathe with his feet. A day would be torture. Two days may kill him. She recalled being given an afternoon of such an exercise as a youth during training. Alena sang songs the entire time.

Thynnes shook his head. "The timber of these crappy puppies makes me wonder. War is a damned good thing, young lady. Every so often boys must learn to be men. We've went a long goddamned time without real action, aside from border skirmishes."

Alena nodded, her eyes momentarily watching Orsen out at the edge of the camp, scribbling on parchment. "The Queen fears intrigue in the transition to another on the throne won't go smoothly in the next generation."

They walked down the pier away from the Admiral's huge ships at the port of Mysoline. The night fading all around them, the screams of the last living pirate pierced the night by a bonfire not far from the docks.

Thynnes grumbled, "Hope they let this one live, fucktwits."

The colonel near him offered, "You mother is nearby, sir."

Thynnes stopped. "Is she? Her skills at persuasion are better than the rack. Go fetch her and tell those assfaces to ease up on that last punk." The General looked at Alena. "We're on the same page, dear." He then stopped and added, "I meant no offense."

Alena looked at the sea. "None taken. Many men don't see me as a woman, not unless you have a tiny waist and tits like melons."

Thynnes coughed. "I'm long past sweet talk, but there are no women in our ranks. I don't mind having one around."

"You respect strong women?"

"Of course. Only a weak man doesn't, but don't get me wrong. I don't want them amongst my men in case of war."

"My sisters and I are excellent warriors."

"You speak the truth. You are. I bet you would be incredible on the field of battle."

"Then why say things like you don't want us in a war?"

Thynnes frowned, but it presently turned to a cynical grin. "You're a woman. I like to look at you. You smell of a woman, even if you have trail dust on you. If a brigade of ones like you came along on a long march, it'd be trouble."

"We could hold our own."

"I think you could, but I want no fighting or mischief amongst my damned army. We can think on women and go for them later, but it's a distraction."

Alena now smirked at the general. "Send a hundred of your stout fellows to assail Queen Garnet's tower. Not a one will live to see her on the top story. I promise you that."

Thynnes chuckled. "I have no fuckin' doubt. I reckon Lady Garnet would rip my nuts off if I got close to her, anyhow."

"You know her?"

He nodded. "Oh, for decades. I still see her at councils. I've seen you before at those things."

"You recognize me?"

"You and your sisters are quite similar but only you have the red highlights in your locks."

She gaped at him as the soldiers came from the nearby hamlet with an elderly woman on a colt.

Thynnes winked. "I'm old, like Gorias, but am not dead just yet. Ah, there's my mother."

The men took the colt right to the man staked down to the ground by the fire. Alena followed Thynnes up to the scene and stood near enough to watch and hear.

The elderly lady, wrapped in many layers of woolen cloth and a headscarf of shimmering fabric stood near the pirate splayed on the ground. The pirate, naked, was staked down, tied at his ankles and wrists. Blood ran from his nose and out from his crotch.

"I'm Louthyn," she told him and took the scarf from her head. Her hair, snow white, tumbled out, but Louthyn bestowed the soldiers dirty looks as she covered the pirate's nakedness with her scarf. "There's no reason to be animals here, is there?"

Alena saw the pirate as a younger man, not even twenty years old. They probably saved him for last because of his youth. Tears ran down his face and he stared at the old woman. "Louthyn?"

"I'm the General's mother, honey," she said gently. "I'm sorry these ruffians treated you so crassly." She sent more sour looks to the soldiers and they backed off some. Her soft look returned when she faced the pirate. "What's your name, sweetie?"

"Declan," he gasped.

"Where are you from?"

"Albion's outer marshes, near Asgardian border to the north."

"How on earth did you fall in with these dreadful sea dogs?"

More tears oozed from Declan's eyes. "I was the youngest of a dozen boys. My mother died giving me life and I was raised by my only sister, Meghan, until she passed my fourteenth year."

"The others all had vocations? Farmer, soldiers, priests or smiths?"

Declan nodded with vigor. "It's like you know my life. Yes, I had no clear path."

"I've heard similar tales. There are too many people in the world these days. Perhaps the stories of the end of time are true? Who can say? But you fell in with pirates?"

"The short of it, yes."

"Dear, there's always a choice. You can join the army and have a life, but that may be another choice for later. Now, my child, tell me, you were indeed here to deliver dragonfire?"

He nodded. "The soldiers here, they never even asked me that."

"That's obvious. They want to know who you were bringing the dragonfire for."

"I'm just a sailor. I don't know who was to get the dragonfire."

"I can understand that. It was silly to torture a boy over something he didn't know. Tell me though, where did you get the dragonfire?"

Declan swallowed hard. "Pergamus."

"Do you know the way to Pergamus?"

Declan told her a long story about navigating by the stars, trade winds and certain islands that would lead you there. A soldier dutifully copied down the words on a parchment.

"What island hides the pirate realm?"

Declan stiffened, looking terrified, but when she stroked her withered hand over his sweaty forehead, he gave that up as well.

"And you don't know for whom the dragonfire is intended?"

Again, he shook his head.

Louthyn leaned down, kissed his forehead and stood. She faced her son and said, "There, was that so hard?"

"Thank you, Mother." Thynnes bowed slightly.

She exhaled and then looked down at Declan. "Keep the scarf. Oh, by the way, he's lying about the receptor of the dragonfire. He knows but won't tell." She gritted her teeth and said, "Crucify him, but use nails. He may find his tongue then." And with that, Louthyn returned to her colt.

Declan screamed as the men untied him and took him to a set of logs.

Alena and Thynnes saw the Admiral and two sailors walking down the pier toward them. Nails hammered into Declan and he cried as Admiral Rosman saluted Thynnes. The sailors eyed Alena. Hands to her hips, she gazed away from them, back at the soldiers nailing Declan to two rude logs and propping him up as best they could in a ditch.

"Admiral, glad to see you."

"General," he replied, then faced Alena, eyes on her insignia and said, "Charmed, Queen's guard woman."

Alena said nothing. Her eyes drilled through the Admiral, but the cocky man with the serpentine eyes looked back to the General.

"Your ships at sea are in motion?"

Rosman nodded once. "Messages are being relayed and in time, we'll catch them."

"Good." They stepped away from Alena, but she didn't

follow. She turned back to the crucifixion, executed not far from the place the errant sergeant was tied up. Alena wondered if the enlisted soldier would ever take his duty light again. She understood why they did what they did near him, so he'd hear the dying pirate cry. He'd hear that voice forever. Alena figured that time and wine would make the wailing Declan's voice fade, in her mind, but that sergeant? He'd hear it on the day he died.

The Admiral and Thynnes talked quietly and Alena walked to the crucified sailor. The soldiers finished pissing on him and walked away, leaving her alone with Declan.

The boy wailed for a bit and then set in to a series of blubberings before falling silent.

"Tell me a name," Alena said softly. "And I'll be merciful."

Declan looked up, blinked and coughed urine several times.

Alena drew out the pig sticker from her right boot and patted the side of his bloody leg with it.

After a few minutes, Declan told her a name. Alena's eyes widened. She nodded and stuck out her weapon. The tip inserted in Declan's throat and after a flick of her wrist, his windpipe and veins ripped loose.

The hanging sergeant gaped at Alena, and pissed himself.

A few soldiers shouted in disappointment, then called to the General, complaining that she slew him.

Thynnes waved them off. "He told us all he knew. The torment only pissed off the gods. Besides, what do you bastards expect from a weak woman?"

She stepped away from the crucified man and walked into the woods. The soldiers giggled and elbowed each other, speculating that the tough girl was going to puke or pass water over her act. Alena ignored their stupidity and got her moment alone at last to open the pouch from Noguria. She took out one of the tiny glowing objects. Eyes focused in, the tiny sliver of glass was no bigger than a huge apothecary pill. However, within wriggled an object like a grub or worm...but it wasn't alive, or at least she didn't think so. The glowing thing was a tiny measure of dragonfire. She squeezed the surface of the glass and it nearly bent. Terrified, she returned it to the pouch, seeing dozens of the objects nestled in.

Alena said to no one, "That's what she tried to slap into Gorias' face." She pondered these and the name the dying man gave her.

Real or not, Thynnes words meant nothing to Alena. She had a name, something they did not. She understood a grander plot more than a gigantic army. She walked away, staring at the sea, unable to suppress her grin.

"You'll want to know that name, won't you, Gorias?" She said. "But which name to give you?"

❖ ❖ ❖ ❖ ❖

"It's really you," Nykia said to Gorias and walked near to him, hands up to his face.

"Yeah, what's left of me."

Eyes tracing every contour of him, Nykia replied, "Are you joking? You're twice the man of any I can name." She turned her head to the pirates exchanging glances. "Yes, I said it. Get over it, Allard." Nykia faced him again. "Look at what you did on the shore, with the dragonfire, with the missile."

Gorias scanned the ship and the crew. He looked farther into the sea and saw an identical vessel further on out. "I survived. I usually do. Just because I don't get myself killed I get called a legend? Whatever."

Her faced gleamed. "I haven't been that excited in years. The dragonfire, it bathed you all over."

Gorias made a fist then opened his hand to remove his glove and patted his chest. "The wyrmling dragon armor protects me. My cloak is gone, I guess, belt too, dammit. Yeah, what were you doing with dragonfire?"

"What were you doing with the army leaders of that land of frogs?"

"Sun bathing, but we got to the beach early. Ya got yerself a stooge on board, Princess, or General Thynnes wouldn't have known where you'd land or when."

138

Nykia's glee faded to a grim frown. "You did know when we'd land?"

"That was guess work, but I hate it when theories come true too easy. We didn't know about the local traitors that would rise up, though. I reckon Thynnes' troopers will torture any good info outta them."

Fists slapping her hips, Nykia said, "Damn. But we made the pick up in the exchange."

Eyes narrowing at her, Gorias asked, "What was the exchange for the dragonfire?"

"Sacred oils for the Albion goddess Rhiannon. Each of these vessels holds a slew of it now."

"You're trafficking in sacred oil to the Albionise priests?"

"They buy from us as well as others and at a cheaper price than getting it direct from Transalpina. If the priests in Albion had the ear of their king too much, they'd want to crush Transalpina and take the means of attaining the oil from the mines at Lascaux."

"Wars have been fought over less. I've heard that when they pour the oil into the pit that the Albion goddess Rhiannon moans like a whore."

"Is Rhiannon really at the bottom of that well in Albion?"

Gorias shrugged. "Dunno. Maybe something is. Seems like a lot to waste on something that isn't there. She must give good results for being fed that stuff. What a weird world, huh?"

"The Albion King isn't a very religious sort, so he doesn't care to send his warriors to dominate a culture over oils. Most kings don't pay close attention to what the minor clergy are up to, though, unless it means to control the masses."

Gorias shaded his eyes a little and faced the other vessel. "Someone gave you a helluva lot of this stuff for the dragonfire?"

"Yes."

"Kinda bad for the Transalpina economy if someone is shafting the market." He dropped his hands and turned back toward the land. He couldn't see the shore any longer. "Who the hell could give you that much oil, barrels of the stuff?"

Nykia smiled again. "Someone with a large supply that had

no more use for it."

Gorias shook his head. "I ain't up on the politics, but I might be able to guess on it."

"A new goddess reigns over Transalpina, Gorias, and that goddess doesn't need the sacred oils that make ceremonies so wonderful as in the past. The fools in Albion use the stuff like maniacs, bathing in it ritualistically, dousing children, but I'm no fool. The Albion military has developed a small projectile in glass, not as bad as dragonfire, but the same principle as you saw earlier."

"An explosion one can throw and have fire spread fueled by the sacred oils of the goddess?"

"Well done! I knew you were sharp."

"Thinking is tougher than fighting. So tell me, who is the culprit? Are you saying the freaking Queen herself is behind it? She couldn't know they are supplying their natural enemies to develop a weapon."

"Don't disappoint me and be thick. My Grandmother has got on board with the new goddess, but she doesn't care about such weapons of war or trade values. No, she has other things on her mind."

"Yeah, I know."

Nykia winked at him as they gravitated down the deck away from others. "I'll get to you in a minute. Who could possibly run a scheme like this, have oil stored, and the means to use dragonfire?"

"The goddamn prognosticator, Yannick? Never trust a wizard, sweetheart." Eyes closed for a moment, he saw the image of Niva's guard, Dola, burning. He doubted Niva and Yannick were in any sort of bed together. Gorias figured exactly who that pointed at. He decided to play along and see where it all led and how much Nykia would lie or was deceived.

"That's the story, anyway," Nykia shrugged. "I could care less who sells it or what they do with it."

"It's dangerous stuff."

"Yeah, true."

As they walked to the poop deck, the pirate ship used its sails and headed out into the open sea. From the bridge, Savage Chad promised they'd be out of harm's way soon.

Gorias stepped away from the rear and wandered over to sit on a bench near the opening to the lower deck. "Where are you all headed?"

Hands on her hips, Nykia said, "Well, we are going to Albion to deliver the oil barrels. This ship contains the cargo barrels below that we got loaded up the coast before the dragonfire exchange could be made."

His look serene, Gorias wondered, "So you got in a couple boats and brought in the dragonfire?"

"Yes."

"Why not make the exchange right when you loaded the oils?"

She sat beside him, trying to contain delight at seeing her hero again, and hugged his arm. "Ever hear that it's better that the right hand doesn't know what the left is doing?"

"I follow ya. Not all understand the mechanisms of this deal?"

Head resting on his arm, Nykia said, "It's better that way. Looks like we were suckered anyhow. The entire deal got fuckered up."

Gorias laughed once. "Such a mouth for a princess."

"Pirate bitch is all I've been for years."

"But I killed your mistress, Noguria."

Nykia's smile faded and her eyes widened. "Yeah, and easily, too." She looked up at him. "I expected no less."

"It wasn't that easy. You belonged to her?"

Nykia nodded, head down.

Gorias assured her, "Not anymore."

She embraced his arm tighter, not caring if it was armor she felt. Her hand ran down and lay atop his huge hand. "I'm yours now."

"Pardon?"

"The pirate way," she winked, hand playing in his beard.

"Aw, shut up."

Nykia giggled. "I've always been yours, Gorias La Gaul.

When I got older I wanted to give you my virginity, to live with you in a castle forever, have your babies…"

"Life isn't like storybooks or tales."

"I know," Nykia agreed, her voice sad. "I know you travel the world and had no time for this pirate girl or fallen princess."

"If I knew you were a prisoner of the Prytens, I'd have come back immediately, true story."

Nykia shrugged. "There was no way for you to know. It's all right."

"No, it isn't, not really, but ain't much I can do about it now."

Nykia smiled up at him. "We can still run away to a castle and have babies."

Gorias leaned back and put his arm around her. "Yeah, there is that."

She snuggled in close to him. "Why are you here in Transalpina?"

"Passing through from Albion, but your grandmother wanted to see me." Her body frame reminded him of another, about five foot four, slender and taut.

"Do tell?"

"She wanted me to find you."

Nestling in closer to him, she mumbled, "Mission accomplished."

"Pretty sure she wants you home from these folks." Eyes closed, Gorias recalled the girl she reminded him of and tried not to call her by his old neighbor girl's name.

"I haven't been home for years. I'd say this is my home amongst these pirates. They stole me from the Prytens years ago."

"With your mistress dead, where's the harm in going home and being an heir to the throne of Transalpina?"

She looked up at him and made a vinegary face.

Gorias nodded. "Oh, I know it's a prissy-assed life, but you'd never want for anything."

"I know. They'll want me to marry some perfumed prick-nose and pump out heirs like a brood sow."

"Still, not a terrible life, is it?"

"You never saw fit to settle down."

"I'm not royalty."

"We both know that isn't true."

Gorias squeezed her tight and then stood. "That's pretty thin, honey. Yeah, my crazy mother was a distant part of the royal line of some country and fit to breed with the aristocracy of any land, but my father was a rough chieftain."

"A king in his own right, no?"

"He sure was, but it didn't go to his head. Just a chief, but he conducted himself well, almost like the royals."

"Weird combination. How did that happen?"

"Troopers escorting my mother were overrun by savages. These savages were enemies of my father, a savage guy himself, and he was set to raid them anyhow. The princess, my mother, just happened to be there and fall into his care. Well, one thing led to another and here I am." He got up, walked away from her and said to the sea, "Not always a good thing, for she was missing a few cogs upstairs." He slapped his head. "Probably all of that royal bloodline inbreeding, really. They say they are so high and mighty, yet screw their relatives like the baser folks in the sticks."

"You'll have to tell me that story, but I want to show you something." Nykia coaxed him toward the rear raised sections of the vessel.

Gorias looked around, seeing the pirates tending the ship and trying to maneuver it better. He followed her through the small cabin door and let it close behind him.

Nykia turned up the oil lanterns. He saw a sparse quarters, a small table for meals, a couple chairs, and a huge hammock large enough to hold two huddled in close. Nykia took hold of the small set of chested drawers and pulled it away from the wall. She pulled out a series of pasteboards, each one had images sketched and painted on them.

"You still sketch me?"

"Looks like you, doesn't it?"

Gorias smiled. "Fighting dragons always."

"Of course. I like it when you smile."

"I've killed more men than dragons, but make the race extinct and they never let ya forget." He reached out and touched her cheek. "I'm honored. You hid these from her?"

She pulled out a strongbox and climbed atop it. Face to face, she slipped her arms about his neck and said, "I'm yours. I always have been. Nykia loves Gorias."

They kissed deep. Gorias couldn't help but think of Alena's kisses, much different than Nykia. Alena tasted of sweet mints, top-end wine with a taste of whiskey. Nykia tasted of smoke from a pipe bowl and stale beer. Granted, Nykia was a more petite woman than the guard for the Queen, and with proper training would've been a gracious feminine girl instead of a rough, tattooed fighter. Her body so reminded him of his first sexual encounter, Jenna, back home, over 700 years ago.

She pulled back, her hands in his mane of hair. Her bottom lip trembled and tears rolled down her cheeks. Nykia's tough façade dropped like the tie that kept her breasts snug under her tunic.

Gorias had to struggle in the tight quarters to undo his armor. Nykia gave him help. With no bed or durable table, Gorias adapted, like he always did, and gave it to her standing. Her arms, stronger than he thought, controlled the action of her hips, as she gripped him in a headlock and lowered her lithe body onto his waiting self. His hands held her backside and gently worked his way into her.

She's not Jenna, he told himself, *even if she feels like her little box*.

He so wanted to have a more passionate encounter, to do more fantastic things with the little princess, but she didn't complain as he entered her slowly, a bit at a time. Her nails dug into his scalp so much Gorias figured he'd find blood dried in his hair in time.

Her mouth open, but no breath exiting, she gaped into his eyes. Her bare legs slithered around him, shaking. Nykia gasped, her breath escaping all at once. She gushed down his member, that she hadn't even taken in all the way, and the warm fluid ran down his legs.

Gorias smiled. He wondered if he got that one from her on just being there in the flesh for the first time alone. A braggart could choose such a moment for smugness or domination, but Gorias understood a more proper way.

"Take your time, sweetheart. As long as you want."

She lofted herself up so that he slid from her, but she reached down with her right hand and gripped him. Holding his shaft, she worked the head of him on herself, slow at first then furious in the slickness. Nykia shook again, glaring into his eyes.

"I just can't believe this is happening," she groaned and came again. Arms again gripping his head, Gorias let her get her breath before he entered her. Once more, she stared into his eyes. "Inside me, you hear? I want you inside me. Every bit of it." Her almost haggard look started to break into a joyous smile. "Take what is yours, Gorias La Gaul."

And he did.

Eyes closed, he heard a distant voice, one he'd forgotten almost, cry out, "Jenna loves Gorias."

His father told him a man seldom forgets his first woman or his last. He smiled as he took Nykia, hoping the gods didn't mess with his head in this fact, making this one here, possibly his last, so like his first.

CHAPTER VIII

BETRAYALS

Before they cast off, the Admiral treated Alena with more grace and pomp than she deserved. She knew it and every sailor knew it, but they kept up the charade like they cared. Certainly, being the only woman on this vessel, the Bahamut, did make Alena start a little, but she shrugged it off, understanding destiny lurked behind every corner. She'd been taught to face that and be ready for what came next. Alena didn't sense death or doom, not exactly. *This was the navy of my own land*, she reasoned. *What do I have to fear?*

She walked the deck before the shore couplings were released, scanning over the docks, watching the troopers from Thynnes' army depart and Orsen lag behind. It didn't shock her that Orsen Riva stayed in the city proper and didn't go back to where Thynnes pitched camp.

Alena also noted Admiral Rosman over by the open gate of the Bahamut, near to embracing a trio of sailors, who nodded at every other word he spoke. They stood back, saluted and exited the ship just before the other sailors pulled in the planks.

Alena secured her wrap about herself, eyes searching the sea from the opposite side of the huge vessel. The wrap felt heavy, concealing the belt of Gorias in its inner pockets. She pondered the complement of sailors it took to run such a massive craft and how many shifts they must run in to accomplish that goal. Never afeared of sea travel, Alena's stomach turned a little as the great ship shifted, the wind pulling the sails and the mechanism of the giant paddles in the rears churning.

"Would you like to see the paddles and how they work?" The Admiral asked as he stepped up toward her, arms folded across his chest.

Thinking his stance rather aristocratic for a man of the sea, Alena said, "I can walk to the back, but I'd rather stay above deck if it's fine with you."

He bowed his head low and then brought his face up to meet hers. "You're my guest. It will be as you say." Rosman then walked beside her to the rear of the vessel, extolling the wonders of the new technology that turned the turbines of the paddles. A new invention, he celebrated, but her mind remained elsewhere. Indeed, the paddles looked beautiful churning and their speed increased slowly, angled by the sails and pushed by the paddles.

"Impressive," she approved. "I've seen this at a distance. Are your other ships so equipped?"

"Only a few," he confessed, hands going behind his back. "In time we'll have the fleet refitted. The vessels further out have been signaled here and there. We will catch up to the pirates in time."

Alena wondered how the pirates ever got in to the Keep with such forces meandering in the sea. Granted, they couldn't be everywhere at once, but she always smelled a rat.

The Admiral offered, "You may recline in my supper cabin, if you so like. It is near the back and above deck. There's a lock on the door and a showering device, also new to this world, in the closet. You won't be disturbed. The cook will have prepared a cold plate for me by now, so if you are hungry…"

"I am a mite," she confessed. "It's been an exhausting night." She thought of how it started out, her riding Gorias like a stallion, and ended here, with her trying to keep her boots steady on a giant naval vessel.

❀❀❀❀❀

The Captain of the great vessel watched Alena disappear into the Admiral's chamber. He soothed back his bald head with his right hand, straightened up his gait and then approached his leader. After exchanging salutes, the men turned their backs and looked toward the rising sun.

"Something on your mind, Captain Jrabesak?"

Still facing the sun, Jrabesak replied, "Awfully cordial, sir, to that woman."

Rosman smiled. "I prefer to clean a cunt before I fuck it, Jrabesak."

"Very good, sir." Jrabesak wiped his brow with a cloth, folded it neatly and jammed it into an open section of his belt. "Sir, you know we have eyes all over the land."

Still wearing a distant look, Rosman replied, "Do these eyes somewhere have an observation, Jrabesak?"

"A runner from Qesot arrived just as we took on supplies. He has reported an attempt on the life of Queen Garnet."

"Gracious," Rosman replied, his comportment mildly amused. "Only an attempt?"

"Affirmative. The assassins were halted by the Queen's choice guards."

"Siblings of that freak we took on board?"

"Yes, sir."

"They are supposed to be excellent warriors for women."

"The attempt wasn't in the tower."

Rosman turned his head at last, his face showing serene bafflement. "That means Garnet is on the move."

"Yes, sir. The Queen made an example of the assassins, a horrible fate, the runner heard."

"No wonder bliss fills our land," Rosman conceded with sarcasm. "There are so many first-rate examples to follow, we should suffer no rationale to step out of line."

❖❖❖❖❖

General Thynnes slept in a large tent surrounded by the tiny tents of his troopers. His own private quarters in the capitol sat amongst the regular army barracks, too. His reasoning always was that he felt safer surrounded by his soldiers, even when bivouacked in the field. If he'd slept in his usual quarters back in the city or in the village near the sea, the men who came for him would've never got near to the aged General, even in the morning's light. It also helped they wore the garb of the Transalpinan Navy. However, two men, each barely five feet in height, slipped under opposite ends of the fifteen by fifteen-foot tent, brandished a dagger in each hand and went fast for the General's bed mat.

If Thynnes had been lying in it, he'd be dead. Thynnes, though, was on his knees in the northwest corner of his tent, kneeling in prayer. The darkness was broken only a little by the flaps rustling as the men entered. The old man held the idol of the god Dagon in his right hand. The idol, made of stone, carefully carved by the artisans of Nineveh where Dagon was freely worshipped, was hardly the size of his hand. He gripped the idol as the men stabbed with four daggers, knowing immediately that they were mistaken in their quest.

Thynnes got up slower than he liked, but fast enough to reach out with his left and grab one of the assassins by their head wrap. Through the wrap started to come loose, the would-be killer fell back from his haunches and lay on the ground before the General. Right hand raised high, the force of a hundred years of military experience and 300 pounds backed up the idol of Dagon, sending it through the forehead of the assassin and four inches into his brains. Thynnes felt the dent and the wetness of the brains, but pulled out fast, knowing the other would-be killer wouldn't be caught so easily.

The virgin daylight slipped in through the main flap and Thynnes roared as he charged, but then stopped in the middle of the tent. He felt the air break as the assassin swung blindly at where he figured the old warrior charged. Once the blades passed, Thynnes kept going, throwing a shoulder into the small man, sending them both out into the daylight.

The assassin fell to his buttocks and his head snapped to the turf between the General's tent and the next one. Thynnes, on his all fours atop the small man, prepared to draw his idol up and strike, but as he did, he smelt something. In a fraction of time, that smell of fish and salt made Thynnes drop and roll. A third assassin's daggers swung past the General and buried themselves in the belly of his comrade. The stabbed assassin screamed. The third man froze, stunned at the happening.

From his knees, Thynnes changed hands with the idol, swiped, and brained the new arrival just above the right ear. Dagon worked magic again, but the idol never broke bone. The third assassin fell over his fellow and then twisted to the ground, grabbing his head, leaving his knives in the other man's belly.

Thynnes stood tall over them. "Piss-poor work, ya little shits." He stomped his bare foot into the area where the gut-stabbed man gripped at the handles of the blades. Thynne's foot drove the blades deeper, through to the ground under the assassin. He then awkwardly stumbled and fell on the man he wounded. "Who are you pukes?" Thynnes saw the men in the tents starting to rouse. "You all? Bring the instruments of torture. And kick the guards of the camp in the balls, would you?"

Colonel Schou glared at the last assassin as two soldiers bound the man's hands.

Thynnes said, "You know who this is?"

The Colonel looked the struggling man over and then at the man dying, fluid welling out of his belly. "Their hair is too long for professional assassins or the military. You think so, Corporal Travin?"

Travin added, "But not the navy. They let them get hair out in the sea. Never knew why." They all looked at the corporal and he stood at attention, saluting. "Uh, Sir!"

Thynnes waved him off. "So, these are the Admiral's little seamen?"

The soldiers laughed as Thynnes got on his knee beside the bound up assassin. "Now why the hell would he want me dead?"

Schou said tritely, "We have not been getting much information from torture, sir."

Thynnes stood up and raged, "We gotta get lucky sooner or later." He pointed at the sailor. "You know you're as good as dead, punk, but it can take a long time to die."

Thynnes used the toe of his right boot when nudging the corpses, which now bubbled black fluid. "What in the hell is that?"

The Colonel stepped forward, leaned down a little and then exchanged looks with each of the officers around.

Thynnes admitted, "Yeah, I don't know. Any of you have any stellar ideas?"

One of the regiment Captains said, "They aren't human."

"Brilliant," Thynnes grunted.

The last living one gaped at his fellow assassin, shocked.

Thynnes reached out to Schou and pulled the Colonel's personal dagger free from the holster. He spoke to the assassin, saying, "A greener man may not have seen that, kid. I know people. They are all bastards, but I know fear and honest confusion." Thynnes looked at the two Captains. "Hold him down." When the two knelt to make sure they held the assassin's arms in place, Thynnes blew on the blade and watched it fog up. He turned to young Corporal Travin. "Here. Cut him."

"Sir?" The corporal took the knife and knelt, but his words only asked the question of where.

"On the forearm."

Travin seized the assassin's wrist and a struggle ensued. With two men on him, the assassin squealed as the corporal slit his arm open. A black, inky fluid rushed out of his skin.

The two Captains released him and Travin jumped back.

Thynnes folded his arms over his chest and then rubbed his bearded chin. "Hmm. Look at him. He doesn't understand it either."

The assassin's eyes grew wide at the wound. He started to scream.

"Wrap him up," Thynnes ordered. "He's losing it. Must be a bitch to realize you're not human."

Travin asked, "Sir, what is he, um, what are they all?"

Thynnes looked at his officers and they again watched each other with empty eyes.

A Major offered, "Sir, perhaps they are Vardogers, you know, the tales of those who can exist in two places at once."

Schou scoffed. "My granny told stories about a Fetch that doubles for people."

One of the enlisted men said, "It's a doppelganger, not a man at all."

Thynnes cleared his throat loud and all talking ceased. "Where is Ellis?"

The men exchanged more uneasy glances and then their

ranks parted. In the open gap stood a soldier barely five feet tall, and so slight, one would mistake him for a pre-pubescent child. His hair so orange it glowed in the lantern and moonlight, Ellis stepped forward and remained at attention. On his hip, he tried to hide his bugle.

"At ease, son," Thynnes said, but the young soldier relaxed little. "What do you make of this?"

Eyes only on the two bleeding assassins for a moment, Ellis stared ahead. "Sir?"

"I know your granddaddy was a damned wizard, Schuler, a great friend of Lady Garnet's uncles. Unfortunately, he refused to adhere to the new edicts and got barbecued for his beliefs."

"Sir?"

Thynnes exhaled in frustration. "Drop the fuckin' stupid act, kid, we all know ya know the things of magic and that path."

Eyes still ahead, Ellis replied, "Possessing such knowledge would mean the rack and the stake for me, sir."

All of the soldiers chuckled and Thynnes glared down at the youth. "Tell me what you think this is, and that's an order. Is it a Vardoger?"

"No, sir. Such a thing is a spirit predecessor, where your self and scent get to a place before you do. Certain sainted figures can perform this at will, but it's just a story for children, not to be believed by rational men."

The Colonel offered, "What about the Fetch?"

Ellis jerked his head slightly. "No, sir. I've heard tell that a Fetch is a double for a man or woman, but it's a signal of that person's death. Once more, these are stories for children."

Weary, Thynnes said, "Doppelganger?"

"I've heard doppelgangers are tangible bi-location body doubles, usually a harbinger of evil times or poor luck. However, these images are not of us, but I would guess they are images of sailors of the Admiral."

Thynnes asked, "Again, son, what would you guess they are, from your years of hearing tales on the wind? This shit jar anything loose?"

Ellis swallowed, clearly understanding how the General planned to get more info loose from him. "Some hold something called a Capgras delusion that a relative or child has been replaced by an evil copy. Some think evil beings place a foundling in the crib and take humans under the earth for hideous upbringing and breedings."

Schou muttered to the Captains, "More like fears that one's wife was lying low with another."

"Quiet, you dickheads," Thynnes shouted and then faced Ellis, wanting him to continue.

"This is more of a homunculus of a sort, an artificial creature grown as a copy." "They don't even know what they are?"

"No, sir."

"Why not send the originals?"

Ellis paused for a while and then said, "Such a copy isn't made and the original set free to live their life, sir."

"Meaning?"

"Meaning their souls and original forms are forfeit somewhere."

"Why would someone do such a thing?"

Ellis drew stiffer at attention again. "In exchange for something. These men were not a part of the bargain, just chips in a game of power."

Thynnes' arms dropped at his sides. "And these men serve the Admiral and were originally sailors. I thought the Admiral out to just silence me if he attempted a military action, but his powers must be on for greater things. He sent these out knowing if they got caught, it wouldn't matter much, but he's showing his damned hand. He has sinister power on his side with a desire for something greater than just military strength." He turned toward the sea, far out of sight. "And I sent that young lady out to the sea with him. Damn."

Schou wrung his hands before saying, "Might I suggest a course of action in catching them."

"You might," Thynnes snapped, jaw tight. "Where's that little ferret that came in with La Gaul?"

"Orsen?" Ellis threw out, still at attention.

"I'm getting too old to remember so many names. Where is he?"

Schou shot hard looks at his Captains until one volunteered, "He stayed in Mysoline at a boarding house this morn."

"Not one for sleeping on the ground?"

Schou said soothingly, "I think he acquired proper lodgings."

Thynnes exhaled. "Twat."

The Colonel blinked. "He's not in the army, sir."

"Palace twat." Thynnes waved at the encampment, his anger boiling at the events of the morning. "Damn it all, betrayal on many levels. Hell. This is what happens when the world goes in the crapper. Damn this very world to hell. May the god of gods truly fill this world with his piss. The sooner the better."

❂ ❂ ❂ ❂ ❂

Once cleaned in the water-spewing closet of the Admiral, Alena pulled fresh underclothes from her roll and donned outer togs once again. She took up Gorias' belt and pulled out the vial she saw earlier. In better light of day from the cabin window, she saw that indeed something humanoid floated in the amber-colored fluid. She couldn't comprehend why Gorias had such an object with him. Revulsion spread over Alena as she wondered if this was a fetus of his own, an unborn child he kept for a morbid cause. True, she admired Gorias but what if something terrible lurked in his spirit?

She checked from side to side, thinking of the previous vision from her crystal and how Gorias' awakening stopped it. Alena had more time now as the Bahamut sailed on.

Alena sat with her back to the door and took a small crystal from her belt pocket, then placed it to her forehead. She held the vial tight with her right hand and then took down the crystal to see what she could.

Images of a robed priest and Gorias appeared in her mind.

The smaller man with the pointed beard said to Gorias, "I know I've done wrong, enriching myself as I attained oils for Rhiannon. This act today will earn me forgiveness. If not, well, my damnation is assured, no?"

Gorias gripped the vial. "This is the way ya want it?"

"It must be so. This is the path to salvation I've heard in my dreams. Please don't fail me, Gorias La Gaul."

"I'll do my damnedest."

The priest mildly laughed. "Our god chose to give us life for simple supplications. The god of the dragonfire, though, sought destruction of all like most of his dire brothers have."

Gorias gazed down at the vial in his hand. "I hope this works."

"From out of the well of eternal harmony, I have drawn the very goddess herself. She has spoken the truth into my mind."

"From what you say she said, it sounds like a fatal, kinda endgame deal between her and Pergamus."

"You don't believe, do you?"

"That they are gods? No, of course not." Gorias nodded. "I do know what they are."

"Perhaps that's why she sent for you, a true apostate, for her destiny."

"Could be."

The vision ceased and Alena blinked, not realizing she hadn't been breathing during her watching. Gulping in lungfuls of air, she tried to clear her mind. Hurriedly, she hid the vial, but in her own belt in the pouch full of dragonfire tablets.

She left the cabin and let the sea air throw her long tresses back. Looking down the deck, Alena spied Rosman and Jrabesak. The Admiral, ever smirking, made a polite bow, then the Captain waved and spoke with his superior. She closed her eyes for a moment, hoping the vision would return. It didn't so she opened her eyes and searched the sea for the pirate vessel.

❈❈❈❈❈

"Ah, look," Rosman murmured as he walked across the deck to join the Captain once more. "The Amazon dries herself off."

Jrabesak offered, "Perhaps I should propose her a more

extensive tour below?"

"Agreed."

"The Queen will take it personally if one of her fine guards is killed."

Rosman nodded, his face composed. "Quite so, Captain. A true pity she is about to be lost at sea."

Jrabesak turned from him. "We will soon overtake the pirates, within the hour, sir."

"Good."

"I'd say they'll never know what hit them, but they'll be well aware of their fate."

"Dead men know nothing, after all. Armory at the ready?"

"They're loading up now."

"Excellent."

Jrabesak cracked his knuckles. "Orders still stand?"

"Yes. Sink one immediately, take the other one alongside us and reclaim the oils. This will be an act of sweetness to our Queen. 'Twill be a shame all lives will be lost."

The Captain's voice dropped. "The Queen's heir, all of that oil, plus Gorias La Gaul will be lost when they go down."

"We will report that they put up a great fight. No witnesses."

"What if Gorias isn't on the one that sinks?"

"You fear a battle with the old fable? He's not immortal. His string of bodies and sloppy tarts would leave one to think that way. He can die like any other."

"Yes, sir."

Rosman cleared his throat and turned toward Alena. He spoke to the Captain, though. "You're from Toblok on the eastern border, correct?"

"Yes, sir, we've talked of it before."

"That's far inland for a man of the sea."

"The army didn't cotton to me so I embraced the navy."

"And why breaking wind to Thynnes' desires doesn't bother you?"

Jrabesak smiled. "Not in the slightest, sir."

"Very good, Captain."

After a salute, Jrabesak walked over to Alena and said, "I'd really like to show you how the turbines work that power our great Bahamut."

Pulling her streaming hair from her face, Alena relented and followed the Captain.

❊ ❊ ❊ ❊ ❊

Nykia lay atop Gorias in the hammock, which stretched nearly to the floor, not meant to hold his great size. She trembled often as if cold, but hugged so close to him he could scarcely breathe. Never one to complain, Gorias held her tight and kissed her hair. She kept her calf lightly pressed on his spent organ as if it would escape. Her weight was light, but Gorias cursed his aged state, knowing that her weight, however slight, tired him a bit after a while. Still, he'd endured worse for less.

"Hope I didn't disappoint you," she said in a soft voice, one not like the tough she-pirate had used before.

Funny, he thought, *I was just thinking that myself.*

His right hand stroking her hair once, Gorias said, "How could you? Wonderful."

She snuggled up closer, reaching down and lightly gripping his limp shaft. "This is mine now, you hear?"

Gorias couldn't hide his smile. "Oh?"

Nykia looked up at him with a serious expression. Her grip tighter, making his manhood stir once more. "Yes. No more whores, no more ladies in waiting, no more pirate girls. Mine, you understand?"

"Huh. Here, and you said you couldn't be royalty."

Nykia blinked, still gripping him. "What?"

"You sound like royalty."

Some humor crept into her expression. "I mean it, Gorias. You're all I ever wanted, all I ever dreamed of when some pig was atop me, or I rode a savage to ruin…or she rode me. I wanted you. I wanted it to be you."

"And a younger man wouldn't do?"

Her eyes focused on his, her hand starting to stroke him. "No. No one but you."

She pulled away and climbed atop him, trying to work his self into her again. As he entered, the hammock broke and they crashed to the floor of the cabin. Both laughed heartily and he seized her waist, recalling how muscular and firm Alena's was compared to Nykia's bony hips. He could feel her bones in his hands as she leaned back, determined to ride him on the floor. She really did feel like little Jenna, all those centuries ago.

A fist pounded at the door and they ceased in motion.

"A ship from the Transalpinan navy has been sighted!" a ruff voice shouted. "Come out here! We will try to evade but our number is up. There'll be no escape!"

"Coming," Nykia shouted and then focused back on Gorias, grinding her hips down on him. "Not yet, but soon?"

Gorias sighed and drove into her, figuring a few minutes wouldn't make much difference if they all were going to die.

❖ ❖ ❖ ❖ ❖

Alena took the Captain's arm and against her better judgment, went below the deck. The vast innards of the vessel impressed her, far larger than any ship she'd ever toured or been near. The hold yawned vast, large enough to hold a hundred horses she guessed, but it sat empty. That pricked her interest, but she let it go. Though some sailors eyed her, it wasn't anything akin to wanton lust a la men who hadn't doused their sea legs ashore in ages. Alena understood they oft went to Albion, where prostitution was legal, and then back home where Yannick's balms for venereal disease were effective.

Jrabesak, a gentle and gracious host, explained they could transport a great deal of cargo, arms, extra men and horses to an engagement.

"How many sailors are on here?"

The Captain pointed to a vast system of bunks and hammocks, all holding slumbering men. "Several hundred. They sleep in shifts and another hundred of them man the vessel."

Alena noted a multi-colored parrot whistling up at the nose of the column, but they were heading the opposite way. After several yards, she paused, nose wrinkling. "You keep stalls for cows here?"

Jrabesak shook his head. "Very astute, miss, but no. Within these stalls are the opposite shifts for the turbine muscle. Our sailors aren't they only thing that sleeps in shifts here."

"Why the bolts and locks on the stalls? Are your cattle prone to escape?"

He led her on past the covered stalls toward the rear of the vessel. The closer they came to what powered the paddles, the louder a grinding sound came to her ears. A sweaty sailor saluted the Captain, eyed Alena, and then unlocked the door at the end of the hall. They walked down a hallway large enough for them to walk two abreast. She noted the long horns on the wall, like ivory trumpets or some trophy gained on a massive hunt afar off.

As soon as the door opened the sound level rose, and the smell of a stable increased.

They walked through and stood on a terrace overlooking the turbines. Two large iron bolts the size of stone columns protruded from the floor, terminating in the ceiling. Long shafts of metal, tipped in rubber grips extended out in four equidistant portions, each manned by a huge figure. Several rows of lanterns lit the scene and she clearly could make out what they looked like, but had no idea what they were. Their bodies, far taller and thicker than Gorias or General Thynnes, were built like muscled men, but sported a thick layer of brown hair...no, it was hide. Their legs, while humanoid, ended in hooves like a bull, their arms ended in hands, albeit sporting three thick fingers and a wide thumb, each. She expected their bovine heads and long ears to have long or curled horns, but these beings bore no such appendages. After a few moments and movements, Alena saw where these horns should be and her mouth dropped open.

Yes, she thought, *they should have them but they've been sawed off at the root*. The Captain still gently held her elbow, but she cursed herself for giving off a chill. She couldn't help it, not at the pathetic servitude of these beasts, but at the fact they had passed their horns on the way in. Did the sailors take them past their old horns each day before lashing them to the turbines? Her stomach turned like the mechanism they churned, somewhere hooking up to make the paddles beat the ocean into submission.

"What are they?" Alena wondered, recalling tales of a Minotaur in her youth and in fables. It was then she noted they had no sets of eyes like a bull, but a single, slitted orb in the middle of their foreheads.

"The Cytaurs are beasts of burden," Jrabesak explained with a flippant tone.

Alena turned, and raised an eyebrow at him. "Really?"

"Well, they are now, my dear."

She noted one Cytaur on each turbine had a diagonal mark burned in his face across the eye socket. Alena swallowed hard, understanding fully that each of these two Cytaurs had their eyes put out, probably with a searing spearhead or iron appliance. Was this disfigurement for a revolutionary act or to remind the others that such things wouldn't be tolerated?

Alena backed away a little from the side, noting the taskmasters down below. While these men had coiled whips and long bamboo rods nearby, presumably to strike the Cytaurs if they slacked in their paces, they sat, read parchment and boredom oozed from their pores.

The Captain's mouth opened, but the Bahamut made a sudden lurch in the sea, stopping his words. Alena registered panic, at first thinking they were struck, but swiftly banished such an idea.

He said, "These rooms are heavily soundproofed. That's why we couldn't hear the mates running above us on the deck."

Still arm in arm with Jrabesak, Alena pulled free, went to the nearest portal and looked across the sea. "The pirates! We've caught up to them!" Her head twisted back to face the Captain. "We've fired on them!"

"Because that's what you do to pirates," he said frankly and swung his right arm around toward Alena's chest.

Her lightning reflexes caught his wrist and stopped the dagger shot he aimed for her heart. He squeezed his left arm around

Alena tight, pinning her right arm, and tried to intertwine his legs with hers. Not a bad fighter, she thought, certainly well trained and experienced. But Alena wasn't a gentle flower. She yanked Jrabesak's right wrist swiftly to her face and did a savage bite into his wrist. He let out a pained groan as she held his wrist in her teeth and released her hand, driving her left in a chop to his groin. His body contorted as the strike to his fruits made him sway in pain. She snatched the dagger from his hand as she drove her forehead into his face hard enough to feel something break in Jrabesak's left cheekbone.

The Captain let go and fell back against the wall. Before he could set his feet and compensate from the blow to his groin, Alena stepped back and kicked, extending her long leg in full, planting a foot in his stomach. This bent him over, so she moved in fast, grabbed him in a front-side headlock with her left arm and drove the dagger into the pit of his back with her right hand. He cried out and gagged as she threw him down.

One of the taskmasters took notice of the action and headed for the steps leading to the catwalk. Alena reached down, tried to grab Jrabesak by his scalp, but her hand slid off. She cursed his baldhead and clutched his ear and the seat of his trousers to throw him down the steps, bowling over the advancing workman, sending them both sprawling down near to where the left turbine churned. A Cytaur looked at them rolling, but took little notice, still trudging onward.

Alena saw the other taskmaster rouse from his sleepy state on his chair, confused as to what was happening. She leapt over the side and used him to cushion her landing. Alena's boots landed in his ribs and collarbones, both of which gave way. The taskmaster gurgled as he fell, arms flailing at her as she drew the pig sticker from her right boot and buried it in his Adam's apple.

Once she went over and skewered the struggling taskmaster in the belly, Alena contemplated her situation. The Admiral had no intent of capturing the pirates, simply destroying them. That was her first thought, for the portal showed one of the pirate ships heavily damaged by the lofted projectiles of the Bahamut.

She tried to figure her next move as the Bahamut shifted, heading in the direction of the surviving pirate ship. She stopped at the bottom of the steps and saw Jrabesak moving. The pig sticker did its bloody work again, this time to his side, as she drove the steel rod in through his short ribs, swirling it around, hoping to take out a lung or other vital organ. The Captain choked and went limp, all life out of him and more blood spilling from his side.

Alena still plotted things out as she opened the door and prepared to run the guard through. However, he stood with a long shield, ready to block, and did so. He rammed into her, throwing Alena back through the doorway onto the catwalk. The guard flipped his shield and chopped with his left hand, forcing her to drop the pig sticker. He swung out with his short blade and Alena caught his forearm, but his heavy shield and weight were pushing her nearly over the side.

Her hand dropped and fell on the pouch, the one Gorias knocked free from the whip mistress of the pirates. Alena's mind lit and she struggled on, not letting him throw her over or cut with his sword. She fished in the pouch and pulled one of the tiny glass pills with the dragonfire within. Sword out and blocking his blows, her hips flexed and she threw him back a bit, but he came forward again to restate his move. This time Alena's hand went across his face and she thrust the tiny glass object into his ear.

Confused, he stepped back, shaking his head.

She jumped up, let go a sharp shout and did a circle-swiping kick. Her boot connected with his ear.

The guard screamed, for the tiny vial broke and his body started to be consumed with dragonfire from his ear across his scalp, then running down his neck. He dropped his weapons as the fiery fluid crept across his body, already turning his head to a boiling mush.

She kicked him in the rump about the time the fire reached his lower back and set him over the railing. The guard fell to the turbine floor, but only his legs would ever see a burial at sea. The tiny fire burnt out at his knees, exhausted.

She again looked to the portal, feeling the Bahamut move

at a great clip to pull alongside the pirate ship. Unable to help, she watched powerlessly as a hail of arrows from the Bahamut slaughtered several on the deck of the pirate ship.

A long set of planks soon bridged the distance and dozens of sailors flooded across. A great battle took place with the survivors, but soon, the deck of the pirate ship was flooded with Transalpinan sailors. Several pirates were brought out into her view, alive. Alena saw Nykia, thrown to the deck.

Then she saw Gorias, swords drawn, bloody, surrounded, looking at the other side of the deck. She smiled for he thought of jumping. A crowbar leveled at the head of Nykia, Gorias threw down his swords and Alena's heart sank.

The Admiral strutted across the planks and stood across from the men who seized Gorias. Alena squinted but could read his lips.

"Take the oil drums back. Fuck Rhiannon. We'll wring what we need from Nykia and her mates." He then looked at his fellows, not Gorias, and said, "And keelhaul the fucking hero. I've had enough of him."

CHAPTER IX

KEELHAULED

"This is as close to a temple to all gods as Mysoline has, young man," the codger said to Orsen as he wavered with a cane in each hand.

Orsen Riva stopped counting the yard-high blocks of stones as they faded off over the countryside. He turned back to the stone circle before him, a small affair, just a dozen rectangles, porous and weathered, set in a perfectly spaced circle with a few smaller jagged blocks atop them.

"Thank you for bringing me out here, sir."

The oldster wiped sweat from his brow, although cool air blew across the fields. "It's part of my daily walk anyway. I wish it were better guarded. Anyone is free to pray here to whatever god they so choose. The way you look and dress, wouldn't you be more comfortable at the small shrine to the goddess?"

"That will be all, thank you," Orsen snipped his words.

The old one took no offense. "Fine, lad. They say the stones out on the line here are older than the rest, soldiers turned to stone by great magic in the war between angels and demons."

When the man turned to go, Orsen said, "Why did you say it needs to be guarded?"

Never turning back, the man waved a hand back. "Oh, the young ones have strange ideas at times. At the full moon last month a danged fool cut open a goat and lay in the guts, sodomizing his girly-friend. Sounds like high magic to me."

The man left Orsen alone at the site so he walked into the middle of the circle. He recalled the words, the idea of the shrine to the goddess he so loved and closed his eyes tight.

"If a man has no faith, the goddess is so much stone," Orsen said to the rocks as if to explain why he couldn't face the image of Ernytel.

Orsen tried to focus his spinning head, but the image in his mind wasn't the goddess but Gorias La Gaul. Gorias frightened him, now more than ever. Orsen thought about what he had to do to be able to strike at a man, to let his sling go or his blade, to really kill another human being. Prayers, physical training and mediation went into his regimen before any engagement or even leaving the room for the day. His courage screwed tight to his goddess, to her strength and forgiveness, Orsen could smack back, knowing the loving graces of Ernytel would both bolster up his spirit and cleanse it from the sin of killing.

Gorias? He struck without hesitation, like one who had no god or had met one and wasn't impressed. Did that make him a murderer, not a warrior? Surely, a murderer doesn't worry on the thoughts of a god or seek forgiveness. Gorias didn't strike him as an evil man at all, just a hard person with no indecision for meeting death, or fear of hellfire. Gorias wasn't a godless man, but imparted lip service to no any special one.

Orsen went to his knees, thinking of Gorias and his godless conscious, and wondered how he slept at night. His hands shook so much he couldn't clasp them together. Orsen didn't like entering a world of Gorias La Gaul, where one had no goddess to lean on or clean one's soul.

"What of the faithless man without such gall?" Orsen asked the stones. In his mind he saw what tore his faith apart: Dola, Niva's eunuch, burning in the fire along with other traitors, providing evidence to any who noted him that the Abbess was in on the dragonfire business.

Gorias saw Dola, too. That ruthless killer was no fool. He'd piece it together if he lived.

If? Orsen tittered a nervous laugh. Of course the old bastard would live through this ordeal. He'd shrugged off a ball of dragonfire and an artillery barrage. Orsen truly believed a mountain could fall on Gorias and the old man would climb out, a little worse for wear. Gorias would figure it out, too. He'd understand it all, one way or another and be out for blood once back in Qesot.

With his faith shattered, the realization that Mavik and

Vincent used him only as ears along with Niva, manipulating a plot he wasn't privy to, Orsen wept alone.

Godless.

❖❖❖❖❖

The salty air tasted better than pussy to Gorias as his face broke the ocean's surface. He never thought he'd taste either again, after being keelhauled. When the naval forces from Transalpina bound him and threw him over the side of the pirate schooner, the former Lord turned mercenary started to be concerned for his fate. He benefited from still wearing his armor, as Rosman's sailors couldn't figure out how to remove it from him. His lungs full of air, Gorias held on as they pulled him under, hands and ankles bound on the line under the ship. Survival instinct being what it was, Gorias wiggled enough as the first pull went, and they allowed him out long enough to breathe again. Rosman shouted not to kill him too soon. He wanted Gorias to suffer, or at least that's what he thought he heard. Drowning would be quick compared to being scraped back and forth, flesh of the body de-gloved and rubbed raw on the barnacled surface of the hull.

Gorias angled his forearms out, scraping a scar with the dew nails of the dragon against the ship. His form popped out the other side, again to the delight of the sailors, but in that instant Gorias saw other activity taking place. In that brief time, he watched sailors with two-wheeled carts approaching the long plank-bridge, preparing to cross onto the pirate ship.

Again plunged under the hull, Gorias set his mind to his course of action. He felt the weakness of his bond and decided to stab his dew nails in deep. This brief snag made the ropes extend. Gorias at first thought his arms or legs might dislocate, but these sailors weren't aces at tying good knots or selecting fine rigging. The ropes broke and Gorias clung to the underside of the ship by his dew nails. He stabbed his way under the wooden hull, trying to get away from an area where the fools would look down and see him. Again, he broke the water, but only with his face, the curve of the ship hiding him.

He took a breath and let his fingernails dig in the creases of the boat's undercarriage nearer to the stern. Gorias understood he'd taste blood before sampling his favorite dish again.

Gorias clung like a spider by his jagged fingernails, trying to stay under the ship so that none above would discover his freedom from the grinding ropes. He praised the stupidity of the Admiral of the war vessel, Bahamut, beside them. Apparently, the much-feared Lady Garnet Peverall, Queen of Transalpina, hadn't employed sailors with an eye for good rope. He recalled her with fondness, figuring she wouldn't have guessed one of her favorite old friends would fall victim to such green sailors, or betray someone she'd sent on a mission.

Eyes closed, he sank, hiding again, plotting his actions, recalling how he got down there. After those on the pirate ship were overwhelmed by the navy vessel and boarded, the invading officers saw Gorias among the skinny pirates. The Admiral wanted no more trouble from him, so he ordered Gorias executed. Rosman's betrayal of those loyal to Garnet didn't surprise him and he figured the seadog wanted Nykia out of the picture, too. Thoughts of the Admiral being in with Mavik and Prince Vincent washed through Gorias' mind, but he'd have to puzzle that out later.

Gorias reckoned a more seasoned sea dog wouldn't have used the worn rigging ropes on the deck for the task. The idea of keelhauling is to scrape a victim across the barnacle-encrusted hull of a ship, thus lacerating him to death and probably drowning him before the wounds killed him. Fingers aching, Gorias grinned, figuring the foolish Admiral had heard much of pirate practices and wanted to employ their own methods to kill the biggest challenge as an example. Gorias wasn't a pirate, a warrior being amongst them being transported to Albion along with oils for the priests of that land. True, Albion was always at odds with her neighbor Transalpina across the channel over religious matters and frontier territories. Like most men who spent most of their lives indoors and shaved their faces, the attitude of the erudite officer from Transalpina was starting to piss Gorias off.

Once he'd breathed, he sank below again and contemplated

his moves until his lungs screamed for air. This reminded Gorias his time grew short. He plotted a course of action and moved further down the underside of the ship before his face broke the water again, seeing that he remained under the crude bridge the navy erected. No one seemed to be looking for him anymore, even after the slack went out of the ropes. He reasoned the minds of the invaders grew excited over other booty on the pirate ship. Still, he figured his time would be short.

He couldn't hold on much longer, nor could he fit through the portals on the sides of the pirate schooner to go back aboard, even if he could figure a way to climb that high. He studied the planks overhead that the naval ship had dropped across the expanse between the ships. They did this to allow easy passage of their troops to the pirate ship. Gorias spied two ropes running under it, slacking down. He didn't recall the end of the plank having pulleys that these ropes ran over, but that must be how they did it, sort of a drawbridge effect. The ropes hung toward the waters and far under the wide planks. Gorias looked at the naval vessel and its gaping portals, some big enough to fit a huge warrior through.

Pushing away from the ship, he held his breath and tried to stay under the ship, swimming in his armor for all he was worth against the ocean current, using crud on the bottom of the hull for handholds to pull himself along. The fool topside would know the rope was broken and the archers would be scanning the waters, Gorias surmised.

Since noontime was on them, no coming darkness helped mask his emergence from the water under the planks. Though busted ropes had come up, they must've assumed Gorias dead under the ship. No one bothered to look any more for him, as other matters concerned the navy officers. Stealing from pirates was an amusing idea, Gorias thought, but not enough to make him grin or give him a hard-on.

He used the dew nails, took hold on the sides of the pirate ship and started to scale the side. It only took a few strides and he hung in place near the drawbridge. Gorias reached out and grabbed the ropes, arms so sore from the struggle already, but he never prayed for strength. When Gorias had broken free under the ship, he nearly called on his god. The vile bellow to entreat a primal god, Wodan, brought fear unto his enemies, power to his limbs and stiffness to his manhood. As he pulled himself along, just out of the water on the ropes, he thought of praying to Wodan's son, Donar, but entreating gods wasn't his style usually. Many did it in hopes they would supply aide or show up literally and end time forever. Gorias wasn't that religious. When they said to keelhaul him, he thought of converting. He'd have kissed the ass of Rhiannon or that uppity goddess of Transalpina, Ernytel, to be free. Now, going hand over hand to the naval ship under the planks, he was cursing those goddess bitches and laughing to himself about it, happy to be alive.

Was it an act of a god he broke free? Gorias blamed shoddy ropes and green troops. He really didn't have time to drop his pants and bend over in any direction for a supernatural force kind enough to douse him in blessings. He still possessed life. Even though life was pain, he hungered to create more.

He could hear the dandy officers above him on the naval ship, the ones too clean to make the crossing, talking of wines and covering perfumed whores later on that night. Gorias nearly lost his grip as the planks swayed, not from the ocean's rhythm, but from large barrels being rolled across them. Grimacing, Gorias assumed they were taking the loot the pirates swapped with the traitors in Transalpina. They were to sell their treasure of oils at the behest of the priests, who took a profit.

Gorias reached the naval vessel. Turning around on the ropes and kicking his legs, Gorias found his boots on the sides of a portal. However, he hadn't seen the metallic stripping and seals that would make it impossible to open from this side. First, he kicked a boot into it. The glass refused to break. The droning of the barrels rolling on the planks overhead was deafening, so he raised both boots and slammed his feet into the glass. It broke into larger pieces and fell back into the room. His boots slid out and he was about to get in closer, but a face appeared in the portal. A young sailor, probably seventeen if he was a day, maybe even on his first voyage, blinked and looked out at Gorias. The savage sneer hanging outside made the youth back up a single step. He froze in place, dumbfounded at what he saw.

Gorias moved close and threw his legs out again. This time, his boots went through the portal sides and grabbed the sailor in a headlock. The youth's surprised look didn't last long. Shock turned to terror and then to panic as Gorias pulled back, ripping the young sailor through the edges of the opening. The jagged glass served his purpose and with great effort, he tore the sailor's throat open. Gagging, trying to scream, Gorias saw the youth's eyes roll back in his head, so he kicked him away from the portal. His first voyage becoming his last, the boy dropped to his knees as Gorias kicked the jagged, bloody glass clear and started to make his own way through the portal. The boy convulsed as he died. Old enough to serve, Gorias thought, young enough to die.

Gorias' thick shoulders could barely fit in the gap afforded him, but his took the scrapes of fortune and made it. Once inside, he checked the room he violated. He'd killed this young sailor in a storage room. Several crates and wooden boxes were stacked around. One could barely fit through the single door of the room. He dragged the dead sailor to one side and unhooked his belt. With some work, he freed the sailor's refined cutlass from its sheath. Since his own swords lay back on the pirate vessel, he'd have to make do. Wondering why the boy was in the room at all, Gorias soon saw a flask wedged between two boxes, hidden from normal view. Grabbing the flask, Gorias opened it, sniffed the neck and said, "Whiskey." He took a swig and nodded appreciatively. "Ya weren't all bad, kid," Gorias said to the dead body and moved on.

Still in the heart of the naval ship, what could he do? His mind raced as he heard footfalls not far away, and even heard the grinding of the rolling barrels again. Suddenly, he thought of these naval men, stealing the barrels of sacred oils meant for the temples in Albion. These oils were for the priests of the King and set for their ceremonies. A cold feeling crept down Gorias' spine as a plan formed. There would be little or no time to execute the idea, so his boldness would have to suffice. He nearly dined with Donar in the great hall of the dead this evening, but hoped the salty pirates and their toothless hookers would suffice.

He opened the door a hair and peered out. Gorias saw another young sailor walking his way. Wondering if the Transalpinan Navy conscripted a boys school, he threw the door open and froze the sailor in his tracks. Gorias reached out, hand over the lad's mouth and the other on the sailor's dagger. Removing the dagger from the sailors' belt, he brought it to the lad's neck and yanked him into the storage room. Gorias had a foot of height and a hundred pounds on the sailor, who looked back at him in terror.

"Tell me, young fellow," Gorias hissed, eyes drilling holes through his quarry. "How many sailors are here? Are they quartered below?"

"Nearly a hundred," he rasped when Gorias barely parted his fingers to let him speak. "We sleep in shifts."

"On either side of the main hold below, that's where they are quartered?"

The boy nodded.

"Is there another way up to the deck aside from the main opening?"

The young sailor shrugged and Gorias nodded, before breaking his neck.

Dropping the body, he moved on.

Gorias didn't need to overhear any conversations with these sailors to figure on their motives. They handled the barrels of sacred oil with entirely too much care to be lackeys for a foreign land. The well-trained men used strange devices he'd never seen, wooden disks with tiny wheels under them, to smoothly transport the barrels over the vast gut of the war vessel. They used many men to lift them into a secure place. They weren't slamming anything down, for they wanted their cargo to be in place and not be harmed. Gorias knew fear when he saw it...fear of their superiors? He doubted it as they'd probably been scourged before. No, such precise behavior reeked of fear of something more, a fear of a god or in this case, goddess.

Cursing all gods, Gorias lamented men were dying over this nonsense.

Licking his mustache, Gorias' hatred of the sea became alive again. A primal man of the earth, he never knew how much he loved the feel of the dirt under his boots until the first bout of sea sickness seized him decades ago. Gorias loathed travel on the ocean, but like any hated foe, he respected it. He surmised crazed acts would only send him into the bosom of the sea, and while ready to die, he wanted to do it on the ground.

Still hidden away, he contemplated his plan. Looking down in the main hold, he backed away and realized he dwelt in a narrow hallway, lined with hammocks. Though dim lanterns lit this end and the other, Gorias could tell dozens of sailors slumbered here. All that fighting above and these men are asleep? He marveled at this, but understood the pirate ship was easy pickings for an armored vessel.

Suddenly, to his right, a shrill shout filled the narrow hallway. Thinking it a serving girl at first, Gorias was not stunned to see it was a large, exotic parrot, colored green and red, tethered next to a near copy of itself.

"Goddamned prick," Gorias grunted, as he moved toward the birds.

Squawking in alarm, it raised its wings. Left arm swinging, Gorias caught this one by the throat and squeezed, crushing its neck in a few moments. Preparing to strangle the other, it squawked, "Damned prick…"

Gorias held up and didn't kill the bird. "You're all gonna die," he said.

Letting out a quiet shrill, the bird mocked him, saying, "You're all gonna die."

A wicked smile spreading on his hairy face, Gorias left the hallway and walked down a connecting path to a like series of bunks on the other side of the vessel. Again, many sailors slept.

Gorias watched as two sailors set a barrel in place and departed again. Figuring his brawn twice that of these little men, he hopped down the steps and bear hugged the nearest barrel of oil. Taking care how he lifted, he slowly rose up, but didn't stand up in full. Not a careless person with his body, knowing he was not as young as he used to be, Gorias set the lip of the barrel on the step and moved around it, taking it up the steps one at a time. He sat this barrel at the end of the narrow row of bunks. He repeated this action on the other side of the ship. In the distance, he could hear the rustle of boots and figured it wouldn't be long before his time ran out.

✿ ✿ ✿ ✿ ✿

Alena saw them tie up Gorias and at first figured them to drop him in the sea tied to the anchor. When the sailors brought over a line from the undercarriage of the ship, she understood that the keelhauling would be next. Such a word, read in books, suddenly became reality to Alena.

For a moment terror crept into her being, understanding any chance for escape or her own existence just fled if they killed Gorias. She considered her options fast, of what Rosman would do upon seeing the Captain dead and his taskmasters done in by the girl they were supposed to kill. She heard them cheer across the way and couldn't look as Gorias fell into the water. She sank to her knees and breathed several times, trying to focus.

"I'm not important to what's going on," she said to no one and looked down at the Cytaurs again. Eyes closed, she focused on her training, the voice of her father, her sisters, their oaths to the Queen, and screwed down a strong courage. Several minutes passed before she said, "Today is the day then." Understanding there was no escape, Alena decided to take as many with her as possible.

In the hallway, she tried to use her sword on the lock of the stalls, but it came to no avail. Holstering her blade, Alena tried the pig sticker to wedge in through the locks. No dice. She then eyed the hanging horns of the Cytaurs, meant as trophies to mock the poor beasts. Alena seized one and aimed the heavy tip at the lock. The angle and force ripped the lock loose from the wooden frame and she slid the stall open.

Within the stalls reclined eight more Cytaurs, two of which were blinded in a similar fashion. They all took note of her, their muzzles expanding at her scent, eyes curious.

She could hear the chatter of footfalls down the steps nearby and she said, "C'mon, let's go! Get out of here!" Feeling stupid, as she doubted any could understand her.

However, two of them got up, their wrists chained together but able to be held a few feet apart, they stretched and looked at each other and then her.

Alena jumped to one side, near to the turbines, and let them charge out. Even the blind ones followed their brothers, all eight ran. Not a damned one returned for their bound up brothers down in the turbine room. "Guess I am the idiot," she muttered as the Cytaurs charged into the sailors and she descended to the turbines. "Giving them so much humanity and emotions."

Using the horn, she freed the Cytaurs down at the turbines, one at a time. Each ran as soon as they were freed. The blind ones she freed sat down on the floor, exhausted, trying to weep but having no tears…or perhaps that's what she made herself believe. She broke the horn on the bonds of the last one, and he only took a few steps, looked back at her and then charged up the steps. Alena followed him at a long clip, hearing the screams of the sailors the other Cytaurs ran into. The last one she freed stopped at the hallway, took up two horns and started down the hall to the main hold.

✦✦✦✦✦

The two sailors returned down the way of the ship with another load. Gorias had pried loose one of the barrel's lids as they peered down the way, seeming to note something was amiss. Behind them strange hails and snorting sounds echoed throughout the halls.

"C'mon," Gorias muttered to the sailors who looked around, unaware. "Both of ya at once."

As one sailor wandered down, noting the rows of barrels quizzically, Gorias got his wish. The other man followed his fellow seaman, questioning his confusion.

"Didn't we start about level with the steps?" the sailor asked, scratching his head. He looked up the steps that led to the bunks, but he chose the wrong stairway. Gorias was behind him and leapt down, barrel lid in both hands like a posthole digger. He drove the lid into the top of the sailor's head. Through Gorias thought he used enough force to split the skull down to the neck bone, only a huge dent appeared as something popped inside the ruined head. That was all right with Gorias, the sailor was just as dead from the cleft to his cranium.

The other sailor gaped at him silently, watching his fellow sailor's brains spill down either side of his ears. Gorias swiped with the lid, clipping the shocked sailor's jaw, turning him around completely. The sailor held his jaw, bent down a little as blood and teeth dribbled from his open lips. Gorias followed up the move by driving the flat of the lid down to crush the confused sailor's head. His scream was lost in his bloody mouth and Gorias never knew if he broke the man's jaw or not. He thought he heard him call for his goddess as the curve of his head became flat, but that didn't matter to Gorias either. He dropped the lid, grabbed the sailor by the throat with his left and reached for the misericorde all sailors held on their belts. In a moment, the lightweight, elegant blade was out.

Noise of fighting far down the ship filtering to him, Gorias still wrestled him about, the man grabbing at Gorias forearm as his fingers dug into his throat. Gorias tried to bury the knife in the man's chest, but it broke.

"Damned goddess. The bitch must've heard ya," Gorias cursed and knelt, still holding him by the neck, and scratched a piece of the broken blade on the floor. Letting him go, he made a surgical insertion by the sailor's Adam's apple and then ripped to the right. Gorias knew the veins to cut to make a man die, even if he wasn't sure of the proper names for them. He didn't have time to salute the sailor for battling on with a crushed head, but he respected his pluck.

He also figured by the cries and shouts the game was up, but somebody else caused that commotion. Sure, these ones would be missed, but in such a timely way? Hurriedly, he pried off the other barrel's lid and then the nearest two on the main floor. Gorias then ran to the first line of hammocks and dumped the barrel over, setting the watery oil to rush down the hallway. A few men in the hammocks started to stir as the noises down the way got louder and went animalistic.

Gorias sprinted to the other hallway and repeated this action on the barrels. He looked at the parrot there as the oil gushed again and released its leg from the stand. It flew on and Gorias laughed, grabbing the lantern beside it. He then threw a shoulder into one barrel in the main hold and then another, setting them to washing down the way.

He was halfway through the hold, almost to the netted lattice where he could make his escape, when he heard the confused voices of sailors.

It was in the wider area he saw the bloodbath caused by monstrous creatures sporting one eye and a group of armed sailors. Bodies of human and creature alike lay splayed about, but Gorias counted six of the one-eyed monsters running up the steps.

Back behind them, he spotted Alena.

Her mouth dropped open.

He held up the lantern and shouted, "Get outta here!"

Sword out, she climbed over bodies, following the last of the creatures, who seemed unconcerned with the bloodbath around him. Alena passed by Gorias and he slapped her ass with the cutlass.

"To Hell with this," Gorias said, jumped on the tops of the barrels, and tossed the lantern back. He lofted the small flame and a few weary sailors, just awakened by a communal confusion, watched the path of the lamp powerlessly as it arched and smashed at their feet in the layer of gushed oil.

Sacred oil burned for a long time. It wasn't terribly flammable, but it was meant to last as adoration of weeks. The tiny spark, though, lit larger and the fluid caught, starting a gradual wave of flame that traveled down the two bunk lines and started on the hold.

Gorias leapt for the netting, seeing the flames washing around the other barrels. Unsure if the workmanship of the barrel makers would be sound, he reckoned his terror was achieved.

Hand over hand, Gorias climbed like a man on fire, for soon, he'd get to experience that sensation firsthand. His helmet back on the pirate vessel, his body may survive the flames but his head would be a cinder. Above his face climbed Alena, and he found himself near enough to bite her ass soon. He couldn't help but smile, wondering if the seawater washed the smell of Nykia off him.

"Hey little girl," Gorias laughed. "Where did you get such handsome friends?"

She playfully kicked back at his head and said, "They are called Cytaurs and they turned the turbines."

The loud cacophony of screams became hushed by a rush of air feeding flames. Gorias leapt out onto the deck and rolled. His appearance, along with the Cytaurs and Alena, drew the attention of dozens of sailors on deck who drew their swords. They never had a chance to step toward him as a ball of flame belched from the hold and rose on the ship up like a mushroom over them into the sails and rigging.

Gorias was up and slashing his way through the amazed faces of the sailors. They were easy prey as they were so afraid. The cutlass blade was graceful, so he made graceful kills, delicately inserting in throats and filching back. Most sailors took no more note of him for they stared at the flames that reached up to the billowing sails.

The Cytaurs reacted badly. A couple ran into sailors, taking them over the edge. One ran for the planks that separated the vessels, but was cut down. A blind Cytaur stumbled around and inadvertently brained a sailor with his swinging hands before they ganged up on him, slicing his hamstrings and throwing him overboard. However, the one who wielded two severed horns stabbed both of these sailors in the backs, gouging holes big enough for a child to stick their arm through. Each sailor fell to their knees on the deck making some of the worst gagging noises Gorias had ever heard.

Alena kicked and fought, stabbing men through and kicking with accuracy with her legs. She twirled her entire body, blade beheading a sailor, sending his noggin rolling to the plank bridge by the feet of the men bringing the last load of oils. These men had stopped to gape at the huge fire belching from the hold of the Bahamut.

Shoving a sailor overboard, Gorias jogged over to the place where the planks joined the vessels. The final barrels had made their way across, but those who rolled them stopped, unwilling to travel farther. Gorias stabbed with the cutlass, but it broke off in the chest of the first sailor. A step back, Gorias took a knee, grabbed the errant head of the sailor by his scalp and rose up. The gaping sailor with the two-wheeler just froze in place as Gorias swung the severed head, smashing him into unconsciousness. Kicking the head aside, Gorias grabbed for the falling sailor's cutlass and attacked the next man on the planks, again going for the throat. He stabbed with the fine blade, swiping out, ripping loose his throat, letting out a vomit of veins and fading bubbling screams.

Giving the barrel a kick, sending it toward the flaming hold of the vessel, Gorias looked back over the planks. Two of the Cytaurs ran crazy down the crude bridge with the one holding two horns behind them. As Gorias started to follow across the planks, the sailor guarding the last barrel saw them, screamed and decided he preferred the embrace of the ocean over the monsters, diving in.

Just as this sailor jumped and Alena got on the planks, a man on the navy vessel retreated from the flaming hold and knocked the securements for the pulleys on the planks loose. The long planks started to draw back up toward the navy ship as Gorias ran up the steepening grade. The Cytaurs all made it across and the shouts of the naval men aboard the pirate ship echoed. Gorias reached the top of the planks, as they were half up in the air. He leapt and caught himself in the rigging of the side sails of the schooner. Beside him, clinging like a spider, Alena arrived with a grunt akin to when she came.

The pirates cheered as the Navy officers on the ship gaped, dumbfounded at the sight.

Gorias swung out over the pirate crew surrounded by sailors and angled himself back. He dropped off the ropes onto the gaggle of sailors already confused by the crazed Cytaurs. Many scattered, but into the embrace of the pirate crew, who picked this chance to fight back at last. They'd been disarmed of swords and obvious side arms, but most of the crew still hid a dagger. They were pirates, after all. Several of the officers fell dead, stabbed in the kidneys first and then disemboweled on the deck of the pirate vessel.

On his knees, then rising like a cobra, Gorias said, "Save me two."

One of the pirates exclaimed, "We have a petty officer and the Admiral of the Transalpina navy!"

A great whoop went up as Gorias looked back at the naval vessel, flames starting to consume it.

"My men," the taller of the two officers yelped, straining against the hold of two pirates. His white breeches stained with the blood of others, Rosman's face turned pale and he shouted at Gorias, "You bastard!"

Nykia emerged from the bloodbath, stepping over the bodies of the two dead Cytaurs. She held out his twin blades. Gorias threw down the cutlass and took up his twin swords. "What's your point? Hell, I hear I got royal blood in me."

The Admiral spat at him. "Those cunts of General Appra have royal blood in them. His mama came from a royal bastard, so what makes you so special?"

Gorias took the embrace from Nykia and ignored the words of the Admiral. "Hey, glad to see ya."

Rosman persisted, saying, "You savage dog, can you know what you've done?"

Gorias grabbed him by the throat, his huge hand nearly encompassing the neck of the Admiral. Nose to nose, Gorias said gravely, "Yeah, I'm pretty sure. I killed all of your crew, burned them like the assheads they are. I hope they woke up in the flames, died, and woke up in the flames of hell again."

"The sacred oils..." the Admiral gasped.

Still holding the man's throat, Gorias said, "Looks like we are both screwed, aye? I'd rather take my chances pissing the King of Albion off than to let a dickhead like you sail away with a drop of that oil. And we're gonna have a long talk now about just why ya wanted it, aren't we?"

Gorias released him and stepped away, looking at the pirates and nodding. They were overjoyed to see him, but they didn't let the petty officer of the navy ship go.

As the pirate Allard handed Gorias a skin of wine, the petty officer straightened up and said, "We are naval officers entitled to fair and equitable treatment under the edicts of the mariner's code."

Wiping his bearded face with the back of his hand, Gorias raised an eyebrow. "Yeah?" He dropped the skin of wine, and squared his shoulders. Gorias took out his member and started to urinate on the petty officer's bleached trousers, then said, "I think all of our copies of that book are lost as sea."

The pirates roared with laughter as Gorias shook off. One of them chirped, "I can't read anyway, sir. Shall I be scourged for my stupidity?"

Gorias wore a dark smile. "Nay, but these two, well…" Gorias looked up on the yard arm, and saw that the sailors had strung up Savage Chad of the pirate schooner. "Cut him down." He faced the officers and then faced their vessel, burning in the night, mayhem ensuing as the masts across the way collapsed and men burned. "You came to steal what we stole. You shed first blood, but never let it be said I am really unfair."

One of the pirates grinned. "Yer a prick, Gorias!"

Not disagreeing, Gorias said, "But a fair prick. Since these two perfumed crap-bags are here…"

The Admiral cleared his throat and said, "I'm a sailor. I desire to die like a sailor."

"I have no time to take you to a whorehouse and let you suffer for years of syphilis."

The pirates roared with laughter, shouting out various methods for him to die and Alena drew her hand across her throat, smiling.

Nykia held up the petty officer by his right elbow and asked, "What about piss-pants here?"

"Don't rush me," Gorias mumbled and gave the Cytaur nearest him a brief look. The creature surged with anger or at least he took it as such. .

Gorias, however, yawned and sat down on the deck and took up the skin of wine. As he watched the neighboring vessel burn, Nykia crawled up beside him. She looked at the flaming ship.

"Want a drink?" Gorias asked.

Nykia eyed him, took the skin of wine and drank.

"Are you taking me to the Queen?" Nykia asked Gorias, offering him the wine skin.

Gorias didn't wipe the blood from the end before he drank. He swallowed and answered her, "Only because we are bound there as well."

"Yeah?"

"I'm not sure what to do now."

"You killed all of those men?" she asked, taking the skin of wine back to drink.

Gorias nodded. "Yeah, Alena helped and the Cytaur things. That big one fought like a sonofabitch. Gimme a thousand of those fuckers and I could lay low any kingdom, by God."

"How many?"

"How many what?"

"How many did you kill?"

Gorias took the wine and upended it. "I don't keep count."

CHAPTER X

GOING TO PIECES

Orsen Riva lay face down on the middle of the stone circle when he heard a voice say, "Get up."

A female tone, his mind buzzed, surely not the goddess come down to speak with him? A strumpet from the port city out here at a religious site? He found amusement at this idea, simply that he'd spent too much time around La Gaul to think of that. Then again, she wouldn't be alone, probably in the company of a thug wanting to get his rocks off. A man like that would strike down a small man blubbering over his religious state. Could it be his goddess?

No, his logical mind said, that rang impossible because he started to accept that his true goddess was just another rock dressed up and polished by Niva. This person also couldn't be Ernytel because it sounded a great deal like Alena.

Up to his all fours, Orsen glanced to where the voice originated, did a double take and got over his shock of thinking it really was Alena, back so soon from the sea. The woman near him stood just as tall, built exactly alike and dressed the same as Alena, but sporting fairer locks, tied back.

"Who are you?"

"Get up, Orsen Riva," the gruff tone returned, and the woman's right boot rustled in the grass, ready to kick him in the rump if he didn't stop pointing it in her direction. Orsen moved to not provide such a target. Again, he came near to tragic laughter, thinking she would assault him for no reason. He had no conflict with the Queen's guards.

Unless…

"What do you want with me?" Orsen sat back on his backside, giving the woman only a slight glance. He'd surmised she truly was one of the Queen's guards, Alena's sister, easily, by her clothes and appearance. Just what one of them would be doing in

Mysoline he couldn't grasp; aside from maybe, a few trailed them, spying on him and ready to strike him down for his secret dealings with Mavik. This idea bubbled in his brain and Orsen understood death came to find him now in this place of empty stones, devoid of gods and him without a goddess.

"I'm Milli. I'm here to remind you that the Queen blessed you with a mission."

Her words provided a bit of light to his situation and he fought the urge to smile at her. Milli didn't restore him to good feelings by a long shot, nor could she have restored his fallen faith in an instant, but she made him more at ease since she obviously didn't come there to kill him. He pondered light, flames or simple annihilation that awaited him beyond his demise. Orsen hoped for the latter.

"I provided you with Gorias La Gaul. The circumstances of his current state are beyond my control."

"The Queen required you near him, to be her eyes in all of these associations."

He wondered what she understood about their situation and decided against telling any grand lies. "Gorias was abducted, taken away by the pirates. Your sister is on a naval vessel with a traitorous Admiral, I hear tell, going after them, probably to slay them all in due course."

Cold and relentless, Milli pressed on. "Why didn't you accompany Alena on the ship? Did you know of this Admiral's treachery?"

"No, but I stayed back with the army. It was pointless to go on."

"Why?"

Orsen threw up his hands and let them drop on either side of him. "It's a matter of faith now for me. I've lost mine and thus, a reason to carry on with this great enterprise for anyone."

"Your religion and faith aren't my concern, nor should you be so fragile as to fold because you are feeling queasy over the afterlife. You have sworn an oath to the Queen and will follow on with it until the end of your life. That was in the pledge, or weren't you paying attention?"

"I need to pray and can't find the words."

"A man can only say so many prayers." Milli's voice returned icier still, her disgust rising to the point she walked in a circle and returned to where she started. No mercy dwelt in her eyes or mannerisms, all cold and rigid.

"It takes a strong man to make them, to pray in earnest through a broken heart, one stronger than me…"

A growl in her throat, Milli reached out, grabbed handfuls of his shirt and brought him to his feet. "Stop that this instant! I don't want to hear of matters of any heart, least of all yours. Listen good, little one, and remember your oaths. You will be going on another trip soon."

"Am I?" Orsen couldn't shake the big girl's grip so he stopped trying. "Tell me all about it."

Still holding him fast, fury barely contained, she said, "I'm going to give you another chance at your faith."

"Yes? This should be splendid."

Milli's nose came near to smashing into his as she yanked him in close to her face. At that angle, Orsen noted her nose crooked a little, as if broken and re-healed badly. "Yes, if you are unlucky, you may get to see if there is a god. Come with me now or you'll find out in three seconds."

❖❖❖❖❖

Rosman seethed, his look fixed to Gorias as the old warrior took a small walk around the perimeter of the deck, swords in hand like he had decided to cut the air itself. "What of me, hero?" Rosman called out, his face churning from boredom to curious wonder. "Will you keelhaul me? That's the warrior code, true?"

Gorias didn't regard him when he said, "Don't rush me." Under his breath, he let go, "What the fuck would you know about a warrior's code?"

"Will you make me walk the plank?" Two of the pirates wrestled him back to the mast as he taunted Gorias, shoving his back into the wooden pole. "What sort of vile buggery do you have in mind for me?"

Sheathing his swords, Gorias replied, "Nothing so droll, ya mouthy ass. Even under wraps ya keep talkin' crap. What gall ya got."

Eyes widening, Rosman offered with a grin, "You will face me in single combat? Yes, you'd enjoy that, swaggering man of the battlefield, a chance to slay a man of the Navy, not skilled with blades like yourself. That would make you appear like such a big man, no?"

"No, ya can shitcan all that talk. Please don't confuse me as a man of honor. I don't confuse you with one."

The sails unfurled and the pirate vessel started gradually to move away from the smoking Bahamut. A few pirates took time to curse the dying ship as it rode the waves, flames running across it out from its center. On occasion, a flaming human form would make it to the deck and collapse. Gorias absently wondered where those sailors hid, but decided he didn't care so much.

"That thing might float for some time," said Gorias to no one particular, his right boot striking the edge of the ship. "The hull isn't ruptured." He exhaled and turned, frowning at the eyes all on him. "What a damned waste of material and men, huh? Cryin' shame for those with tears."

Hands bound and his waist hastily strapped to the mast, the Admiral watched his vessel smoke and turned to the other man left from his crew. After this single look, the man stood taller. Rosman then turned the opposite way, his eyes aiming north and to the open sea.

Gorias left the pirates to their rigging and stretched his legs with a walk further down the deck. The pirates melted away from the sector of the deck the tall man trod. Gorias came near to walking into Alena. She crossed the rear deck and threw herself at him, half hugging him, but drawing back fast, slapping his arms hard, her head shaking from side to side fast.

"What? Ya thrilled they didn't kill me?"

"I could never make myself believe that you'd die easily."

Gorias stared deep into her gleaming eyes and turned to face the sea instead. "It took guts to get on the Bahamut along with all of those guys."

Alena joined him watching the burning ship. "They are men from my navy, from my homeland. That didn't take courage. Usually, such men are honorable, all sea dog jokes aside."

"Kinda looks bad now."

"True, but I'm sure many of the sailors were just following orders."

"Yeah, but that's a shitty excuse for bad behavior. I ain't gonna argue about my actions. People die. It's a part of life. The last part."

Again, she turned to him, beaming. "I'm glad to see you."

Nykia stomped past, shouting orders to the other pirates and stopped to hug Gorias' left arm, then moved on down the deck.

Alena's smile faded and she focused on the flaming Bahamut.

"Many men died because of these assheads in charge, doing bad things, so I'm short of sympathy for men doing their duty for bad folks right now."

They took a few steps and stopped at the sight of the brooding Cytaur.

The Cytaur let the long horns in his grasp rest on the deck. He took many breaths and didn't face anyone on the ship.

Nykia stepped up to the creature and showed no fear. "The Navy used you, not us, understand, Cytaur?"

Gorias thought the Cytaur bore a malevolent eye, but he felt no threat in the lone creature. He did note the pirates pointing at the Cytaur and whispering, saying words like, "unnatural" and "monster" many times.

One young pirate with a dirty-blonde ponytail mumbled, "I've never seen such a thing."

An older pirate, balding and red-faced from the sun stepped up and spoke loud enough for even the Cytaur to hear. "I have. They lived in lands beyond the hills of the Varangians, far to the east of here even beyond the territories once occupied by the Kolbias, Karelians, and the remains of the Tavastians."

Nykia wondered, "Once occupied, Allard?"

Allard nodded. "The current King of Albion slaughtered those tribes. Anyway, down the river Lyrcenda dwell a people called the Kalevalans who once were assailed by Taurons." He looked to Gorias. "You know what they are, right?"

Gorias cleared his throat. "Taurons. They are bigger than the Cytaurs, more human in appearance about the face, but similar in body style and an assload more aggressive."

At his words the Cytaur turned, his single eye focused on Gorias.

Gorias went on, saying, "The Taurons were killed off, for the most part, when they turned on the peoples out there. The Cytaurs were naturally docile." He then turned his head, staring at the streaks of blood on the horns the Cytaur held. "Most of them, anyways."

The Cytaur stepped away from them, obviously wanting space.

Gorias leaned over and Alena drew close to hear him whisper. "His manhood still swings long, even if he's castrated."

"By the way that he fought," Alena confided. "I'd guess they didn't quite cut off all of his balls."

When the pirates laughed at Alena's words, the flat of Gorias' right hand slapped over his heart. "Balls are in here, too, ya filthy seadog bastards. Alena here has a hairy set in her chest."

Her frown so deep the jovial nature of it drew guffaws from the pirates, Alena said smartly, "Keep talking like that, you'll get me excited."

"Tell me I don't know how to make a woman feel special." He then walked over to where the pirates had covered Savage Chad's body in a dirty sheet. Nykia knelt beside him, wiping the back of her hand across her eyes. "So Albion, is it?"

Nykia nodded, not answering.

"Rhiannon's priests might feel shortchanged, part of their load at the bottom of the sea and all."

Alena stepped up. "Will they give us trouble?"

"Dunno. Religious folks are screwy. They can be forgiving

and then go to war damned fast. Who can say?"

Nykia let out a mild sob and said, "Savage Chad was a good guy, not a proper fellow, but not evil. He was…"

Gorias offered, "Just?"

"He did good by us, fair. He deserved a better death than hanging by his own yardarm."

"We all figure we have a better death coming than what arrives, I suppose. Live seven hundred more years and see how many ways to die ya can imagine."

"I'll try."

"Folks in these parts don't live as long as the ones raised in Shynar or spending time elsewhere. I dunno why, maybe it's all inbreeding. A hundred years ago Garnet was a damsel. She's gettin' on in years now, but not feeble yet. I know gals back in Shynar that are 500 years old who still bear kids, and look half Garnet's age. The world is screwy."

The pirates traded looks, unsure of his words.

Gorias strode over to Rosman. "So what's your story, Admiral? Were you a career military man, tired of a set ol' life and deciding to upset the apple cart of the homeland? Don't wear that snotty high-handed look. I'd say your time for dignity has passed."

His eyes scanning the warrior, Rosman replied, "Lecture me not of dignity or any matters of a higher sort. The Queen will not appreciate your slaying her sailors or sinking her ship, no matter what your standing in her heart."

"Who is gonna tell her? They're all dead and who will believe the word of a pirate or a traitor?"

The sailor near the Admiral swallowed hard, fully accepting his fate.

Rosman still maintained his stern manner. "You're a fool, no matter if you won this battle with boldness or not."

Gorias stepped a bit closer, nostrils flaring wide. He shot the Cytaur a dour look and then faced Rosman again. "You think I don't know things, but you really delude yourself…Admiral." Gorias said the title as if he addressed anyone but an Admiral worthy of respect.

This exchange made Alena frown.

"Why do this? Why destroy half of the pirates, send the oils to the bottom of the sea? The Transalpinan navy isn't known for acts of savagery." Gorias pointed with his right index finger at the corpse of Savage Chad. "Why try to kill the Queen's friends, bodyguard and heir?"

Rosman turned his head, his slicked-back hair resting on the mast.

Gorias frowned. "Still no words? They'll wring them outta ya back in Qesot." After a few moments, Gorias focused in on where he noticed Rosman looking. "Searching for something, ol' son?" The horizon to the north on the sea lay blank and listless.

Alena stepped up, anger in her voice as she said, "He's not in charge of anything. He's a pawn of Mavik and Vincent."

His resentment at being spoken to harshly boiling, Rosman's eyes bored into Alena's face. "A pawn? How silly, you ugly bitch. You think me a minor player in a game, not a tentacle of the board itself."

A pig sticker slid from Alena's boot and she let the serrated tip rest in the cleft on Rosman's chin. "I'm sure a little more scarring on him won't matter to the boys back home. They won't mind a few extra bruises or cuts."

His grin wide, Rosman said amiably, "Then by all means, go ahead, act like the man you wish you were."

"Alena," Gorias gently pulled her hand away and stepped up closer to him.

Rosman snapped back at Alena, "My father died on the Somme, serving his land."

Alena interjected, "And serving my father, General Appra?"

Gorias muttered, "Lotta guys left babies behind, dyin' on the Somme."

Rosman turned to Gorias. "But you survived, didn't you? Always the hero, always the survivor."

Gorias sighed. "You grew up all right by the look of ya."

"We were part of the aristocracy and my education, while granted by wealth, expanded my mind. I was an apt pupil but didn't want to be a soldier in an army that never killed anyone. In the navy, well, I could be King."

Nykia stepped near to Alena and whispered, "I can't add it all up yet either."

With a slight nod, Alena kept her central point on the exchange.

Gorias asked Rosman, "I don't suppose yer gonna be a nice fella and just tell me what this is all about, huh?"

"You'll kill me no matter what."

"True, but we can do this the easy way or the hard way."

Chin jutting, the Admiral scoffed. "I won't break under torture."

Nykia walked over. "They all say that at first, but they always talk, elsewise, who'd use torture?"

Gorias shrugged. "You misunderstand me, Princess. I'll get no jollies over seeing this prick suffer. Dead is dead and he can do no more harm."

Rosman eyed Nykia. "You, a princess? Please. They better drop the ban on magic and call in an alchemist. They'll need one of those to get a pearl necklace out of a boar's nutsack."

Right on cue, Nykia leapt at him, punching Rosman across the jaw, but only earning his laughter and Gorias' disdain as he shoved her back.

"A princess? The future Queen?" Rosman continued laughing as he spoke, near to the point of being unable to talk. "My word! Such a prize for stiff Garnet you will be! All covered in ink and the vaginal secretions of your mistress. Oh yes, I know about your bitchly nature, little sow. Queen? You're not even a proper cumal wench."

"Shut up," Nykia raged and Gorias pushed her back into Alena's restraining grip to her elbows.

"You? On the throne of Transalpina? Producing what? A brood of piglets? I'll gladly die to not have to see that."

"Let me go," Nykia struggled with Alena's hold. Garnet's guard did let her free, but Gorias stopped her from attacking Rosman, his left arm up between them. "You're Vincent's bitch. He's hardly a man."

Rosman replied, "But his wanker only has to work once to produce offspring better than anything to crawl out of that awful thing between your legs. Who knows what the future holds?" Again, he looked away from them to the open sea, but quickly back to Gorias.

Nykia still spoke, though. "They'd never have accepted you as King no matter who you killed or married."

Gorias conceded. "Yeah, true, there'd be a fight at the sword rack among the Appra sisters to see who gets to die assassinating you first."

Humor draining from his face, Rosman hissed at Gorias, "To be so strong and yet so stupid."

Gorias squinted at the Admiral. "Something is amiss here."

Rosman grinned. "You can sense it, can't you, old sinner?"

"Somethin' about ya makes my skin crawl and it ain't the usual thing I get near members of the aristocracy."

"Top show to you then, old sinner, for that, your long life and senses."

"Someone in Transalpina trades the pirates sacred oils, a slew of it, for tiny vials and then a huge portion of dragonfire. I know that this fire is kept animated only at Pergamus."

Grinning still, Rosman scoffed. "What an old wives tale. Pergamus indeed."

"The ol' gals got it right and ya know it. Not many around would know or believe such a thing. That's how deception comes so easy to this generation."

"If you say so." Rosman feigned an innocent look.

"What I wanna know is who is doing that, and what do they want the damned dragonfire for?"

The Admiral looked off, serenely watching his vessel die.

Alena stepped up and suggested, "Who in Transalpina can have that much oil on hand? How can they get rid of it and not be noticed?"

Nykia offered, "There are many dissidents in the land, dividing favor for Queen Garnet and her sister. These are those that traded with us. It wasn't personal to Gramma, just for the money.

The fools in Albion pour it down a hole to feed a god that isn't really there. It's so pointless."

Gorias rubbed his left eye. "But the dragonfire deaths in Transalpina aren't even close to the Queen. Somebody is rubbing out castellans and those kissing ass at court. A good blade does that just as well. Why all the high drama with the fire? Seems like alotta trouble to go through for what other means can accomplish."

"That depends," Rosman said steadily. "On what one chooses to achieve with the fire, in the end." He turned to look at them each for a moment. "Humans are such feeble fools, present company excepted. They have ostentatious ideas, but are effortlessly swindled by those superior in breeding and aptitude."

Gorias rolled his eyes. "He talks a lot for an innocent guy, huh?"

"If given a boon of power, they will indeed use it toward their dream, but along the way, the human emotion of revenge is too great to pass on. Plus, the dragonfire deaths keeps one on their toes, no? Keeps them praying to the goddess?" He spat out a single fake laugh. "Such scum you are. It is not a wonder a third of the stars of heaven fell at your creation."

Gorias stepped back, looked at Alena. "He ain't the Admiral."

The Cytaur moved closer, hooves emitting deep thuds on the deck, his eyeball scanning Rosman, up and down, over and over. Nostrils distended, the Cytaur stopped and didn't blink for a full minute.

Gorias broke the silence by saying, "See? Even the Cytaur knows."

His face momentarily screwed into an acerbic expression, Rosman soon scoffed at Gorias, "You mean to leave my fate to cattle on two legs?" The Admiral spat at the Cytaur, who didn't react to the slur. "To the privy pot with you, freak. You're not even worth making a good jacket. You and your kindred, all dumb, soulless beasts created on the whim of some Nephilionic idiot."

The Cytaur's nostrils squished in and out once, the long horns gripped in his thick fists bounced off his sides.

Smelling trouble, Gorias' eyes narrowed at Rosman. "What

would you know about such things, more than lore?"

"The angels who fell crossbred with fair women; the others may have humped cows like the mother of this eyesore."

The Cytaur stepped between them, his eyelid dropped near to closed as he scanned the Admiral. Huge jaws parting, a sound not unlike a man underwater drawled out. "I don't have a soul, so when I close my eye forever, it's done. You? I can send you to Hades, a place prepared for the Devil and his angels."

Gorias stepped in fast, hands out to grab the Cytaur's wrists, but his move couldn't stop the creature's momentum. The Cytaur swung its two horns out and then stabbed them down, the one on the left entering the Admiral under his left collarbone and then stabbing into the mast behind Rosman...the other horn jamming directly through the Admiral's heart, also protruding out his back with a splash.

While the Admiral's face registered inconceivable shock, it was all of them looking on that soon shared this expression, for the wounds created by the Cytaur all bled an inky, black essence.

The Cytaur stepped back, pulling the horns with him, astonished by what it saw. The pirates holding the Admiral released him, staring at the wounds and the black ink solution running out.

Alarm fading, sneer returning, the Rosman's lips peeled back from his teeth, which started to drip a black fluid. "Stupid beast, indeed." He turned his gaze to Gorias and the pirates. "All of you."

❖❖❖❖❖

Thynnes and his men lined the docks of Mysoline, some stowing gear, others praying, many more gaping at the Cytaurs being taken up the planks to power the sister ship of the Bahamut, the Kamira. When a courier rode up astride a white horse, dressed in togs of the police of the capitol city Qesot, Thynnes wasn't impressed. However, when he read the dispatch, Thynnes told his men to load up on the ship and he'd join them shortly.

The General and Colonel Schou walked to one of the cargo depots. He stopped before entering the long warehouse, seeing ten horses hitched up outside and a beat-up coach. Thynnes walked over to the coach and opened the door. Within was opulent beauty, cushioned interiors and a velvet plush place to lie while the stage moved on.

"Nice, scent, huh?"

Schou stood rigid, nose wrinkling. "That smell familiar to you, sir?"

"Yes, she is…yes, it is, Colonel."

He walked back to the door and it opened inward fast. They were met by two tall figures in dusty, hooded robes. They motioned him to come in.

Schou drew his sword, but Thynnes waved him off. "No fear, son," he chided Schou and walked in, unarmed.

Though several shutters stood open, letting the sunlight lighten the room, a single lantern on the table was all Thynnes needed to know royalty existed here. At the table, on a chair modified with a purple cushion, sat Queen Garnet, sipping from a ceramic bottle, munching a tiny cake with a frosted top. All around her and behind the Colonel by the entrance stood those in grimy robes, who shed them promptly, revealing ten of Alena's sisters, all near copies of herself in size, bearing and armaments.

Thynnes stepped forward as his Colonel took a knee. "Queen Garnet," he grunted a little. "A pleasant surprise."

"I do so like to travel," she said, her voice stronger than he recalled. "So many think me a relic in my tower. Oft, I travel unaware with my girls here."

"They would surely see you safely along."

"They do," Garnet affirmed and daintily wiped her mouth. She extended her right hand and Thynnes stood, walked over and bent down to kiss her signet ring. "Now, General Thynnes, can you guess why I'm here?"

"I doubt it's for the local cakes, however good they are."

"Not bad, but not as good as the ones Alena makes. She's a wonderful girl, don't you know?"

"She has my respect."

"But I don't see her here."

Thynnes stood, sighed and relayed the story to the Queen. She listened intently, a few times shooting dagger looks to the girls who exchanged looks when their sister was mentioned.

"So, you think the Admiral up to no good?"

"Vile witchery is closer."

"And Alena is on the Bahamut?"

"Yes," Thynnes reaffirmed.

"Lord La Gaul with the pirates?"

"Yes."

"And?"

"I'm about to set things right, ma'am."

Garnet rose and Schou bowed his head. Thynnes remained at attention. "I expect no less. All of these players are very important to me."

Thynnes nodded and spoke low. "I understand, ma'am."

Her voice rose and she explained, "I am here to view some horses and take in the countryside. I do so tire of palace life, but in these days of traitors, one can never be too careful."

Thynnes eyed the girls. "Might I suggest a simple test of loyalty?"

Garnet blinked. "After what you explained of these copies, go ahead."

Thynnes held out his hand to the Queen. "Your hair pin?"

The Queen pulled loose her coiled locks and handed Thynnes her pin.

He took the saucer from her table and dumped the partially eaten cake off it. He held his large hand over the dish and pricked his middle finger. Red blood dropped on the saucer. He turned to Schou and motioned for him to arise and come on over. He stabbed the Colonel with the pin, getting red blood.

"Ladies?" Thynnes said, wiping the pin on a flap of his shirt exposed from the mail.

Ten girls offered their long fingers to Thynnes and all ten bled red.

"Well, that's good," Thynnes remarked to the last girl, probably the youngest he guessed by her expression. "I'd hate to have to kill one of you."

Garnet sighed. "I don't doubt my girls but this deviltry won't do." She then extended her hand to Thynnes. "I won't be known by any to not be myself."

Thynnes jabbed the Queen and the Appra sisters all gasped at once, but Garnet bled red, too. "Ma'am, I suggest you get back to the palace."

Garnet held out her hand and one of the girls quickly applied a small wrap to the spot. "And I suggest you cast off and don't fail me.

⁂⁂⁂⁂⁂

Though the rest backed away from the bound up Admiral who bled black, Gorias stood his ground, disengaging his swords.

Flanking Gorias, but back a few yards from him, Alena and Nykia took up defensive poses. Alena shot Nykia a look, almost comical. Gorias knew this was no time for disgust at raw fighting tactics versus well-trained warriors.

Confusion spread as all had no idea what they faced. All eyes soon focused on Gorias, his blades at the ready.

Eyebrows high, prim as ever, the Admiral clucked, "Still think I might tell you something?"

"No," said Gorias, stepping forward and leading with his right sword, slicing the Admiral's left arm off at the shoulder. The abrupt move made a peculiar sound, like a boot pulling from mud. Gorias quickly followed this move by striking off the Admiral's other arm. Both limbs fell to the deck, and everyone save for Alena and Gorias jumped back. Black ooze bled from the fresh wounds, and Rosman didn't show a clear sign of being in any pain. "You see, Alena, the dead know nothing, or the copy of a dead man won't talk much."

Rosman started to laugh, but Gorias crossed his swords and sliced the head from the thing lashed to the mast. The head dropped with a plop to the boards, soon followed by his legs, in three pieces each. Gorias then chopped the torso in half and it fell from the bindings.

The right hand started to move on the deck, making the arm crawl slowly and one of the pirates cried out for his god. Gorias hadn't heard of that deity and wished him the best of luck. "Kick 'em in the drink." He waved his word, trying to remove the black substance before wiping it off on the Admiral's right thigh.

Many of the men aboard shrank from the task Gorias outlined, but after Nykia stepped up and booted the Admiral's left arm into the sea, several more ran forward to help. In a moment, only the head remained, and it still smiled.

From high in the crow's nest a voice shouted, "Something coming up fast."

Allard offered, "Can it be another ship? Are we sailing in circles?"

The pirate shouted, "Island, coming up fast!"

Gorias looked over at Nykia, half smiling.

Confused, Alena also demanded of Nykia, "How is that possible?"

A small distance existed between the pirate vessel and the burning Bahamut, but north of them a jagged island loomed, coming up fast.

Alena glanced on either side of the ship. "We aren't moving that rapidly. How is that thing getting so near us so fast?"

"Because," Gorias said with resignation. "It's moving, not us."

Allard shouted, "That's impossible! Islands can't float!"

Nykia went to the edge, held the rail with one hand and raised a scope. "Damn!"

Gorias turned from the sight. "It's not an island."

While Alena registered terror at Gorias' reaction, Nykia dropped her scope and declared, "It's Pergamus."

"So you say," Gorias mumbled.

Nykia's expression jerked from amazement to concern. "But it's not supposed to be here."

"Nope," Gorias replied, hands fondling the pommels of his swords.

Mouth open, no words emerging, Nykia thought for a few

seconds before she looked back at the sight again. "I've been there, Gorias. It looks just like that!"

"I believe you," Gorias replied, then folded his arms.

A bubbly croak made Nykia and Alena jump back, for they knew in an instant the Admiral's severed head laughed. The mouth opened, pitch-black goop running out, the voice croaking, "Tell them, hero. Tell them what I was…tell them what it is."

Gorias cocked his leg and kicked the Admiral's head into the sea. Once he turned around, again, all eyes focused on him.

"The Admiral was a doppleganger of sorts, a copy made for the thing that powers the island. It collects souls of men, then makes a copy and sends them out to do its bidding. God knows how many are there in the world."

Alena asked the obvious question, "Why?"

"Because it cannot leave the island, no matter how hard it tries, for all the magic and souls it collects. It sends out the copies so the humans it deals with will not double-cross the power, and it needs the souls anyway to maintain a veil of secrecy."

Nykia wondered aloud, "For what?"

"Pergamus moves and needs power because it needs to hide. What it's up to in Transalpina with dragonfire and oils, I dunno, but I do know this. Pergamus isn't an island." He paused as the pirate ship stopped next to the huge rock cliffs of the island. "It's a *he*."

CHAPTER XI

AT PERGAMUS

Allard stood by Nykia and Gorias, gaping as the island loomed next to the ship. The men scrambled as Allard shouted for everyone to hang on. Allard wasn't the Captain of the pirates, but he started to act like one and they all obeyed.

Confusion seized Alena's face but it only took a moment for her instincts to understand the waves would near to topple the ship. She grabbed the mast pole as the waves caused by Pergamus' arrival came close to capsizing the ship. Gorias stumbled and fell to the deck, Allard and Nykia crashing on his back and rolling off as the ship tilted by 45 degrees.

On his own back soon after Gorias threw him off, Allard shouted, "This is goddamned impossible!"

Gorias patted Nykia on the thigh as if in small apology for dislodging her a moment before. He rolled back over as the ship shifted the other direction. He thought Allard's grasp of understatement a plus.

Fists on the wet deck, Nykia exclaimed, "But it is Pergamus! It can't be here!"

In the minutes that followed, the waves calmed and the island stopped moving. Allard got up, looked over the side and rubbed his beard.

Gorias said, "I wouldn't grapnel to that thing. If it moves off fast again, we'll be hauled along and torn apart."

"Agreed," he said and motioned the pirates to drop anchor. "What do we do?"

Gorias faced Nykia and then Allard. "You have had many dealings on Pergamus before?"

Both nodded, word still difficult with the manifestation of the island far from where it should be located.

"Who is it? Is it a person who hands you the dragonfire or

do you hear a voice?"

After a few moments of silence Nykia said, "Noguria, Savage Chad and the former Captain I slew usually did the dealings."

Gorias closed his eyes and rubbed them both. "Gods. This is gettin' better all the time." Eyes on them again, he said, "You gotta understand that this thing showed up, savvy? It wants something. I wonder what."

Allard mused, "The dragonfire didn't make it to Transalpina."

Gorias shouted, "So?!"

Eyes fluttering, Allard recovered from his shout and stated, "They wanted the dragonfire in Qesot. It exploded on the beach."

Hand up to his face for a moment, Gorias demanded, "I get what everyone else exchanged. What did you give at Pergamus to get the dragonfire?"

Nykia said, "We always had to bring in a person, man or woman, and they'd never return."

"Who took them in, Savage Chad or Noguria?"

Nykia shook her head. "It was a different crewman each time. That was the decree."

"Do you recall which ones?"

Nykia turned and scanned the crew surrounding them. "Many were on the other ship that sank, oh, you!" She pointed at a pirate with drooping mustache and his left eye sealed by a cataract. "Evigan! You took the sacrifice in the last time, right?"

The pirate shrugged as he stepped closer to Gorias and Nykia. "Yeah, I did."

Alena asked, "What happened to the captive? Were there people there? Was there a sacrifice?"

Evigan opened his mouth by Gorias cut him off. "Don't listen to him." His swords slid out and he moved toward Evigan. The others stepped away as Gorias grumbled, "He's a liar. Let me test a theory."

Gorias spun his swords and stabbed down, skewering both of Evigan's feet through to the deck.

A wave of gasps escaped from all onlookers, but when Gorias pulled his swords and showed the black liquid on them from

Evigan's feet, everyone else drew their blades.

His right blade aimed at Evigan's face, Gorias said to the crew, "You have all been suckered, used by Pergamus and made to do his bidding. His price was more than just a soul you won't see again, but another set of eyes into the outside world."

Evigan blinked, glanced down at his boots, then opened his mouth. However, the simple accent of an Albion sailor didn't fall from his mouth. A baritone voice echoed out, telling Gorias, "Come as see me, La Gaul. It'll be wonderful to see you…Again." Evigan then wilted like a hacked off weed, crumpling to the deck, his body liquefying to black tar.

Alena was the first to look from the body up to Gorias. "What will you do?"

"There's no escape. I don't think we can get away from the island. I might as well go see Pergamus."

Nykia shook her head. "You've seen him before?"

"Those fuckers lie," Gorias shrugged. "We'll see."

Allard said, "You take your fate in stride, La Gaul."

"Fate goes as it must. I'd rather face it than hide and piss myself."

✷✷✷✷✷

Gorias climbed down the rope ladder and set his boots on what they called Pergamus. He hopped a little, testing the rock beneath him.

Allard wondered, "Expecting it to shift?"

"Not really. I think it wants us here, but the idea of a mobile island goes against my natural instincts." Gorias took a few steps along the edge of the rocky beach and then walked further inland. He stopped. "The color is different."

Alena stayed near him. "You've been here before, haven't you?"

Gorias didn't turn to acknowledge her, still observing the distant formations. "Yeah, well, not exactly here, but here, nonetheless."

Nykia dropped off the rope ladder and shouted, "Some of the men refuse to come off the ship."

Gorias muttered, "It's their funeral."

Alena gaped at Nykia then to the pirates still aboard. Many had descended the ladder to join them, but others backed away even from the edge at her look.

Gorias shrugged. "They're afraid. Can't blame them."

Nykia joined Gorias and Alena. "Are you afraid?"

"Sure. A man ain't human if he has no fear. I'm probably going to my death on this rock, but I'm ready for that." He tore his look from the landscape and eyed them both. "Sorry, but I think that means you're both gonna die, too."

Alena's manner grew stern and her chest expanded, courage screwing tight, but Nykia smiled. "You can't die, Gorias. I'll be fine with you."

"You're talkin' stupid, Princess." He turned and started to walk toward the stone outcroppings in the distance.

Once everyone had climbed from the ship, Gorias eyed Nykia and then her new Captain, Allard. "Something wanted us off that damned ship."

Allard replied, "That never happens. We've been here, well, not exactly here, many times and…"

Gorias straightened up, rubbed his back. "I doubt the island ever came to you before, huh?"

"Nope," Allard answered, looking all around at the broad paths and distant choppy mounts on the rocky surface. "But this is the place, no doubt about it."

"Ask yourself, chief," Gorias said with anger in his voice, "why would it come to you? Ya always made deals with it, the entity of the island, Pergamus, right? I'll ask ya again, do ya think it's pissed that your last loads got shitcanned? Ever think it ain't givin' dragonfire in glass orbs out for goodness and picnics on the palace grounds?"

Allard's look hardened. "I suppose we didn't give a shit, Gorias La Gaul. It's easy being a hero and all that, but remember, we are dubbed pirates, reavers or whatever the fuck. We deal both sides of the fence and don't have a loyalty."

Gorias let his hands dangle near the pommels of his swords. That act alone made the captain's ire fade some. "I suppose that's the way of piracy. I couldn't expect morals outta such folks. I ain't got much time for morals my own damned self, but I do have common sense. Ya'all ever consider what the endgame was for dealing with something that lives in a mountain and gives out dragonfire?"

The Cytaur pointed toward the largest spires in the distance as Allard replied, "We made a pretty profit up until we ran into you."

Gorias smirked. "Sorry to fuck up your deal." He then turned to where the Cytaur aimed. He saw something in the air, wings working hard, and hoped it was a large bird. "Cap, how does Pergamus contact you? How do ya know what to do and what to bring?"

Allard saw the image too and blinked. "After each transaction one of the crew, usually Justin over there with the stripe shaved down his head, well, Pergamus speaks through him."

They all watched as a figure the size of a large crow flapped into clearer view. The sunlight glittered off the hawkish thing, making it appear orange like the rock formations.

Gorias drew his swords as the bird approached.

Alena drew her sword as well, hissing at Gorias, "What is it?"

"I just wanna make sure it goes for Justin."

Oblivious, Justin stepped forward as if he'd been called to dinner. The bird fell, its joints grinding, sounding like stone on stone. Its right leg stabbed down, talons springing out, pursuing Justin as he started to backpedal, understanding his danger at last. Too late, he turned, but the creature stabbed the long leg through his neck, pulled up off the ground and let his legs run a few times, then turned him around to face the others. Talons protruding from Justin's jaws, his mouth moved and a voice echoed from within a bottomless well.

"Come unto my mountain again, travelers, and we shall talk."

A couple pirates ran back for their vessel, but Allard shouted for them to stop. Before they could reach the planks of the pirate ship the ground gave way just around the edge of the island. The two pirates plunged into the sea, their screams hushed in salt water.

Gorias said, "I guess we gotta go see Pergamus."

Justin's eyes focused on Gorias and then he smiled just before the stone bird released him. Justin fell dead to the rocky surface and the bird flew away.

Allard looked at Justin. "Well, that's different."

Gorias said, "His mouthpiece is dead. Makes ya wonder if he ever needs one again, huh?"

Nykia looked to Allard. "We are all kinds of fucked, aren't we?" She then faced Gorias. "But with you there is always hope."

"I ain't unkillable, sweetheart, just fortunate. We'll see how it goes. As long as yer alive, there's a chance." He again started to walk toward the mountains.

Nykia caught up to him as Allard and the others joined them. "But this island approached us. It wants us for something. Why let us walk in if it could've overrun us?"

"You bet your life on that?" Gorias grunted once. "Pretty flimsy."

Nykia frowned, head shaking violently. "It wants something."

Gorias nodded. "Yes, he does."

Allard wondered, "He? You said the island was not an it but a he?"

Alena asked the obvious. "Who is he? Pergamus?"

"Yeah," Gorias replied, never breaking stride.

Nykia sounded demanding as she put forth, "Who is Pergamus?"

"Just another fallen angel, wanting to be God, playing at it in his own way. That's pretty much what all the angels did who fell during the war in Heaven, although not in the same regard. Many were shocked in their new existence, fallen from grace and the heavenly abode, all that, and curled up into balls of fright, became evil spirits, the lot. Some cause bad dreams, others hide in cisterns and make the rainwater bad, it happens. Many were aware, though, and while their resentment toward their Creator for creating man is what made them fall, they discovered a similar ambition when confronted with humanity."

They stopped at the edge of the stone beach area, overlooking a small valley of glistening shale stones. The sunlight made the loose rock glisten like a sea of diamonds.

Allard rubbed his chin, eyes up at Gorias. "So what did Pergamus do after he fell?"

"Same thing that mankind did," Gorias explained as he started to walk down in the valley. "He did just what pissed him off about God. He tried to start his own race, to create a populace to worship him. Many of the others of the fallen did so, as well, and soon discovered their destiny."

Alena wondered, "That humans would worship them?"

"Yes, but also that something else was watching them. You see, the angels, now demons, weren't meant to be on the earth. They have another destination. The abyss."

At his words the dozen pirates, Alena and Nykia stopped, but Gorias kept walking in the glimmering gravel. At last, Nykia spoke up. "The abyss?"

Gorias stopped, turned, his face sour at the expanse between them. "Yeah, 'course. Ya mean ya don't believe in the war in Heaven story 'bout angels and demons fighting over Heaven? Well, ya better think on it really well because one of the losers who thinks he's a little god is on this island. All your gold and reasoning can't pay him off or pray him off."

Alena walked to Gorias. "You said they were being watched and didn't count on something."

"Yeah. The abyss, the eternal pit of Hell itself is their destiny, but many fell to earth and found a way to hide out."

Allard chuckled. "All that is folly, but I'll bite. Hide from who? God? Which god? Are you a believer in one supreme one? Isn't he all powerful, all knowing?"

"There is only one, really, all the rest are punters." Gorias turned and started to walk again. "Sure. He made a place of free will, though, and the humans would have their choice to worship him or not. Some angels didn't like the abundance of choice afforded humanity and embraced the darkness. Well, that is the scheme of the universe in a nutshell. Congrats, I just solved it all for ya."

Allard spat, "Preposterous."

Gorias still trudged the shale, eyes forward. "And yet, it happened."

Nykia threw up her hands. "So tell us, why didn't God just pull them from the earth? Why all the terror and letting them do bad things to his new children?"

"God's an odd duck, but I won't presuppose his reasoning. He's God after all, and we are maggots to him. He let free will go and let his angels have charge of it. So, if a demon just appeared himself for worship by the masses, an angel would show up and ofttimes dispatch him to the abyss, where there is no escape. They want to be on earth, not there."

Alena nodded as she kept close to Gorias. "I imagine."

Allard faced the looming mountains of rock and asked, "Suppose I buy all of this argument of fancy tales. Are the tales of the fallen angels breeding with women true? Are the Nephilum children of the Cherubim?"

"Pretty much," was all the answer Gorias gave. "But not all decided to try and breed a race of giants with comely ladies of the creator. Some got screwy."

All but Gorias now looked to the Cytaur.

Gorias said, "Yeah, s'true, God didn't mean for something like him to be bred, that's one reason for the end of the world coming. The world is full of evil mistakes and things God never intended. I think he is gonna scrub us all and start over."

Allard shook his head. "Then why the gap? Why not just kill and restart?"

"That's a good question and I don't have an answer. However, you are missing my point here about alternate breeding. In all the kid's tales, what is Pergamus?"

Nykia said hastily, "The homeland of the dragons?"

Allard guessed, "Pergamus is the father of the dragons? Are you saying he mounted up lizards and created beings to spew dragonfire?"

Gorias stopped and took a few breaths. "Pretty much."

Alena cracked her knuckles and scanned the spires of the

rocky mountain-scape. "And you slew many of them and made sure the last are gone."

"Yeah."

Alena bit her bottom lip. "Pergamus must love you."

"Dearly."

Allard put his hands over his face and rubbed with fury. "This is silly. Why doesn't he just make more?"

Gorias started walking again. "He can't. His power has lessened. The sin birthed by the darkness on this earth is taking its toll. Things are breaking down, dying. Once, men could live 900 years, but that's shortening up the further away from the cradle of creation one gets. We are in the sticks out here. 150 or 200 is great here. Back in Shynar, 900 is the norm."

Allard asked, "You are saying the more sin grows, the more we and everything else lessens or dies?"

"Yer on the right track. I've lived a long time and traveled far. I know. Accept it if ya like. The power of the demons isn't getting stronger, but weakening. The angels will ferret them out, which is why a weaker Pergamus hides in a mobile island."

Nykia grinned. "If he manifests, comes forward into the material plane, the angels will get him."

"Yup."

Alena frowned. "Then why the subterfuge with the balls of dragonfire? What is this all about?"

"Not all demons or fallen host are as mean or petty as Pergamus to want mischief. Others, like Rhiannon in Albion, really felt rotten for what they did and did try the god or goddess route. They are all guys, just some more than others. That's a long story too. Anyhow, Rhiannon is a remorseful fallen one, but there's no redemption and Rhiannon knows it. She, um, he, realizes the abyss is his destiny and time is tight."

Allard chuckled. "All that oil, pouring down the well of Rhiannon, for what?"

"Maybe it soothes its heart or injuries?" Gorias threw up his hands. "Who can say? But I'm unsure of what Pergamus has in store and why this is happening. If we have come this far, he wants to talk and tell us something."

Allard laughed loud. "He'll want to kill you!"

Gorias stopped again, turned and grinned. He wiped sweat from his forehead and told him, "I'm counting on it."

❖❖❖❖❖

The valley leveled out fast and the loose rocks dispersed back into a rocky plain. The rising surface took on a steeper grade, full of lines like a dry riverbed. These grooves served as a natural set of steps for the walkers as they moved nearer to the towering rock spires of the island.

Allard whispered to Nykia, "He knows where he's going. We didn't have to tell him where the others were led to."

Nykia replied, "He amazes me so. I know I sound like a punk bitch about him, but could he have anything else to prove himself to me? Good night, look at him and tell me there's no God?"

Allard did watch Gorias stomping on the stones ahead of them like he had a grudge on them and sighed. "You do sound like a girl again, Princess."

"Oh, shut up."

"If he is even half right on that angels and demons story, we're doomed, I'd say. Gorias is a helluva fighter, but can he take a demon, even a weak one?"

"He'll think of something."

Allard nodded. "He sure carries himself like he's not afraid. He'd be a great card player."

"Probably."

"He's had the Amazon, you know."

Nykia's head snapped to face him. "What?"

"The tall gal walking behind him? Gorias has screwed her. I can tell these things."

"That's just stilly. She's half a man."

Allard shrugged. "She looks at him the same way you do. She wants to embrace him every so often but doesn't. Her hand goes out and stops, drops. It's true. She wants him and tries to hide it." Allard looked over at her. "You do too, but it's brutally obvious."

"I've not hidden my feelings for Gorias."

"But look at one who struggles to do just that."

Nykia waved him off. "Don't be stupid. You're messing with my head."

"They have a great deal in common, a powerful will, great warriors..." Allard broke into laughter. "...lots of balls..."

"Piss off."

"If I cannot laugh in the face of my own demise, when can I?"

Nykia moved up close to Alena and they exchanged a look. After a few moments of silence, Nykia asked her, "Why are you here? You defend me like I'm your sister."

"My sisters don't need me to defend them," Alena replied, eyes forward.

"But why? I'm nothing to you."

"For a girl of the world, you're thick in the head." Alena stopped and looked down at Nykia. "I made an oath to my Queen and I shall fulfill it. I promised to see you back to Transalpina, alive, and that I'll do. It's my duty."

They turned back and continued. Nykia said, "What of Gorias?"

"What of him?" Alena said, eyes going to the rocky ground beneath her boots.

"I see how you look at him." Nykia glanced at Alena, but she kept looking down. "What is he to you?"

"I'd never met him before the other day. One always hears of Gorias La Gaul or sees the reliefs painted or sewn about him in school, but I never set eyes on him until he came to the tower."

"Do you love him?"

"I said I just met him."

Nykia cleared her throat. "And I've loved him truly my entire life, before I met him and the moment I set eyes on him dragging men to death on the beach."

Alena's jaw jutted, grinding. "He's an incredible warrior, worthy of his legend, but he's an old man."

Nykia smiled. "It's all right to care for him, many women can't help it. It's his--what is the word?"

"Charisma?" Alena offered.

Nykia nodded fast. "That's good. Charisma. You can touch it a yard away from him."

"I'm a palace guard of the Queen's inner circle, descended of a General unable to father sons. Father made his life count by making a deal with Queen Garnet for his daughters' lives. Rather than be pimped out as brides or sold to the cloister, they became warriors and the best cover a Queen can have. I have no thoughts of settling down and fathering a brood with a warrior 675 years older than myself."

Like she heard little of the speech, Nykia said dreamily, "But you think of him, don't you? It's impossible not to."

"What is your point?"

Nykia shook her head but couldn't stop smiling. "It's natural."

"You want him for your King, don't you?"

"Now that would be a dreamy thing for a dirty pirate girl to think on, no?" She laughed sarcastically. "I think that'd be the only thing to get me back there."

Alena glanced back toward the ship. "We aren't out of here yet."

Nykia assured her, "I've been to Pergamus many times, relaying the dragonfire to the contacts in Transalpina. This won't be any different."

"The island ever float up and arrive for you before?"

Nykia's face darkened. "I have to admit, that is strange. Pergamus Island isn't exactly as we recall it, location-wise, but many attribute that to drunken navigation."

Alena didn't speak and a more sullen look formed on her face. Nykia jogged up to Gorias and slapped his elbow. She turned and saw Alena watching her and a chill flittered across her arms.

❈ ❈ ❈ ❈ ❈

Nykia said to Gorias, "I've met some strong women but that one…hard as some men I've met."

Gorias agreed. "She's all woman."

She pondered the look on Gorias' face when he said that, decided against thinking on it longer and said, "Her sisters all serve the monarch, correct?"

"Her personal guard, yes."

"They will serve any heir, then, or monarch?"

"Who can say if Prince Vincent will feel protected by such ladies? Hell, I would, but that'd be like putting the wolf behind a wall of bitches in heat. Vincent may change the guards. Garnet did in favor of these ladies, knowing they'd all die for her."

"That's a helluva code."

"Still, it's a code. Mine has changed a lot over the years. Ya gotta if ya wanna stay alive."

"Would they serve Vincent?"

"I don't see why not, but I doubt they have concubine on their list of ethical behaviors."

"Would they serve me if the old gal drafts me as her heir?"

Gorias glared at her for a moment. "That *ol' gal* has plenty of starch left in her collar and was always a great lady, even as a girl. She had that, well, strength and all that stuff. It can't be taught. Well, maybe it can. She'll try to school you in it, I suppose. I'd listen if I were you."

"You think I should take up palace living?"

"Why not? You've had your time as a slave, a warrior and all that. It'll help make better choices later in life."

"But I'll have you at my side."

"Listen, sister…"

Nykia reached out and clasped his hand. "I won't let you get away again, Gorias La Gaul. You're mine and I intend to keep you."

"Let's talk about this when and if we get off this rock alive."

✤✤✤✤✤

Nykia hung back and talked to a few pirates, but Allard stepped up, muttering to Gorias, "Has it all figured out, doesn't she?"

"Good ears on ya, old fart."

"You should take up palace living."

"Piss in your hat. She'll never keep me."

"She'll try."

"Her and what army?"

"The Transalpinan one."

Gorias sighed. "Yeah, I reckon she will at that. I hate this long walk. I hope Traveler is alive back there on the mainland."

Allard looked around them at the party walking the long rocky trail toward the spires ahead. "Gorias La Gaul, why is it you do what you do?"

"You fuckers all want a story, huh?"

"Sure."

"One really doesn't plan to live to be 700. Even in this age of men who can live for centuries, it's not something ya think on while younger. I hear there was a bastard that made it to near a thousand. Can ya image how boring that musta got?"

"I'm sure."

"He probably was a godly man, clean living and all that. But hell, in that case, I shoulda never broken 200. I didn't really have a tragic life, but I hear my birth was marred with drama...not on my part. My father carved me from my mother before she could sacrifice me."

"I thought your mama was nobility?"

"Have ya ever met a noble that didn't get weird later in life? Anyways, I grew up in a more tribal area, not barbarian bad, but danged close."

"I heard you're from Thule."

"Well, not all stories are exactly true. Aside from the fighting and raiding, we farmed quite a bit. No one ever hears about that. I even went to the bigger lands to get educated, took part in some wrestling matches and got trained up pretty well with weapons, better than the tribesmen taught me, well, or damn near as good.

Then, some asshead threw me in the arena with the national champion. I didn't know I was supposed to take a dive."

"What happened?"

"I killed him. He was a damned good fighter. Maybe he held back and thought I was gonna fall or was easy pickings because I was young. Still, he died, right there in front of his wife & mistresses, blood kin and bastard children. They all didn't take it too well."

"I bet."

"They hanged me," said Gorias, gazing across the rocky plain.

"Really?"

Gorias nodded. "Under my beard ya can still see a rope burn scar. The rope broke, by the way."

"I figured as much."

"The rule is if that happens, they have to let ya go. Well, the nobles weren't having any of that crap, so they locked me up so they and their priest could fight it out. I never had much use for clergy, but in that case, cheers."

"What happened?"

"A lady of the garter came and offered me freedom if I promised to have sex with her and kill her husband, an abusive lawmen."

"I can guess what happened."

"A small price to pay to get to run away. She slipped me out and I slipped in her. Her ladies in waiting apparently were obsessed with preserving their virginity via the oral cure, and seemed to take it up as an addiction. That's how she plied the guards."

"Yes, yes…"

"Or at least distracted them. Anyhow, I killed her asshead husband with the axe they intended to use on me the next day. I got caught killing him, and had to kill the chief deputy, his buddy, the local doctor and his daughter."

"His daughter?"

"If ya saw the bitch, ya woulda killed her too, but she was armed and swinging at me."

"Had you ever killed a woman before?"

Gorias pondered that. "Not with a weapon. An aging whore once passed while…"

"All right, all right. What a youth."

"I wasn't even twenty yet at this time. I ran away after I covered the lawman's wife. A deal is a deal."

"I see."

"I've been running ever since. I did stop a few lands over and really got book-educated. I learned from scribes and went to class, no kidding. I learned a great deal about the world from that education and those tablets in Shynar. I earned my pay as a guard and took up training swordsmen for a bit too."

"Did you ever settle down, have a family?"

"A few times. It wasn't me. I wasn't any good at it."

"Did you have children?"

Gorias' face darkened. "Can we talk of something else? Alena wants to screw me like I was a teen and you wanna talk me to death."

"The great whore-taker has no children?"

Gorias grimaced. "I have several. But it's a terrible thing to produce something the world can do without. I have some grandsons that are good men. A youngun, Maddox, lives way off across the world in Shynar. I oughta go see him one of these years."

"Why did you slay dragons?"

"I hadn't set out to, for real, and killed the first one by accident. Those nails of theirs?" Gorias pulled up his sleeve to show the dew nail on his armor. "These things cut through their scales like paper. You'd be surprised the lengths ya go to to get what ya want. I got this armor and killed that dragon to kill someone else, but that's another story"

"Are your swords made from the wings of angels?"

"I'm gettin' tired of talkin' about my life."

❈ ❈ ❈ ❈ ❈

The group arrived at the crest of the hill and they stood on a level plain of stone.

Alena observed, "This surface is almost polished."

Gorias mumbled, "Yup," as he raised his head, looking at the broad spires of jagged stone spread out in a semicircle. "They look like wings, don't they?"

Allard smiled. "Don't tell me Pergamus is really the mountain, his wings of stone meant to hide his location from angels? Those angels need to bring along bloodhounds if they are that stupid."

"They're more attentive than smart-assed pirates, but no, I'm not saying that. It almost looks like a temple, really."

Nykia wondered, "Why would he create something like that to surround himself? The God complex?"

"Maybe. Could be that he's recalling something he saw somewhere."

Allard chuckled. "We're walking into a bastard version of Heaven, Gorias?"

"If I could figure his reasoning completely, I'd be further ahead of this, Allard."

They took a few steps but all stopped when pinpricks of light appeared down in the deep darkness of a cavern stretching into the belly of the rocks.

"Well," said Gorias and rubbed his hands together, seeing the tiny lights increase in size and give luminosity unto the robed figures that carried them. "We might as well see what passes for the throne of God, huh?"

Gorias in the lead, they walked in closer to the thirteen figures in red velvet robes, all with their faces covered, all holding a tiny orb of dragonfire in their right hands. These figures drew back, six to each side, but one remained before Gorias. This figure turned and led them into the realm of Pergamus.

CHAPTER XII

SHOWDOWN

Several of the pirates drew their swords as they followed Gorias. The ones that didn't draw a weapon were too busy staring at the hooded figures lighting the way with balls of dragonfire. They soon broke from this stupor and armed themselves.

Allard and Nykia followed suit, taking slow steps to begin.

Alena let her hands rest on the handles of her sword and knife, but never pulled them clear of their scabbards. Gorias thought her clearly concerned about their escorts, but she didn't let her eyes stray far from his actions.

Gorias walked casually, not slow, but not in a hurry, letting the hooded folk lead them and illuminate the path into the inner realm of Pergamus Mountain.

The temperature dropped slowly, lending a chill to his skin. Gorias noted the others shiver, but his armor kept him warm. Waves of warmth washed out from the interior, but mostly the cold air reigned. He expected no heat from the dragonfire, it being housed in balls of glass, after all.

The walls vaulted up, what he could see of them, reaching above and not smooth. They reminded Gorias of castles in the sand made by children, fingers running grooves down, deep like small trenches.

Ahead of them, the smooth flooring extended out, but soon the darkness broke more. The chamber widened, gigantic in itself, and a centerpiece became clear to any eye. They walked up to a towering image. From a distance, Gorias thought it possibly a cloaked giant, skinny on top and tapering down to a low, shrouded base, but as they came closer, he saw the image emitted light exactly like the dragonfire balls. The tower soon drew kinship to tall pine trees he'd seen in the northern lands, not unlike where he grew up. In the winter, the glistening ice crystals made the limbs appear to light up. This image reminded Gorias of similar sights during the winter solstice when some would adorn such trees with candles and shrunken heads from their conquests.

Nykia stepped up closer to Gorias, hissing quietly, "What is it?"

Gorias spoke plainly, not shielding his tone. "It looks like a tree." He then glanced back and stopped. All of them halted as well before he spoke. "No reason to whisper. Pergamus can hear us. He's all around, right?" Gorias shouted his last word and a vibration like thunder rippled around the room, causing even Alena to pull her sword and the pirates to wear bewildered looks.

Allard wondered, "Is this where the dragonfire comes from? It's all over the tree, but…"

Gorias completed his thought, "But missing in places?" He walked closer to the tree but the rest hung back, save for Alena and Nykia who wandered in the gap between. "What's in the empty spots?"

Eyes wide, marveling, Allard mumbled, "How many different types of angels are there?"

"Many argue that point, saying varied bands or divisions based on numbers of wings and duties they perform. A priest once told me that wasn't important and that there are only two types."

"Yes?"

"Good and bad." Gorias took a deep breath. "That's really all that matters in the end."

The tree bore many limbs, but the branches had neither wooden grain nor leafage. The texture ran in scaly lines, punctuated by porous gaps. The color, black as night, held a mystery of the globes of matter in the places where no dragonfire glowed.

Eerie and beautiful, the tree held dozens of glass balls of the fire, some as large as the one the pirates wasted back at the Keep, others small like those held by the priests.

Gorias stopped, hands to his hips. "Well, I ain't gettin' any younger."

They then heard the voice, a deep tone so imperious it nearly caused a panicked run by the pirates. "I'm delighted to perceive you again, Gorias La Gaul."

"Wish I could agree. It's been quite a spell."

Pergamus' voice echoed all around them, saying, "Not many live that know of the olden times and ways."

"That's why ya can dupe so many now."

A slight pause and the deep voice agreed. "True. Human stupidity is my ally. They forget their history and thus can be manipulated into falling again, over and over, for the same lines. Child's play, Gorias."

"Nice tree."

"Have you comprehended my play yet?"

"Seeing the lights missing, I'm starting to get it."

"It's long past time I left here, skulking about the sea and shifting my ways."

"Taking up quarters elsewhere?"

Pergamus paused. Gorias waited for a laugh. He didn't get one. "Not by choice."

"I reckon."

Nykia looked to Alena, confused, but the tall woman waved her off and even slashed across her mouth with her sword to make sure she understood that silence was a great idea.

"The end is near, well, the end for the world, for a while." Pergamus said reflectively. "Soon, many of us on the world will cease to be, the bodies they inhabit will drown and all of their bastard children will be swept away."

"A good flood will get rid of the problem."

"Many of us have other plans. Many will go to slumber in crypts under the sea in balanced animation, waiting for the stars to be right and to be awakened by followers in the future. The angels will not uncover us in that way."

"So that is your plan? To go to ground and hibernate like bears? What's with the tree then, with the dragonfire and the rest?"

"My being, my soul and spirit feeds the dragonfire. It is the dragonfire. Each dragon carries a portion of my soul, and thus, every piece of the fire is a soul of the dead dragons you and others slew."

"You're moving your children into the world?"

"In a way."

"What's with the copies, the doppelgangers?"

"You so amuse me, so I'll tell you. I require the souls of men, not just for sacrifice but for spies in the material world, a better form of possession and trusting against the rise of human will. Many can fight a spirit if they have faith or knowledge. These still think they are who they are and are my eyes, do my will, oft unknowingly. I use them to further my programs, to make sure my place will be ready."

"You're moving yourself, one piece at a time, to Transalpina to hide? To wait out the flood?"

"Your words are crude, Gorias La Gaul, but not unwarranted. In time, the place will be ready for me to sleep and I shall be able to be all together, safe, and then slide my essence from this self-made prison of rock."

"Why are we here?"

"You are going to help me further, these little squids with you and all. They will make excellent carriers. You see, the conflicts of men, the passions of the Admiral and all the rest mean nothing to me."

"I doubted they did. Why is someone using dragonfire in Qesot?"

Again, Pergamus paused. "Perhaps our benefactor is siphoning off power for their own use. It's of little matter as soon, I will be complete there."

"It looks like you have a ways to go on the tree here."

"I have time. There's no great rush." Many limbs of the tree stated to move, to bend and snake like serpents. "Long have I wanted to add Gorias La Gaul unto myself."

Gorias drew his swords. "Ya know that ain't gonna be easy."

"Of course. I truly expect trouble from you and your group. It is of little matter. I'm immortal and even if you cause trouble here, you cannot destroy the tree. Can you stab a forest and kill it?"

"Maybe I can chip the bark a little."

"You rail on me, La Gaul, at what I'd doing. In your mind, it may be petty, infantile or useless to your little lives. I have eternity to play my games as you say. So do you all, really, as you all carry an eternal spirit, yet are shackled by a material life. But a life in flesh is not a complete life. You may understand the range of a thousand years, but you cannot conceive of a hundred thousand years or a million. Once a million years passes, not the first moment of eternity has gone by, thus, I have plenty of time to scheme against you. I have no doubt the Creator's homunculi will pass away in time, but he'll do it again. It's his nature, like it's in my nature, now, to be away from his ethereal presence."

Gorias shouted, "It wasn't always as such, was it? You could've stayed on the side of the angels."

The rocky floor quaked under them. "You speak of angels, a man standing there with the shards of angelic wings as your swords. Can't you appreciate my stealth, avoiding them so long in my prison?"

Nykia hissed, "What does he mean?"

Gorias said, "Pergamus fell to earth like the other defeated members of the heavenly host. A third of all angels did but many were cast into the abyss by the victors."

The voice roared, casting many of the pirates to their backsides. Nykia fell to a knee, grabbing Gorias to hold herself up. Alena snapped into a defensive stance, erect still, but near to a fallen Allard.

"Your words and understanding mean nothing. Can't you see how pointless it all is now? You are doomed and there is no escape from my course. You have come unto this place because of my will. I have allowed these pirates, each time, to come unto my self and take out the dragonfire." The tree of lights and its slithering limbs glowed brighter at the words. "I have sent the souls of the dragons into the world again to be made manifest by my servants. I live in every point of dragonfire. Soon, their father will follow."

Gorias said, "I know ya bred with saurian beasts here and created the dragons, unlike yer fallen brothers who mounted up real women, creating the Nephilum giants. You want a cookie?"

Pergamus replied in a modest voice, "We all have our desires fostered by the imperfection sin brings. Some became desirous of the Creator's puppet women, others saw greater icons rise in the dusk abroad. My mind saw the images our master took on, the serpent, the eternal dragon, and thus, I have worked to create more of the same." His conceited tone fell. "Until you slew them all."

"I had help."

"You had guts for an ungodly man. Your ego is such that it wasn't about doing good, but fostering your own legend. My compliments. You could be demon material if not for the stench of the heavenly host on you."

"Thanks." Gorias slid his blades across each other.

Nykia whispered, "Can you kill him with those?"

Gorias looked at the swords. "I can piss him off, but no, I can't kill him."

Pergamus chuckled. "So young, so silly, no? You cannot kill that which isn't really alive."

Alena said, "Pergamus is a demon and has no material life."

"Ah, the girl with the thighs speaks. My brethren would love one like you." Pergamus' humor faded and he snarled, "I have eternal life."

Gorias added, "In the pit, though. Not much life to be had in the abyss, once you're there, huh? Ya can't even reach out and screw with humanity then, or a lizard as the case was here."

Nykia grabbed the dew nail on Gorias' forearm. "He's fallen from heaven, but not damned, not yet, so…"

Gorias said, "So he skulks about the ocean, pretending to be an island, dreaming up schemes to destroy more human souls to Hell? Yeah, that's it."

Nykia gasped. "Why doesn't he just fly across the world and burn them all?"

"He can't," Gorias affirmed. "Can you?"

Silence reigned about them.

Gorias said, "Ya see, if he comes out and plays like that, the heavenly host will sense him, find him and then send him to the abyss."

"How has he got by so long?"

"Angels aren't everywhere."

Nykia frowned. "That's crazy. If there is a God and he knows all, why leave him running amok?"

Gorias smirked. "Good question. All a part of personal choice inflicted on humanity." Gorias raised his voice. "That Creator you hate so much, ya exist at his leisure and ya keep pissing up his leg!"

Pergamus spoke calmly. "It's a game, but you wouldn't understand."

"I understand plenty," Gorias replied as he pulled from Nykia and started to jog toward the tree. He snapped the handles of his swords together, making one double-bladed staff. "I understand that deliverance will come."

Gorias pulled on his helmet and dropped the visor, moving up fast, preparing to strike at the base of the tree.

A limb of the tree, black and naked, slithered out like a snake and snapped at Gorias. Blades spinning, Gorias twisted and sliced through the slapping tendril, sending the piece of the tree soaring over the heads of the pirates.

Gorias swung his joined blades about and swept his other arm about the room. "Defend yourselves and kill them all! They can't be much more than dupes as servants!" After he spoke, he swung the blade hard, striking the base of the tree like a lumberjack at work. Gorias' blade went in only an inch and popped back out, but the tree surged brighter than before.

In this new light, the others saw the hooded men drawing back with their globes of fire. The Cytaur wasted no time, attacking the nearest hooded figure with his horns. His fast moves sent the ball of dragonfire flying off to the right, crashing and causing a burn near one of the servants who'd already flung his ball at the pirates. The Cytaur's pointed horns passed through the body of the hooded figure, and pulled out, covered in black fluid. The Cytaur watched the figure next to the one that he dropped, the fire consuming it, the form of a man melting away like so much candle wax. Under the hood, no distinct features existed on the faces, yet each was different in a subtle way.

Although Nykia ran to attack the nearest hooded man, she felt a hand grip her collar. Before she could react, she was flung sideways, head over heels, and rolled out of the gut of the fight. In the very moment Alena threw her out of the way, the hooded man threw his ball of fire. Once Nykia got clear, Alena shoulder rolled on the floor under the flying ball of flame. The move, at her size, appeared near to impossible, yet Alena executed it with grace, her long legs flying up, boots boxing the ears on either side of the hood of the thrower. Stunned, the man moved a few steps to his right, but Alena was up, dagger in her left hand buried in the kidneys of her target, pig sticker out and quickly inserted into her enemy's sternum. Choking, the man fell, his hood off. Nykia stood by Alena when she rose, looking at the face of the fallen man.

"By the gods," Nykia said. "It's Vallen, one of our spies."

Alena eyed the conflict. "It was."

Many of the pirates faired worse, but they didn't have Alena to guard them. A half dozen of the robed men threw their balls of fire and killed just as many of the pirates. The Cytaur waded into the conflict, butchered two more of the hooded men, impaling them and pulling out their guts with the horns, making a lurid, ropy knot before kicking them down. The Cytaur turned and one of them reared back, threw a ball and got him, dead to rights in the chest. His one eye blinked as the ball bounced off his chest and never broke. He immediately backpedaled with his hooves as the ball dropped and flamed up between him and the hooded man.

Gorias continued hacking on either side of the tree, looking up at the slithering forms on the branches and seeing that these shapes started to take on humanoid forms. He also could hear Pergamus' voice give out a loud sigh, bored by it all.

Alena went to work, using her sword with two hands on the pommel, deftly avoiding the thrown balls, chopping the head from one hooded man and nearly cutting another one in two at the waist.

"You bore me, La Gaul," Pergamus said. "You came all this way to cut my tree down? You make me laugh."

From the branches, figures started to fall, all covered in black liquid, all landing, sliding but soon standing fast again. They were men, rubbing the blackness from their eyes, but not awakening into confusion. Clearly all of one accord, they started to surround the survivors.

One of the glass balls of fire on the tree fell and landed near Gorias, shattering, bathing him in dragonfire. Like before, the fire churned and gained in mass, writhing about Gorias like serpents. Gorias turned from the tree and faced Alena.

The tall girl reached into her pouch and pulled the vial from Gorias' belt. She jogged toward the tree a few paces, reared back and flung the vial into the air.

Gorias fell to the stone floor, rolled, came up with his swords spinning, whipping the dragonfire into a malleable tiny vortex with his left hand. His right reached out, but didn't catch the vial. It flew past his grip and dropped near his boots. Gorias flipped over, casting the dragonfire back at the tree, and let his blades fall to the floor, still joined. He sprawled out, cursing, extending his left arm and smashed his forearm into the vial.

He faced up, seeing the tree tremble as another ball of dragonfire fell. He flipped over, cursing himself, knowing that as a youth he'd have turned about four or five times, but he only managed one roll and that was to avoid the glass ball. Again, fresh fire bathed the scene, but when Gorias stood up, he wasn't alone in the flames.

Allard stabbed at one of the inky figures attacking but soon shouted out, "There's another in the fire with him!"

Gorias saw what they all did, a humanoid shape rising up in the flames, tiny at first, like a dwarf, but soon gaining the stature of a full-grown man. Lean, almost feminine in a way, the hairless silhouette in the fire took on features, bearing slanted eyes and an almost serpentine quality to the mouth and nose.

Pergamus growled all around them. "You damned worm! Delight in your trickery, La Gaul. You've brought the god who thinks himself a goddess, Rhiannon, unto my realm. What of it?"

While the fire dissipated, Gorias moved away from the lithe form of Rhiannon. Staring up at the tree, Rhiannon spread out skinny arms.

Pergamus rumbled, "Bah, go to Hell."

Rhiannon's voice, high pitched but oily, echoed all around them, saying, "Oh, dear, you along with me."

From the tree fell more objects, but none of the dragonfire.

This time dozens more bodies bathed in inky blackness dropped. Gorias recognized Admiral Rosman, but he was no longer himself. All of the original bodies that Pergamus harvested souls from wore empty stares, blank, devoid of their selves. However, they moved fluidly and encircled Rhiannon.

Hands clapped together, a dozen profiles appeared and surrounded Rhiannon. Each new image pulsed in emerald hues, each a different height, but all wearing the robes of Rhiannon's priests, but close to being transparent of mass.

Backing up and hacking his way through a few bodies from the tree, Gorias joined Nykia and Alena. "Pergamus ain't the only one who can take a body, use its soul and have the energy left to use later."

Nykia fought off one of the servants, striking a blow to the heart and wrenching her sword around. "What are those things with Rhiannon?"

"Probably his priests, many suicidal martyrs to follow their god into his final mission before eternity." Gorias took a knee, slashed the knees from two of the attackers and allowing Alena to use him as an obstacle. She flipped across his back, her boots striking the chest of an attacker before landing to strike another with her sword.

The priests fought well, too, striking out with their arms made of energy, evaporating the reanimated bodies seeking a closer grip on Rhiannon. The inky shapes fell to dust as if struck by lightning.

Alena grabbed at Gorias, but he pulled away, armor still smoking from the dragonfire. "Look! One of the bodies!"

Gorias gestured for them all to get back. "Yeah, I see him."

Alena stood frozen, seeing the form of Prince Vincent trying to attack the priests of Rhiannon.

The stone base under them lurched, sending all tumbling, even Rhiannon. The mountains of rock overhead burst the ceiling of the cavern, flying in all directions, letting the sunshine in fast, but soon this light was partially obscured by the massive form of Pergamus.

Although hundreds of feet high, dwarfing even the tree, the spectacle made Gorias recall gargoyle statues seen outside Nineveh: both thick limbed and finned at the joints, covered in a scaled, reptilian hide. In proportion to a human shape, Pergamus' frame ran twice as thick as standard size.

Gorias saw the father of dragons and understood their faces as they resembled the avatar above, savage teeth, protruding nostrils, finned ears and spikes over his head (probably snaking down his back, but Gorias couldn't see). His manhood swung between his stout legs like a great, limbless trunk.

The silence broke as Gorias heard Alena remark, "He doesn't have any balls."

"Why do you think demons are so pissed?" Gorias said, from a push-up position.

"How did he…" Alena wondered but Pergamus' roar at Rhiannon muted her words.

Gorias got back to his feet, figuring her wonder came at how Pergamus bred the dragons…but she understood little of magicks and the desires of the demonic horde in one-upping their Creator.

Rhiannon's chin turned up, taking in the spectacular sight of Pergamus towering over his form. "You're such a braggart," Rhiannon said, delicate features drawing but into a wicked grin.

The last of the hooded servants of Pergamus fell along with the bodies fallen out of the tree. The dozen forms surrounding Rhiannon snapped around like a bowman notching an arrow, their arms up and aimed at the towering Pergamus. Rhiannon raised his arms just as each priest started to glow red. Their arms shot beams of light up and at an angle, all forming like rain off an awning over Rhiannon, who let go beams of focused power that gushed like spouting water. Their beams congealed and shot at Pergamus' midsection.

Pergamus shuddered, and a layer of stony rock peeled away; however, he didn't fall or cry out in pain. Right fist balled up, Pergamus swung down, striking atop Rhiannon.

Nykia gasped and the rest drew back some, save for Gorias. "Rhiannon's gone!" She declared as Pergamus' fist arose, showing no more priests or god.

Gorias waved at them to retreat. "Go back. This isn't over yet."

226

Pergamus stood up and focused his glowing eyes on Gorias. The moment of focus lasted just that long, for Rhiannon erupted from his chest, hands ripping open the stone covering like an earthquake splitting the ground. Rhiannon somersaulted to the floor and swung about, catching a hunk of the falling cover and throwing it back, kneecapping Pergamus. His leg near to collapsing, Pergamus limped and then roared with fury.

Like a dog shaking off water, Pergamus shuddered all over, shards of rock flying off and falling in fine pieces like a blizzard, his mass diminishing to nearly ten feet tall. His body was now sleek and muscular and more akin to a large man, but sporting long wings flapping like a wind-disturbed tent.

Rhiannon's bare back suddenly sprouted twin appendages, uncoiling like leather and fluttering fast like a hummingbird. When Pergamus struck out again with his fists, Rhiannon elevated and flew past him, leaving his strike to fall on the polished floor. Rhiannon turned, kicked Pergamus in the head and came near to wearing a smile.

"It's time to go," Rhiannon told Pergamus. "Our time is at an end." Rhiannon swung about again, clocking Pergamus' face with his other foot. "I won't go unto the abyss alone."

Pergamus turned about, grabbed Rhiannon's ankles and extended his own wings. A fast spin, he threw Rhiannon into the mountainside. Rhiannon fell hard to the stone surface, an avalanche crashing on his head, but only making him shake off the dust and debris. Airborne, Pergamus flew at his demonic brother and never paused when the images of the twelve priests appeared, all joined at the head like spokes in a wheel. When Pergamus flew through the tangible images, a golden glow rippled across his form, tearing apart more of it, reducing him to the same size as Rhiannon, sending him off his intended path. Pergamus crashed into the wall at near to the same spot as Rhiannon. He also fell, but was met in the air by Rhiannon, who seized his legs and twisted them across each other, clearly breaking the limbs.

This move drew another gasps from the crowd, but Gorias shouted, "Its all crap, their bodies aren't real."

Alena's head dropped as the forms crashed to the surface, wrestling. "Then what is the point of this?"

Gorias backed away and waved for the rest to do the same. "They have to take on shapes and shells to affect material objects. I'd have not been able to keep him busy like Rhiannon."

Nykia shouted, "Busy? Why busy?"

"Even a demon can be distracted, have an ego, and forget. They aren't gods, no matter how much they wanna act like it."

Hobbled, Pergamus got to his all fours, head quivering. Rhiannon stood behind and by the smile on his face, he didn't expect Pergamus to curl his wings back and lock up the god's arms. Pergamus used his wings to flip Rhiannon over his head, planting him into the surface with a thud. Pergamus sprang to his feet, legs restored and unbroken.

The last of Pergamus' fancy additions peeled away, he resembled Rhiannon on a larger scale. Gorias' heart sank as Pergamus crushed Rhiannon to the ground, foot in the pit of his back, and ripped the two leathery wings free. Rhiannon screeched and Gorias felt the tenor down to his toes. Pergamus held up the wings and laughed. He flapped them and mocked the fallen Rhiannon in a rapid series of curses Gorias couldn't keep up with.

Though Pergamus dropped the wings and reached into the holes of Rhiannon's back, a flapping sound still echoed across the rocky land. Pergamus tilted his head, looked around, curious at the sound and planted a knee in Rhiannon's back.

Those on the ground started to scoot backwards, eyes to the sky, frozen in fear at what floated there.

Three forms levitated above them, all in the shape of tall men in white linens, but the one in the middle stood out as different... for his body was born up on six wings instead of two like the beings that flanked him. Their wings weren't made up of layered feathers, but glittered like a series of polished metal shingles. The sound of beating sliced the air like the falling of a thousand swords. Their faces shone like flickering lightning, thick beams of white light pouring out and spreading, never ceasing to stream from their faces.

By his expression and from the yelping gasp, Pergamus

showed fear at last.

Gorias turned from the scene and got to his feet. "Run, you fuckers! This is the end!"

Nykia exclaimed, "But they're here for him, er, them, right?"

Gorias shoved her so hard Nykia almost fell. "They don't give a shit about us, so run for the ship!"

The beating of the gleaming wings stabbed into their ears, sharp and near tangible.

Gorias' ears popped as seams formed in the floor of the island. Everyone turned and ran for the ship, and Gorias followed suit, the last one out of the area as the two demons and the angelic host clashed. Radiance poured from the heavenly beings and their shine overlapped the struggling figures on the floor.

"Damn you, Rhiannon!" Pergamus wailed. "Damn you, Gorias La Gaul! I'll be waiting for you in the abyss!" His voice then became lost in the buzz of wings and crackles of energy. "I'll be waiting, you hear me? For you and all of your children!"

Gorias didn't look back and followed the rest as they ran down the slope that had led to the cavern. The hike up had taken several minutes, but the scramble down went quickly. A few fissures developed and Gorias saw one of the pirates fall down into the gap, then be spewed back into the air as ocean water exploded up in a slicing wave.

The shaking ground sent them all sprawling again, but the sight at the edge of the island made their hearts sink. The pirate vessel was no more, partially sunk, a portion moored to the trembling rock surface, busted asunder. A series of boulders had pelted the ship, destroying the masts, and breaking its spine.

Pinned to the rocks by an invisible force in the air, Gorias couldn't breathe as the mountains around them became dust and light belched up into a bubble around the caves. Under his shoulders, the shaking ground lost its hardness and turned to sand, then, to mud, and then, alas, water.

Gorias closed his eyes as the seawater rushed all around him. His armor heavy, he prepared for this final descent, but still spread out his limbs to best try and ride the waves. However, the current pulled him from the water and he broke the surface again. He thought it the backwash of the falling pieces of the island and thus, that he'd soon plummet into the deep anyway. True to his thoughts, the water sucked him down again. In moments, though, he broke the surface of the water and crashed across a sector of the destroyed pirate ship. Shaking his head free of water, clasping the piece of floating debris like it were gold, Gorias looked up and saw a yard above him the floating being with six wings.

"Fare you well, Gorias La Gaul. We keep our bargains." The baritone voice rippled across the waves, currents that peeled back at the beating of the lower four wings. The perfect, nearly sculpted face showed no emotion as it said, "Deliverance will come."

And the Seraphim was gone. He didn't fly into the sky; he just disappeared.

For a moment, Gorias buoyed along alone. He closed his eyes and breathed deeply. He never cried but almost felt like it. Almost.

CHAPTER XIII

LONG WAY HOME

Gorias clung to a floating section of the hull, bobbing in the water with Nykia suddenly up and on his back. "Get next to me, Princess, I ain't that strong."

Nykia slid off and swung a leg over the hull. Higher up in the water, she pointed to a few other survivors. "Look, Alena swims this way."

"I knew she'd make it."

"Knew or hoped?"

Gorias took great gasps of air. "Don't argue absolutes now."

Alena swam up and never took hold of the debris, content to trend ocean water for a moment. "Glad you two made it."

"Show off," Gorias laughed, betting those thighs of hers could crush a beer mug at will.

A loud bellow echoed and some of the glass balls of dragonfire bobbed to the surface with the Cytaur riding two of them. His one eye blinking fast, the creature gasped for air and hugged the balls of flickering light under his arms for support.

Allard rowed up in a small life raft undamaged from the destruction of the pirate vessel.

Gorias frowned. "That fuckin' guy and his luck, better than Orsen's." He thought for a moment and asked, "Where did Orsen get to?"

Alena took hold on the hull and swept her long locks out of her face. "He stayed with the army."

"Huh," Gorias pondered it but a second more. "Weird."

Nykia climbed in the boat and Alena started to, nearly tipping it over, but she made it in. In a few minutes, Gorias and the Cytaur also got inside the craft.

After several minutes of breathing hard and Allard rowing them a little distance from where they started, Nykia scanned the water and asked, "Is that all?"

Alena replied, "It appears so."

Nykia looked to Gorias. "Now what?"

Taking measured, deep breaths, Gorias motioned toward Allard. "Looks like we are headed back to Transalpina. I think with the old man rowing, we'll make it there in a couple years."

Alena slapped Allard's thigh and leaned back. "Relax a minute. We survived the wake of the island sinking. If anything else pops out to kill us…" She faced Gorias. "Are they gone?"

"Pergamus and Rhiannon? I'd say so, from this realm at least. Stories abound that the fallen ones who are reined in go to the abyss and can't get out again."

Nykia said, "I'd think if the angels are so powerful they could easily track down errant demons. Don't they leave footprints in the ether realm or give off signs of their evil ways?"

Gorias shrugged. "One would think. However, maybe they have better things to do than always be on patrol for their fallen brothers."

Alena asked, "Why wouldn't God or the gods tell these angels where the demons are hiding? Doesn't he know all?"

Gorias sighed loud. "I don't really feel like religious discussions now. What's next on this damned raft? Politics? Gardening?"

Alena and Nykia looked away opposite directions, miffed, but Allard smirked.

Gorias kicked Alena's boot. "Lighten up. Even the Cytaur is laughing at you two but ya can't tell."

Once she shot the Cytaur a hard look, Alena said, "It's not a wonder so many fall into false practices when the gods give out confusing signals."

Gorias settled back and breathed regularly. "It's a big universe, darlin' girl. We all try to put our visions of right, wrong and God in a tiny box. There's a day coming soon in the world, so they say, when if one has a little faith ya better get ready to whip it out and polish it finely."

Allard said, "Is it really true they say the gods will destroy the world for its wicked ways?"

Gorias rubbed his eyes. "That's the story. It's an old one."

Nykia asked, "Do you believe it?"

"Who knows?" Gorias yawned. "These things come in ages, if ya live long enough. Every generation thinks theirs is the last and they've got it all figured out. Who the hell could ever know?"

Alena stated, "For a man known to the angelic host, by name, have you ever heard tell of it?"

"The angels don't know dick about such things. They follow orders and take care of things."

Allard put down the paddle and pointed with his right hand. "I see our deliverance is at hand!"

All eyes stared at the sight of the huge naval vessel approaching on the sea over the horizon.

Despite the fact that Nykia and Alena exchanged glad looks, Gorias scowled. "The last time we saw the Transalpina navy, what happened?"

Deflated, the girls fell silent.

Allard offered, "Perhaps we can hope for the best?"

"Yeah," Gorias grunted. "If they ask us if we've seen the Bahamut, just act natural."

❖❖❖❖❖

They'd all talked it out and readied themselves for a couple eventualities. When Gorias saw Thynnes' face high up above them, he burst into laughter.

"Well, I've never been so happy to lay eyes on a prick, aside from the day my eldest son was born. Hey up there, ya old dog!"

Allard grabbed Gorias' wrist. "Don't you think kindness might be better than jovial slams?"

"Meh, he came all this way for us."

Nykia offered, "Hopefully not to make sure we're dead."

Thynnes cupped his hands around his mouth and shouted, "Ho down there! We're letting down a damned ladder for you all! The Queen will be overjoyed you are alive."

Gorias shouted back, "Not half as glad as we are."

In minutes, the rope ladder unraveled. Allard was quick to grab it and climb on. Nykia and Alena exchanged a look as Allard climbed fast above them.

Alena said to Nykia, "You go first. That way I'll break your fall if you drop."

Nykia blinked. "You're serious."

Alena replied, "Yes, Your Majesty."

With a sigh, Nykia climbed on the ladder. Alena waited until Allard got aboard before she put a boot on the first wrung.

Gorias slapped her ass and she twisted, grinning at him. He then got on the ladder after Nykia went up a ways.

Starting to climb up, Gorias heard Thynnes laughing. "Just what I need, another set of hands to turn the turbines." Gorias looked down to see the Cytaur, one hand on the rope ladder, one hoof still in the boat. Thynnes yelled down, "C'mon, ya bastard. I can use ya like always."

The Cytaur took one of the long horns and nudged Gorias' boot. Gorias reached down and took the horn, reading much in the look he received from the Cytaur. The creature then let go of the rope, turned his back on the vessel, and stepped into the sea. He sank like a stone, holding the other horn to his chest. A silence swept the scene, broken suddenly by Thynnes' laughter. Gorias looked down, armed up the horn under his armpit and shook his head.

After Thynnes chuckled at the Cytaur dying instead of returning to servitude, Gorias shook his head again and gazed across the sea.

Thynnes jeered him as he climbed, saying, "The mighty warrior of renown laments the passing of a creature not meant to be alive?"

"That's the easy way around it for some folks," Gorias replied, still looking away. "Those things, by common belief in humanity, shouldn't be alive in the first place, so, it's easy to treat them like monsters."

Thynnes' smile faded. "They're stupid beasts, not far from the cattle they were bred ill from."

Gorias shrugged and handed the long horn to Alena. "So you

say. It's a strange justification for abusing that which is different, granted. That one there under the waves? He fought like a warrior and was a pretty noble creature, all in all. I respect nobility wherever I can find it." Boots on the deck at last, he faced Thynnes. "God knows the upper crust in this world is lacking in what they drape themselves in, nobility."

Thynnes smiled again, then hooted heartily. "I'm glad you're alive, ya old sonofabitch, to bitch about the passing of a cow."

Orsen emerged from among the sailors and solders. Alena smiled at first, but her look hardened when she saw her sister, Milli. The two tall ladies said nothing to each other but took up positions flanking Nykia. Orsen walked over and smiled at Gorias.

"Kid, glad yer alive."

"And you as well, Lord La Gaul."

Nykia approached Gorias. "I never did tell you who the dragonfire was for in Transalpina, via our contacts."

Gorias stretched, then leaned back on the guardrail of the vessel. "I'm damned curious and have a few targets in mind. Any time ya would care to enlighten me with your version of the truth, go ahead."

Alena stepped in front of Nykia. "When Thynnes crucified one of the pirates, I gave him a merciful death and he told me it was the wizard, Yannick." She turned and faced Nykia. "Correct?"

Nykia blinked, mouth open, and nodded. Eyes cast down, she affirmed, "The same wizard who inked my tats here and those of Orsen, yes."

Gorias frowned. "That lying little twat. I'll gouge out his eyes..."

Alena added, "I suspected him from the start, Gorias. He must barter the fire to whoever is doing the killings in the capitol. I doubt he could sneak around and do such things, being who he is and all."

"Damn him," Gorias raged, fists clenched. "Make 'em a prognosticator and they still wanna roll the bones and do bad things. Rotten bastards." Gorias held out his arms. "I smell like Dagon's ass. Anywhere to get cleaned up on this berg?"

Thynnes turned to his officers and Colonel Schou stepped forward to say, "I believe there are shower facilities powered by a new device that purifies the sea water."

"Fantastic," Gorias replied, and then looked to the girls. "Alena, you and yer sister oughta get her a bit more presentable before meeting the Queen."

While Alena eyed Nykia, the pirate girl popped back; "I guess I have no more say in the matter?"

Hands dangling at his sides, Gorias snapped, "Not really, sister. Your friends and owners are dead or at the bottom of the sea." He looked at Allard and then back to Nykia. "I aim to see you deposited back into the safe graces of Queen Garnet and that'll be that." Gorias' eyes narrowed at her. "What? With all yer talk of me staying around…"

Thynnes chuckled. "She is contemplating riding off into the sunset with her hero, not staying behind to be a monarch."

Nykia's chin snapped up and her eyes blazed at the General. "Your future monarch, if you think about it long enough, old man."

Thynnes humor faded, but he took up no anger. "You aren't Queen yet, missy, and besides, I'm about too old to be a threat or scared of much."

Alena added, "It'd be wise to cultivate the respect of the military, ma'am."

Nykia trembled for a moment, like walls enclosed her.

Gorias said gently, "You'll be fine. Garnet ain't dying any time soon. She'll learn ya good like it should be. Now, go wash up and let's get something to eat. I ain't nowhere near as young as I used to be." He then looked across the waters. "And this thing ain't quite done, yet."

Alena started to loosen her tunic and asked Gorias, "Once this is over, where is next for you?"

"I might just go see my grandson in Shynar. I haven't seen him in a long time."

Thynnes coughed and spat. "Shynar? Cradle of the world? Bah, there is bad witchery from Lord Nosmada's realm near there. I'd stay away if I were you."

"But you aren't me," Gorias reminded him. "It's a bitch being me, but hey, it's been fun so far. Kinda. Naw, Maddox is a good lad and I need to see him."

Alena's head tilted at Gorias, reading much into his words and mannerisms. She turned away and started toward the captain's cabin.

While the others shrank away, Nykia approached Gorias. "You say you're going to see your grandson in Shynar. That's halfway around the world, from what I remember. Will you come back?"

"Sure," Gorias said with a smile. "I promise."

"Please don't lie to me."

"I'm not, but I'm gettin' old, sweetheart. I might meet God on the plains of Shynar. If I do, well…"

"He might be pissed?"

Gorias shook his head. "God loves guys like me. He has a hard-on for warriors, for we send so many souls to Hell for him."

"That's just crazy."

"Kinda sounds funny, though."

⁂⁂⁂⁂⁂

Several hours passed before Gorias La Gaul again stepped onto the deck. He'd cleaned up down below deck in the sailors' quarters and even let one of the lads wipe down his armor. He'd watched the sailor, maybe sixteen years old, probably simple if in the service so young, caress the nails on his armlets. Surely, dreams billowed in the head of that sailor, he mused, but Gorias didn't ask.

After he cleaned up and took care of necessities, he lay down in one of the sailor's bunks. His joints ached and tremors stabbed across the left side of his chest. Eyes closed, he breathed steadily, trying to recall mental games he'd learned to lower the pounding in his ears. In minutes, this dissipated, but as he laid his forearm across his face, Gorias understood his time was limited.

Eyes closed, he slipped into slumber, dreaming of times gone by, but awaking with a start as the simple sailor spoke to him.

"Lord La Gaul?"

"I'm not a...what is it?"

"Your breathing was so shallow, sir, I thought maybe..."

"I passed on? Soon enough, kid. How long have I slept?"

"Over an hour, sir."

"I see."

"Your armor is done."

"Thanks."

"It really is from a baby dragon, isn't it?"

"A wyrmling, yeah."

"You skinned it and hollowed it out?"

Gorias looked over at the youth. "I'm sure ya have heard stories about it."

"I wouldn't have thought I'd ever see it, sir."

"I can't say that I thought I'd live this long, son. Be of good cheer. Ya have many years left."

"I've heard tell the world will end someday."

"Everything dies, son."

The sailor looked both ways, his voice lower. "What have you heard?"

"That the world will be destroyed by the supreme God."

"Why would he do this?"

"Why not? If he made us, our bitching about fairness doesn't matter a helluva lot, does it? Enjoy life while ya can, kid. Now, come back and get me in an hour and I'll give ya some coins. I won't need them when I leave this land."

Once re-dressed and ready, Gorias indeed gave the sailor a small bag of coins from the belt Alena saved before he strolled onto the deck.

Near the aft portion of the vessel, staring at the paddles, he found Orsen. Also cleaned and re-dressed, Orsen only gave Gorias a slow look, returning his gaze to the turbine's efforts.

A dull silence reigned for many minutes before Orsen said slowly, "Aren't you going to ask me how I am?"

"Naw, I can smell ya and tell that you're drunk, but even not so, I wager ya ain't well."

Orsen held up a flask and then upended it to the deck, showing it empty. "It's a wonderful day."

Gorias thought, *Yeah, sucks when everything ya believe in gets turned around.* "What are ya gonna do?"

"I got drunk. That was first on my list."

"Couldn't hurt."

"But I'll be straight soon enough. There are many things to decide, soon."

"I can guess what's on your mind."

"Really?"

Gorias nodded, hand on the rail. "You're gonna kill Crown Prince Vincent, aren't ya?"

"I must discover if he's a copy."

His voice tired and showing some anger, Gorias snapped, "I saw his form on the tree in Pergamus. Prince Vincent is a fake, just like Garnet thought he was. Weird, huh?"

"I know," Orsen muttered and fell silent, sucking on the flask again, hoping for more liquor.

"Just let me do it, or Alena. She'd love that, I bet."

Orsen shook his head. "I must. You two would rouse the guards. Mavik will be expecting me back. She will let me right in. Her guard Harlan will kill me soon after."

"Better take Alena or her sister along."

"Maybe. Mavik won't say much if I do bring her."

"I wonder if she knows, ol' Mavik."

"I wonder if she cares. She has her son, that's all that matters to an aging royal right now, no?"

"Yeah, I suppose. She'll take it hard. Reality is a bitch."

"I must do this to show the Queen I'm loyal to her."

"Ya think Garnet won't figure ya were in bed with Mavik and her offspring, all for the benefit of Niva?"

Orsen twisted his head, facing Gorias. "Only you could work that out, you and Milli, I think."

"A lucky guess, though I have no proof. Watch yer ass, son. This drama will end really badly for somebody. I just got a feeling. If it's me, that's fine. I've lived long enough."

Up from his backside, Orsen grimaced. "As you might say, sir, how fucking noble of you."

Gorias gave a mock bow.

Orsen said, "You will ride off and we'll be left to patch up Transalpina."

"Ya guys let it get all screwy in the first place."

"I understand, but it's easy for you. Arrive, kill and leave, no worries."

"There're always worries."

"I must do what I must do, Gorias."

"I salute ya for it."

Gorias thought of Orsen in his double dealing with the monarchs, serving both and ready to stay with who won. However, Mavik wouldn't take his destruction of Vincent well, even if Garnet did. He wondered what Mavik would do with Orsen when he exposed her son. Gorias swallowed and stared at the sea, understanding Mavik would never get a chance to expose Orsen.

"Ya got yer work cut out, Orsen."

"As do you," he replied placidly.

"You have been one lucky bastard, though, so I reckon you'll be fine."

"If you think this terminates at the cottage of the wizard, you're mistaken."

"I've been wrong before."

❊❊❊❊❊

Alena entered Nykia's cabin, seeing her naked, wiping herself down. Clean and wearing naval togs herself, Alena walked across the room, grabbed a large metal pitcher and poured water into a cup.

Nykia wiped her legs down and said blithely, "You were lying your ass off on the deck about Yannick."

Alena took a drink. "Of course, and you went right along with me, like a good monarch being led by her advisor."

"Why did you lie?" Nykia demanded, not covering her

241

nakedness to her.

Eyebrow raised, Alena looked her over. "Why did you, Princess?"

Nykia's eyes narrowed, "I hate the damned wizard and Gorias will kill Yannick now."

"Not Niva, as you know to be true, and what the dying man told me."

"Correct."

Alena pointed at Nykia's pelvis. "Does Gorias realize you have that?"

Towel away from her pubic ridge, Nykia's fingertips touched the tattoo of Gorias La Gaul that straddled the tip of her clitoris. "No, he failed to examine me that close."

"Yannick?"

Nykia nodded, head down.

"Gorias doesn't realize its magic and he was compelled to have sex with you?"

"I doubt if he needed magic."

"True."

"I've drawn images of my hero my entire life. Years ago I had Yannick do this, hoping someday his magic would compel Gorias to be near me."

"I don't think that little thing can make him stay with you, though."

Nykia covered herself and turned away. "I'm sure you're right."

Stepping in a semicircle, Alena related, "I have no love of Niva, but Yannick, I agree, he's trouble."

"If Niva is behind the dragonfire deaths and the use of it like Gorias said, to build some portal for dragon souls, the transfer of Pergamus for hiding in the coming destruction of the Earth..."

"Her supply is cut off now," Alena quipped fast. "She'll heel into line seeing the wizard fall."

Nykia patted the sailor togs laid out for her. "Would that both were gone."

Alena smiled. "Patience...Your Majesty." She performed a

mild curtsey.

"I'm sure I'll ever be at ease seeing people do that to me."

Boots flat on the floor, Alena's brows lowered. "I'm better to have as a friend, a confidant and a defender than an enemy, your highness." Menace flowed from the tall woman as she explained, "I won't mention that again. You should think about the future, really."

Nykia turned from her, eyes closed, doing just that.

"Let's get some air, Your Majesty."

Only a few steps later on the deck, Nykia and Alena approached a smaller soldier, heaving his guts over the side of the ship.

"Alena tells me you're called Ellis?"

The youth wiped his mouth with a sleeve and turned from the side of the ship. "Yes, miss."

"You're not much of a sailor."

Ellis looked down at his army uniform. "I'm not much of a soldier, either."

"Alena tells me you were an apprentice and your father was a magus, even more powerful than Yannick, which probably explains his death."

Head shaking, Ellis denied it. "No, miss, not me."

Nykia glanced down the way at the other soldiers and stepped closer, her voice low, though no one could hear, and said, "Oh, stop it this minute. You can trust me. I'm not one of them."

The green tint in Ellis' skin faded some and he disagreed. "On the contrary, miss, you will soon be the head of them. I am no necromancer."

Hands to her hips, she asked, "Do I look like a typical monarch?"

"Absolute authority changes people, miss. I'd hate for you to recall me years from now and decide you needed to illuminate your garden with my burning flesh."

Alena held her hand to her mouth, suppressing a laugh but Nykia raged, "Oh stop it. I'm not that tight-assed."

"Why do you care? What is it you want from me?"

"Tell my fortune, or give me a horoscope. Such things aren't completely forbidden."

Eyebrow raised, Ellis shrugged. "I can try. Let's go inside, please? This sea air makes me wretch."

"You get used to it after a while," Nykia replied, motioning him to follow her to the captain's cabin.

"I fear the ground is my ally like the stars of heaven would be, if I were indeed a prognosticator prime."

Nykia winked. "If I am ever Queen, you may well be."

"I don't know…"

"Do you want to be in the military forever?"

"No."

"Then stick with me, kid. We might go places."

Clearly thinking her words over, Ellis followed and seemed elated to sit down at the table of the cabin. He jumped a little when Alena opened the door and closed it behind her.

Nykia assured him, "It's all right. You can say what you please in front of her."

Ellis' face flushed, more frightened of the Queen's guard than Nykia.

"Do either of you have a hairpin?"

The women exchanged a look, but Nykia said, "We aren't too proper, neither one of us."

Alena asked, "Do you need a pinprick of blood?"

Ellis nodded. "Sorry, but it's required."

With a fast move that made Ellis jump, Alena yanked her dagger from his belt. "Do you want to me to do it?"

Ellis shook his head. "I must be the one." He took the knife, raised his eyebrows at the point. "It's seen action."

"Surprised?"

"No," said Ellis and wiped the tip on his own pants, then licked the tip. "My fluid cleanses and will set the magick to work. Nykia? Your left hand?"

"Why not the right?"

Ellis blinked. "I'm the prognosticator, miss. The left hand is always the way. It is in opposition with the rest of the body, the left hand path and all. It will betray your truth. It will show the things you hide, even as simple as a future."

Nykia rolled her eyes and let her left hand lay flat on the table.

Ellis then inserted his left hand under hers in the opposite direction. He took the knife and posed it above the center of her palm. "The cut will be slight and I only need a drop. Once I draw blood, please turn it over and let it drop to my hand. Ready?"

Nykia sighed. "Get on with it."

With a few words the women couldn't understand, Ellis made the cut, twice like a small cross. He then took the knife and wiped the bloody tip on his right eyelid. With his right hand he rubbed his eye and then nodded for her to turn her hand over. Nykia did so, letting the blood drip into his palm.

"Spit into my hand," Ellis told her.

"What?" Nykia laughed.

"Spit on the blood."

Nykia glanced at Alena before doing so.

Ellis then spit into his hand and promptly made a fist. Right eye closed, the other rolled back, Ellis muttered more words in a tongue they found pointless. Right eye open, the whites full of blood, Ellis then looked down and opened his hand.

"Your life line bears a fracture, more than one. That's not surprising. I see glories in your life and much death and pain."

"Will La Gaul stay with me?"

Ellis breathed shallow. "Gorias' time is near to done. I can't see him spending a future in Transalpina or anywhere else."

Frustrated, Nykia grimaced, but Alena raised her hands, begging indulgence.

Ellis' face twitched, his narrow chin fell and he said, "You're future is cloudy, but full of light, however…"

Nykia slammed her hands on the table. "What?"

Eyes slowly moving up from the bowl, he said, "You're not alone in your flesh."

"Huh? I'm possessed?"

"Not with demon, with child." Ellis shrugged, smiling a little. "I don't know if that's good news, but you're pregnant."

Nykia blinked several times, rapid. "But…" her look of shock became one of excitement and she faced Alena. "I've only been with Gorias! Never another man for years!"

Emotionlessly, Alena said, "Congratulations. The Queen will get an heir and more, then."

Nykia stared at Ellis. "Are you certain?"

"Fairly sure. The portents and magic don't lie. However, I'd wait to see if you miss your time."

Nykia headed for the door and Alena stepped aside, saying, "Be careful depositing such news on the old hero."

"What?"

Alena reflected, looking at Ellis. "He may not think its wonderful news considering all he's been through. You may choose to ignore my words, but I advise you to wait until you're sure before blurting that out to him."

Deflated somewhat, Nykia pondered her words. "You're right, I guess. I'll see if I can live with all that."

"It's natural to be elated, miss," Alena nodded. "To be sure is better. You can do as you desire, though. He's so very tired and grim, now, as he knows there's more to do in this ordeal."

Nodding vigorously, Nykia agreed. "You're right." Head down, Nykia departed the cabin.

Ellis rose up but Alena took a few steps toward him, right hand resting on the hilt of her dagger. Ellis swallowed and gaped at her. He looked at the open door and saw a near replica of Alena fill the frame. This blonde woman closed the door.

Alena said, "There's something else I need you to do, prognosticator." She then pulled her dagger again and licked it clean.

CHAPTER XIV

RECKONING DAY

The wizard exited his cottage and walked into the herbal garden. He stopped cold at the sight of Gorias, Nykia, Alena and Orsen. Yannick's look of horror couldn't be denied. He gaped and tried to backpedal, but Gorias bridged the distance between them with a few strides.

"You little cocksucker," Gorias fumed, his right hand seizing Yannick's robe near the hood, and his left hand jabbing the old man in the belly. Yannick gasped and lurched, but Gorias refused to let him fall. "Stand up, you lying fuck."

Yannick winced. "I'm no warrior."

Gorias bellowed into his face, "I don't care. Your damned games sent me nearly to my death. All of that other bullshit and games with the throne are one thing, but you nearly killed me! That's something I cannot forgive."

"I may have misled you a little…"

Lifting Yannick from the ground, Gorias snarled close to his face as if to bite him. "You misled my balls!" At this Alena, who'd been standing smartly with her hands on her hips, had to cover her mouth with her right hand, and she even wore a wry grin as Gorias threw the wizard to the cobblestone path through the plants.

"Please…"

"The guards aren't coming and if they did, they'd die as well."

Yannick gasped in several breaths. "You mean to murder me here?"

"Why not? Give me a reason not to cut out your heart and stomp it in the mud."

Yannick looked up, his gaze stopping on Nykia.

Gorias stepped closer to him and the wizard cowered down again. "That's right, this is the real one, not a copy running around or a bitch delivering dragonfire. I've brought her home, contrary to the wishes of you and whoever it is you serve here that doesn't want a proper heir to the throne."

Yannick rasped, "She'll need an heir herself."

Reaching down, Gorias fumbled in the folds of Yannick's hood until he grabbed his ear. He lifted Yannick up and pressed his mouth close to his ear. "Maybe I've already taken care of that. Now, tell me who is really the slave to Pergamus? Tell me the truth and I'll think about maiming you and not ripping your head off."

"You think my life matters to me?"

Gorias raged loud again, drawing the attention of guards on distant walls, whom Alena waved off. They still looked on as Gorias said, "Don't bullshit with me. You feared death so damned much you went to extraordinary lengths to prolong your miserable existence. You endowed someone here in Qesot with dragonfire, someone with an ire for the world, anyway. Who is it?"

"Niva," Yannick whispered, breaths coming in and out fast.

Gorias dropped him and blinked.

Alena's jaw dropped. "The Abbess of the temple?"

Nykia said, "He could be lying again."

Over and over, Yannick shook his head. "No, it's her. You can see the proof in her flesh. I marked her deep with the images of the dragon and the fire within. You will see it and know I speak the truth."

Gorias looked at Orsen, who stood frozen in shock by the gate. "I guessed Mavik. Ain't I the squirrel's nuts?"

Orsen agreed. "That was my fear as well."

Nykia said, "Mavik is a dupe, if you think on it long enough. She got what she wanted, a pittance in the world as a whole. Her darling son reborn."

Alena swallowed. "A fake son? How can she live with that idea?"

Gorias said, "I'd bet Traveler on it. I doubt Vincent knows."

Orsen swallowed hard, eyes closed. "We all assume she even knows. She might be ignorant of that reality. I shall deal with Mavik and Vincent."

All eyes looked to the youth but when they looked in his

eyes, they took him at his word.

Alena said, "I'll take Nykia to Garnet. She'll want to see her, but in time. I will get her washed up a bit and changed in the lower tower."

Nykia smirked. "You're hot stuff yourself, sister."

Her good-natured grin fading, Alena replied, "I'm not your sister, just a servant of the Queen. My duty will soon be discharged."

Nykia wore a blank look as she turned to Gorias. "What shall you do?"

"I have to stop Niva. This has to end here."

Alena stepped forward. "You can't go alone. Wait until I take Nykia in and then..."

"No, that is somethin' I cannot wait for." Gorias said with firmness. "You girls go on back to the tower. Orsen, this is the day your Lord has made for you. Use it as ya must. I advise takin' Milli Appra along if ya wanna live to see tomorrow. That may make it more interesting." He looked down at Yannick. "I'll be back for you, ya lyin' prick."

Nykia pointed at the wizard. "How can we trust him? He may run."

Gorias shrugged. "Where's he gonna go? The guards aren't gonna let him out, not now, so let him brood here."

Nykia gave Yannick a look near to fright. "What if he uses his powers?"

"By all means, let him if he still can. If he does, though, then I'll keep my promise and see him cut to pieces, slowly."

❖❖❖❖❖

In the apex of Garnet's tower, Alena curtseyed and stood back a few paces from Nykia. Hands clasped behind her back, clad again in fresh togs for her position, she saw the Queen's disappointment when she studied Nykia. Alena felt glad Garnet did not burst into tears and rush to embrace her granddaughter, for laughter would've been impossible to suppress.

Her floor-length skirts making no sound on the polished

floor, Garnet took a few steps toward Nykia. "I'm glad to see you again."

After a sheepish shrug, Nykia said, "I'm here."

"And here you will stay," Garnet said smartly, eyes riveted to the girl. "I comprehend the life you've been subjugated to and the things learned in exile amongst the pirates, but that time is past. You must see to finishing your education, training and means of being the proper heir."

Nykia opened her mouth, Alena figured to object, but never said anything. *Good for you*, Alena mused.

Her voice still stern, but dropping a bit in force, Garnet said, "I know I cannot drive a nail into rock, at least not with ease, my dear, but you were born better than most. I've returned you to me at a great cost to our land, whatever the public will be told or chooses to believe be damned. You are the last heir to the throne of Transalpina." Garnet took a step closer. "I understand young Ellis has told you there is another heir already."

Nykia nodded.

The Queen said gently, "You may speak. I'm flattered you've held your vile tongue, but I'm no simpering maid. Speak freely for we will be near often in the future."

"Ellis the wizard, um, prognosticator…"

"Very good," Garnet said with a sardonic smile.

"…cast the forecast." Nykia's thin fingers ran over her belly. "I've conceived."

"And Gorias La Gaul is of a royal house, whether he cares to admit it or not."

"I'm proud to carry his child."

Garnet's smile faded. "Don't act like an idiot, girl. Legitimizing the bastard will be interesting work, but we can do it. The world may think this the seed of some pirate, not a royal line, and see fit to object."

A hurt look on her face, Nykia said, "Gorias wouldn't deny it."

Garnet threw back her head for a moment when she laughed, then faced the girl. "Gorias doesn't give a good damn, Princess. A great thing about being royalty is that sometimes, your will can be absolute. We'll make an announcement and massage the truth a little."

Nykia watched her turn away and said, "Gorias said he is off to Shynar soon, to see his grandson."

Garnet didn't turn back. "That may well be, but he'll not leave without making the declaration of parenthood and matrimony. He'd not disappoint me." She never looked at Alena, but said, "Take care of her, Alena. Get her in proper quarters, rewashed and ready. She's your responsibility now."

Alena nodded. "Yes, mum."

The two departed the Queen and went down several steps before Nykia asked, "How long will I be your responsibility?"

"Until you die."

* * * * *

Orsen dressed himself properly in his best attire. After all, he was going into the presence of royalty. He brought along two of Alena's sisters, Dani and Milli, the former a brunette, but a near copy of the tall fighter he'd been around for days. The guards and staff in Mavik's home and estate made no great deal of these ladies, as Mavik wasn't her sister's enemy. Orsen oft visited Vincent and Mavik with one of the tall girls or a castellan, like he did that day. The bodyguard Harlan, his manner smart and taut, followed along, bored, hands behind his back.

Castellan Turenball walked along with Orsen as well, his shaven head glistening in the lanterns' light, and greeted Mavik warmly as they entered. Two male guards gave Dani and Milli questioning looks, but didn't stop them as they followed Orsen into the inner lounge chamber. Harlan stopped by the door, blocking the exit. The girls flanked the doorway, which Orsen left open to the receiving hall where Turenball and Mavik chatted.

Vincent sat in a recliner chair by the window, the warm sun on his face, placidly reading a parchment and enjoying his afternoon.

Orsen bowed and left this head low as Vincent turned to face him.

"I'm glad to see you back," Vincent said softly. "Is this terrible business nearly over with?"

Still bowed, Orsen stood up sharply, his right hand sweeping out with a curved blade, slicing Prince Vincent's neck clear across. For a brief moment, nothing happened, only ruptured skin. Orsen feared he erred badly, but soon, a black ooze ran from the injured Prince's throat. Vincent made no hasty move of distress, nor did he cry out and feign terror. He looked down at his tunic, touched the silky fabric with his hands, and marveled at the black liquid on his fingers.

The two guards outside drew their short swords and shouted in alarm. Harlan swung his arms out and ran forward past the Appra sisters. The guards' surprise ended fast as Dani and Milli swung into their paths on opposite sides of the door, gutting them from crotch to their sternums, each starting and stopping with two daggers apiece, cutting equal-sized trenches in flesh.

Harlan pulled his knife and his sword, stopping not a yard from Orsen. When Orsen turned, he saw Harlan's face frozen with shock at the state of Prince Vincent. Orsen passed his blade to his left hand and made a swipe at Harlan while he reached for his pants pocket. Harlan quickly swiped his sword, knocking the curved kill knife away, but in the open space his extended arms provided, Orsen withdrew his hand from his pocket. Hardly any momentum was needed as the experienced slinger flung the tiny bolo up at Harlan, who did react fast, stabbing out with his knife. The bolo wrapped about his left wrist, but one of the steel spheres on the ends of the flying string swung about, striking Harlan in the teeth, knocking two out. This moment of shock was all Orsen needed as two pig sticker blades popped from Harlan's chest. Confused, the powerful man gaped down at the bloody metal rods coming out of his chest. His knees wavered as scarlet gouted from his wounds and he fell to his knees.

Dani and Milli drew out their pig stickers as Orsen grabbed Harlan's knife from his hand. He slit the bodyguard's throat with his own weapon and stood back as the big man fell, his blood puking all over the finely woven rug.

Lady Mavik took a single step forward, mouth agape at what Orsen did to her son, but stopped her advance upon seeing what the Appra sisters did to her guards. Gagging on her words at first, Mavik screamed, "Vincent!" at last.

Orsen said calmly, "This isn't Vincent, ma'am. He's dead with the rest of the souls on Pergamus now."

Still confused, Vincent looked to Mavik. "Mother?"

Uncaring of the guards, Mavik pulled up her huge skirts and ran to her son, just as Orsen stabbed him in the belly with an uppercut swipe and pulled up. The new seam in the Prince allowed a gush of black fluid and tendrils to slip out, long things that masqueraded as intestines, but looked like stems of weeds. Tears soaked her face and Mavik wailed, stopping short of her son.

Orsen oft wondered which direction her trembling breakdown came from that resulted in dropping to her knees before her unraveling son. Was she thrown into the fit due to the revelation that her son really was a false object and that all of her faith in Niva had been a lie? Did she know Vincent was a glorified puppet and not really care, as long as she had her son, or means to power? Alas, he pondered, they'd never know. The old girl clasped her face with both hands, smearing the tears and her make-up before her hands clutched her chest. Mavik's gasps became short, then sounded awfully winded.

When Orsen drew a fresh dagger from his belt and turned toward her, making his intention painfully obvious, Mavik saved him the vile act and fell to the floor shined with blood and wax. Her eyes open, the pools of black liquid dripping from Vincent making a border around her face, Mavik breathed her last.

Vincent looked down at her and squeaked, "Mama?"

Milli gritted her teeth. "Finish it, Orsen."

Orsen turned back toward the thing that was a Prince and stabbed him with the fresh blade. Vincent made no move to stop him, nor did he fall from the gouge to his kidney.

Dani declared, "Stand back, we'll cut it to pieces."

As the two women waded in, chopping at Vincent like he was a practice log, Turenball shouted, "Leave the head in tact! We'll need proof beyond just my witness to this form of the truth!"

Orsen stepped back and let the sisters vivisect Vincent into over a dozen parts. He rubbed his eye, watching the power hungry Castellan, more than happy to throw in with them to get Garnet's will done. Orsen thought of La Gaul and his words, knowing Turenball's tongue couldn't be trusted for very long and that he'd end up killing him soon enough.

But not today. Today was a day of exposing all evil in Transalpina. He hoped Gorias La Gaul had luck. He'd pray he had luck, but Orsen didn't have anything left to pray to. He looked to his tattoo for luck and saw it had all but disappeared.

❖❖❖❖❖

Standing before the long wooden doors of the shrine to Our Lady of Great Sorrows, Gorias thought about returning to the garden to chop Yannick's head off. Surely, the wizard lied about the Abbess of this temple, Gorias thought, and the worker of the dragonfire couldn't really reside in this convent. A burly man in a black overcloak opened the door. Gorias bowed his head and thought, *They even have eunuchs as doormen, what a joint.* No other sort of man would exist in such a place where women were cloistered. The name Metrose walked across Gorias' mind, but he let it go.

"Is Mother Niva in?" Gorias asked the thick-set man politely, hands shifting an oblong object in a sack lodged under his right arm. He laid eyes on him, recognizing him as the other of two he'd seen before, opposite of the one he'd watched burn at the Keep. "I hear she runs this devotional establishment, correct?"

Pushing his cowl back, the eunuch gave him a suspicious look, up and down Gorias' closed new cloak. "Abbess Niva? You are from Her Majesty, the Queen?"

"Is that hard to believe?"

"That she would send a warrior instead of a Castellan for recompense transfer, yes, that's odd."

Gorias let the words *recompense transfer* turn in his brain a moment before saying, "My turn came up, brother, so ya gotta take what ya get."

The head of the eunuch seemed to change color as the torches within the stone sanctuary reflected off his bald pate. With a confused look, he let the long doors swing out and gave Gorias a welcome sign from his goddess.

Stepping into the foyer of the massive holy place, Gorias' eyes focused on the rows of kneeling benches that led toward the front of the sanctuary and the great image of the goddess Ernytel. Though he'd seen many smaller icons of the deity Ernytel in his life, seldom outside the west-coastal realms of Transalpina, Gorias was impressed by the main representation of said goddess. Though swathed in robes and winding cloths, it was clear that Ernytel sported wide hips, an enormous bosom, and full lips. He face in person was far more alluring than the dull icon reliefs, he noted. Behind her flickered many candles, by the shadows on the distant wall, a place hard to access because of the heights of benches and no ready-made steps.

Holding the oblong pouch in both hands, Gorias said to the servant, "Awful nice for such a brow-beating goddess of morality, aye?"

The bald man frowned and said, "I will send an acolyte for Mother Niva. I doubt she conducts personal audiences for such matters."

"I'm a new courier," Gorias lied to him. "This kinda of transaction happen a lot?"

Raising a thin eyebrow, the eunuch replied, "Only when there is need." The eunuch adjusted his cowl, turned and departed.

Waiting until the servant left, Gorias walked closer to the goddess statue. Ernytel stood behind a thin, velvety retaining rope, before a half dozen rectangular holes in the floor. On closer inspection, Gorias guessed they were ritual baths or cleansing points for new converts. Unsure of all of the tenets of Ernytel's religion, aside from the behavioral purity rules he heard joked of in taverns, Gorias surmised the baptisms as akin to any other religion. Each small chamber was devoid of water, though.

His curiosity at a high ebb, he leapt up like a kid climbing a fence and climbed over the barrier. His legs swung down and he walked around toward the back of the great idol, thinking he'd behold devotion candles. He stepped about the goddess and let out a mild groan. Up the entire opposite side of the figure was a mimicked copy of Pergamus' tree, all made up with flickering dragonfire in glass balls, but so many slots were empty.

He climbed down and stood before the backside of the goddess, shaking his head. Gorias then bowed his head, his hands pushed together at odd angles, and he prayed. His breaths steady, but deep, Gorias thought in his mind about words to God, and asked for him to make him strong.

"Your mind is in awe of the goddess, and my Tree of Life behind her," a low, feminine voice filtered out in the vast chamber. "She makes the hardest man consider his place in the universe."

Gorias looked around the goddess toward the doorway where the eunuch disappeared. Of course, Mother Niva wouldn't come to see him from there, he said to himself with a flippant voice. She'd make a grander entrance.

Not to disappoint Gorias' theories, the tall form in dark vestments fluttered around the left side of the giant idol of Ernytel. Unlike the common, cowled robe of the servants, Mother Niva wore a long houppelande gown made from silken damask fabrics. Gorias thought the black-work embroidery on the edges of the outfit, right up to the barbe under her chin, were a bit much for such a modest deity.

"She's sort of hard to miss," Gorias replied, looking up at the goddess' image. "No matter what a fella believes, that there stands an impressive work of art."

"Ernytel's image inspires and enthralls better than any artist's handicraft," Mother Niva said shortly, her arms folded under her gown. "But you're not here to admire her self nor to take up her edicts, are you?" Her voiced lowered, but held no fear as she said, "Gorias La Gaul."

"Ma'am," Gorias nodded at her recognition. "A wizard or prognosticator tells me you are who I'm looking for in this mess. By the dragonfire balls decorating the back of your goddess in a mosaic, I'd say he may be telling the truth this time."

Her arched nose rose as hazel-colored eyes widened at him. "I see. Now, I wonder why that old devil has confessed such a thing to you, La Gaul."

Gorias shrugged and his fingers flexed on the canvas bag he held. "Well, he was beholden to you at first. He performed the service you required to get enough gold to buy the balms for his own mystical cure. He gave what you wanted, the magic even your goddess couldn't give."

Niva's long fingers touched the top of her gown. Her manner was icy as she responded, "My goddess…"

Gorias' right hand fumbled with the straps on the pouch as he said, "Your goddess is so much stone, save for the sacrifices and belief ya put in her. She couldn't give you the feeling you needed, that feeling that only revenge can give."

Eyes flaring, she snapped, "How could you know any of that?"

"I've been everywhere, sister, um, mother…" Gorias opened the pouch and held it gingerly. "…nothing quite as passionate as religious furor, save for religious folks who get really pissed when their god or goddess comes up short. What did those castellans do to you to merit such death? Ya got gold here and plenty of means. Ya mean to tell me ya couldn't have hired them guys' throats slit? Why burn 'em to death with dragonfire? That seems like overkill to me."

Fingers digging into the gown under her neckpiece, Niva said, "Hard to get one past a legend, eh, La Gaul? Certainly, you comprehend retribution and the lengths one will travel to make the world right."

"I understand plenty, sure. Barbecuing these politicians with dragonfire, well, I cannot say if their crimes warranted such a death or not, but the means to do it…why go that far?"

"I'm a woman, La Gaul," her pale skin flushed pink as she unbuttoned her gown at the top. "My strength is only so great in my arms, no matter how strong my heart is. To hire these men killed, well, that wouldn't be the same as doing it myself, no?"

Gorias put his hand in his pouch. "Yeah, I know the sentiment. I like to see the look in a man's eyes when he knows the gig is up. That's something I readily confess to, but it kinda grows on ya once you've seen a legion of men die."

She nodded. "You see? We're not so different! You understand it well, this feeling to be better, and one my goddess couldn't accomplish."

Gorias watched her hand work the gown open and then both of her hands spread her dress wide. The abbess dropped the gown and Gorias beheld the images tattooed on her body. From Niva's knees, curled up her thighs, over her belly, curling about her breasts were the depictions of dragons, blue and red. Almost mirror images on either side of her body, their mouths and lips terminated at the nipples. Unlike artist's imaginings Gorias' had seen, these were more reptilian, finned and scaly...just like real dragons. The detail was high quality, for Gorias knew the number of wings on a red dragon was six, not two or four...and this rendering had it right.

"Great work that Yannick does," Gorias commented as he drew the oblong shape out from his canvas bag. "So, Yannick endows you with dragon fire, mystically placed in the images of the dragons, called forth from beyond with his magic. That comes at a heavy cost, ma'am."

Niva looked at his hand and saw the dragon-skinned object he held. She grinned. "The bastard in my belly was created by one of them. No loss that life, so the exchange was simple, a life for a life, but not mine. The lives of the men who wronged me were promised to the forces beyond along with their bastard."

"Which Castellan was the father?"

Niva retorted, "Doesn't matter. All of them could've been. They were all guilty in using me back then. They are men, typical hogs, and wanted no responsibility." She leered at what he held. "You think that will save you, don't you?"

Gorias dropped the bag and held up his helmet, an object created from the hollowed-out skull of a wyrmling dragon and placed it over his head, securing it to the neck plates of his armor. The visor was still up as he said, "I've fought authentic dragons, sister, breathing fire and trying to crush my ass for jollies. Yer a jilted bitch with an attitude problem about her own goddess and her own failings. I'm not a horny castellan, out to get points in Heaven by screwing the Mother Superior of the temple, so I ain't gonna go to a secluded tavern to get my ass roasted alive."

"What do you care?" she asked simply, no anger in her words. "You don't like Yannick. You could care less about our territory, to be exact. All you yearn for is enough gold for your own whoring, La Gaul, or are the legends about you counterfeit? The great swordsman is also a lover of enormous capacity, yet spends no time to fall in love. He goes the easy route."

"Your judgment doesn't amount to crap in a satchel to me, Niva," Gorias said and put his visor down. "Deliverance will come."

Gorias disengaged his swords and Niva's hands went to her bare hips. The lines of the tats glowed orange like the sunset. Her smile ceased as the areolas of her breasts glowed ginger and dragonfire sprang forth from her nipples. Gorias turned, placing a forearm over his face as the two jets of flame struck his frame. The liquidy fire saturated his body as he took a few steps toward Niva. As the fire continued to rage, Niva laughed, challenging La Gaul.

Arms to his sides, Gorias' new cloak fell in tatters, almost completely consumed by the dragonfire. Gold coins fell from the burning cloth, jingling on the stone floor. However, the fiery substance was repelled by his dragon-plated armor.

"Let's dance, sister," Gorias roared, unsure if the woman spewing dragon flame could hear him or not. Swiping his swords, and advancing, Gorias met two new streams of the liquidy fire as they erupted from her bosom. She screamed, backing away, as Gorias pushed the streams off with his mysterious blades like a man would push through heavy bracken in a forest. The lines of dragonfire peeled off like dead snakes, but only coiled about the base of the statue, not burning out right away.

Soon, it was clear what Gorias aimed for and Niva backed up, waving a hand to repel the attack. Niva stepped back again and aimed herself at the floor, bathing a soup of dragonfire on the slick flooring. The warrior waded through the fire. Gorias boots walked in the sloppy substance of the gelatinous inferno, but were not consumed.

He swung his blades at her, but missed, although breaking off the lines of fire at her breasts.

Niva's hands clutched her breasts, mouth gaping in surprise, stunned that he came so close to maiming her. She ran around her goddess with the fluidity of one sliding on ice. "Come chase me, La Gaul."

Gorias stopped, looked up at the goddess and wished he had the strength to topple the giant idol. "Squishin' yer ass would be too easy," He muttered and took one step to follow her around the goddess, then instantly twirled about, blades striking the opposite sides of the goddess' base. The blades passed through a new blast of dragonfire released by the Abbess. Her words filthy, she cursed him as she again used the goddess as a barrier.

"I wasn't born yesterday," Gorias shouted. "Fool punks and bitches with that tripe." He quickly placed his right sword back in the housing and leapt down from the main platform. He grabbed up one of the kneeling benches. His ears picked up the release of her fire as he turned and slung the bench. Niva aimed high, expecting the bench to be thrown at her face or upper body. Gorias aimed low, though, the bench falling and sliding to her feet. Niva hopped up to miss it and recognition lit up her face. Gorias charged at her, both blades swinging down, meaning to remove her arms when she landed. Her breasts fired off again, striking each arm of the charging warrior, propelling her but a few inches away, just far enough to be missed by his attack.

She landed and moved back, but Gorias didn't yield. Though pushed back a little, he charged on again, this time striking lower to mutilate her ankles. Niva turned, cartwheeled and again avoided the strikes from the blades; this time they knocked loose the gilded edges of the goddess' base. Just as she settled and turned, trying to speak but short of breath, Gorias stopped, looked up and stabbed at the lower hem of Ernytel's gown. The goddess' stone edges cracked, dislodging a huge ball of glass containing dragonfire. Gorias dropped both swords and the echo of their clatter made Niva smile, but her happiness became muted as Gorias caught the falling ball and drew back.

"You think I can't handle it?" she screeched at him. "Go ahead and throw it."

He did. He lobbed it slow, not fast.

Niva reached, then had to grab again, clutching the glass ball. Her face angry, perhaps getting that he didn't mean to break it and figured she could handle such a blast. No, he occupied her hands and dived toward her. Niva held the ball as Gorias leapt and seemingly missed his target, sliding between her legs to the waist. She started to back up and raised the ball high to spike it on his spine. Gorias slid his arms back as she did so. Bathed in fire and not caring, he pulled his body back. In this act, Niva screamed, not from the fire, but from agony in her calves. She tried to walk but her left leg gave out. Her hand to the spot, she struggled in the flame to see and feel what happened. Gorias held aloft the dew nail of his armor on his forearm. In the flames and amid her cries, she could hear him laugh. He turned around in the fire and reached for his swords.

Hands on his swords, Gorias twisted around and sliced many times in the air. The flames died some as he swung, shearing off four fingers of Niva's left hand as the woman struggled to fend him off. She howled in misery, clutching the hand to her tattooed stomach, directing fresh jets of dragonfire to the floor, away from La Gaul. Funnels of flame whipped up, licking the stone garments of the goddess. Clearly, she wasn't a trained fighter, Gorias reasoned, but one endowed with power for retribution.

Looking up in terror, she saw that Gorias was on her, close. Both blades fell in overhand arcs, but neither found the exact mark they desired. Though he meant to remove her arms with the blows, his left sword struck her elbow and passed through. The right blade missed her shoulder and sliced halfway down Niva's arm against the bones, ripping loose the biceps down to her elbow.

Cursing the terrible aim of old age, Gorias stepped back once, took another round of stabbing dragon fire swirling at his gut and swished the blades, aiming for her neck. Again, he missed his target, but mutilated her collarbones, snapping each, turning them upwards like wishbones. She pushed away, her ruined legs flailing.

Angry and weary of the dance, Gorias howled, striking home

a third time. This double shot, straight forward, struck her sternum. His circular motions cut her breasts loose so they hung off at crude angles, but it was the act of driving the swords through and out her back that caused the screams to cease. Helm close to her face, her eyes filled with a strange look, almost like bliss, as he let Niva go. She fell at the feet of her goddess and died with one shudder.

Gorias stepped out of the gooey dragonfire that started to eat away at the velvety ropes around the goddess. He raised his visor to breathe a bit better. Squinting his eyes, he saw Niva move.

Slamming the helm down, he watched her body split apart. Niva's ribcage rent open and each side of her flesh fell away, dropping into the empty ritual bath holding tanks. Still maintaining their complex images in the fire were the dragons, red and blue, as if outlines or crude cave wall renderings of such a species. On all fours, these beasts unfurled their wings and blinked at each other, taking cautious steps on their two dimensional claws.

Unsure what nightmare would come from these beasts out of their human cell, Gorias sliced at them with his swords. The blades passed through them. This action only made the two creatures of light aware of his presence. The red dragon jumped on Gorias' chest, knocking him back to the floor, swimming in a puddle of the oozing fire. Gorias felt the force of the beast, but couldn't put his hands on it to eject it off his frame. Likewise, the creature was angry that it couldn't affect La Gaul any more. It looked all over Gorias for a seam to exploit, but lost interest fast. Along with its brother fiend, it roared and flew up into the spires of the temple, spewing fire and braying.

Retrieving his swords, Gorias holstered them and ran for the door. As the dragons in light-lined bodies kept screaming, the eunuch emerged to see what ailed the sanctuary. Gorias threw a forearm into his bulbous face and ran out the door. It took him moments to get to Traveler. Once in the saddle, Gorias rode for a three city blocks before he looked back.

The heavy bricks of the temple, a newer structure for certain, gave way at the pressure of the freed dragons, whose mass increased to proportions larger than a horse. The grand shrine crumbled away, falling apart like a child's game of blocks. Within the main sanctuary, around the placid stone goddess, great tornados of fire brewed hot. These wicked flames licked at the frame of Ernytel. Around the goddess' blackened image arose a halo of fire that belched into the sky. In this circle of fire these winged ones emerged. Every so often, an explosion rocked the night, perhaps more dragonfire balls erupting at last in the storm. Two crazed screams echoed into the cosmos, as if falling into that void, forever, signaling their freedom.

Gorias breathed deep, knowing his mission was at an end. Almost.

✿ ✿ ✿ ✿ ✿

"I wasn't always a pirate, you know," Nykia told Alena as the Princess of Transalpina turned in front of the long mirror.

Alena leaned against the closed chamber door and nodded. "I know. I know all about your history and life."

Almost glowing in her new, resplendent long gown and powdered make-up, Nykia replied, "Do they sing stories about my abduction?"

Alena pulled away from the door and slowly paced across the room. "I've never heard any. However, in class, on the history of our land, you are a footnote on the current royal family." She unlatched the shutters and opened them, allowing more sunlight to pour in and bathe the princess.

"They teach it in class?"

Alena shrugged. "It added credence to your right to the line if that ever happened. There was more about Gorias La Gaul."

"I see." Nykia's hand soothed down her chest to her waist. "I could do without the corset."

"You don't have to wear that all the time, but we need you in excellent form for the Queen and the public."

"I could do without the women dressing me."

Alena half smiled. "They are made for such duties and love their tasks. Enjoy their company, but be careful who you trust. They show up fast if you call on them, just like they lit out of here when we told them to go."

"How will I know who to trust?"

"Ask me or my sisters. We will tell you."

"I can trust you?"

Alena winked. "You have to. We are your life now. You are ours. If anything happened to you under my watch, my life would be forfeit fast. That is the way of Garnet's will."

Nykia's hands touched her stomach again. "I wonder if Ellis is accurate."

"Probably," Alena shrugged and walked behind her to look in the mirror as well. "Gorias is what he is, but his ability and potency, heh, what a fortuitous development. It saves you the awful trouble of being pimped out to a punk or a surviving relic of the approved royal lines of other lands."

"Do you think Gorias will agree to be my consort and husband?"

"He has little choice. Garnet won't let him leave right off, and for appearances alone, I can see the ol' boy going through the motions."

Nykia beamed, her freshly scrubbed teeth radiant.

Alena added, "I'd also prepare to face the fact that he'll soon ride out to Shynar, like he said. Gorias won't sit still long and you have to face that."

"But if we are wed, can't he stay?"

"For a tough pirate girl, you sound like a mooning child at times."

Nykia turned and gave her a pouting look.

Alena said, "I'm your servant but not your slave. I will tell you the truth and keep you honest. I won't blow smoke up your skirts, ma'am."

Nykia nodded. "It's better that way."

"I concur."

Nykia looked to the window. "We are awfully low to the ground here. I wonder what that glow in the night sky is?"

"Who can say? This is a dressing room, usually locked, and we are on palace grounds. I doubt the pirates will abduct you here.

In fact, I'd lay money on the idea that Garnet has had Thynnes exterminate every pirate hovel, tavern and outpost along the coasts. If you did have any friends or enemies, they are soon to be no more."

"That's terrible. Was that necessary?"

"Yes. That part of your life is over. We couldn't destroy them all before for fear of killing you, the heir."

"What of Allard?"

"I think they are offering a position as a groom or work at one of the ports. It's better than banishment but not many trust pirates."

"You wouldn't lie to me and just off Allard?"

Alena let her right hand rest on her pouch, and then her index finger snapped it shut. "You need to fear other things now, like political intrigue, trouble with the temple and malicious wizards."

Nykia turned to face Alena. The tall warrior took a few steps toward her. "The wizards? I thought they were all dead or burnt."

Alena smiled wide and reached out her hand to caress Nykia's right cheek. "Oh, in time, they'll all burn." Still wearing a smile, Alena reached out fast and shoved her right thumb in Nykia's mouth. Her right hand quickly slid to the Princess's throat and then gripped the back of her neck. Alena's left hand shot forward, her index and middle fingers jabbing into Nykia's mouth like darts.

Confusion and terror in her face, Nykia's hands gripped Alena's shoulders, but she couldn't kick back due to the hoop skirt about her legs. Although strong, she was no match for the Queen's guard.

Left hand squeezing Nykia's nose and then her hands holding her neck, Alena said steadily, "Thus should it be for all enemies of the Queen." The pressure in her hands increased until she felt a sufficient amount existed to break the capsules she's shoved into Nykia's throat. Alena then jumped back as the glow of the dragonfire erupted from Nykia's mouth and nostrils, starting a flood of liquid fire that coursed all over the young lady's body.

In a few moments, it was over. The fire consumed Nykia and her smoking clothing fell in a heap. Not a single bone remained, just dust, and not a drop of blood existed of the princess.

Alena opened the dress cabinet and took out a grappling

hook. She walked to the window, secured the hook under the shelf and threw the rope out into the empty yard. Alena looked at the vacant lot and then at the wall just across toward the cottage of Yannick. She walked out of the room, glancing at the smoldering heap briefly. Alena then stepped to the door, closed it in front of herself, and dropped the bar over the frame. She pulled her short sword, inserted it under the bar and pulled back. Her knee beside the door, she cracked the bar and then threw it on the floor. She left the room, closed the door and promptly kicked it open, busting the latches.

Alena screamed, "The Princess! By the gods! Sound the alarm!"

EPILOGUE

Queen Garnet ascended the steps of the curtain wall tower, a half dozen of her personal guards before her, a half dozen behind. Alena stepped beside her and let the aged monarch lean on her a few times.

"They won't strike the flames until I'm aloft," Garnet called to the warriors jogging before her. "No need to hurry, ladies."

Alena kept her head down as she said, "Gorias will be off soon."

The Queen walked the many steps, every so often a male guard on the wall bowed. "I'm glad he signed off on the nuptials before doing so. That was mighty kind of the fighter."

"It'll be proper that way and affirm all we've fought for."

"The old sinner, he's a sport, no?"

Alena let a sardonic smile play on her lips. "Yes, mum."

"Terrible business with Mavik and Vincent," Garnet said under her breath.

"Yes," Alena agreed. "Orsen should be recognized for his gallantry in ferreting out these imposters, so close to seizing the crown of Transalpina."

"Indeed. I shall add him to the Order of the Garter at least, perhaps an allowance for his trouble?"

"That'd be fitting, mum."

"What's done is done and had to be done," Garnet declared as they stepped to the top of the curtain wall. A huge cheer filtered across the masses gathered below, all terminating to their left at the pile of wood with a wooden pole erected in the outer yard. "Burn them all, that's what my father used to say."

"Yes, mum, mine as well."

"General Appra was wise and a good man."

Still in his robe, Yannick had been strapped to the stake. Four of Alena's sisters stood around the pile of wood with torches, waiting.

Gorias La Gaul stepped away from the pile of wood and climbed onto the saddle of Traveler. The crowd applauded him and many bowed as he started to move away from Yannick.

"Terrible thing," the Queen sighed, arms folded under her breasts. "Yannick murdering the Princess Nykia like that with his dragonfire tablets."

"I found the pouch of them in his cottage," Alena said gently, eyes on Gorias, her hands folded at her stomach.

Garnet looked at Alena and then down at her clothes. "You look spectacular dressed as a Princess, Alena."

Alena curtseyed in her hoop skirt. "Thank you, mum."

"The land respects you, knows of your lineage and the royal blood of General Appra, plus, you too carry the child of Gorias La Gaul, according to Ellis." The Queen peered down the wall at other dignitaries, one, the short youth Ellis, now re-outfitted in the doublet of Queen's prognosticator. "I'm sorry your husband must now leave us, but I'm glad he left the heir within you."

Alena smiled at Gorias, who also looked up at her. "Do you think he knows?"

Garnet raised an eyebrow, reading Gorias' face. "Do you think he cares? I think his exact words to me were, *The world will end soon, so enjoy that kid while you can.*"

"Is he serious?"

"It will be another two hundred years or more in crazy theories, so that is a lifetime even in this era of long-lived men. Who can say if all of those tales are for certain? Maybe the supreme God is really talking to that fool in Shynar, but maybe its more demons having a boy's rag. Who can say? I refuse to live life afraid for tomorrow. Worry is crushed by action."

"No regrets, mum?"

"Only that I held my virginity away from that man down there. Still, my life was wonderful and God has shown me a new way to solve life's disappointments. Gorias indeed will have a son on the throne." She faced Alena. "Or a daughter that will tear out the lungs of anyone who dares stand against her."

"Do you love him, mum?"

"Oh, in a way. One cannot help but love Gorias. Do you love him?"

Alena smiled and waved at Gorias. He lifted his chin and bowed his head with pageantry. "In a way, I always will."

"It's no sin to love him. It's just foolishness to try to fence in the wild wind."

✻ ✻ ✻ ✻ ✻

Gorias La Gaul rode down the main avenue of the capitol city in Transalpina, weary of those who pointed at him, looking away from the rising dust cloud still lingering after the final fall of the temple of Ernytel.

The enormous throng around the spectacle in the street cheered him as he left. Of course, when he looked back toward the castle, he again saw the figures up on the curtain wall. The Queen and her Princess, wrapped up tidy. Seeing as the destruction of the temple of Ernytel was seen as a disapproving sign of the gods, Garnet proved rather accepting of a new reality. She even came down to let the people see her watch Yannick put to the pyre.

"Goodbye," Gorias mouthed at them, unsure if they could tell, uncaring if they could. He hated long goodbyes or goodbyes at all.

The wizard was tied to the stake with metallic bonds to insure he would stay in the flames long enough to burn. The mound of wood and debris flung from the crazed crowd fed the small fire the Appra sisters lit.

Gorias stopped Traveler as he turned back, watching Yannick's mouth open and close. The wizard stared at Gorias, face pleading emphatically. Mouth agape, no sound emerged as the flames grew higher. The old legend sat for a moment, his hand on his saddlebag full of gold pieces, both from the Queen's coffer and the wizard's larder. Gorias' other hand was a fist and he smiled at it. The crowd had witnessed Gorias' final action to Yannick seconds before, and cheered it. They understood Gorias' act on Yannick ensured the wizard would cast no spell to free himself, call down no rains to mute the fire, or worse, bring out any evils capable of releasing him.

La Gaul opened his right hand and looked at Yannick's tongue. It still felt warm to the touch. Gorias kicked Traveler, cast the tongue to the dogs in the gutters and rode out.

THE END OF

OVERKILL

But Gorias La Gaul will return

In

BORN OF SWORDS

ABOUT THE AUTHOR

Steven L. Shrewsbury, from Central Illinois, enjoys football, books about history, guns, politics, mystery shows and good fiction. 365 of his short stories have been published in print or digital media. His novels *THRALL*, *STRONGER THAN DEATH*, *HAWG*, *TORMENTOR*, *BAD MAGICK*, (collaboration with Nate Southard), *BEDLAM UNLEASHED* (collaboration with Peter Welmerink), *HELL BILLY* and *GODFORSAKEN* run from horror to historical fantasy.

Connect with Steven online at:

www.stevenshrewsbury.com
or add his Facebook page at:
www.facebook.com/stevenlshrewsbury

Check out the following pages to see more from

All Seventh Star Press titles available in print and an array of
specially priced eBook formats.

Visit www.seventhstarpress.com for further information.

Connect with Seventh Star Press at:
www.seventhstarpress.com
seventhstarpress.blogspot.com
www.facebook.com/seventhstarpress

MORE FROM STEVEN SHREWSBURY

Look for the hard-hitting, heroic fantasy novel THRALL, featuring illustrations and cover art by fantasy artist Matthew Perry!

Trade Paperback ISBN: 9780983108634
eBook ISBN: 9780983108641

FOR GORIAS LA GAUL...
DELIVERANCE WILL COME

Set in the mists of ancient times, *Thrall* tells the story of Gorias La Gaul, an aging warrior who has lived for centuries battling the monstrosities of legend and lore. It is an age when the Nephilum walk the earth, demonic forces hunger to be unleashed, and dragons still soar through the skies ... living and undead. On a journey to find one of his own blood, a young man who is caught in the shadow of necromancy, Gorias' path crosses with familiar enemies, some of whom not even death can hold bound.

Thrall is gritty, dark-edged heroic fantasy in the vein of Robert E. Howard and David Gemmell. It is a maelstrom of hard-hitting action and unpredictable imagery, taking place within an incredible antediluvian world. In Gorias La Gaul, *Thrall* introduces an iconic new character to the realms of fantasy literature. Thrall invites the reader to go on a perilous journey where it is not a matter of whether one has the courage to die, but whether one has the courage to live.

All Seventh Star Press titles available in print and an array of specially priced eBook formats. Visit www.seventhstarpress.com for further information.

Now Available from Seventh Star Press, D.A. Adams'
fantastic saga *The Brotherhod of Dwarves Series*, featuring
illustrations and cover art by fantasy artist Bonnie Wasson!

Book One: <u>The Brotherhood of Dwarves</u>

Trade: 978-1-937929-91-6
eBook: 978-1-937929-93-0

Roskin, heir to the throne of a remote, peaceful kingdom of dwarves, cravesexcitement and adventure. Outside his own kingdom, in search of fortune andglory, he finds a much different world, one divided by racial strife andoverrun by war. The orcs to the south want to conquer all dwarves and sellthem as slaves. The humans to the east want to control the world's resources. Caught in the middle, Roskin finds himself chased by slavetraders and soldiers alike as he discovers that friendship is the bestfortune of all. Just when he thinks he has triumphed, an act of betrayalsends him into bondage. His only hope of escape is the faltering courage ofa disgraced warrior whose best days are behind him…

Book Two: <u>The Fall of Dorkhun</u>

Trade: 978-0-983740-25-4
eBook: 978-1-937929-90-9

Crushaw, Molgheon, and Vishghu have liberated the Slithesythe Plantation. They must make their way to safe lands before being caught andreturned to certain bondage. Across the orc lands, they and Roskin recruitand train an army of freed slaves, for between them and freedom arethousands of well-armed, well-trained orc warriors. Near the Pass of HardHope, in the shadows of the eastern mountains, they make their desperatestand. But even if they succeed, Roskin's ordeal is far from finished, ashe is haunted by visions of something awful back in Dorkhun…

Book Three: <u>Red Sky at Dawn</u>

Trade: 978-1-937929-92-3
eBook: 978-0-983740-25-4

The Fall of Dorkuhn, the third installment in The Brotherhood of Dwarves series, continues the adventures of the dwarf Roskin. Having escaped slavery, and survived the Battle for Hard Hope, Roskin returns home to a kingdom divided by war with the ogres.

On one side, his father desires to restore peace. On the other, Master Sondious, hungry for revenge after having been crippled, seeks to escalate the aggression. Roskin and his friends hasten to the capital, to make a desperate attempt to resolve the growing rift, but unknown to the dwarves, new and powerful menaces threaten to destroy the entire kingdom…

The Brotherhood of
DWARVES
Book 1

D.A. Adams

The Fall of
DORKHUN
Book 3

D.A. Adams

Red Sky at
DAWN

D.A. Adams

Now Available from Seventh Star Press, Jackie Gamber's fantasy novel REDHEART, featuring illustrations and cover art by fantasy artist Matthew Perry!

Trade Paperback ISBN: 9780983108672
eBook ISBN: 9780983108696

Enter the lands of Leland Province, where dragon and human societies have long dwelled side by side. Superstitions rise sharply, as a severe drought strips the land of its bounty, providing fertile ground for the darker ambitions of Fordon Blackclaw, Dragon Council Leader, who seeks to subdue humans or wipe them off the face of the land.

As the shadow of danger creeps across Leland Province, a young dragon named Kallon Redheart, who has turned his back on dragons and humans alike, comes into an unexpected friendship. Riza Diantus is a young woman whose dreams can no longer be contained by the narrow confines of her village, and when she finds herself in peril, Kallon is the only one with the power to save her. Yet to do so means he must confront his past, and embrace a future he stopped believing in.

A tale of friendship, courage, and ultimate destiny, *Redheart* invites readers to a wondrous journey through the *Leland Dragon Series*.

Now Available!
Jackie Gamber's Book 2 in the Leland Dragon Series: Sela

Trade Paperback ISBN: 9781937929893
eBook ISBN: 9781937929893

Peace is fleeting. Vorham Riddess, Venur of Esra Province, covets the crystal ore buried deep in Leland's mountains. His latest device to obtain it: land by marriage to a Leland maiden. But that's not all.

Among Dragonkind, old threats haunt Mount Gore, and shadows loom in the thoughts of the Red who restored life to land and love. A dragon hunter, scarred from countless battles, discovers he can yet suffer more wounds.

In the midst of it all, Sela Redheart is lost, driven from her home with only her old uncle to watch over her. As the dragon-born child of Kallon, the leader of Leland's Dragon Council, she is trapped in human form with no understanding of how she transformed, or how to turn back.

Wanderers seek a home, schemes begin to unfurl, and all is at risk as magic and murder, marriage and mystery strangle the heart of Esra. A struggle for power far older and deeper than anyone realizes will leave no human or dragon unaffected.

In a world where magic is born of feeling, where the love between a girl and a dragon was once transformative, what power dwells in the heart of young Sela?

Now Available from Seventh Star Press, Stephen Zimmer's epic fantasy Fires in Eden series, featuring illustrations and cover art by fantasy artist Matthew Perry!

Epic Fantasy-Fires in Eden Series

Explore the lands, seas, and skies of Ave in this epic fantasy adventure, as eleven individuals from the modern world find themselves in lands both wondrous and dangerous. The enigmatic figure known as The Unifier has unleashed a war to end all wars, but the nature of it is far more insidious than any of the kings and rulers supporting it can possibly imagine. The fate of Ave hangs in the balance, as the eleven exiles discover the reasons for their presence, and the choices that they will have to make in response.

Book One: Crown of Vengeance
ISBN: 978-0982565612

"This is definitely a book for people who like character driven stories with gorgeous and detailed descriptions of a fantasy world and their inhabitants mixed with beings who follow devious plans who will face more resistance than expected…"

-Only the Best SciFi/Fantasy

"For me to say so many great things about a fantasy book is an accomplishment as these types of books used to be towards the bottom on my list that I was willing to read. This book with the help of Mr. Zimmer has restored my faith that fantasy makes for some thrilling reading."

-Cheryl's Book Nook

Book Two: Dream of Legends
ISBN: 978-0983108627

"Dream of Legends is a solid installment to the Fires in Eden series and left me hanging on to read book three."

-Bookworm Blues